Dear Aaron

Mariana Zapata is a *New York Times*, *USA Today*, and a multiple No. 1 Amazon bestselling author. She is a five-time Goodreads Choice Awards nominee in the Romance category. Her novels have been published in thirteen languages.

Mariana lives in a small town in Colorado with her husband and beloved Great Dane, Kaiser. She loves reading, anime, and dogs. When she isn't writing, you can usually find her picking on her loved ones.

Website: **www.marianazapata.com**
Facebook: **/marianazapatawrites**
Instagram: **@marianazapata**
Twitter: **@marianazapata_**
TikTok: **@marianazapataauthor**

By Mariana Zapata

Under Locke
Kulti
Lingus
Rhythm, Chord & Malykhin
The Wall of Winnipeg and Me
Wait for It
Dear Aaron
From Lukov with Love
Luna and the Lie
The Best Thing
Hands Down
All Rhodes Lead Here

Dear Aaron

MARIANA ZAPATA

HEADLINE
ETERNAL

First published in 2017 by Mariana Zapata

First published in Great Britain in this paperback edition in 2022
by HEADLINE ETERNAL
An imprint of HEADLINE PUBLISHING GROUP

6

Cataloguing in Publication Data is available from the British Library

ISBN 978 1 0354 0283 0

Book Cover Design by Letitia Hasser, Romantic Book Affairs
designs.romanticbookaffairs.com

Editing by Hot Tree Editing

Formatting by Jeff Senter, Indie Formatting Services

Typeset in 10.75/13.75 pt Minion Pro by Jouve (UK), Milton Keynes

Printed and bound in Great Britain by Clays Ltd, Elcograf S.p.A.

HEADLINE PUBLISHING GROUP
An Hachette UK Company
Carmelite House
50 Victoria Embankment
London EC4Y 0DZ

www.headlineeternal.com
www.headline.co.uk
www.hachette.co.uk

*To my Isaac,
the greatest nephew
in the history of nephews*

Chapter One

June

June 3, 2008

Dear Aaron,

My name is Ruby Santos, and I'm your new pairing through the Help a Soldier Foundation.

I'm not sure if you've participated with Help a Soldier in the past or if this is your first time, but if you aren't familiar with the fine print of the program, I'll break you in so that you aren't wondering why this person named Ruby from Houston, Texas is e-mailing and sending you letters. (It'll probably be a month or so from now before you start getting mail from me, so this might get a bit awkward. After we get the hang of this, I'll try not to send you the same message that I also e-mail because that would get boring.)

According to the foundation's guidelines, I'm supposed to reach out to you once a week while you are deployed . . . wherever it is you're deployed. They don't tell me these things. All I know is that you're a staff sergeant. Please don't feel obligated to tell me where you are unless you want to. It doesn't matter to me. Since I'm not sure if you prefer e-mails or getting letters, I'll do both in the meantime. You can let me know which you would rather get.

I'm not even close to being rich, but hopefully every once in a while, I can send you a care package. Hopefully you understand. I'm sure you're busy, so I won't bore you too much now.

Since we're in this for the long haul, I'll ask you a few questions so we can start getting to know each other. Hope that works for you. ☺

1. Do you go by Aaron or something else?
2. How many months do you have left in your deployment?
3. If I could send you one thing from home, what would it be?

I look forward to hearing from you, but if you're busy, that's okay, too. I promise I'll write every week anyway.

All the best,
Ruby

June 8, 2008

Dear Aaron,

It's your new Help a Soldier pairing, Ruby from Houston.

I hope you're doing well and that you received my e-mail and/or letter.

I'll answer the questions I asked you last week so you can get to know me a little.

1. I go by Ruby. Rubes. Rubella (only my mom calls me that). Squirt (everyone I'm related to or knows me through family calls me that).
2. N/A since I'm not the one deployed.
3. If our roles were reversed, those packets of microwave-ready macaroni and cheese would be exactly what I would miss and want more of. Please don't ask how many I can eat in a single sitting.

There isn't much to tell about me, but if you have any questions, ask away.

All the best,
Ruby

June 15, 2008

Dear Aaron,

It's Ruby again. I hope you're doing well. Have any of my letters shown up? Are my e-mails coming through? I won't send you anything new via e-mail until I'm sure the messages are going to the right place. They haven't bounced back to me as undeliverable, but I would rather play it safe. ☺

If you've sent me a response through snail mail, I haven't gotten it yet, and if you haven't, that's okay, too. I know these things take a while.

I know I already asked, but have you participated with HaS before? You're my third soldier that I've done this exchange with and usually we trade questions back and forth to get to know each other. Hopefully you don't think

I'm being intrusive. I had pen pals in other countries when I was a kid through a program at my elementary school and I thought it was fun. HaS is like a grown-up version of it.

I have more questions for you.

1. Do you play video games?
2. Are you an only child or do you have siblings?
3. Pizza or cheeseburgers?

Hope to hear from you soon,
Ruby

June 23, 2008

Dear Aaron,

It's Ruby Santos, your Help a Soldier pair again.

I'll answer the questions I sent you last week below if that's okay.

1. Video games: I really enjoy playing video games when I get a chance. My old Nintendo still works, and I've been known to play *Duck Hunt* for hours at a time if I'm stressed.
2. Siblings or no: I'm (un)lucky enough to have two brothers and two sisters. I'm the fourth in line.
3. Pizza or cheeseburgers: Cheeseburgers all the way forever.

Hope everything on your side of the world is well.

Best wishes,
Ruby

June 29, 2008

Dear Aaron,

It's Ruby.

I hope you're doing fine. I haven't heard from you, and I know this kind of thing happens, but I worry anyway. I'm still sending the same e-mails and messages, so I hope I'm not boring you.

I'm not sure what to send you, and more questions seem annoying, so I'll give you a break. I hope you don't mind terrible jokes because they're my favorite. Here's a military one:

Sergeant Major to a young soldier: "I didn't see you at camouflage training this morning, soldier."

Soldier: "Thank you very much, sir."

All the best,
Ruby

Chapter Two

July

July 5, 2008

Hi Aaron,

It's Ruby, your "adopter" from Houston.

I hope you're doing well. I'll spare you from jokes this letter just in case you didn't appreciate the one last week. So more questions! Again!

1. Pretzels or chips?
2. Summer sports or winter sports?
3. Dogs or cats?

Hope all is well.

Best wishes,
Ruby Santos

July 12, 2008

Dear Aaron,

It's Ruby, your HaS pairing/the broken record.

I really hope you're doing fine. I still haven't heard from you through e-mail or by letter, but I hope my messages are coming through some way.

I'll answer the questions I asked you last week.

1. Pretzels or chips: Chips, preferably Fritos.
2. Summer sports or winter sports: Winter sports.
3. Dogs or cats: Both, but mini pigs trump dogs and cats.

Hope you're hanging in there.

All the best,
Ruby Santos

July 19, 2008

Hi Aaron,

It's Ruby. Sending a postcard this week to spice it up. I'm in Orlando with my family (see: the Mickey Mouse on the other side.) Hopefully Mickey makes you smile as much as he makes me smile.

–Ruby S.

July 26, 2008

Dear Aaron,

It's Ruby. I'm back home in Houston. If you're curious, my vacation went great. I even got a pretty serious tan. That was my sixth time going to Orlando with my family, and it never gets old.

I have some more questions for you:

1. Have you ever been to Orlando/Disney?
2. Apples or oranges?
3. Cake or pie?

Best wishes,
Ruby

Chapter Three

August

August 2, 2008

Dear Aaron,

I hope you're doing okay. I contacted the Help a Soldier foundation to make sure you're fine and to double-check the address/e-mail I have for you since I haven't gotten a response. Hopefully I'm only overreacting. I know I've told you I've done this before, but every other soldier has always reached out to me at least through e-mail once a month (not that I'm putting pressure on you, I just want to make sure I have all the right information and I'm not sending things to the wrong person or address).

I just realized how clingy that sounds, but I don't mean it in that way.

I hope you're fine, and I'll leave you with another joke since I spared you from one last month. ☺

A group of soldiers were standing at formation when their instructor said, "All right, all you dummies fall out."

Only one man in the squad stayed at attention while the rest wandered off.

The instructor walked over to the soldier who hadn't left and met him eye to eye. The soldier smiled and said, "Sure was a lot of them, huh, sir?"

Best wishes,
–Ruby Santos

August 9, 2008

Dear Aaron,

I decided to switch it up this week again and send you something different. The picture I've sent along is one of my favorites in the whole world. I bought it when I was eighteen. My sister took me with her to Iceland for her college graduation present and I found the print at a little store. I bought three copies and gave one to my best friend. Sometimes when I have a bad day, it's nice to remind myself that the world is a lot bigger than I am and whatever crap I have going on in my life, and the Aurora Borealis has that effect on me. Isn't it beautiful?

Hope you're doing well.

All the best,
Ruby

P.S. I still haven't heard back from the foundation.

August 19, 2008

Aaron,

The Help a Soldier foundation got back to me a few days ago, and they said they confirmed that you're still deployed and that they provided the correct information to reach you.

I've thought it over and maybe we didn't hit it off, or I did/wrote something wrong, and that's okay. This will be my last letter/e-mail to you. They're going to switch me out with someone else in the foundation, so you should continue getting mail on time.

My brother was a marine, and I joined this program because he told me how lonely and bored soldiers get when they're overseas. It's easy for me to forget that not everyone has a big, overwhelming family like mine. Writing back and forth while he (my brother) was in Iraq made us really close. Loneliness even when you're surrounded by others is something I understand well.

I'm wishing you the best while you're stationed somewhere in the world. Thank you for your sacrifice and bravery. Take care.

Best wishes always,
–Ruby Santos

From: Aaron.Tanner.Hall.mil@mail.mil
Date: August 24, 2008 1:08 p.m.
To: RubyMars@mail.com
Subject: RE: Help a Soldier

Ruby,

This is Aaron with Help a Soldier.
    All your letters and e-mails have come through . . .
sorry for taking so long to reach out.

–A

From: Aaron.Tanner.Hall.mil@mail.mil
Date: August 28, 2008 1:46 p.m.
To: RubyMars@mail.com
Subject: RE: RE: Help a Soldier

Ruby,

This is Aaron again. Haven't heard back from you . . . Can
we start over?

–A

Chapter Four

From: RubyMars@mail.com
Date: September 1, 2008 2:05 a.m.
To: Aaron.Tanner.Hall.mil@mail.mil
Subject: Hi

Hi Aaron,

My name is Ruby, and I live in Texas. I was paired up with you through the Help a Soldier foundation.

If you aren't familiar with the program, I'll break you in so that you aren't wondering why I'm e-mailing and sending you letters. According to the program's guidelines, I'm supposed to reach out to you every week. I am not even close to being rich, but hopefully every once in a while, I can send you a care package.

I'm sure you're busy, so I won't make this long.

Since we're in this for at least a few more months, I'll ask you some questions so we can get to know each other.

1. Do you go by Aaron or something else?
2. How much longer do you have left of your deployment?

3. If I could send you one thing from home, what
   would it be?

I look forward to hearing from you.

All the best,
Ruby

P.S. Does this count as starting over?
P.P.S. It's okay that you didn't reach out until now. I kept
putting off writing back to HaS about the reassignment.

From: Aaron.Tanner.Hall.mil@mail.mil
Date: September 5, 2008 2:17 p.m.
To: RubyMars@mail.com
Subject: RE: Hi

Ruby,

Thanks for writing. You're the sixth match I've made
through HaS, and the second one on this deployment.
You're the first one that lives in Texas. Are you originally
from there?

Letters and e-mails are enough for me. I appreciate
you taking the time to write. You don't need to do anything else.

Here are the answers you asked about.

1. My friends and family either call me Aaron or
   Hall, nothing original . . . sometimes asswipe.
   Why does your family call you Squirt?
2. I have 8 months left before my deployment ends.

3. If I could get something from home it would be a pizza . . . mac and cheese is number 2 on my list of things I miss.

Hope you write back soon.

–A

P.S. This counts as starting over. Sorry for not writing you back before. I don't have a good excuse. I had some personal mess going on . . . nothing to do with you. Hope you understand. Sorry again.

From: RubyMars@mail.com
Date: September 7, 2008 1:55 a.m.
To: Aaron.Tanner.Hall.mil@mail.mil
Subject: Texas and Nicknames

Dear Aaron,

You're welcome for writing. I'm sure you're busy. It's no biggie. All I wanted was to make sure someone was getting my mail.

You're my third soldier I've "adopted." That's a strange word, isn't it? Like you're not an adult. If I'm your second pairing in this deployment, does that mean you have another person or family who still messages you or did things not work out with them? Don't feel obligated to answer that.

I was born in California, but I've lived in Houston since I was four. Are you from Texas by any chance?

I'll stick with calling you Aaron. I'm curious and you don't have to tell me, but who calls you asswipe?

Squirt . . . Everyone calls me that because I was the baby in the family for almost six years. I'm also the shortest. My little sister was an "accident" I don't like to think about. :)

You've got me in a pickle with sending you pizza. I'll have to think about how to make that happen, but luckily, I like solving a good problem.

Okay, here are three more random questions (I switched one up from that time before we're pretending didn't happen. Reactivating my amnesia after this.):

1. Do you play video games?
2. Are you an only child or do you have siblings?
3. What kind of movies do you like to watch?

Hope you're okay.

Best wishes,
Ruby Santos

P.S. All is forgiven. Don't worry. You don't have to write me back every week. I promise I wasn't trying to guilt trip you. I really was just worried I had offended you or my messages weren't going through.

From: Aaron.Tanner.Hall.mil@mail.mil
Date: September 8, 2008 2:17 p.m.
To: RubyMars@mail.com
Subject: RE: Texas and Nicknames

Ruby,

Were you paired up with your other soldiers their whole deployment? The other family I have in the program writes me every week. I think HaS hasn't had as many soldiers signing up this year like they have in the past and that's why some of us have multiple families that write us . . . not that I'm complaining.

I was born and raised in Louisiana, but I've moved around a lot since enlisting. Been to Texas a few times with friends.

My best friends call me asswipe.

I'll stick with calling you Ruby, if that's all right.

Here are the answers to your questions.

1. If it wasn't for video games, half my platoon would be bored out of their minds. Somebody here is always having a *Halo* tournament.
2. I have one sister and one brother.
3. Favorite movies . . . I like 80s action films, but I'm not picky. I'll watch anything. What about you?

Hope to hear from you soon.

–A

From: RubyMars@mail.com
Date: September 12, 2008 12:05 a.m.
To: Aaron.Tanner.Hall.mil@mail.mil
Subject: Movies and Stuff

Dear Aaron,

Before you, one of the soldiers finished his tour and went home. We were paired up for eleven months. The other one . . . I had to ask HaS to switch us. Things got weird. That's great you have more people messaging you. I was talking to someone I know about the pen pal thing with the military and they told me that there's a lot more dating websites for military personnel and civilians than there used to be. I bet that might be why there are less soldiers signing up. Don't take my word for it.

Where in Louisiana are you from if you don't mind me asking? It's okay if you don't want to answer that.

Ruby is fine. ☺

80s action movies like what exactly? Jean-Claude? Arnold? Steven? I'm not judging, just asking.

My favorite movies? That's a tough one. I've watched the original *Cleopatra* a hundred times, *Alien* a thousand times, *Beetlejuice* a million, and the *Star Wars* trilogy even more. You?

Do you guys play anything besides *Halo*?

One sister and brother sound nice. I have two sisters and two brothers.

Here are more questions for you:

1. Pretzels or chips?
2. Summer sports or winter sports?
3. Dogs or cats?

Wishing you the best,
Ruby

From: Aaron.Tanner.Hall.mil@mail.mil
Date: September 17, 2008 1:17 p.m.
To: RubyMars@mail.com
Subject: RE: Movies and Stuff

Ruby,

Weird how?

I've seen a lot of ads about those dating sites. I bet that might be why there are less, never really thought about it I guess.

I lived in Shreveport until I was eighteen. You been there?

All of the actors you mentioned in movies . . . You also missed Bruce.

There's a movie about Cleopatra? I haven't heard of that one.

The three games we have on repeat are *Halo 3*, *Rock Band* and *Bioshock*. *Call of Duty* and *Guitar Hero* are runners up.

Here are the answers to your questions.

1. Chips, but not Fritos. Salt and vinegar mostly.
2. You said before winter sports—why? I like summer sports, I guess. We don't have a lot of winter sports in Louisiana. I played ball in HS.

3. Dogs, but I got you on the mini pigs from the e-mail we're pretending didn't happen . . . they're cute. My dad has a king shepherd back home. Love that dog.

Four siblings sounds . . . interesting. You all close? Talk to you soon.

–A

From: RubyMars@mail.com
Date: September 20, 2008 2:05 a.m.
To: Aaron.Tanner.Hall.mil@mail.mil
Subject: Video Games, Siblings, etc.

Dear Aaron,

About my other soldier pairing: weird like *weird*. It was inappropriate and . . . weird. LOL. I'll tell you if you really want to know.

I can't say I've ever been to Shreveport. I've been to NOLA once for Mardi Gras, and driven through Louisiana on vacation but only stopped for gas. Once in New Orleans was good enough for me.

How could I miss Bruce? My mom calls him her boyfriend. *Cleopatra* is an old movie. It's a classic from the 60s. The costumes were amazing. That's why I've seen it so many times.

Halo and *Bioshock* I get. *Rock Band* though?

What kind of ball did you play in high school? The only sport I ever watch is figure skating. I'm not into any other sports unless watching *Friday Night Lights* counts. (That's a TV show.)

I had to look up what a king shepherd was. I've only heard of German shepherds. What's his/her name? As much as I love mini pigs, the only pet I have is a ferret named Sylvester.

My brothers, sisters and me all get along really well. I say this, but tomorrow I'll complain about how one of them did something to make me mad. You're probably familiar with that, and if you're not, consider yourself lucky.

Do you want me to keep asking you random questions? Is there anything you'd want me to tell you about? Or talk about? I'm a good listener. Whatever you want.

Or do you want more jokes? You tell me.

Hope you're doing okay.

Best wishes,
Ruby

From: Aaron.Tanner.Hall.mil@mail.mil
Date: September 22, 2008 3:17 p.m.
To: RubyMars@mail.com
Subject: RE: Video Games, Siblings, Etc.

Ruby,

Now I really want to know what happened with that soldier you were paired with. You've got me imagining things.

I've never been to NOLA for Mardi Gras . . .

Cleopatra still doesn't ring a bell, but I haven't watched any classics either. The only classic I can think of is *Gone with the Wind*, and that's only because my stepmom used to watch it at least once a month . . . I hated it. You're into costumes in movies?

You know what *Bioshock* is? You said you played *Duck Hunt* before so that's what I was expecting. You into gaming?

I played football. Not because I loved it . . . or thought I was going pro or anything like that, but it was something to do.

Figure skating is the only sport you watch? Does that count as a sport? Hockey, yeah. Figure skating, no. Why? I've never watched *Friday Night Lights* the show before but I watched the movie.

Aries is the dog's name. If I wasn't in the army, I'd bring him to live with me, but I'm gone too much . . . It wouldn't be fair to him.

Why'd you name your ferret Sylvester?

I get the sibling thing. We all get along. I don't see them much, so that's probably why. You said you're almost the baby, how old are the rest of your brothers/sisters?

You can talk to me about anything. My other pairings in the program write to me about their lives and their kids. It's just nice to have an escape sometimes, anything is welcome even if you think it's boring because it's probably not compared to things here.

Do you have kids?

I shared your jokes with some of the guys in my squad. Feel free to send more. You can message me about whatever though.

Can I ask why you're always awake in the middle of the night?

–A

From: RubyMars@mail.com
Date: September 24, 2008 3:05 a.m.
To: Aaron.Tanner.Hall.mil@mail.mil
Subject: Hi Part 2

Hi Aaron,

I'll tell you what happened with the other soldier if you insist. He started sending me "crotch" shots (or if you want to be technical, the words I'm looking for rhyme with "tick licks"), and asking for some in return (not "tick" pics but you know what I mean). There's only so much I'm willing to do for my country. Nudies isn't one of them. Please excuse me for talking about private parts. You asked.

You're smarter than I am. Mardi Gras was an experience I'd be fine not ever reliving. I thought I had an idea of what to expect. I didn't.

I don't know who would have the nerve to be sarcastic about *Lethal Weapon*, but it wouldn't be me. My mom would beat me. I'll second your hate for *Gone with the Wind*. I hated the plot and the characters, too, but I liked the wardrobe. And yes, I like movies with great costumes and makeup. I'll tell you two things about *Cleopatra*: it's one of the most expensive movies ever made and the main actress had 65 costume changes. Crazy, huh? (You don't have to answer that. I know not everyone thinks that kind of thing is interesting and that's okay.)

Lol! *Duck Hunt* is my favorite, but I've played *Bioshock* a few times before. Two of my friends are real gamers—one likes PC gaming and the other console gaming—so I know a little.

What's wrong with figure skating? They wouldn't have it at the Olympics if it wasn't a sport. They're really athletic. You should probably know my little sister is a figure skater, that's why I'm into it. It's the Santos family official sport.

Aries is such a perfect name for a king shepherd. Did you choose it or did your dad?

I had to change my ferret's name after two months because his original name, Logan, wasn't cutting it. He didn't have a "Logan" personality. He's a mess. Ferrets have a lot more personality than you'd imagine.

My oldest brother is 29, then there's my sister who is 26, my other brother is 25, then there's me at 23, and my little sister is 18. Do you miss your brother and sister while you're gone?

Getting to know someone is always a little strange, but I'm sure we'll figure this out. I don't really do much. I work, watch TV, and go out to do random things with my friends or family a few times a week. I travel with my little sister sometimes and for work every once in a while, but not that often.

You can ask me just about anything that you think of, if you think of anything.

I don't have kids yet, but hopefully one day in the future I will. Do you?

I have a good joke for you:

Grandson: Were you in the war, Grandpa?
Grandpa: Yes, I was a fighter pilot.
Kid's mom: Weren't you stationed in Illinois, Dad?
Grandpa: Yes, and I'll have you know not one enemy aircraft got past Missouri!

Good in a cheesy way, right?

Last but not least, before you fall asleep from boredom, I'm a night owl and do my best work then, that's why I'm up late every night.

Best wishes,
Ruby

From: Aaron.Tanner.Hall.mil@mail.mil
Date: September 27, 2008 2:14 p.m.
To: RubyMars@mail.com
Subject: RE: Hi Part 2

Ruby,

Let me get this straight. The soldier before me was sending you pictures of his "tick"? How did that even get started? Would it make it any better if I told you that your country appreciates your dedication, nudies or not? . . . that was supposed to be a joke.

What happened at Mardi Gras? You've got me imagining different scenarios again and it could be any of them . . . Most of them aren't good. There's a reason I've never been.

Cleopatra is one of the most expensive movies ever made? When I first read the 65 costume change thing it didn't seem that . . . cool . . . but now that I'm thinking about it, that's a lot of costumes, and they weren't jeans and a T-shirt I'm guessing.

Don't get me started on gaming. I needed an intervention to get me off *WoW* . . . *World of Warcraft* . . . on my last long leave. I didn't leave my spot in front of the computer for two weeks unless it was to use the bathroom or grab food. You ever played it?

Your sister's a figure skater? Like the ones on TV at the Olympics?

My ex-stepmom named Aries. She used to teach mythology and folklore.

Why'd you name your ferret Logan? For Wolverine?

You're only 23? I thought you were older. Ten years between the oldest and youngest isn't so bad. Did you drive your parents crazy? I do miss mine but not that much. I'm the middle one.

I'm sure your life is a hell of a lot more interesting than mine. For real. It's the same thing every day. Work, eat, work out, sleep, video games.

I don't have any kids either. Are you married? Don't mean to sound like Soldier #2, just curious since you said you hoped to have some.

That joke . . . :] Cheesy good.

What do you do for a living where you can stay up all night?

–A

From: RubyMars@mail.com
Date: September 30, 2008 1:05 a.m.
To: Aaron.Tanner.Hall.mil@mail.mil
Subject: Tick Licks and Other Nosey Stuff

Hi Aaron,

Of course you want the story behind the dick pics. (Excuse my French.) I don't really know how we even got to that point in our e-mails. I'll call Soldier #2 "Smith." Smith and I had been e-mailing each other for about five months when he first started sending me pictures of himself. No biggie. He'd always been nothing but polite, asking me questions about myself, normal getting-to-know-you stuff. About two months after he started with the head-shots, he started sending me some full body pictures that were a little funny in not a good way. I didn't say anything. The next thing I knew, I had a version of half-mast on my cell phone screen. Then, I had the full sausage and eggs, if you get my drift. No thank you. I would rather volunteer as a nurse on the front lines than send some random guy a picture of my no-no parts.

I already told you about the soldier, you tell me what you think happened at Mardi Gras, and I'll confirm or deny.

The only movies I can think of that have been more expensive are *Titanic*, *Pirates of the Caribbean*, *Waterworld* and *Spider-Man*. Those all came out thirty years after *Cleopatra* did. Crazy, huh? You're right, none of the costumes were jeans and T-shirts. They were all really intricate. I want to say I read somewhere they spent almost two hundred thousand dollars just on her wardrobe alone.

Have I ever played *WoW*? I led my own *WoW* guild when I was 18, thank you very much. I finally had to go cold turkey my second semester in college because I started to see I was going to fail if I didn't get my shit together. MMORPGs are dangerous. I can't even look at the game in stores without starting to itch. I can relate to Smeagol's obsession a little too well. No joke. (Smeagol is a character off *Lord of the Rings*, FYI.)

My sister is trying to eventually qualify for the Olympics. She's won a bronze medal at a major junior competition two years in a row. She didn't start skating until she was nine, and most that go professional get on the ice when they're barely learning how to walk, so you can say we all think she's pretty amazing for going so far in such a short time. I could talk all day about her, if you can't tell.

In high school, we spent a whole semester on Greek mythology in English. I still remember a lot of it. I read a lot, too.

I didn't name him after the *X-Men*. Logan is a character on one of my favorite TV shows, *Veronica Mars*.

How old are your siblings? Do they still live in Louisiana? You're right, five kids in ten years is a lot. I don't know how my mom survived, but I feel like that's part of the reason why her and my dad's marriage didn't make it. They could never agree on how to deal with us. My mom is bananas too.

How old did you think I was . . .? How old are you?

As boring as your life may or may not be, if you ever need to vent with someone, I'm here. I'll keep my judging to a minimum.

I have one niece. I'm not married, but I do have a boyfriend. The whole having-kids thing is a dream for some time in the future, but I'm not rushing or anything. I want to have four. Are you married?

What do I do for a living? I'm a seamstress. My aunt is a manager at a dry cleaning place, and I get a lot of alteration work from her. (A LOT.) I have another aunt who owns her own bridal shop, and I help her out there, too. I've done wedding dresses, sweet sixteen and quinceañera dresses . . . If anything needs to be sewn and made, I can and have done it more than likely. I do freelance work too, costumes and things like that, but that isn't steady. Apart from two days a week where my aunt with the bridal shop asks me to come in to help out, I can work any time I want. It's nice, but I don't sleep much.

How long have you been in the military?

Best wishes,
Ruby

Chapter Five

October

From: Aaron.Tanner.Hall.mil@mail.mil
Date: October 1, 2008 4:17 a.m.
To: RubyMars@mail.com
Subject: Tick Licks?

Ruby,

Half mast . . . sausage and eggs . . . I scared half the room
from how hard I laughed. I can't remember the last time
that happened. All serious, "Smith" can get into a lot of
trouble for sending you things like that. What's his name?
I don't know what to say to you regarding your no-no
parts. Just going to let that one go. :]

I'm game to guess what happened to Mardi Gras. Did
someone throw up on you at the parade?

I did a search on your movie before I replied just now.
It says the film almost went bankrupt. Now I'm guessing
you liked the costumes in the other movies you've watched
a thousand times too?

You took *WoW* to a whole new level. You led your own
guild? No wonder you almost failed. Did you go days

without showering? One of the guys I went to AIT with . . . advanced individual training after boot camp . . . used to be really into it. When we talked about it, his eyes glazed over. I stopped bringing it up. I know who Smeagol is. I've seen *LoTR*. You can give me some credit. I don't only watch 80s movies.

Your sister is trying to qualify for the Olympics? Wow. I'll be honest, I've never watched any figure skating in my life, but everybody knows you can't get to the Olympics unless you're the best at something.

Is *Veronica Mars* the reason your e-mail is RubyMars?

My sister is 25 now and my brother is 31. They both still live in Shreveport. Your parents are divorced?

I told you most of the people who sign up for HaS have families. I assumed you'd be closer to 30, I guess. I'm 28.

You don't hear that very often any more (women wanting to have kids). Whatever makes you happy. I'm not married either. Do you live with your boyfriend?

I don't want to come off as an asshole, but that's your job? Sewing?

I've been in the army for almost eleven years. Time has gone so fast . . . You said your brother was a marine in one of your e-mails. How long was he in for? Where had he been deployed or on tour?

Hope to hear from you soon.

–A

From: RubyMars@mail.com
Date: October 3, 2008 5:05 a.m.
To: Aaron.Tanner.Hall.mil@mail.mil
Subject: Tick Licks for Sure

Aaron,

I appreciate the concern, but don't worry about it. I'm sure my "Eww. What's that?" comment did enough to traumatize him for a while. :) Plus, the HaS people kicked him out of the program, or at least that's what they told me. I thought about looking him up on Myspace a few months ago but decided against it. I've seen enough of him for a couple of lifetimes.

Yes, someone did throw up on me at the parade, but that was just my best friend and it was only my shoes that got yacked on. Continue with your guesses.

Is the shower question a trick question? Since we're [pen] pals, I'll tell you the truth: yes. The longest I went was five days without a shower when I was really into WoW. My sister paid me fifty dollars to put the whole family out of their misery and bathe.

The costumes are exactly why I like all those movies. The wardrobe, visual effects, makeup . . . it's pretty amazing when you think about it. If you can't tell, I do. :)

Did you read the LoTR books or only watch the movies? I'm not judging, just asking. You will get bonus points if you read the books.

I doubt you have time to browse the web, but you can look up my sister's videos. Her name is Jasmine. Same last name.

Ding, ding, ding on the Veronica Mars connection. I have a grown-up e-mail too for work-related purposes. This is my fun/spam e-mail.

That's nice your siblings live in the same city. Does your dad still live there? All of us still live in Houston, too. Yes, my parents are divorced. They have been since I was 8, but they were separated for a year before that.

My older brother gives me so much flak every time I say I want to have kids, like he can't believe why I'd want them, and not be single and ready to mingle for the rest of my life. He has one daughter (and she was an accident if I'm going to be honest). I figure, it's my life and my body, I can do whatever I want with it. I don't judge other people who want different things out of their lives, why should he have a say with what I do with mine, you know what I mean?

I went pretty deep with that. It's obviously not a soft spot. :)

You aren't married but do you have someone special in your life? I don't live with my boyfriend.

You have no idea how many times people ask me that. "That's what you do?" "You live off that?" It's normal. If you want to know, I started sewing when I was 6. I wanted a Sleeping Beauty costume for Halloween that didn't exist, so my mom shoved a bunch of random clothes at me she didn't wear anymore and told me to figure it out. (That's how she's taught all of us almost everything. I'll tell you how she taught me to ride my bike another day.) Another one of my aunts had been a seamstress and she helped me when I told her about the costume I wanted to make, and she kept teaching me as I grew up. I loved it. When I got old enough to work, I needed a part-time job on the weekends and my other aunt (the one who manages the dry cleaner), hired me. After that, I just kept making my own costumes on the side . . . Then other people would ask me to help them with theirs . . . the rest is history. My bridal shop aunt hired me, etc., etc. I also make ice-skating dresses like the ones my sister wears for competitions. My mom couldn't afford to keep buying her dresses, so I started making them for her. (For the record, the first few things I made her were crap.)

That might be more information than you wanted to know. :)

Do you want to be career army? My brother was in for 5 years. On his last deployment, he had an accident with an IED and was seriously injured by shrapnel. I'm pretty sure he almost died, but he and my mom were so secretive about it, they never said for sure. He has a limp and he's too much of a prude to show anyone his scars. I think he would have stayed if that hadn't happened, but who knows? I'm just happy he's alive and fine. He had stories about plenty of other guys he knew who didn't have anyone there for them. If it weren't for him, I wouldn't be here writing to you. I figured, how many other people are out there alone, needing some kind of interaction even with a stranger?

Hope I didn't bore you to death. This is a lot longer than I had anticipated.

Best,
Ruby

From: Aaron.Tanner.Hall.mil@mail.mil
Date: October 5, 2008 1:17 p.m.
To: RubyMars@mail.com
Subject: Eww

Ruby,

I think half the men in here thought I lost my mind from how hard I laughed at your "Eww" comment. I'm still laughing. You're going to make me start expecting to crack up first thing with every e-mail you send. If you change your mind about me reaching out to "Smith," let me know. The offer stands.

Continue? More happened at Mardi Gras?

Less than a week without a shower? That's rookie level. I've gone over a month while on deployment in the past. I was in Iraq at one point in 2003, and we didn't have showers for a long time. Imagine a whole company who hadn't used soap on their armpits in almost 6 weeks. We didn't change our uniforms or socks all the time either. Think about that.

What other movie has the best costumes?

No bonus points for me. I've only seen the Rings movies. I'm going to take it that you've read the series? I've only read a few fantasy books, all of them while on tour.

I'll look your sister up on my next day off when I get more time.

You're the first person I've heard of with multiple e-mails, but most of my friends wouldn't need to have more than one. Nobody wants to e-mail them anyway.

My brother works for my dad and lives on his own, but my little sister still lives with him. She's on the Autism spectrum. I think one day she'd be fine getting her own place if she really wanted to. For now she's good with him.

I've never thought about having kids or not having kids like that. Why's it anyone's business what you want or don't want? It's your choice. I like kids. Maybe one day I can have one or two . . . I don't know about four.

I don't have anybody special in my life anymore. To be honest . . . that's why I didn't write you back for a while.

My girl broke up with me right after I got here. It came out of nowhere.

How long have you been with your boyfriend?

Ice-skating dresses? In Houston? That's the last place I could see a figure skater coming from. I figured they'd all come from up north. Are there classes you take to get better at sewing or something? Not trying to come off like a dick again, but I had no clue "ice-skating outfits" was even a thing. I can sew a hem all right, but that's it.

I'm sorry about your brother. That kind of thing happens a lot more than you'd think. Between us . . . I don't know what I want to do. Some days, especially when things aren't great here, I'm ready to do something else. Other times I think I could handle more years of it. I don't know. This is all I've ever done besides working at a pizza place when I was in HS and helping my dad out. What else could I do?

Like you said, that was a lot deeper than I thought it'd be. Not a sore spot or anything. :]

You didn't bore me at all. I like my letters from my other "adopters" like you call them, but yours make me laugh. You can tell me anything and I'm sure it would be funny.

You can send more pictures like the Aurora Borealis one anytime you want . . . if you have any.

Hope to hear from you soon,
Aaron

From: RubyMars@mail.com
Date: October 6, 2008 2:05 a.m.
To: Aaron.Tanner.Hall.mil@mail.mil
Subject: Showers, Costumes, and Things

Aaron,

You should know one of my favorite things is making people laugh. And by "people," I really mean myself. Game on.

Yes, more things happened. I can't even say getting puked on was the worst. Keep guessing.

A month and a half without a shower? Eww. :) If I don't shower every day, a one-mile perimeter needs to be cleared. Did someone higher up than you finally order a shower to be built when the smell got too bad? I faintly remember my brother mentioning shower trailers. How many men are in a company? I hope I don't regret it, but how long exactly did (or do) you wear the same uniform?

Best costumes in movies . . . *Memoirs of a Geisha, Moulin Rouge, Gone with the Wind, LoTR.* There are so many. Those are just a few of my personal favorites for wardrobe. Have you seen any of those?

I did read the *Lord of the Rings* books, but I haven't read them over and over again like a lot of people I know. Only once. Do you read at all while you're overseas?

The videos aren't going anywhere. She has a big competition in two weeks in Moscow. I'll tell you how it goes.

Please don't feel obligated to answer any of my intrusive questions about your family. I've met a couple people with high-functioning autism before. One of them is married and has a good job.

Your ex breaking up with you while you're gone is really lame. I remember my brother telling me that kind of thing is really common when you're deployed or on a tour. What do they call them? Dear John letters? It wasn't like she didn't know what she was getting herself into when you left. Were you together long? I want to ask if she had a good reason for breaking up with you, but if it was unexpected, I can put two and two together. There I go asking questions that aren't any of my business again. Don't answer that if you don't want to.

Designing and alterations is all I do. If something needs a needle and thread or a sewing machine, I can tackle it, and no, not everything ice-skating related I sell is for people in Houston. I'm about to blow your mind: I have a website. People order my work on there. They send me measurements and I get it done. It's a small percentage of work I get though. I have to turn down work because I either can't take the time off to get outfits done within a certain time frame, or can't go take measurements in person. I've sold ice-dancing dresses and outfits to Russia, France, once to Japan. Mostly, I make things for a discount to younger figure skaters who can't afford the bigger name designers in the industry. It's an expensive sport, and it used to be that most skaters come from wealthy families, but now a lot more don't. I help some ice-skaters resell their costumes when they can't use them anymore, too.

You asked about getting better at sewing/designing. I started taking classes at my community college by my house as soon as I could for needlecraft, pattern making and fashion design, and have gone to a couple workshops. I even did an internship once with this Ukranian lady who yelled at me half the time, but she sure did teach me a lot.

I was so surprised at seeing just how many wounded vets there are. My brother goes to these meetings twice a month, and I've gone with him once. It breaks my heart.

Not every injury is physical. People don't realize that. I'm sure you'll figure out what you want to do whenever the time comes.

What made you go into the military?

I have a few other prints I've collected over the years I could send you, if you wanted. I overheard my brother once tell my other brother about how many topless photos of women the guys he was in the marines with put up on their walls. This is a judgment-free zone. You can put your photos next to whoever or whatever you want.

This is already really long, but you wanted me to tell you something funny so let me do that. I was talking on the phone to my friend this morning (early afternoon, same difference) and was so distracted I poured orange juice into my cereal bowl.

Best wishes,
Ruby

From: Aaron.Tanner.Hall.mil@mail.mil
Date: October 8, 2008 2:17 p.m.
To: RubyMars@mail.com
Subject: RE: Showers, Costumes, and Things

Ruby,

. . . did somebody pee on you? You should know I couldn't type that sentence with a straight face.

No one ordered a shower to be built. The shower trailer had burned down. A few of the guys got desperate and found an industrial coffee maker that they rigged up to warm water, and built a shower out of that. It didn't work great, and you had to stand in mud the whole time, but it was better than nothing. Last deployment I brought one of those bags you fill up with water and let sit in the sun so you can shower outside just in case the same thing happened . . . it worked. Two hundred sweaty men were in my company. I was swapping out T-shirts and socks every other week . . . It was just as bad as you're thinking.

I haven't seen any of those movies. I'll have to take your word that the costumes are cool. Maybe when I get home, I'll look them up.

Are you going with your little sister to Moscow for her competition?

I read some . . . didn't really get into it until I started going overseas and had nothing to do. A lot of us read while we're here to pass the time. When I'm home, I'd rather watch a movie.

You aren't being nosey. I would have asked too. Paige has HFA. My dad worries about her a lot . . . and I guess I do too . . . but I know she could be on her own if she wanted to someday. Social cues give her trouble, but anyone who can't appreciate how honest and kind she is doesn't need to be in her life anyway.

Are you some famous designer and you're playing it cool? Where was your internship with the Ukranian lady? Could you get another internship or do you know . . . everything there is to know? Send pictures of these . . . costumes . . . you've made.

You're right. The worst injuries a person can take aren't always on the outside.

I joined the army because I had nothing else going on . . . still don't, if you want to get technical. I didn't want to sit in a class all day in college and didn't have a trade school I was interested in back then. I didn't want to work for my dad either. The military seemed like a good idea. Looking back on it now, I know I did the right thing joining. If I would've stayed home, who knows what I would've ended up doing or how I would've turned out. Maybe good, maybe not. Who knows.

The military is what keeps a lot of magazines operating. No joke. For the record, I haven't had a "topless" woman on a wall in at least eight years.

I had a bad day today, but your message made me feel better. Maybe everything will work out. I still have almost two years left on this enlistment. I'll figure it out.

The orange juice story made me laugh. You're on top of your game. What else do you have?

–Aaron

From: RubyMars@mail.com
Date: October 10, 2008 3:05 a.m.
To: Aaron.Tanner.Hall.mil@mail.mil
Subject: Jimmy Rigging

Aaron,

Bingo. Someone did pee on my shoes at Mardi Gras. I think that was worse because it was a complete stranger. Continue with your guesses. The crap show retelling isn't over.

A shower out of a coffee maker? Something is better than nothing. Do you have a shower trailer where you're at now? I'm also not going to make a comment about changing your clothes every other week.

No, I'm not going with her to Moscow. It's too expensive. She only travels with her coach to international qualifying events. If she moves on to a final, I'll charge the trip onto my credit card. That's what I usually do.

Now you have me curious. What do you guys read? I know you said some fantasy, but what else?

I hope I don't regret asking, but are you close to your dad? Does he or your siblings write you while you're gone?

Famous. Now you're trying to make me laugh. I'll send you a picture of the dress I made my sister for her short program (that's one of her routines. It's the shortest one if you can't tell from the title.) I could do another internship. There's always something more to learn, but I don't know. Everyone cried last time I left, and that had only been to Philadelphia where my cousin lives. I'd been 19 back then. I have more responsibilities now. I'd be scared to quit my jobs.

Joining the military for that reason makes a lot of sense. Who knows what they want to do with their lives when they're 18? Maybe a few people do, but most don't. With my brother, he learned discipline and grew as a person. It gave him more stability and accountability than my mom gave him. She let him get away with *everything* when we were younger. She'd never admit it, but he's her favorite.

I don't blame anyone for putting up topless pictures of women on their walls. You might as well have something nice to look at while you're over there. :)

Sorry to hear about your bad day. Like I've told you before, if you ever want to vent, I'm here. Just tell me you don't want a response, and I won't even say a word. I know sometimes you just have to talk and don't necessarily want an opinion back.

I'm glad my ruined breakfast made at least one of us happy. :P This isn't that funny, but last night I was trying to put pepper on my dinner and the entire cap came off. There was literally what looked like three tablespoons of pepper on my plate. My little sister and I play pranks on each other, so I know it was her doing. I purposely didn't call to blame her. I don't need her to know she got me. I'll plan my revenge so she doesn't expect it.

Hope you're okay,
Ruby

From: Aaron.Tanner.Hall.mil@mail.mil
Date: October 13, 2008 1:22 p.m.
To: RubyMars@mail.com
Subject: RE: Jimmy Rigging

Ruby,

Crap show . . . are you trying to tell me something? Did you go with anyone else other than your friend? I want to ask if you got rained on, but that's too obvious. Did you step in crap? Human crap if you want to be specific.

We do have showers. The water isn't the best; they tell us not to open our eyes or get any in our mouths, but you deal. At one point on another deployment, they paid a water truck to spray us down because we were in the same situation with no shower facilities. You really grow to appreciate hot water over here.

If she makes it through the qualifying rounds, do you already know where the final is?

What do we read . . . there's a lot of fantasy, thriller, mystery, court drama stuff . . . some romance books too. *Halo* is the most action a lot of us like to deal with. The rest gets our mind off things going on around us. We share books around here all the time. Do you read? I can't remember if you told me you do or not.

Me and my dad get along all right. He isn't a fan of me being in the army, but we talk and message at least once a week. I can't complain much. My sister and brother both write, but not as often . . . Maybe once a month.

That picture you sent me of your sister's ice-skating costume looks like something that belongs in a museum. You made that? For real?

I'll tell you why I was upset. You might have seen it on the news already, but two soldiers were killed while on patrol. I've known one of them for a few years. We'd been stationed in Germany together. Our Internet gets blacked out every time an incident like that happens, to give the military time to identify the bodies and contact families. This time, they blacked it out for two days. One of the guys' sisters messaged me after she found out because he'd told her we were here together and he had given her my e-mail "just in case." "Just in case" are the worst three words in the world, don't let anybody tell you different. You can't not expect the worst . . . that would be stupid, but . . . I don't know . . . What's messed up is that a part of me wishes he hadn't done that. How do you tell someone's sister . . . somebody who doesn't want to believe her little brother is gone . . . that it's true? Not going to front, writing her back gave me stomach cramps.

Pranks are a big thing here, even though half of them go wrong with all the high emotions and the stress everyone is under all the time. A few days ago, someone got a care package and offered to share things he got and it almost caused a fight. He mixed bags of M&Ms and Skittles in a container. Separate, great. Together? Not so much.

Hope to hear from you soon.

–A

From: RubyMars@mail.com
Date: October 15, 2008 1:05 a.m.
To: Aaron.Tanner.Hall.mil@mail.mil
Subject: Poop water?

Aaron,

. . . how did you know I stepped in a pile of poop? Has it happened to you?

I'm scared to ask and sorry to bring up the "P" word again, but is there poop in the water? Is that why they don't want you putting it in your mouth? What do you do about brushing your teeth? Bottled water?

If my little sister makes it through (and I think she will), the final will be in France in December. My mom and her husband told me they're going to Russia with her. They had applied for a visa, but it hadn't come through until now, so they're scrambling for plane tickets. She's the baby and everyone spoils her.

Sharing books makes a lot of sense. That's nice to hear you all aren't greedy. You could start a book swap for money. Not saying that you need it, but you could make it work. I think I've heard of people doing that in jail, setting up a bartering system type thing. Romance and fantasy novels floating around base doesn't sound crazy at all.

Everyone needs a happily ever after. Now tell me the truth. I'm not judging. How many of them have you read?

I like reading anything and everything. :)

You're flattering me to death. Yes, I made that dress. It took me almost a hundred hours to make it.

You have a heart and a conscience, losing someone you know is going to be hard. I doubt it's ever supposed to be easy. I'm really sorry about your friend and the other soldiers. I don't really know what to say besides I'm sorry, and even that sounds lame, but I hope you understand where I'm coming from.

Mixing M&Ms and Skittles? That's mean. I would never do something like that. I'm lying. My sister and I rigged up an airbag once for my brother who isn't a marine. That was the best $100 I've ever spent.

Hope you're doing all right.

–Ruby

From: Aaron.Tanner.Hall.mil@mail.mil
Date: October 19, 2008 1:44 p.m.
To: RubyMars@mail.com
Subject: RE: Poop Water

Ruby,

The server has been down for the last few days. Sorry for not writing back sooner.

I've never admitted to anyone except to my friends who were with me, but yeah, I've stepped in a warm pile of crap once. Appreciate you joining the club.

There's all kinds of things in the water, not limited to

the brown stuff. You're supposed to rinse out your mouth with bottled water. They purify it so fast to meet demand it isn't really filtered at all, but it's gotten better than it was years ago. Some of us have gotten kidney stones from how many minerals there were in it at one point. Add that up with getting constipation from the MREs and it's a party on your intestines.

Why do I have a feeling you're a hustler? Trying to get me to start a bartering system . . . It made me smile. This stays between us, right? I've read four romances. Two of them were pretty cheesy, but the others weren't bad. I get why the shelves at the grocery store back home are stocked. Sometimes it's nice to deal with things that aren't all about life and death.

What do you like reading?

A hundred hours to make one dress? Is that normal?

What did your brother do to deserve getting the airbag trick?

Sorry this is short. Everyone wants to check their e-mails.

Hope you had a good week.

–Aaron

From: RubyMars@mail.com
Date: October 22, 2008 3:05 a.m.
To: Aaron.Tanner.Hall.mil@mail.mil
Subject: The Poop Club

Aaron,

Don't even worry about it. I'm glad you're fine.

Thank you for inviting me to this exclusive club I regret admitting being a member of. :) When and why did you step in it? It = poop.

Kidney stones from the water. Whoa. You guys drink a ton of it too to stay hydrated, don't you? I had a friend who passed stones once. She said it was almost as bad as giving birth, and she doesn't have your . . . parts . . . genitals . . . you know what I mean.

Me? A hustler? Busted. After my parents split up, money was tight (remember I mentioned making my own Halloween costumes?). I made lemonade and babysat every weekend. When I was old enough to get a job, I didn't have a car so I couldn't get a normal job, and we lived too far away to walk anywhere (don't get me started on my mom thinking if I took the bus I would end up on a milk carton—keep in mind people haven't been putting kids' faces on milk cartons since the 80s). What I made during the weekends helping my aunt do patch-up jobs and making random ice-skating outfits for my sister and other girls in her classes was enough to make up for not working after school.

If you want, you can tell me which two romances you read that you enjoyed. I'm curious, and by curious, what I'm trying to tell you is that I want to read them.

No judging, right? I've read *Twilight* more times than I can count, *The Alchemist*, *Pride and Prejudice*, and *The Chronicles of Narnia* over and over and over again.

The fabric I used for her dress is really hard to work with, but the adorning (the beads and crystals) were a giant pain in the butt. If anyone else had asked for it, I would've charged them an arm and a leg or said no, but I couldn't say no to my sister. I didn't want her to skate in front of hundreds of people looking raggedy.

My brother switched the salt with the sugar the day before Thanksgiving. Every dessert was ruined and the turkey . . . no. No. He deserved what he got. We ended up having to go to KFC to buy food. I have the video on my phone of him and the airbag if you want to see it. It's just about my favorite thing in the world.

My dumb story of the week: I walked into a glass patio door yesterday. There's still a red mark on my forehead. Enjoy that.

Take care,
Ruby

From: Aaron.Tanner.Hall.mil@mail.mil
Date: October 26, 2008 1:41 p.m.
To: RubyMars@mail.com
Subject: RE: The Poop Club

Ruby,

Did you pee in a dark corner at Mardi Gras too? I stepped in crap at a music festival once. Pissed me off for days, and I had to throw away my shoes.

It's tough staying hydrated in the desert. I drink gallons a day and pee all the time. You sweat nonstop for hours, but on some days, even if you think you're drinking enough water, you might only go twice. Those are the days you have to worry.

I can't remember the titles of those books I read. Not lying, I'm being for real. The names were familiar though. I'm sure they carry them at the grocery store.

The only one of those you mentioned that I've read has been *Chronicles of Narnia*, but the rest I haven't. Sparkly vampires aren't my thing. :] The only book I've reread in my life was *Ender's Game*. Have you read that one?

The thing about your mom thinking you were going to get kidnapped made me laugh. If she didn't love you, she wouldn't worry. Did you use your lemonade money to buy a sewing machine? My sister used to have one of those things that puts beads on clothes. Did you have one of those? I just realized you've mentioned being close to your brothers and sisters but not your parents. Do they live close by? Did they remarry?

You stitched each bead on your sister's dress? It looks like there's a thousand on there.

All right, the thing with your brother makes sense. You don't ruin Thanksgiving dinner. Did he learn his lesson? My family was never into pranks. If I would've done that, they all would've lost it, and not in the same way.

Send a picture of your forehead.

–A

From: Aaron.Tanner.Hall.mil@mail.mil
Date: October 30, 2008 12:17 p.m.
To: RubyMars@mail.com
Subject: Thank you

Ruby,

I got your package in the mail today. Thank you for my pizza kit. Freeze dried cheese? I read your instructions step by step twice. How'd you figure out melting it would

work? I've already had people trying to buy it off me . . .
the movies, pictures and snacks too. The salt and vinegar
chips will be gone in two days max. Thanks a lot.

Hope you're okay.

–Aaron

Chapter Six

November

From: RubyMars@mail.com
Date: November 1, 2008 2:01 a.m.
To: Aaron.Tanner.Hall.mil@mail.mil
Subject: Surprise!

Aaron,

I'm glad you got the package! I wasn't sure how long it would take to get there. Besides sending my brother things (and he'd never tell me he got them or say thank you), I've only sent one other person care packages (not the "tick lick" guy). I dragged my brother with me to Target and made him help me choose things for you. I put my thinking cap on to figure out how I could send you cheese that wasn't perishable (there aren't that many options) and then experimented a lot. I ruined a pound of the freeze-dried stuff before I got the measurements for the water to cheese ratio correct to rehydrate it. It isn't the best tasting pizza in the world, and if you hate it, my feelings won't be hurt. :)

I bought and sent you a few books yesterday. Only

books, nothing else, don't get too excited. Hope you don't care about surprises. I don't.

Me? Find a dark spot to pee in? Busted. I'm crying laughing. I made my friend keep an eye out for me while I did it. Now I need to text her and remind her about it so she can laugh too. Did someone you know tell you they had to do that? There's nowhere to pee!

Worrying about how much you pee in a day is something I never even thought about. Do they give you bottles of water or do you reuse them?

You "don't remember the titles." Okay. Right. I pinky swear I won't judge whatever your read. Hint, hint, hint.

I read *Twilight* right after it came out. I was 19. This is a judgment-free zone, remember? ☺ Have I read *Ender's Game*? Is there a moon in the sky? I'm kidding. Yes, I did, and I enjoyed it a lot.

I know my mom loves me. You can't be that overprotective if you didn't love someone, and there's no one more protective than my mom. If she could have given me everything I ever wanted, she would have. After my parents separated, we all stayed with her. My dad moved back to San Francisco. That's where most of his family lives. He has a sister who lives here in Houston. The only reason my parents moved here (Texas) was because of my mom's family. My dad hated living here. He says the humidity reminded him too much of the Philippines when he was a kid.

I still see my dad at least once a year. He comes down to visit, and I try to go see him sometimes in Cali. He got remarried a few years ago to a nice woman with three kids who are cool. My mom on the other hand . . . she's been remarried three times since him. Husband #4 is five years older than me.

There's one thousand two hundred and four beads/ sequins on the dress I made her. Good guess.

My brother didn't learn his lesson. On Christmas that year, he brought a pan of brownies. Pot brownies. Everyone except my little sister ended up high as a kite. It was probably the best Christmas I've ever had since I was a kid. It was a lot of fun even though my mom got really mad afterward.

Why weren't your parents into pranking? Are they really serious? Not that there's anything wrong with it, just curious.

No picture or video of running into the door, but it happened. Ben, husband #4, was on the floor laughing. My mom walked out of the kitchen. Luckily it was only them who saw it, otherwise it would take two lifetimes to live it down instead of one. My mom texted everyone to tell them what happened. That's my family for you.

I just got home from a concert. I left my earplugs at home and don't think my ears will ever be the same. I'm about to pass out. Hope you're okay.

–Ruby

From: Aaron.Tanner.Hall.mil@mail.mil
Date: November 3, 2008 3:27 p.m.
To: RubyMars@mail.com
Subject: Strange stuff

Ruby,

I really do appreciate you sending me the box. I reread the message I sent and it didn't sound half as appreciative as

I wanted it to. Don't know how you even thought to try dehydrated cheese, but it was genius. I already ate one pizza and have zero complaints. It was a little piece of home I needed after this crap week. I nuked everything in the microwave like your instructions said . . . Debating whether to stretch out what I got left or eat more tomorrow. I try not to save things just in case there isn't another time, know what I mean? I'm looking forward to seeing what books you sent. Thanks. Really.

Ruby, I had just been kidding about peeing . . .

I've been through a patrol where we only had a canteen a day. We can get as much water as we want. I don't take it for granted. They tell us to crush the water bottles when we're done with them so that the company who does the bottling doesn't try to reuse them.

I swear I don't remember the titles of the books. If I see the covers, I'd recognize them. I'll tell you if I see them.

Ender's Game is one of those books I wish they'd make into a movie . . . but I bet it wouldn't be as good as the book.

That's good you still keep in touch with your dad, but I can't get over your mom being remarried to someone a few years older than you. Is that weird? Do you care?

Your brother got all of you high?

Growing up, my parents were strict Baptists and both their parents . . . my grandparents . . . were . . . uptight. I don't remember any of them ever laughing or smiling. My dad's a good guy. I wouldn't call my birth mom a good person though, but she was all right when I was real little. Nothing seemed . . . off . . . until I was in middle school and started spending time at my best friend's place that I noticed how different things were. It isn't a big deal now. My dad's happy enough, and my birth mom . . . I don't know if she'll ever be happy, but that's on her.

What concert did you go to? Did you have a good time? What do you do when you don't work? I know you said you kill ducks for fun, but what else?

My ex e-mailed me. She wanted to let me know she added me as a reference on a job application. I don't know why she would think that's a good idea. Does she expect me to answer my imaginary phone or write back an e-mail telling someone to hire her? Would you ever ask an ex for a reference, or is that as stupid of a request as I think it is? My mind is blown, but maybe I'm that tired. You tell me.

You don't have to answer my question ^^^ if you don't want to. Sometimes I feel like I don't understand women and never will. No offense . . . I don't mean you.

–A

From: RubyMars@mail.com
Date: November 4, 2008 1:05 a.m.
To: Aaron.Tanner.Hall.mil@mail.mil
Subject: No

Aaron,

Your message was fine, and I'm relieved my cheese experiments weren't in vain. :) I had my mom's husband try some of it to give me a second opinion. Not that it says much because I've seen him eat food with mold on it after he scraped it off.

If you were anyone else and our conversations were any different, I would feel more embarrassed than I do right now, but I think we're past that. I peed in public. I'll own up to it.

Speaking of peeing . . . do you pee in the bottles? My brother told me when he was in Afghanistan and it was cold, that there was no way he was getting out of bed to go to the bathroom. He'd roll over and pee in one instead. Not that he learned that in the military or anything. He and my brother mastered that art on family road trips when my mom would refuse to stop to use the bathroom, unless she needed to go, to save time.

I agree. I'd love for them to make a movie, but I doubt it would be as good. (But the costumes!)

Lol! Each husband has gotten younger and better looking. My mom was twenty-eight when she had me, so get that into perspective. After my dad, husband #2 was three years younger than her. (My mom is ten years younger than my dad). They were together for two years. Husband #3 was ten years younger than her, and they stayed together 8 years. He was my favorite. Husband #4 has been around a year now. They work at the same company and met that way. The next thing I knew, she was bringing him over for Thanksgiving, and by Christmas, they were married.

My older sister isn't a fan of how many times she's been married, and she hates that the men have been so young. The rest of us though don't really care. I don't. My mom doesn't look her age. If you look up cougar in the dictionary, they would have her name as an example in a sentence. Who am I to tell her not to snag some young guy if she can? I think for a long time, she was hurt because of splitting up with my dad and wanted to make a point, but she didn't let it keep her down. Honestly, I think my dad still gets jealous over it. Maybe I shouldn't pick favorites, but . . . go Mom, you know?

That was an info drop.

We were high out of our minds thanks to those brownies on Christmas, Aaron. I'm not exaggerating. Usually people have family get-togethers and you know there's going to be leftovers that everyone has to take home, right? There weren't any. NONE. If the grocery store would have been open, I'm sure we would have taken a taxi to go buy snacks. We laughed the entire night. I should've known something was up when my little sister was going to break her diet for once to get a piece and he didn't let her. Part of me hopes he'll do it again this year, but we'll see. Maybe I can hint at it. Please don't call the cops on us.

I understand the religious point. I have a friend who was raised with a cult-type religious family. She couldn't wear skirts, tie up her hair, or watch television. She ended up running away when we were in high school. My mom was a pretty strict Catholic up until she and my dad got divorced. Then she decided the church wasn't so important, lol. The only time she goes now is for family baptisms and maybe Easter. I am sorry to hear that your relationship with your birth mom isn't the best.

How long have you and your best friend known each other?

I went to see my favorite band. They're called The Cloud Collision. You probably haven't heard of them. They're indie rock with an even balance of screaming and amazing vocals. It's kind of hard to explain. I've been a fan for a few years. Every time they play close by, I go watch them.

When I'm not killing ducks on television, reading or playing pranks on my family, I like to go to the movies. I used to be pretty big into cosplay (if you don't know what that is, I can explain, but I don't want to assume you don't since you play video games), but my friends have kind of chilled out on going to conventions, and since I work so much, I don't make costumes for fun like I used to. I like trying new things too. I was taking some kickboxing classes recently, and before that I did aikido for a while. I like going to festivals and museums too.

I hope I'm not crossing the line when I tell you your ex has lost it. What was she thinking trying to use you as a reference? If you two had gotten off on good terms, I would understand, but from the little you told me, that doesn't seem like the case.

For the record, I've been a female for twenty-three years and I still don't understand myself half the time. Good luck.

Hope you're okay.

–Ruby

From: Aaron.Tanner.Hall.mil@mail.mil
Date: November 9, 2008 2:51 p.m.
To: RubyMars@mail.com
Subject: Yes

Ruby,

Sorry for the delay again. We had another blackout. It's been a rough week.

I think we're good to say we can talk about body . . . stuff at this point. :]

I've got peeing into water bottles mastered. I could teach a class on doing it without standing up. Winters in Afghanistan are no joke, your brother was right. You don't roll out of your warm cot to pee outside there.

You and your costumes. Some of us watched *The Dark Knight* and I caught myself looking at what all the actors wore. I'm blaming you.

#4 is more than twenty years younger than your mom? Your dad has got to be jealous. I would. She must be a hell of a woman.

Good call on your brother not letting your sister have any. I bet they drug test her, right? I haven't had special brownies since high school. If your brother brings some for Christmas, I'll have to live through you. Record it. I wouldn't call the cops on you.

Don't apologize about my birth mom. She hasn't been in my life for twenty years.

I have two best friends. The one I mentioned I've known since seventh grade, that's about eighteen years. My other best friend, I met freshman year of high school.

I haven't heard of The Cloud Collision, but I like the name.

I know what cosplay is. Which characters did you do? I've always wanted to go to one of the big conventions they have. Why did you start taking aikido classes? The only kind of festivals I've ever been to have been music ones . . . remember the stepping in crap accident . . . but I've only been to two, and one was in Germany. It was . . . wild.

I don't know what my ex was on writing me that. She has other people she could ask . . . I don't get it. You ever had any exes do stupid stuff like that? Say yes, I wouldn't mind knowing someone else has had it worse than me sometimes. Every girl I've ever dated has been the devil. My best friend says I'm a magnet for the crazy ones and liars.

Hope you're all right.

–Aaron

From: RubyMars@mail.com
Date: November 10, 2008 12:05 a.m.
To: Aaron.Tanner.Hall.mil@mail.mil
Subject: Hi

Aaron,

I'm sorry about the blackout. I hope it wasn't someone you know again.

What's your tent situation like? My brother told me once, and this was a few years ago when everyone was in the Middle East, that a lot of reservists who were stationed where he was had to sleep outside because there wasn't enough room. He'd complain about how bad the mosquitoes and the mice were. Yuck. I just picture them crawling all over you while you're sleeping on the floor.

I'm stupidly pleased at you appreciating the wardrobe for Batman. I remember reading the designer had to make her own material for the suit. It's dorky, but I think that is so mind-blowing. I like movies where I can enjoy those details.

My mom is a hell of a woman. I'll send you a picture as long as you promise not to become my new stepdad. I like #4.

Lol! I'll have my phone on me Thanksgiving Day just in case anything goes down worth recording. I'm sure it will. To answer your question about drug testing, yes, my little sister does get tested. She's paranoid and only takes aspirin and basic antibiotics whenever she gets sick.

So are all three of you BFFs? What do they do?

I love cosplay. I've done a lot of costumes, but my favorites were during my *Fifth Element* phase. Have you seen it? I've always wanted to go to the big conventions too! I've only been to local ones. The only reason why I started taking aikido was because I was bored and this gym by my mom's house was having a New Years' deal. I got my older sister to do it with me, but she quit after a few months. I've never been into sports; if I see a ball anywhere close by, I'm going to turn around and walk the other way, but I like martial arts.

Aren't those festivals in Germany insane and just packed with people? How long was your tour there?

How long were you and your ex together?

^^ You don't have to answer that. As for you being a magnet for crazy girls and liars, I don't want to say you only have yourself to blame, but you're the one who decided to date them, right? :) I'm messing with you. Kind of. I'd think you were full of crap about the kind of women you attract, but my oldest brother is the same way. My older sister says he gets all the "batshit crazy" ones, and it's true. He's had his car keyed three times by three different women. My niece's mom is the devil. He's had stalkers. You guys either like the crazy or need a new radar.

It's been a while since I shared a joke with you. Here you go:

What do you call fake spaghetti?

. . . an im-pasta.

You're welcome.

Hope you're okay.

–Ruby

From: RubyMars@mail.com
Date: November 10, 2008 12:25 a.m.
To: Aaron.Tanner.Hall.mil@mail.mil
Subject: I'm Sorry

Aaron,

I hope you'll forgive me for not telling you the truth, but I can't keep going with it. I feel so bad. I can't handle the lies anymore.

I don't have a boyfriend. I've never had a boyfriend. I made him up when we first started messaging each other because I was paranoid after the incident with the "tick lick" guy. Now that I've gotten to know you and like you, I know you aren't anything like him. I'm sorry for not being upfront with you to begin with, but I hope you understand why I did it.

The repentant liar,
Ruby

From: Aaron.Tanner.Hall.mil@mail.mil
Date: November 12, 2008 12:07 p.m.
To: RubyMars@mail.com
Subject: RE: I'm sorry

I'll write back everything else later, but I wanted to write you back about your fake boyfriend first.

I'm not pissed you did it. I get it. I thought something was up with how vague you were being talking about him. Most girls always bring up their boyfriend unless they're . . . trying to get with someone else on the side. It's no big deal if that's the only thing you haven't been honest about, but I'd be surprised if there was something else. You don't seem like that kind of person.

But that is the only thing you've lied to me about, yeah?

I saw there had been a hurricane heading toward Texas a few days ago. You make it through all right?

–Aaron

From: RubyMars@mail.com
Date: November 12, 2008 4:05 a.m.
To: Aaron.Tanner.Hall.mil@mail.mil
Subject: So Sorry

Aaron,

I cross my heart that's all I've lied to you about. I just couldn't keep going with it.

I'm sorry. I've been making myself sick worrying about lying to you.

–Ruby

P.S. The worst of the hurricane didn't hit us. We only got a little rain. The hurricane last year was the one that was a pain. That's nice of you to ask.

From: Aaron.Tanner.Hall.mil@mail.mil
Date: November 14, 2008 1:32 p.m.
To: RubyMars@mail.com
Subject: RE: So Sorry

Ruby,

It's all good. I get it. It isn't like you told me anything else except you having a boyfriend and not living with him. :]

–Aaron

From: RubyMars@mail.com
Date: November 14, 2008 2:05 a.m.
To: Aaron.Tanner.Hall.mil@mail.mil
Subject: I'm Sorry Part 2

Aaron,

I thought of something else I didn't tell you about. I still live with my mom and #4. That's it. Everyone knows I do, it isn't like I try to hide it, but I feel like a fraud not actually telling you that. Looking back on it, I never made it seem like I lived anywhere else but . . .

–Ruby

From: Aaron.Tanner.Hall.mil@mail.mil
Date: November 16, 2008 1:37 p.m.
To: RubyMars@mail.com
Subject: RE: I'm Sorry Part 2

Ruby,

That's not you lying. What's wrong with living with your parents?

–Aaron

From: RubyMars@mail.com
Date: November 17, 2008 1:02 a.m.
To: Aaron.Tanner.Hall.mil@mail.mil
Subject: So Sorry

I don't think there's anything wrong with it, but I know people who have told me it's been time to move out since I was eighteen. But the rent is cheap (I pay the electricity and water bill), and I have my own room and another room I can work in. Plus, my mom still cooks dinner most nights. She doesn't care I still live at home. I think she prefers it. I promise that's all I haven't been upfront about.

–Ruby

From: Aaron.Tanner.Hall.mil@mail.mil
Date: November 19, 2008 2:42 p.m.
To: RubyMars@mail.com
Subject: RE: So Sorry

Ruby,

Time for you to move out? Why? I'd still live at home if it wouldn't drive me crazy. Don't listen to anybody else if you're happy and like living there.

–Aaron

From: RubyMars@mail.com
Date: November 20, 2008 3:05 a.m.
To: Aaron.Tanner.Hall.mil@mail.mil
Subject: RE: RE: So Sorry

You're right. My older brothers and my sister had all moved out by the time they were 18. My oldest brother and sister went to college in Austin, and Jonathan joined the marines. I decided to go to school here in Houston, so I never left. They're all successful, and I know I shouldn't compare myself to them, but I do, even knowing it's dumb to do that. They all tell me I'd be an idiot to move out. I'm happy. For the most part. Usually. I don't want it to seem like I'm complaining.

–Ruby

From: Aaron.Tanner.Hall.mil@mail.mil
Date: November 21, 2008 12:41 p.m.
To: RubyMars@mail.com
Subject: RE: RE: RE: So Sorry

Living on your own is different than living with your family, Ruby. If you're not happy . . . you should look into getting your own place, maybe with a friend. It's your life.

–A

From: RubyMars@mail.com
Date: November 22, 2008 2:08 a.m.
To: Aaron.Tanner.Hall.mil@mail.mil
Subject: RE: RE: RE: RE: So Sorry

It isn't that I'm unhappy, I'm not. I am happy, but . . . sometimes it'd be nice to leave the house and not have my mom still treat me like I'm 16 when I'm not home by midnight (I'm exaggerating. She only calls if I'm not home by 2). I know she means well, but every once in a while it gets to me. They're all overprotective. I'm grateful. I shouldn't make it seem like it's a burden.

Anyway, can we start over?

–Ruby

From: Aaron.Tanner.Hall.mil@mail.mil
Date: November 23, 2008 11:41 a.m.
To: RubyMars@mail.com
Subject: RE: RE: RE: RE: RE: So Sorry

I'll let it go, but all I'm saying is, it's your life. Do what you want with it. If that's living at home or not. My dad didn't want me joining the army, but I did it anyway because I wanted to.

We can start over.

−A

From: Aaron.Tanner.Hall.mil@mail.mil
Date: November 23, 2008 11:51 a.m.
To: RubyMars@mail.com
Subject: Hi

Ruby,

I didn't know the soldier who died, still sucks . . . leaves a knot in my chest because it could happen to anyone at any time.

The tent situation here isn't too bad. There are twenty men in each. The best part is we have AC. It gets hot here . . . about 130 degrees during the summer. We're in the desert, but in the winter it's still warm during the day and gets cool at night. I've done deployments early on in the war without AC . . . it's a blessing.

The mosquitoes are the worst. They're smarter than the ones back home. We've had hours-long conversations about them here. We have mosquito nets, but they crawl under them to get inside. They know how to do it. The mice can get bad, but a lot of us try to be careful. Where there are mice, there are snakes, and I don't care what anybody says, you don't want a snake hanging around. I check my bed every night.

You are a dork, but it's cute you notice things like costumes and get excited about them. I get what you mean, but for me it's the other way around. I can't enjoy war movies anymore. I criticize everything in them.

Scout's honor, no matter how good-looking your mom is, I won't try and steal her away from #4.

All three of us are friends. Max, the one I've known since high school, works at a refinery. Des, the one I've been friends with since middle school, is a firefighter.

I've seen *The Fifth Element*. Give me some credit. What costumes did you do? I had this thing for Mila in that orange outfit for the longest. What belt did you have in aikido?

Festivals in Germany are insane. I don't have any pictures with me, but imagine a ton of people and then multiply it by three.

We were "together" two years, but we probably only spent maybe two months of that face to face . . . saying two months is a stretch too, I bet. I had a tour in Italy for a year, and before that she didn't live anywhere near where I was. We met through a friend of a friend when she visited base. It wasn't anything that serious, but . . .

I'm not going to say you're right about me choosing to date them. :] I've only had my car keyed once when I was twenty and had a couple of exes who were borderline stalkers. I feel his pain.

... what did you mean by you've "never had a boyfriend"?

Hope you're okay too.

–Aaron

P.S. Does this count as starting over? :] We can pretend I've always known the truth.

From: RubyMars@mail.com
Date: November 24, 2008 1:11 a.m.
To: Aaron.Tanner.Hall.mil@mail.mil
Subject: RE: Hi

Aaron,

Mosquitoes that know how to get under nets? Mice and snakes? How can I say this? No thank you? You would think, because of Sylvester, I'd be okay with mice, but that is a negative. Snakes? No way, Jose. I feel stupid, but I didn't put two and two together and figure that it would get cold in the winter on that side of the world. You think "desert" and think "hot" and "dehydration," not jacket weather.

I'm attaching a picture of my mom and #4 from our trip to Orlando a few months ago when I sent you the Disney postcard. Don't make me regret it. ;)

Do your friends still live in Louisiana?

You'll be happy to hear I did a Leeloo costume—that's Mila's character. I still have the wig and everything. I've also done Diva Plavalaguna, the opera singer. The makeup took a stupid amount of time to do, but it came out well. I only got my yellow belt in aikido.

Excuse me for saying it, but your ex seems dumb. She was fine with you being stationed in Italy but wasn't okay with you being on deployment now? Sounds fishy. I'm really sorry that happened to you.

I'll tell you some stories about my brother's exes if you're ever down and need a laugh. :)

"I've never had a boyfriend" means exactly that. I've never had a boyfriend.

Hope the mosquitoes aren't getting you too bad.

–Ruby

P.S. I forgot you'd asked if I ever owned a Bedazzler, the answer is no. We were broke back then. She bought me glue and gems from the dollar store. Same thing. :)

From: Aaron.Tanner.Hall.mil@mail.mil
Date: November 25, 2008 3:17 p.m.
To: RubyMars@mail.com
Subject: RE: RE: Hi

Ruby,

I have one soldier who gets heat exhaustion really easily. I have to keep an eye on him and ask almost constantly if he's drank enough water, otherwise he gets sick. It's so hot it's suffocating. When you're sitting in an HMMWV, it's almost like you're sitting in a sauna all day. The mice can get into everything. About a month ago, one got into my bin and ate my ramen.

There's no way that's your mom you sent a picture of.

Both my friends still live in Shreveport. When I get leave, that's who I go stay with. They come and visit as often as they can wherever I'm stationed, but usually I go visit them, and then we go somewhere.

How did you pull off the opera singer look? Was your entire body blue? You got any pictures of the Leeloo costume?

I never thought about how there wasn't a big difference between being in Italy and here . . . that bothers me a lot more than I figured it would. She never really lied before, but I guess if she had, how would I know, huh? I'll have to think about it. I was pissed off for so long after . . . I made myself stop. I've been pissed enough. I'm done with it.

You've never . . . ever . . . had a boyfriend?

The bugs aren't the worst they've ever been, but they're still bad enough.

What kind of dresses are you working on now? Wedding or ice-skating?

–Aaron

P.S. That's not your mom.

From: RubyMars@mail.com
Date: November 26, 2008 12:38 a.m.
To: Aaron.Tanner.Hall.mil@mail.mil
Subject: Gross, Yes and Yessss

Aaron,

Do you have to stay on top of a lot of your soldiers? You're a noncommissioned officer, aren't you? If a mouse got into my bin, I would throw everything away. :) Can you set up traps to catch them?

That's 100 percent my mom. She's 51. I'm sending a picture of her and my dad when I was a kid. She hasn't aged, has she?

That's nice of your friends to go visit. Do you think you'll ever end up back in Shreveport? I hope I'm not being rude asking, but why don't you stay with your dad when you go?

A LOT of body paint was what it took to pull off the Diva costume, and a bodysuit that I had to special order and almost ruined twice. That was the most stressful design of my life. The material was a nightmare. I would rather make my sister a dozen one-hundred-hour dresses than ever make that costume again. I'll attach a picture of the opera suit. It's hanging in my closet. My best friend was really into makeup effects and helped me do it.

I feel like a jerk for bursting your bubble with your ex. I shouldn't have said anything, but who knows what she might have lied to you over. People say "everything happens for a reason." I'm not sure if that's true, but it was probably for the best. Maybe. If a little distance is all that it takes to tear a relationship apart, that should tell you something. Anybody would be mad. There's nothing wrong with that.

If you want to get technical, I've had one boyfriend . . . in elementary school. Damon White. We were together for all of a week.

I'm working on two dresses right now. One is a wedding dress for my aunt's shop that she was having a lot of problems with, and she asked me to take over. The other thing I'm working on is for an eight-year-old who might win a gold medal in the future. I'll attach pictures of them after the one of my parents. The ice-skating one is my favorite. I like doing those more than wedding dresses, but don't tell anyone I said that. What do you think?

My dad is coming to visit tomorrow for a few days. I'm excited.

–Ruby

P.P.S. Promise that's my mom.

From: Aaron.Tanner.Hall.mil@mail.mil
Date: November 28, 2008 12:15 p.m.
To: RubyMars@mail.com
Subject: More Lies

Ruby,

I am an NCO. Most of the men under me have their "stuff" together, but I still check on them all the time. If I failed to remind them about something, even if it's something I would assume they wouldn't forget, I'd never forgive myself. If I tried to throw anything else away other than the ramen packets they got into, the other soldiers would dig through the trash for it. I used some of the baby wipes you sent to clean everything up. It's all good . . . least until I get sick.

Now you're lying. There is no way the woman in that picture is 51. She looks like she's in her thirties. She's your sister, isn't she?

We'll go with nice to describe my friends. Heh.

It's just easier to stay with Max. My dad turned my old room into a workout room.

That costume looks like it's straight from the movie. Have you thought about going into costume design for movies? What else have you got?

You didn't do anything wrong. Thanks for saying something. I'm over it all now for the most part, but . . . goddamn, Ruby. It was rough. I was so pissed after she e-mailed me . . . but you made a good point. I've been thinking about her a lot lately . . . not like that but in general . . . and there's a million different times I can think back on now and realize how fishy the things she'd do and say were. Who she would be hanging out with . . . why she wouldn't answer the phone when I called . . . Maybe I'm imagining it, but I've got this gut feeling. I'd be lying if I said I wasn't angry about it all over again. I hate feeling like a dumbass. I've been in enough shit relation-ships, you'd figure I'd know and be used to it by now.

Don't think I haven't noticed you being vague about your boyfriend situation. It only makes me more curious. Why haven't you dated anyone? By the time I was 23, I'd had . . . a lot of girlfriends.

The wedding dress is all right if you're into those giant princess dresses . . . are you? I like the skating dress a lot more. Does work ever slow down for you or do you always have something to work on?

^^ You don't have to answer that. It's none of my business.

Hope you're having fun with your dad.

–Aaron

P.S. Tell me the truth about that picture of your "mom." You're pulling my leg, right?

From: RubyMars@mail.com
Date: November 29, 2008 2:22 a.m.
To: Aaron.Tanner.Hall.mil@mail.mil
Subject: Lies? Never (Not Anymore)

Aaron,

I'm picturing you as a momma bear with your soldiers, but if your nagging keeps them alive, they can deal with it. It's a lot of responsibility, isn't it? Have you thought about doing school and becoming an officer? Maybe you've already done school. I hate to generalize and assume.

Lol! No! I'll attach a picture of my older sister. They're almost identical, but you can tell my mom is the older one. I'll give you that; they look like sisters. Cross my heart she's in her early fifties. It's all good genes, facial products, and she claims it's helped that she's never smoked anything in her life and doesn't drink more than wine at dinner.

I might have believed you and your friends were good until you decided to use "nice." You're full of it, and it isn't pizza you're full of. You and your friends got into all kinds of mess when you were younger, didn't you?

I've attached a couple more pictures of cosplay costumes I've done and still have. One is the female version of Ghost Rider and the other is Darth Maul. They've both been hanging in my closet for years. I think I might see about selling them online. I've done that for other costumes I've done and knew I'd never use again. There's a lot more girls who like cosplaying than you would think . . . There's also a lot of parents with senses of humor who are willing to buy costumes for their kids.

I'm not creative enough to do costume design full time, plus . . . relying on big gigs to get paid is intimidating. What if I can't find work consistently enough? Or what if I can't come up with ideas? At the rate I'm going, I know that one day when I'm ready to move out, I can afford to have my own little place (with a roommate) and still eat with my jobs right now. It's good enough for me.

No one likes to feel like a dumbass. Do you really think she cheated on you?

I should've known you'd keep bringing up the boyfriend thing. No, I have never ever, ever in my life been in a relationship with someone. I've gone on a few dates, but that's all. I was into this guy for a long time. It wasn't until recently that I decided I wanted to try and really date someone who wasn't him.

How many girlfriends is a lot?

I'm always asking you questions that aren't any of my business. But to answer your question, I do have enough work at all times to stay busy. I'm almost too busy. My aunt with the bridal shop used to make a lot of the dresses herself. Then she started getting "busier" (lazier) and would leave the more time-consuming things to me. The last year, she hasn't been doing hardly anything and has me do the entire dress. My other aunt that manages the dry cleaning business is my main priority. It's getting harder to balance both and do my side work.

My dad's gone. He was only here for five days, but we had a good time. He stayed with my marine brother. We went to a few museums together, took a trip to this pier nearby, and went to the movies. I was waking up early to spend time with him since I don't usually have things to do during the day, that's when he was free since everyone else was at work or practice at that time. At night, he would spend time with everyone else. I promised to go to California to visit in a few months.

Hope you're okay.
–Ruby

P.S. Yes it is my mom. Deal with it.

From: Aaron.Tanner.Hall.mil@mail.mil
Date: November 30, 2008 1:22 p.m.
To: RubyMars@mail.com
Subject: Not Dealing With It

Ruby,

I would never want to be an officer. I already deal with enough political BS. Being commissioned increases the BS to levels I'm not willing to handle. Plus, half the officers I've met have been entitled pricks. Not all of them, but enough.

Your "mom" and your "sister" look like twins. What does your grandma look like? Do you look like them? I don't mean that in a sketchy way. I won't be sending you any "tick lick" pictures all of a sudden. Don't worry.

Heh. Yeah, we did get into all kinds of . . . things when we were younger. The problem was not getting caught. We used to make napalm, mess with electrical stuff . . . Good times. Don't know how I didn't lose a finger at least thinking back on it now.

Your costumes are amazing. I don't understand how you think you aren't creative enough. I don't know anyone that could do what you've made. Do you go all out with your makeup when you cosplay? My favorite was your Ghost Rider outfit.

You're really talented. I'm not just saying it. Remember that.

I'm not the jealous type. I don't know . . . maybe I didn't pay enough attention to her. It wouldn't be the first time an ex has told me that. I wouldn't sit somewhere and expect her to go behind my back while we were together, but now? I wouldn't be surprised. I should've expected it. She broke up with me out of the blue. I e-mailed her to ask if there was someone else right after . . . I was angry. She said that wasn't it, that there wasn't anybody else. I can't talk myself into asking any of our mutual friends what she's up to and if she's with someone else. Should I?

Hold up . . . you were into someone for so long that you never wanted to date anyone else? Why wouldn't they want to be with you? You seem like a great girl. Why would you wait for somebody anyway? How long did you like him? This all sort of blows my mind. I've never known anyone over the age of 18 who hasn't been in a relationship, even if it was a bad one.

I don't kiss and tell. Heh.

I'm kidding, I'll tell you. Girls I've called my girlfriend since I was like 16? Around 20. I've lost count. Not more than 30.

Glad you got some quality time with your dad. California is pretty nice. When are you thinking about visiting?

Hope you're doing all right.

–Aaron

P.S. I'm not dealing with it. That woman isn't old enough to have a kid your age.

Chapter Seven

December

From: RubyMars@mail.com
Date: December 1, 2008 5:05 a.m.
To: Aaron.Tanner.Hall.mil@mail.mil
Subject: Get Over It

Aaron,

I talk to my brother about our e-mails sometimes, and he laughed when I told him your views on officers. He said, and I quote, "Nobody likes officers but other officers."

My mom and sister are both beautiful. I don't have any pictures of my mom's mom. She didn't like having her picture taken. I think she thought they stole your soul or something. She was pretty old school from everything I've heard. I'm not even kidding. She died before I was born, but supposedly, she was a beauty queen. I don't look anything like her. She's got that red hair and mine decided it didn't want to be red like hers or black like my dad's, but I have closer to her coloring minus the freckles and inability to tan, and her eyes. I don't look like either of my parents, more like both of them and neither one of them at the same time. My brothers call me "the milk man's baby" because the rest of them look like one or the other, except me.

You guys had the *Destruction Cookbook*, didn't you?

Thanks. I'm glad you liked my cosplay. With the exception of the Leeloo costume, I usually always do characters who have their faces covered. I don't like being the center of attention. When I put the face paint on, it's like I'm taking on the character and it makes me more outgoing, if that makes any sense. Like I'm not myself. It gives me a boost of confidence. That makes me sound like a weirdo, but it's true.

Not that you're asking, but I think you're better off just living with the doubt. Unless you're planning on getting back together, why torture yourself and get more pissed off? She did what she did, or she didn't. Either way, I'm sorry . . . do you want to get back together? Not judging, only asking.

You're making me feel like an idiot. Here's the thing: everyone knew I had feelings for this person. My entire family did. It wasn't something I tried keeping a secret. I'd liked him my entire life. Besides fictional characters, he was the only person I had ever been in love with. Or at least, it felt like I was in love with him. I don't know anymore. I'd like to blame it on just being young and dumb, but that seems like a cop-out to say that. It was the classic in-love-with-your-older-brother's-friend situation . . . except it was real life.

I'm the only person I know who's never had a boyfriend either. It wasn't like I didn't know that. Even my little sister, as busy as she is, has had a couple of them.

Twenty-something girlfriends. Hmm. What was your longest relationship? I'm trying to do the math in my head and you would've had to have at least 3 a year for a while.

I was thinking about going to visit my dad sometime next year. April maybe. Have you lived in California?

–Ruby

P.S. I swear on my life I came out of her almost 24 years ago. Accept it.

From: Aaron.Tanner.Hall.mil@mail.mil
Date: December 4, 2008 2:39 p.m.
To: RubyMars@mail.com
Subject: Never (Getting Over It)

Ruby,

Your brother's comment about officers made me laugh. Take our word for it. It's true. It takes a certain kind of person to want to be an officer. If you ever meet one, you'll understand.

I bet your sister will be like your mom, picking up guys half her age later on. If you do or don't look like your mom, I'm sure you have nothing to worry about. I got a question: did your brothers' friends ever hit on her?

. . . how did you know that was the book we had?

Your face paint reason I get. It's like you're stepping into a role . . . nothing wrong with that. :] Whatever makes you happy. For some reason, I have a hard time imagining you being shy, but I'll take your word for it.

I know you're right about my ex, but it still doesn't sit right with me. I keep telling myself that it doesn't matter what she did, but it doesn't change anything. Did I waste years of my life? That's what bothers me the most, I guess. No, I don't want to get back together with her. We're done.

You're not an idiot. I didn't mean to make you feel that way. I hope you know that. You're a nice girl. You never said anything to him though? What finally made you give up after so long? You're not lame or stupid. I'm just . . . surprised . . . shocked. You had to feel some kinda way to put your life on hold like that.

I'm sure you weren't missing out on the love of your life or anything like that by not having a couple boy-friends. Sounds like your life has been pretty good if you ask me.

The longest I was ever with someone was that ex.

I've never lived in California, but I've been to visit a few times.

–A

P.S. I don't know if I'll ever believe you.

From: RubyMars@mail.com
Date: December 5, 2008 1:13 a.m.
To: Aaron.Tanner.Hall.mil@mail.mil
Subject: My Name is Ruby and I'm an Idiot

Aaron,

Well, my sister won't be picking up guys half her age. She's gay. Her last girlfriend she had for a few years, but she wants kids and the girlfriend didn't. I hadn't really liked her in the first place. She wasn't good enough for Anatalia (my sister). Having a little sister, I'm sure you'd feel the same way about her having a boyfriend.

My oldest brother's friends were always hitting on and checking out my mom. It was really weird and uncomfortable and more weird. I remember them always calling her a MILF and stuff behind my brother's back. My other brother, the one in the marines, is gay and so were half his friends, so it wasn't as bad with them. They were all busy drooling over my oldest brother. :)

Ha! I know you had that book because my brother, Jonathan (the marine) did too. I told you I read everything. Sometimes he'd let me watch from a distance while he tried something. Sometimes I even got to suggest things he could try.

Yeah, I'm only shy when I'm half naked and people are paying a lot of attention to me. I've had enough people pay too much attention to me for a lifetime. I'm over it. It makes me uncomfortable. Usually I dress like an eighty-year-old (those are my little sister's words) but it's fun to put on a costume, even if it's a little more provocative than I'm used to. It's fun to pretend to be something I'm not without expectations or judgments. Like during Halloween when women wear really sexy costumes but it's totally okay because it's Halloween, you know where I'm coming from?

You had to have learned something from the time you guys were together. It couldn't have been a total waste of time. Make a list if it makes you feel better. Everything happens for a reason, remember? :)

I told you . . . everyone knew I liked him. It wasn't a secret. He knew. I made it pretty obvious sometimes. One time more than any other, but . . . the next day he made it seem like nothing had happened. I'm embarrassed just thinking about the things I used to say and do to him for attention, especially when I was younger. I got more discreet when I was older, but . . . ugh. I don't deal with rejection well, and that's how him not liking me seemed like back then. I know that makes me sound like a coward, but why lie to myself? Months ago, he finally started dating someone regularly. He brought her to my mom's birthday and it looked serious. My heart broke a little (a lot) and I cried that night and for a few nights afterward—about thirty nights if you want to know the truth—but I'm glad it happened. I needed to move on with my life. He'd always dated people, but it never seemed serious back then.

I'm pathetic.

I know you didn't mean to make me feel that way. It just feels like I wasted so much time. Like you said, and then I said—no one likes to feel stupid. Then I think about how my entire family was aware of it and how they had to have known nothing would ever come of it, and that makes me feel worse. It wasn't like there was a ton of guys knocking on my door to take my mind away either, so there's that too. Now I'm just making excuses for being a dummy.

Oh well.

Hope you're okay.

–Ruby

From: Aaron.Tanner.Hall.mil@mail.mil
Date: December 8, 2008 12:09 p.m.
To: RubyMars@mail.com
Subject: You're Not An Idiot

Ruby,

That was a plot twist I didn't see coming. Did your brother and sister always know they were gay? Did you know? I can't imagine how hard it must have been for your older brother having a hot mom. One of my best friend's moms was smoking hot too. He would get so pissed anytime anyone brought her up. Of course that would only make us comment more.

What did he make from the book?

What exactly does an eighty-year-old dress like? The way I'm picturing it is you in a pink sweater and black shoes with glasses. I'm not exaggerating when I tell you, you don't seem like you're shy at all, "half naked" or not. You feeding me a lie?

You said to make a list, so here it is.

Things I learned while in a relationship with my ex (and every ex):

1. Don't trust anyone.
2. Keep the toilet seat lid closed when you're sharing a bathroom with your girl.
3. Everyone lies.

We both know who the pathetic one is, and it isn't you.

Feeling like your heart is broken happens to everyone. My first real girlfriend in high school cheated on me and we stayed together. Then she cheated on me again a month after the first time. Of course I felt stupid for giving her another chance. Fool me once and all that crap, you know? You were a kid. There was no way you could play it off if you liked him. You figure that game out when you're older. :] That guy didn't deserve your tears or your time if he knew you had feelings for him and never did anything about it, even if all he did was break your heart by telling you he wasn't interested. I think mine broke a little at you crying over him. That had to be a reality check. What'd you tell me? Everything happens for a reason?

Not that you're asking for my opinion, but I think you should try to date someone. Multiple someones. You have a lot of things to make up for. I know some people in great relationships.

–A

P.S. Live your life for both of us while I'm over here . . . hear me? Don't let some idiot "rejecting you" make you think everybody will. It's hard for me to believe you didn't have a long line of guys trying to hook up with you.

From: RubyMars@mail.com
Date: December 9, 2008 3:33 a.m.
To: Aaron.Tanner.Hall.mil@mail.mil
Subject: Hi

Aaron,

They both have always known they were gay, but my sister was the first one to come out. My sister announced she was a lesbian when she was like . . . sixteen or seventeen, right before my brother, but my mom says she always knew without a doubt about Tali. There are videos of her making her Barbie dolls kiss and she used to say they were married. Sorry for busting your bubble with my sister . . . not. Lol. My brother came out when he was sixteen I want to say. I think he was worried about how my mom would handle it (remember she was a strict Catholic for a long time and he's her favorite), but she did fine. Better than fine. She claimed she always "had a feeling." He had a couple girlfriends before he came out, but they didn't stay together long for a reason. Him and his friends who were gay were all in the closet and hid it really well. Looking back on it, it makes me sad they had to do that.

I don't remember exactly what my brother attempted. All I know is that nothing ever worked and he almost died each time he tried something from the book. It wasn't until he burned his hands and eyebrows off that my mom figured out what he was doing and put a stop to it. If you're wondering what "putting a stop to it" means, it means she whooped his rear end. Fifteen years old or not, she beat him. That was the one and only time she ever disciplined him I bet.

^^^ It still makes me laugh. :)

Lol! You make it sound like I'm a Pink Lady in *Grease*. I don't wear glasses, but the flats and cardigans happen when I have to do something work-related.

You need help. Here's a list in response to yours:

1. You can trust your best friends, right? (And you can trust me, if you ever wanted to.)
2. Keeping the toilet seat up while you pee is nice. Try sitting on a wet one when you're half asleep.
3. Not everyone lies (but your ex did . . . and I did too. I'm still sorry about that).

Was that girlfriend that you forgave for cheating on you your first love or just a first girlfriend? I was a sad mess for about two months after the girlfriend thing. It wasn't just a few days or nights. I cried and I cried and I cried more. One of my friends thought someone in my family had died. It had felt like it. You picture being with someone for so long, even if you know it's a fantasy, and it's tough. A part of me thought he'd come around some day, but that was me living in la-la land. It was a learning experience. He really is a nice, great guy. I couldn't stay mad at him. Not that I even had anything I could really get mad at. It was my fault.

I do want to date, and I will, but I don't really know where to start. Do you have any suggestions? So far the five guys I've gone on dates with were friends of my friends. I already know meeting guys at bars is a bad idea, and I don't even like going to bars to begin with. So? Any suggestions, your holy dating, twenty-girlfriend highness?

I know plenty of people in good relationships too, but I know a lot of people in really bad relationships as well. I don't want to waste my time on a crappy one.

Hope you're okay. I saw a German shepherd today and thought of you.

–Ruby

P.S. Yes, I'll live my life for both of us. Lay on the guilt trip. :)
P.P.S. Trust me, there was no line of guys trying to ask me out ever. There's only a small fraction of guys who like girls like me. Most of my male friends who I thought liked me had been too shy to ask me out, and I wasn't brave enough to go after the one I did like. Funny how that works.

From: Aaron.Tanner.Hall.mil@mail.mil
Date: December 19, 2008 1:11 p.m.
To: RubyMars@mail.com
Subject: RE: Hi

Ruby,

Internet blackout again.

Is your brother in a relationship? How did he keep it a secret while he was enlisted?

The image of your mom beating on your brother cracked me up. She really is something else, isn't she?

There's nothing wrong with being conservative. You have your reasons. Wear whatever you want whenever you want.

Here's another list for you:

1. I can trust some of my friends. (You included.)
2. It isn't a big deal to wipe the seat down before you use it.
3. Everyone lies, even me. (And I've forgiven you for your lie. I thought we were pretending it didn't happen?)

She was my first love. My first everything if you get what I mean. I'm not going to front, back then it felt like the world had ended, you know? Every few years, she messages me asking how I'm doing. She married one of my high school friends and has a couple of kids now. I'm happy for them.

I think you're giving that guy too much credit. He had to have known how you would handle him bringing someone over to your mom's house. Either way, you did nothing wrong. He was older than you, he should've known better and done right by you. It's BS. A nice guy wouldn't have done that. Just saying.

Definitely don't meet guys at any bars or clubs. Don't date friends of your friends either if you can help it. That always gets awkward. What about at kickboxing class? Or a cosplay thing? Let me think about it more. Every idea I have of where I'd met someone wouldn't work for you.

Every relationship turns into a bad one unless you find somebody to stay married to you for the rest of your life.

This puppy showed up in my tent a couple of days ago. We've been taking turns feeding it. We're not ... allowed ... to have any pets, but some other units have found dogs, kept them and got their paperwork together. He's a cute thing. One of the guys here has a camera. I'll try and get a picture and send it to you.

–A

P.S. What's "girls like you" supposed to mean?
P.P.S. I feel zero remorse for guilt tripping you.
P.P.S. You never told me about your sister's skating competitions. Did she make it to the finals?

From: Aaron.Tanner.Hall.mil@mail.mil
Date: December 20, 2008 2:17 p.m.
To: RubyMars@mail.com
Subject: Thank you

Ruby,

I just got your next box. I thought you were only sending books? :] Little liar. I'm going to make a pizza tonight and go through what you sent. The guy in the bunk above mine was already trying to look through them and choose one. I told him he could wait until I read them first. Can't trust anybody here.

The candy, socks, and mac and cheese packets are great too.

I appreciate it.

–Aaron

From: RubyMars@mail.com
Date: December 21, 2008 2:55 a.m.
To: Aaron.Tanner.Hall.mil@mail.mil
Subject: You're welcome

Aaron,

Liar, liar, pants on fire. That's me. I'm glad your box made it! Do the socks fit? I'm not sure how tall you are. I tried looking you up on Myspace to get an idea, but I couldn't find you.

^^^ I just realized that makes me sound like a stalker, but my intentions were good. I wasn't going to try and friend you or anything.

I know you didn't mean anything by the comments about my mom or sister. :) My brother is in a relationship. He met his boyfriend about three years ago, and they've been together for the last two. He's great. He's so hot and funny and friendly, my sister and I are both a little in love with him. Actually, I think everyone in the family is in love with him. It annoys my brother to no end. The marine thing . . . he just didn't tell anyone he's gay. I think it was really hard for him to pretend to be something he knew he wasn't since he had for so long, but . . . he did it. He'd always wanted to go into the service even if it meant having to lie. (There we go with liars again.) He worried about how accepting people would be toward him if they knew.

You have no idea how bad my mom is. You should have seen her when we were kids and anyone would say or do anything remotely unpleasant about us or to us. She could call us ungrateful, lazy, dumb brats, but if a teacher said we needed extra help, you'd figure we were geniuses by how offended she got. No one can talk shit about her kids but her.

I have my own list for you:

1. You can trust Aries too. :P (Why can you only trust some of your friends?)
2. Try sitting on a toilet seat that's been peed on and tell me it isn't a big deal for the pee-ee (person guilty of peeing) to not be conscious about it.
3. Maybe we all lie, but there's a difference between a white lie and a being-an-asshole lie. Think about that.

Your first girlfriend was *that* girlfriend. I see. My two best friends each had boyfriends in high school and those guys all cheated on them. Now that I think about it, every relationship I know of in high school had that happen, not that it was always the guy who did it. I think that's just the norm. We all have to grow up. Have you ever cheated on anyone?

That person I was goo goo gaa gaa over is a nice guy. Honestly. I don't have love glasses on. You're right though, maybe he could have handled the situation differently, but then again, so could I. I could have accepted he didn't like me a long time ago and not . . . forced myself on him. "Every idea I have of where I've met women wouldn't work for you," oh brother. Going to try not to judge, but it's hard. Lol. I already told you I know meeting people at a bar or a club is a bad idea, sensei.

"Every relationship turns into a bad one unless you find somebody to stay married to you for the rest of your life." That's an interesting way of looking at the truth. :)

Send me a picture of the puppy if you have a camera! If not, it's not a problem. I'm attaching a picture of Sylvester, my ferret, in exchange.

Also, my sister (Jasmine) didn't do so well at her competition. That's why I never brought it up. After her short program, she placed third, which wasn't so bad. She got sick the night before and was really weak. In her free skate, the nerves got to her and she fell twice. She came in sixth. No one in my family is bringing it up. Can you tell it's a sore subject?

–Ruby

P.S. Girls like me. That sounds worse than it is. I'm not "sexy" or really confident or even really funny. I like doing dorky things, and I'm okay with all that. Most guys want someone who has a big rack or a big butt, or at least think or act like they do, or they like funny, outgoing girls. I'm not any of those. It is what it is. I'm just Ruby.

From: Aaron.Tanner.Hall.mil@mail.mil
Date: December 24, 2008 1:01 p.m.
To: RubyMars@mail.com
Subject: RE: You're welcome

Ruby,

First off, Merry Christmas, crazy stalker girl.

Second, the socks did fit. I was relieved you bought XL ones instead of going down a size. For future reference . . . and not that you need to buy me anything again . . . I wear a size 12 in shoes. I'm six foot two.

I cancelled my Myspace account a while back, but if you'd friended me, I would have accepted it.

So you know . . . I read *The Alchemist* since I wrote you last. I'm sure you wouldn't mind, but I let a friend of mine borrow it already. I started that *Darkness* something book you sent last night . . . the title is long and I can't think of it. At the rate I'm going, I'll be done with all the books you sent in two weeks.

Where did your brother and his bf meet? I don't know how he managed to keep it a secret for that long, but it had to be tough. Can't say I blame him though. There's an equal amount who would and wouldn't care.

Does your mom boss everyone around? Even her husband?

There is a difference between a white lie and a being-an-asshole lie. I'll give you that. And I can only trust some of my friends because once somebody screws you over once, there's always the chance they'll do it again.

Talking about lies, I'll tell you I wanted to be an ass-hole and lie to you, but I'll tell you the truth. When I was younger . . . and dumber . . . I cheated on a couple of girlfriends. It's been at least ten years since then. I'm not that same person. I was a teenager.

I don't think I'll ever believe you about that guy being "nice," but whatever floats your boat, Rube. I'll judge silently . . . and out of our judge-free zone. Just saying, I still think if he'd really cared about you, he would have said something to let you move on.

What? It's the truth. Most bad decisions involve bars. Take it from me. I'm glad you know that. I've picked up women at them before . . . and parties. Don't do that. Don't trust anyone who would do that to you either.

All right maybe that was dark, but half of marriages end in divorce. At least a girlfriend can't take half your money and kids.

^^^ Just because I've had a shit streak doesn't mean you will.

Sylvester is cute. He's browner than I figured he'd be.

Here's a picture of the puppy. I don't have a camera, but a PFC . . . private first class . . . with me has one. The pup's already gained some weight since we found her . . . it was a her, not a him like we thought. We named her Ax.

That blows about your sister. Is she bummed?

Merry Christmas again. Tell me how it goes with the fam and if you got "special" brownies.

–Aaron

From: RubyMars@mail.com
Date: December 25, 2008 5:05 a.m.
To: Aaron.Tanner.Hall.mil@mail.mil
Subject: Happy Birthday to Jesus

Merry Christmas, soldier boy. :)

I'm glad I did go with the XL ones. Something told me you weren't short. I could only hope my sixth sense was right. Worst case, I figured it would be better for them to be too big than too small.

Why did you cancel your Myspace account? I hardly ever get on mine anymore, but I have it. Now I usually just get on Facebook.

What did you think about *The Alchemist*? I hope you love *The Left Hand of Darkness*. It gave me a giant hangover. I'll have to send you more books in the future. And you're right, I couldn't care less that you share them. They're yours. Spread the goodness.

Depending on the secret, I usually can't keep one for longer than a day before I have to tell someone. It depends. I agree though, how he managed to not let it slip is beyond me. He and his boyfriend met at a bar one night. They're probably the only relationship I know of that started that way and they've managed to last. I think it helps that his boyfriend is ten years older. He's got his life together and doesn't let my brother get away with his usual crap, AKA blowing up over things and then not wanting to talk about them.

My mom is super bossy. I think her husband likes it though. Let me go throw up in my mouth now. Lol.

I don't want to be a hypocrite, I told another lie today. Jasmine, my little sister, asked if I could see through her dress and I told her no. But I could see her underwear right through it. That's what she gets for the pepper incident a few months ago. Remember I told you about that? No regrets.

Wait a second. I feel like maybe I'm missing something here. You don't have to tell me anything you don't want to, but what has someone done to you in the past to make you not trust them, and why are you still friends with them even after that?

That sucks you cheated on your exes, but at least you've come to terms with it and don't do it anymore, I guess. You aren't the only one judging silently. (Kidding.)

I'm not trying to convince you the guy I liked is nice at this point, because you aren't going to believe me, but . . . he did used to help me with my homework. He did it for me a couple of times. I'm trying not to think about him anymore. I really do want to move on.

Regarding where to not pick up guys (bars and parties): I'm going to die alone. Great. Thank you.

I guess you do have a point about half of marriages ending in divorce, but . . . you know my mom is on marriage #4. #2 was a bad divorce, emotionally for her at least, but #3 was pretty amicable. Even knowing all that, I hope one day I can still find someone to be in a long-term relationship with me. I know I'm the last person to tell anyone to take a chance, but you never know unless you try, right?

I love Ax! Why that name though? Does she sleep in the tent with you guys? She looks like a mix of a lab and an Akita, even though her coat is blonder. You can tell by her smile she's sweet as cherry pie.

Was my sister bummed about not moving on? She invited me to go to Golden Corral (a buffet, in case they don't have those where you've lived) with her, and we went for donuts afterward. This probably doesn't mean anything to you, but if you knew her, you would know she has the discipline of a samurai when it comes to her training and diet. Once, a cousin offered her one hundred dollars if she'd eat a slice of cake and she said no. It's safe to say we're all worried about her. You've never met a sore loser on the scale of Jazz.

We're meeting for Christmas in a little bit. I still have gifts to wrap. :) Wish me luck.

Merry Christmas again, Aaron the Not-Asswipe.

–Ruby

From: Aaron.Tanner.Hall.mil@mail.mil
Date: December 28, 2008 2:59 p.m.
To: RubyMars@mail.com
Subject: RE: Happy Birthday Jesus

Ruby,

Why would you think I wasn't short?

I've heard of Facebook but don't have one. Maybe when I get back, I'll look into it. I canceled my Myspace because anyone I really want to keep in touch with can just e-mail me . . . Also, my ex got jealous over the girls I was friends with . . . not that there were a lot . . . and I got tired of hearing about it. Seemed easier just to cancel it than fight all the time.

I spoke too soon: I haven't gotten too far in *The Left Hand of Darkness*. We've had some long days lately, and by the time I get back to my tent, all I want to do is sleep while I can. I'll let you know how it goes once I'm done. *The Alchemist* really got me thinking about choices and where they'll lead you. I'm planning on reading it again.

I've never heard of a relationship between two people meeting at a bar working out either. Usually those are just hookups.

You gave me a mental picture I shouldn't be having about a fifty-something-year-old woman whose daughter is my friend. Thanks.

I can't believe you let your sister walk around with her underwear for everybody to see. That's shady . . . but I like it. :] Remind me never to prank you.

I'm still friends with people who have done me wrong because I know they're sorry. Doesn't mean I have to trust them as much as I used to.

Telling you about what a douche I was made me stay up thinking about it. I'm tempted to reach out to my exes and apologize for being a prick. What do you think? I'm really not that person anymore.

He did your homework for you but still led you on. Not convinced. Seems like he felt guilty. He sounds like a dick.

I laughed out loud at your "I'm going to die alone." You aren't going to die alone. What if you went to church and found someone there?

I get where you're coming from with your whole "you don't know unless you try" thing, but I guess I've always known that if I ever got lonely once I'm out of the army, I'd just get a dog. I've seen what a divorce will do to a person and I don't really ever want to put myself into that position.

It was the birthday of one of my soldiers, so we let him choose the pup's name. That was the best he came up with. I didn't realize how much you get from a dog until lately . . . how much joy they give you. The unconditional love . . . you can't get it from anywhere. Overall, everyone's mood has improved since Ax showed up. I'm not exaggerating. We still haven't gotten all the fleas off her, but I'm sure when we do, she'll be napping on someone's cot.

We didn't do much here for Christmas. Some guys hung up Christmas lights a few weeks ago, but that's all. My commanding officer gave some of us each a cigar. I'll be saving mine for a special day.

I didn't think about how strict her diet has to be. Hope she gets back on her feet. Nobody wins all the time.

They just let me know I can take my midtour leave in February. I'm heading to Louisiana for two weeks to see my family and friends. I miss plumbing.

In case I don't message you before, happy New Year.

–Aaron

From: RubyMars@mail.com
Date: December 29, 2008 3:05 a.m.
To: Aaron.Tanner.Hall.mil@mail.mil
Subject: Hi

I just had this feeling that you weren't short. I don't know how to explain it.

There aren't that many people on Facebook, so you aren't missing out on anything. When I first signed up, it was only for college kids.

I hope you love *Darkness*. It's one of my favorite books of all time.

Every bad decision my friends have made has been with guys they met at bars. If I wanted to make a bad decision, I'd go to the grocery store on an empty stomach.

You had a mental picture of my mom? Now I have a mental picture again. Let me go throw up one more time, thank you.

I'm a lot of things, but I take my pranks seriously. :)

I'll drop the questions about untrustworthy friends for now but I will tell you that I'm a very trustworthy person. I've never done anything mean or bad to my friends before. :)

I'm not judging you too bad for being a cheater when you were younger. Contact them if you want, or don't. If you hadn't changed, I'd tell you to do it, but it's up to you. I don't know what to tell you. This goes beyond my expertise.

Listen to me. Trust me. It was my fault for how things worked out between me and that guy.

Meet a guy at church? Did you really suggest that?

I can't fault your logic with getting a dog if you get lonely. When has a dog ever broken someone's heart? But . . . never mind. I'm not going to try and tell you, you should get married one day if you don't want to. You know what you're doing and what you want. I have a single aunt who's supposedly never been in a relationship and her life is awesome. Like you said, half of marriages end in divorce. I know how bad my mom's taken some of hers. It sucks. Do whatever makes you happy. You can love someone and not marry them. It's the same thing. At least it should be.

Dogs really are the best. One day I'll have one. My mom is allergic. I'm glad all you guys are being cheery with Ax around. It would take forever but I could send you flea shampoo. Tell me.

Do you smoke?

Christmas was great. Luckily in the custody paperwork, my niece's mom is the one who gets to spend Christmas with her every year so she didn't witness our show. No pot brownies, but my older sister made jello shots, which then led to the liquor cabinet getting opened and we all got hammered, even my little sister. Everyone had to spend the night. I woke up passed out on the recliner and there were people on the floor and the couch. I found my brother asleep on the stairs. Attaching a picture because it's too funny not to share.

Jasmine is still sulking, but we've only gone to a Chinese buffet once lately, and when we went to the soft serve ice-cream section, she only had one cone. My goal is to talk so much smack to her, she gets riled up and starts skating again to spite me. I don't really want to do that because I'm not good at talking bad to anyone, but I don't know how else to get to her. I hope I don't regret this decision. I'll let you know how it goes.

I'm excited for you getting to take leave. Are you going to make any solid plans other than taking plenty of showers?

I'm starting to feel pretty crappy, sorry if this message is short. Hopefully it isn't food poisoning.

Hope you're okay.

–Ruby

From: RubyMars@mail.com
Date: December 31, 2008 5:05 p.m.
To: Aaron.Tanner.Hall.mil@mail.mil
Subject: HI

Happy New Year, Aaron! :)

–Rube

Chapter Eight

January

From: Aaron.Tanner.Hall.mil@mail.mil
Date: January 7, 2009 12:01 p.m.
To: RubyMars@mail.com
Subject: Stuff

Ruby,

I can't wait until I'm out of here . . . It's finally hitting me
hard. This happens every tour, but this time it's worse
than usual and happening earlier. Everyone's been on
edge lately. We got woke up two days ago when someone
started shouting by the tents in the middle of the night. A
soldier had his AR with him and was pacing . . . ranting
and yelling . . . crying . . . I don't know how to describe
what it was like exactly. Scary if I'm going to be honest. Everybody's cried at least once when they're out
here . . . It's just the way it works. When the homesickness
gets bad or when things are happening back home, that's
"normal," but not like that. Not like that soldier. Like
there's no hope left. I don't know. I could go the rest of my
life without seeing that happen again. It really fucks with

my head seeing in person how close everybody can be to reaching that breaking point when you're out here . . . you try not to think about it, but it happens. You're fine until . . . you're not. And you always kind of worry and wonder if it'll happen to you.

I can tell you're trustworthy, Ru. :]

I haven't contacted my exes. Chances are I won't. I've thought about it. I don't want to spend my time calling them because I don't have any other way of communicating. I doubt I scarred any of them. It wasn't like we were in love or anything.

^^^ Does that sound like a shit excuse?

What's wrong with meeting a guy at church?

Like I told you, just because I'm done doesn't mean you need to be. Maybe you'll find a good relationship. I hope you do.

If you wouldn't mind sending some flea shampoo, I can pay you back when I get home on break. I'd ask a friend, but it'd be a month before they got around to it.

Your entire family is out of control. Who brings jello shots to Christmas and then gets drunk? For real, I think I was jealous for a sec. The picture of your brother was hilarious. Did you draw the "tick" on his face?

Talking bad to your sister is how you get her to do things? I can see someone with a strict diet taking their anger out on food.

I just want to do a whole lot of nothing for those two weeks of RR leave. I want to take a real vacation once I'm back home for good.

I hope you're feeling better.

–Aaron

From: Aaron.Tanner.Hall.mil@mail.mil
Date: January 14, 2009 1:11 p.m.
To: RubyMars@mail.com
Subject: Hey

Ruby,

I haven't heard from you. You all right?

–A

From: Aaron.Tanner.Hall.mil@mail.mil
Date: January 18, 2009 2:09 p.m.
To: RubyMars@mail.com
Subject: Hey

Ruby,

Everything good?

–Aaron

From: Aaron.Tanner.Hall.mil@mail.mil
Date: January 22, 2009 1:55 p.m.
To: RubyMars@mail.com
Subject: Please read

Ruby,

If I did or said something to make you mad, I'm sorry. At least let me know you're all right.

−A

From: RubyMars@mail.com
Date: January 23, 2009 12:44 p.m.
To: Aaron.Tanner.Hall.mil@mail.mil
Subject: RE: Please read

Sorry for scaring you. I'm really sick but mostly alive. Dropped my phone in the toilet on New Year's and hadn't gotten a new one.

   Happy belated 29th birthday. I meant to send you a message but hope you understand.

−R

From: Aaron.Tanner.Hall.mil@mail.mil
Date: January 24, 2009 12:58 p.m.
To: RubyMars@mail.com
Subject: Finally

I was worried. What happened?

Don't worry about it. Thank you. I don't make a big deal about it.

–Aaron

From: RubyMars@mail.com
Date: January 25, 2009 1:05 a.m.
To: Aaron.Tanner.Hall.mil@mail.mil
Subject: Dying a Little

A cold turned into bronchitis then pneumonia. I know I'll live, but it doesn't feel like it. Feels like I died and somebody did a Buffy and pulled me back from the dead but only halfway.

Really sorry for scaring you. I've been too sick to do anything and my phone busting didn't help. Finally got my sister to go buy me a new one.

Missed our e-mails. Hope you're okay.

–R

P.S. ^^ Buffy from *Buffy the Vampire Slayer*

From: Aaron.Tanner.Hall.mil@mail.mil
Date: January 27, 2009 2:22 p.m.
To: RubyMars@mail.com
Subject: Not allowed

Ruby,

I've missed hearing from you too. I thought I did something to make you not want to write anymore.

How do you get bronchitis and pneumonia? Did you go to the doctor?

Hang in there. Sorry you're feeling so bad.

–A

P.S. I know who Buffy is. I watched it a few times. She was hot.

From: RubyMars@mail.com
Date: January 27, 2009 5:55 p.m.
To: Aaron.Tanner.Hall.mil@mail.mil
Subject: RE: Not allowed

A,

You didn't do anything wrong. Even typing this exhausts me. I'm so weak. Lost fifteen pounds. Everything hurts.

Don't know what got me sick, but I waited too long to go to the doctor. My whole family was worried I would die in my sleep.

Are you okay?

–Ruby

P.S. She was hot.

From: Aaron.Tanner.Hall.mil@mail.mil
Date: January 28, 2009 12:18 p.m.
To: RubyMars@mail.com
Subject: RE: RE: Not allowed

Ruby,

How do you lose 15 pounds in a month? That's a lot of weight. You're not helping me worry about you any less with your "they were all worried I would die in my sleep" BS.

I'm fine. Same old crap as usual. I'm too busy wondering how you're doing. Can't you die from pneumonia?

Eat chicken noodle soup and drink a lot of water.

–Aaron

From: RubyMars@mail.com
Date: January 28, 2009 3:28 p.m.
To: Aaron.Tanner.Hall.mil@mail.mil
Subject: RE: RE: RE: Not allowed

My brother the marine has been calling me Skeletor. You know how some people say they could afford to lose ten pounds? I could've done maybe ten. Not fifteen. The scariest part is I'm not hungry. I'm always hungry.

I told you my family is overprotective. They're all worry warts. Any time I get sick, they all try to stand vigil. They were trying to get me to wear a mask . . . in my room.

You can die from pneumonia if you're older or don't get treatment. Don't worry. I'm taking my medicine and trying everything everyone is telling me to do to boost my immune system. It just feels like I'm starting at –100 now.

Got out of breath going downstairs. I've been brushing my teeth sitting down. Pathetic.

My brother's boyfriend has brought over chicken noodle soup twice. Organic everything. No wonder I love him.

How's Ax?

Aren't you going on leave soon?

–R

From: Aaron.Tanner.Hall.mil@mail.mil
Date: January 31, 2009 12:01 p.m.
To: RubyMars@mail.com
Subject: EAT

Ruby,

Your brother calling you Skeletor isn't helping any. You eating now?

Wear a mask in your room? Really? Are they like that with everyone or just you?

Is there anything I can do?

Ax is fine. I'm sending you a pic. She looks like a new dog. She slept with me last night.

I'm supposed to be leaving next week, but I'm not holding my breath. I won't believe it until I'm on the transport. I've got this feeling . . . We'll see.

–Aaron

P.S. Eat something.
P.P.S. Eat a lot of something . . . anything.

From: RubyMars@mail.com
Date: January 31, 2009 4:05 p.m.
To: Aaron.Tanner.Hall.mil@mail.mil
Subject: Not Hungry

My appetite isn't totally back but it's getting there. I had toast twice today. I'd step on a scale, but I don't want to. Please don't worry about me. I'll be okay.

Yes, wear a mask, lol. No, they're only like that with me. It makes me feel special sometimes . . . at least not when it drives me crazy. I had to take medicine for a while. I had surgery a few years ago and that just made them more watchful and worrisome. I'm fine, but . . . I can't cough without one of them freaking out. I'm not complaining, I swear. I'm lucky they love me and care.

Writing me when you can is good enough. It keeps me company since I can't do anything except marathon shows my brothers have on DVD.

Ax looks like a brand-new dog. She's so cute. Send more pictures.

I hope you get your leave. If I don't hear from you until you get back, have fun and enjoy your plumbing.

–Ruby

P.S. I put some butter on the toast.

Chapter Nine

February

From: Aaron.Tanner.Hall.mil@mail.mil
Date: February 4, 2009 2:38 p.m.
To: RubyMars@mail.com
Subject: Toast and Superman

Ruby,

Still here. They're telling me I can leave in three days. We'll see.

I'm going to worry about you "almost dying." Who else would send me pizza materials? :]

You're celebrating toast? I'm shaking my head right now. Find some vegetables or fruit at least.

What did you need to take medicine for and what kind of surgery did you have? Don't think I didn't notice you being vague again. That never means anything good.

When I'm the one entertaining you and it isn't the other way around, that's sad as hell. There's nothing new or interesting happening over here. Last night, some of the men in my tent talked about who would win in a fight, Superman or Jesus, for an hour. I couldn't sleep, and I ended up thinking about that for too long.

Did you have to push back all your dress/costume making and sewing stuff?

More Ax pics attached. She's one of the few things making me smile here.

–A

P.S. At least put some cream cheese on your toast. Calories, girl.

From: RubyMars@mail.com
Date: February 5, 2009 5:05 a.m.
To: Aaron.Tanner.Hall.mil@mail.mil
Subject: RE: Toast and Superman

Aaron,

Still there?

I walked downstairs twice today. That's an improvement. I've had two pieces of toast with butter and some chunkier soup. Happy? :)

I'll make sure to leave a note in my imaginary will that someone in my family keep sending you pizza materials in the case of my demise.

. . . I was being vague on purpose. How you could tell through a message is a little amazing, to be honest. I don't usually tell everyone about my health, but that's only because I worry people will react the same way my family does, and like I said, it isn't that it isn't great but . . . I sound like a whiney baby. I had a heart disorder. I had surgery for it a few years ago. I'm fine now. :)

Superman versus Jesus. I've never paired them up. (It's blasphemy, but Superman would win, wouldn't he?) My brother told me when he'd have trouble falling asleep, he'd stay up counting all the aircraft that flew over the camp. Have you done that before?

All my designs on my own were moved back or canceled. You should have read some of the rude messages I got from a few of the skating moms that were "understanding." You'd figure that I intentionally got sick and wanted to miss out on making money. My alteration work through the dry cleaner had to go through someone else, and my aunt with the bridal shop . . . she chewed me out. I'm trying really hard not to think about how much money I lost, but it's hard and it makes me panic. I felt really bad about letting everyone down. When I give someone my word, I try to keep it.

Thank you for the pics of Ax. I'm going to print out the one of her on top of the big tractor tire and frame it. It's beautiful.

Hope the mosquitoes and mice are treating you well. :)

–Ruby

P.S. I put butter. Real butter, not the fake stuff. Good?

From: Aaron.Tanner.Hall.mil@mail.mil
Date: February 8, 2009 12:45 p.m.
To: RubyMars@mail.com
Subject: Sometimes I wonder

Ruby,

Still here . . .

You're being vague again, Rube. A heart disorder and you had surgery? If that's all you want to tell me, it's all right. I know it isn't my business. But if you do want to tell me, I'd like to know. I searched for heart problems and there's . . . a lot of them. Kind of wish I wouldn't have done that now.

At this point, I hope you've walked further than just downstairs and eaten more than soup. The Internet was down for a little while and we got sent out on a patrol.

Make sure whoever inherits me sends books too.

^^^ You know I'm messing with you, yeah?

Superman all the way . . . but some guys put up some good points on Jesus to be fair. We're both going down if it's blasphemy. Down, get it? Heh.

The aircrafts constantly going over the camp is unreal. You have to learn to zone them out, otherwise you'd never stop counting them or get sleep. They're always there. Literally always.

Do you have money saved? Can you borrow some from your family if you needed? Tell those moms to leave you alone. If you cough all over their dresses, you'll get their kids sick . . . then they can't skate. Your aunt has no business giving you hell over not being able to work on dresses for her. Didn't you say she already makes you do a lot more than you should?

I'm keeping the mosquitoes fed and Ax is keeping the mice away. She tries to play with them.

–Aaron

P.S. Stress isn't good for you recovering. Just saying.

From: RubyMars@mail.com
Date: February 9, 2009 11:11 p.m.
To: Aaron.Tanner.Hall.mil@mail.mil
Subject: How did you do tours without my e-mails? Kidding.

Aaron,

I'm sorry for not telling you everything. It's a touchy subject. I guess I just didn't want you to think of me any differently. Not that you would, but . . . I'm sorry. I had no right to expect that. If you were the one who'd had surgery, I would want to know everything too.

Here's the story. I used to get dizzy and lightheaded when I was younger, and my heart would start beating really fast. I didn't say anything for a while. Young and dumb, I know you know what I mean. :) I finally told my mom one day about it, and they took me to the doctor and did some tests. You're not supposed to feel that way when you're a kid, apparently. It turned out I have this syndrome called Wolff-Parkinson-White. To make a long story short, I had an extra electrical pathway between the upper and lower chambers of my heart. There's a node that's bypassed because of the pathway and it caused my heart to beat fast. I took a beta blocker for a while to deal with it, but a few years ago, I had surgery to fix it.

Everything went fine. I'm okay. I should be okay from now on. My mom blamed herself for not knowing. Remember I told you her mom died before I was born? She had sudden cardiac death and the doctors think she might have had the same thing as me and never got treated for it. That's why they all freak out over my health, even if it isn't anything to do with the old ticker.

I hope you didn't fall asleep reading that.

My mom and her husband have been taking turns coming home on their lunch break to check on me. I swear she takes better care of me now than she did when I was little (before my heart thing). She'd make me go to school even if I had something contagious back then. You'll be happy to know I made it through a grocery shopping trip and only felt like dying the last half of it.

Pizzas and books. You got it. All romance. Lol.

(I know you're messing with me. I think you'd miss me for the rest of your deployment if I wasn't around, see the subject line.)

I guess the aircrafts don't ever let you forget where you are, huh?

I have some money saved. I've been reinvesting most of it into ads in magazines and a couple of websites, and more expensive materials to work on. If I needed money bad enough, I could ask my mom or oldest brother, Sebastian. They'd let me borrow it with only a few snarky comments. The rude parents I can handle, but my aunt with the bridal shop is a different story. I got a voice mail from her the day before yesterday that made me cry. I couldn't tell my mom or my dad (his sister) because they would've lost it. She pretty much told me she was going to be broke this month because I hadn't finished the dresses she needed. I feel bad, but it wasn't like I got sick on purpose.

I just thought about it, can't you get malaria from mosquitoes?

Have you heard from your friends lately?

I want to ask about your leave, but since you haven't brought it up again, I'm worried it didn't work out.

–Ruby

P.S. I'm eating more. I've gained three pounds back.
P.P.S. While I've been busy coming back from the brink of death, I started signing up for this dating website. I haven't hit publish on my profile, but I will soon. Baby steps.
P.P.P.S. Sorry for being such a Debbie Downer this e-mail.

From: Aaron.Tanner.Hall.mil@mail.mil
Date: February 14, 2009 4:17 a.m.
To: RubyMars@mail.com
Subject: We'll go with that.

Ruby,

You know your heart is the most important part of your body, don't you? I get why you didn't want to tell me, but I'm not going to treat you any different. Mostly :] I get your family being overprotective even more now. Your grandma dying from a heart problem doesn't help anything either. What kind of surgery did you have to fix it?

Were you faking being sick when you were a kid and that's why she made you go to school? Or did you genuinely feel bad?

I got this feeling I'd miss your e-mails even if I wasn't on deployment.

No, you never forget where you are with Apaches flying overhead at all hours of the day.

I hope you don't have to ask them for money, but I'm glad you have people you can reach out to for it. About your aunt . . . didn't you tell me that she used to make those wedding dresses herself? Why didn't she work on them while you were sick? I don't know anything about the dress industry, but I know if someone couldn't come into work at my dad's business, he would pitch in. Don't let her get to you. It sounds like she made a bad decision and wants to blame you for it. She isn't worth crying over, Ru. Some people you can never make happy no matter how hard you try.

My first time in Iraq, they made us take anti-malaria pills that gave everybody messed-up dreams and constipation. Now they figured out it isn't a big deal here, so we're good. Mosquitoes are just annoying.

Both my friends e-mail me once a week. Not as much as you do. It's more of them just making sure I'm alive than wanting to talk. Not like our e-mails.

If you think you're eating enough, you probably still aren't.

What site did you sign up for? What's your profile like?

I haven't heard anything more about my R&R leave again . . .

–Aaron

P.S. For real though, don't cry over your aunt's BS, all right? You didn't do anything wrong.

From: RubyMars@mail.com
Date: February 15, 2009 10:55 p.m.
To: Aaron.Tanner.Hall.mil@mail.mil
Subject: Friends

Aaron,

I know how important my heart is, smarty pants. Everyone else freaked out so much over the diagnosis, I couldn't. Do you know what I mean? I'll never forget hearing my mom crying in her bedroom or my older brother, Seb, blubbering to Jonathan (marine) about it in the kitchen while I eavesdropped. My dad flew to Houston right afterward, even though there wasn't anything he could do about it. I felt so guilty over it. The surgery I had is a procedure called a catheter ablation. It's with wires that are called catheters, with electrodes at the tip of each. They traveled through a vein into my heart and the electrodes emitted a radio wave that created heat and destroyed the extra tissue that caused the problems. I wasn't even technically asleep during it, and I got to go home the next day. :) See? It wasn't that bad.

I didn't fake being sick, thank you very much. That was both my brothers, lol. I was the good kid who never did that.

For the record, I'd miss our e-mails too.

I would rather chew my arm off than ask anyone for money, but I will if I have to. The last time I asked my older brother to let me borrow twenty bucks because I'd forgotten my wallet, he tried to tell me I'd borrowed thirty. I know he was just messing around, but that's how all my family members are. They'll tease me for it forever. It isn't a hassle asking for favors. It's just a pain in the butt.

My aunt used to make all the dresses herself that weren't from a catalogue. It was her who taught me the basics.

I guess I just feel like I owe her or something. She used to be really nice, but she stopped being so nice when I was about ten or eleven for some reason. I know you're right about how I shouldn't let her bother me, and I know she could've handled that situation differently so that they could've gotten finished, but I can't tell her that. She wouldn't listen and I would just piss her off more. I'm dreading calling her back. I'm a little sensitive. I cry over all kinds of things. Just yesterday I watched a video about baby elephants and cried. You've even made me cry before. I just didn't tell you.

Constipation on top of already getting dehydrated back then? That sounds like a nightmare. At least you don't have to take the medication anymore.

Want me to start writing down what I eat every day so it can pass your approval?

. . . . . .

(Chirping crickets.)

I signed up for pairsmeet dot com. One of my friends has done the dating site game and said this one had the least amount of creepy guys. They ask a ton and a half of questions first, and I still haven't gotten through them all. I got a free three-month trial. They ask things like how do you feel about kids, what's your ideal date, put in order the traits most important to you . . . etc., etc. I'm kind of excited, but it might just be the caffeine I had today for the first time in weeks. There's this free website another friend told me about . . . I don't know about it though. It kind of seems sleazy.

I hope you still manage to get to take your time off. :) I hate to seem nosey, but how many months do you have left on your deployment now? 3?

–Ruby

From: Aaron.Tanner.Hall.mil@mail.mil
Date: February 16, 2009 12:08 p.m.
To: RubyMars@mail.com
Subject: RE: Friends

Ruby,

Wires going to your heart that release heat and kills heart tissue, no big deal.

I'm being sarcastic if you can't tell. I'll keep my mouth shut for now, but . . . I get it. You already have two brothers, you don't need another one.

Don't let your aunt upset you or make you feel bad. You didn't do anything wrong. If she doesn't get that, it's her fault.

Send me a link of the baby elephant video. :] Don't cry for me either, Ru. I can handle it all.

Better constipation than diarrhea resembling a busted fire hydrant. Once, a lot of us got food poisoning from bad meat in the mess hall. Imagine all those porta-potties being used to the max. You could smell them from a hundred feet away.

I wouldn't mind a list of what you eat . . . Have you gained more weight?

Did you finish your profile? If you're talking about the website I'm thinking of, don't do it. Go to church. Volunteer at a hospital or an animal shelter or something. Don't do that site.

They've told me I can still take my leave, but this isn't the first time they've told me it was going to happen and it didn't. If one of the guys here has a wife and kids and can get the leave to see them, I'd rather be the one who stays. I don't want to be that selfish. I don't have anybody who cries when I'm not around. I'll be home in less than three months. I'll live.

Are you feeling any better?

–A

P.S. A new picture of Ax is attached.

From: RubyMars@mail.com
Date: February 17, 2009 4:15 p.m.
To: Aaron.Tanner.Hall.mil@mail.mil
Subject: Diarrhea like a trumpet

Aaron,

I don't know what to tell you about my heart thing. So let's settle on :) :) :). Thank you for caring. I promise I try to take care of myself. It's rare I'll get an arrhythmia in the future, but if it happens, they can fix it. I've lived so much of my life with everyone else making a big deal about it . . . making me worry and be more scared than I should have . . . making me double think everything I do . . . I'm trying not to let it control me so much anymore. You should have heard my mom when I started taking aikido. Remember when I told you about how I've been to Disney a bunch of times with my family? For years I couldn't get on hardly any of the rides because everyone worried. Even now, we go to take my niece and I only get on the little kid rides. I've always wanted to go skydiving, but I haven't, for the same reason. I've built it up so much subconsciously that I've gotten scared to do things for the last ten-plus years that I think me as a kid wouldn't have thought twice about.

I'm sorry if I make you feel like my therapist. Let's continue.

My aunt is the biggest drama queen in the world. She genuinely kind of scares me, Aaron. My older sister and I think she's bipolar. She left me a voice mail yesterday telling me she'll "think" about giving me more work soon but she's "really" upset with me. Honestly, I want to quit. I've wanted to quit for a long time now. I'm tired and her attitude bothers the hell out of me. I figure if I do quit, I can probably pick up more random work that I usually turn down to keep up with her projects. I'm going to think about it.

Diarrhea? In a porta-pottie? No. Once, we were on vacation and we all got food poisoning. 8 people sharing two bathrooms. Never again. I almost threw up from the smell alone.

Har har har. I'm back up six pounds. Still feeling like road kill and I have zero energy but better. I have a few ice-skating dresses I need to finish that I'm going to try and survive through. Wish me the best.

No, still haven't finished my online profile, but I will. What is with you and me going to church? Have you ever been to church? There're no single guys there. I'm going to pretend I didn't read your suggestion about volunteering at a shelter either. Now I know you've never done that before. Finding a decent guy is a lot harder than it seems. Half the time it feels like they're all already in a relationship or they're just scrubs or players. (No offense. You're not a scrub or a player.)

I'm sorry, Aaron. That blows you can't leave, but it's really admirable of you to be so selfless. Most folks wouldn't. I'm sure the next months will go by fast at least. Do you have anyone picking you up when you land? Am I jumping the gun by asking? You said you wanted to go on vacation, did you have somewhere in mind?

I'm feeling a lot better but still not anywhere near 100%. I pricked my finger ten times yesterday just sewing a few beads. That's a record, and not a good one.

I can't stand how cute Ax is. Has anyone started the paperwork to get her to the States?

–Ruby

From: RubyMars@mail.com
Date: February 17, 2009 11:50 p.m.
To: Aaron.Tanner.Hall.mil@mail.mil
Subject: [no subject]

Aaron,

I'm sorry for bothering you, but I want to throw up and I don't know who else to talk to.

My mom told us all today that they found a lump in her breast and they're going to do a biopsy. They think it might be cancer.

I want to cry.

That's a lie. I'm crying right now.

–R

From: RubyMars@mail.com
Date: February 18, 2009 3:15 p.m.
To: Aaron.Tanner.Hall.mil@mail.mil
Subject: Sorry

Aaron,

I'm sorry about that e-mail last night. You have enough
things to worry about, and I'm supposed to be here for
you, not the other way around. You were just the first person I thought of to tell.

Forgive me for crossing the line.

–Ruby

From: Aaron.Tanner.Hall.mil@mail.mil
Date: February 20, 2009 2:22 p.m.
To: RubyMars@mail.com
Subject: Stop

Ruby,

You didn't cross any line. Don't apologize. We're past
being pen pals. I thought we went over this already? :]

I am so damn sorry about your mom. When are they
doing the biopsy? Did she tell you out of the blue?

I'm going to respond to your first message.

No, I don't have anybody coming to the base. It's fine.
I'm used to it. It's funny you ask about a vacation because
I just wrote back an e-mail about it. Max, Des, and I just
started making plans last time I e-mailed to go to Scotland since I couldn't get my RR. Max's family is Scottish,

and he's been talking about going for years now; this deal popped up for a tour and he invited us to go along. His little sister, her friend, and another guy we all know are going too. The more people, the better the deal. Have you seen pictures of it or been there before? It looks amazing. We might stay at a beach house for a week after that in Florida, but it all depends if they can get the time off.

Are you one of those people who gets offended if someone asks their weight? What are you up to now? Hope everything is going okay and you're feeling even better.

Why are you so against going to church? There's got to be single guys you can meet there. Since you asked, it's been a long time since the last time I've been to one. You've got to know I laughed at you writing "scrubs." Haven't heard that word since HS. I'd like to tell you you're wrong about the guys being douches part, but . . . you aren't. Some of the soldiers under me are all right, but the rest . . . I don't know how they've made it to their twenties.

Haven't heard anything about Ax's paperwork, but we should get on figuring it out. It's tricky because we're not supposed to take animals back with us, but I know I've told you other soldiers have done it.

I'm really sorry about your mom again. Technology and medicine are improving . . . And she has all of you to support her. You can't expect the worst. I'll be thinking of you all. Write me whenever you need. You're past being shy with me, remember?

–Aaron

From: RubyMars@mail.com
Date: February 21, 2009 12:58 a.m.
To: Aaron.Tanner.Hall.mil@mail.mil
Subject: RE: Stop

Aaron,

You made me cry. I've been so much more emotional lately than usual, I didn't think it was possible. Thank you for being so nice. I thought we were past being pen pals, but I didn't want to assume how much I could share with you. I really enjoy talking to you. Like I said, you were the first person I thought of to write. (If my best friend or anyone else in my family ever saw me write that, they would kill me, so that's something to think about.)

The biopsy was done yesterday. They should have the results soon. Her husband and I went with her to get it done. She told me to stay home, but I wasn't about to do that. It's gotten all of us shaken up. We're all so close, the idea of something happening to her . . .

I'm crying just thinking about it, and I feel like a jerk complaining when I know you've lost friends. I've never lost anyone, so that might be why I'm being this way . . . but how the hell do you come back from that? I don't understand how anyone could ever be okay with it. I'm a mess. I'm sorry. Everyone was over for dinner on Tuesday, which should have been a sign because she never invites the whole family over for food during the week, and we were eating at the table when my mom suddenly busts out with "They found an abnormality in my mammogram. I already went for blood work and now I have to get a biopsy," all while eating lasagna like it was nothing. I don't think it's ever been so quiet at the dinner table before and something tells me it never will be again. Usually everyone but me is yelling over each other to talk, and it was completely silent.

I've hijacked the conversation. Let's get back to it before I cry again.

No, I'm not offended by the weight question. I'm just not going to tell you how much I weigh. :) I haven't gained it all back. The costumes came out fine. I've done three more since then. I'm still really far behind on my day job work though. I've slept about 8 hours total over the last two days.

There are no single guys in church! What is this? The 1800s? Lol. Single men don't go to church period, at least not any of the churches I've ever gone to. Give me a break. Do you know anyone who does? I bet not. I'm better off trying to pick up a single dad at my niece's school. Now that I think about it, I could make a good stepmom.

The worst part of everything with my mom is that I know chances are she's going to be fine, but I still can't help but think of the worst every night as I'm lying in bed. It's an endless circle. My little sister doesn't want to talk about it. She went on this long rant about how she needed to be checking her breasts every month and not waiting until her yearly mammogram to make it happen. I wanted to kill her. It's already done. There's nothing we can do about it. Why did she need to comment?

Hijacking this conversation again. I'm sorry.

Can you get in trouble with the local government for trying to take Ax?

-Ruby

From: Aaron.Tanner.Hall.mil@mail.mil
Date: February 22, 2009 12:01 p.m.
To: RubyMars@mail.com
Subject: Stop again

Ruby,

Don't cry. I tell you things I don't even tell my best friends. Don't tell them I ever said that. :]

Any word on the biopsy?

Don't feel bad about bringing this up with me. What happened to my friends . . . I'm all right talking about it. You're close to your mom. You're going to be upset. Look, if I really thought something was going to happen to her, I'd tell you how I've learned to deal, so I'm not going to say anything. Be strong for her right now and the rest of you all can lean on each other.

I'm always here to talk to if you want. You got IM or something? I have a Skype account I signed up for but never used.

That's good to hear you're getting back to work. Get your day job work done when you can. They can't expect you to be better overnight. Have you talked to your aunt with the attitude problem?

There has to be a single man at church you can ask out. Come on. I'm not going to answer your question about knowing anyone who goes to church. What kind of guy are you looking to date anyway?

Imagining you as a stepmom made me laugh. You'd be too busy playing with the kids to be strict. Bet.

Your sister's rant probably wasn't what your mom wanted to hear. I got you. You're worried about her because you love her. There's nothing wrong with that.

There's no point appreciating something or someone after they're out of your life. That always seemed pretty fake to me.

We can take Ax out of the country. We just need to make sure not to get caught is all. :]

Hang in there. Thinking of you all.

–Aaron

From: RubyMars@mail.com
Date: February 23, 2009 9:11 p.m.
To: Aaron.Tanner.Hall.mil@mail.mil
Subject: Bet

Aaron,

You tell me not to cry, and then I cry more. It's a curse.

She's fine. The lump is benign. I've never been so relieved in my life. I cried when she told me the good news. It felt like a hundred pounds came off my shoulders and it wasn't even me that's sick.

You don't have to call, I'm sure you have better people to call, but my number is 832-555-5555. My Skype IM name is . . . guess? RubyMars.

Look, I'll e-mail you tomorrow. Right now I'm mopey for some reason and you don't need that. I'm going to go cry a little now in relief. Maybe I'll play some *Duck Hunt* to unwind. Nothing celebrates life like picking off innocent digital ducks.

–Ruby

From: RubyMars@mail.com
Date: February 24, 2009 10:04 a.m.
To: Aaron.Tanner.Hall.mil@mail.mil
Subject: Sorry for the millionth time

Aaron,

I'm sorry for the e-mail yesterday. I feel like I'm halfway back to normal, but thinking of my mom being sick left me with the worst stomachache. It's easy to forget how uncertain life can be. What you said about not appreciating people until they're gone really struck home.

You asked what kind of guy I'd be interested in dating. I just want him to be mostly nice, funny, likes to do things with me, and be honest. And have a job. It'd be nice if he was taller than me, but it wouldn't be a deal breaker if we were the same height. That's not asking for much. What do you think? I know what I don't want better than what I do.

If I were a stepmom, I wouldn't have to be the disciplinarian. Get it? I'd win the kids over by being the one who plays with them and is fun.

Thanks again for putting up with my babbling and everything. I appreciate it.

I haven't shared a joke with you in a while. Here you go:

What did the ocean say to the shore?

. . . nothing. It just waved.

Hope you're okay. Give Ax a rub for me.

–Ruby

Chapter Ten

March

March 3, 2009

12:08 p.m.
AHall80: you awake?
RubyMars: Yes?
RubyMars: Aaron?
AHall80: Hey
RubyMars: Holy crap.
RubyMars: Hey. You caught me off guard, sorry. How are you?
AHall80: All right . . . you?
RubyMars: Still alive, I can't complain too much. :)
RubyMars: I can't believe you actually messaged me.
RubyMars: I'm still trying to catch up on some work.
AHall80: If you're working, I can let you go
RubyMars: No, don't worry about it. I'm tired and my eyes are starting to cross. I should take a break before I mess up so bad I give myself more work to do fixing it.
RubyMars: Is this really you?
AHall80: Yes lol :]

A Hall80: What are you working on? Costume stuff, day job, or wedding dress?

RubyMars: Day job. Can you sense my excitement?

A Hall80: All the way over here. Got a lot left?

RubyMars: Define a lot.

A Hall80: You got days left of work?

RubyMars: Not as much as I should, which is stressing me out, but I think I'm just being paranoid. Who complains about not having enough work?

RubyMars: I'm rambling. Sorry.

A Hall80: Heh. It's all right. How you feeling?

RubyMars: Compared to how I was feeling three weeks ago, a thousand times better. Compared to how I felt two months ago, still like crap.

RubyMars: :)

A Hall80: You eating?

RubyMars: Yes, Mommy Aaron. I'm back up ten pounds.

RubyMars: Am I being too . . . familiar with you? I don't want to make you feel weird.

A Hall80: No. You're how I expected

A Hall80: You're packing on that weight quick.

RubyMars: . . . . .

A Hall80: I'm messing with you. Glad you are

A Hall80: Am I being too familiar now?

RubyMars: No, you're just like I expected.

RubyMars: :)

RubyMars: How's the constipation?

A Hall80: . . .

RubyMars: . . .

A Hall80: . . .

RubyMars: No? You didn't like that question?

A Hall80: . . .

A Hall80: Did you finish your dating website profile?

RubyMars: I'll take it you're still constipated.

AHall80: Who are you?

RubyMars: I'm tired. I haven't been sleeping much. My sister says I get feisty when I'm tired.

AHall80: I see. Now I know for next time. I'll be prepared.

AHall80: Why can't you sleep?

RubyMars: Stress from catching up. I went to bed late. The ice-skater I'm doing a dress for wanted me to personally measure her after she was done practicing for the night and didn't want to pay for my hotel room, so I had to drive to Austin to measure her last night and drove straight home afterward. By the time I got back and managed to fall asleep, I only got a three-hour nap in before my little sister started banging on my door to get me to go have breakfast with her. I got back and went straight to work. I'm not made for early mornings.

AHall80: What time you usually wake up?

RubyMars: I plead the fifth.

AHall80: I see how it is.

AHall80: I thought this was our no-judging zone.

RubyMars: It is . . .

AHall80: Then you know I'm not going to judge you. What time do you usually get up?

RubyMars: 11 a.m.

AHall80: I thought you were going say 2 p.m. or something. 11 isn't bad.

RubyMars: I only wake up at 2 p.m. on Sundays. :)

AHall80: Lol. That's more like it.

AHall80: I'll drop it. What'd you do for breakfast?

RubyMars: This Mexican food place close by. I had a couple of barbacoa tacos. She annihilated two burritos on her own. I didn't know she had that appetite in her. Maybe it's years of watching her diet so closely that now she's making up for it.

AHall80: She's still not skating?

RubyMars: No. Her coach has been calling her every day to see when she's going to hit the rink again, but she's ignoring her calls.

AHall80: You think she's going to quit?

RubyMars: I hope she doesn't, but who knows. Most figure skaters have really short careers. She already started years later than the majority of them do, and I told you she's a sore loser.

AHall80: I thought you were gonna give her the tough-love treatment?

RubyMars: My mom asked me not to.

AHall80: Why?

RubyMars: Because she thinks it might go the opposite way we want it to. I'll make her mad and she'll decide she really wants to quit. Then the whole dream is dead.

AHall80: Hmm

RubyMars: Yeah . . . I still think I might do it even though I'm worried, but I'm not sure I can talk crap to her. She's just getting more and more pissy. I'd love her if she skated or if she'd didn't, but it would be a shame if she quit. Everyone knows she has a gift that not many people have. You have to watch her skate to know that's what she was born to do.

RubyMars: I know that sounds corny, but it's true.

RubyMars: I'm rambling. Sorry. How's Ax?

AHall80: You're not rambling, and I like hearing about your sister's skating. Hope she figures it out on her own though.

AHall80: Ax is good. She's taking turns sleeping by all of us. I think I'm her favorite.

RubyMars: Aww.

AHall80: Every time I see her, she makes me smile . . . Didn't realize how much I didn't smile until she started hanging around more often

RubyMars: Do you guys need a collar or a leash for her? I'm sorry I never got around to sending the flea shampoo, but the pneumonia . . .

AHall80: Nah. Don't worry about it. One of my PFCs had his wife send things over for her.

RubyMars: How are the books coming along?

AHall80: I finished all the ones you sent. I started rereading *The DaVinci Code.*

RubyMars: I knew you'd like it!

RubyMars: Barter for more books . . .

AHall80: You and your bartering lol

AHall80: I did see somebody reading *The Hobbit.* Maybe I'll trade for that one.

RubyMars: Do it.

RubyMars: I sent you more books, but I'm not sure when everything will arrive.

AHall80: Thanks, Rube. I appreciate it. My friends sent me a package last week. No books in it though.

AHall80: Hey I gotta go. I'll message you again soon.

AHall80: Sorry for leaving so quick

RubyMars: It's okay. Take care!

AHall80: Thanks

AHall80: Bye

March 8, 2009

AHall80: Hey

RubyMars: Hey

RubyMars: How's it going?

A Hall80: Fine. Same old like always. You?

RubyMars: Eh. I've been better, but I'm okay.

A Hall80: Eh? What's the matter?

RubyMars: I got fired yesterday.

A Hall80: What?

A Hall80: From where?

RubyMars: From the dry cleaner place.

A Hall80: Why? I thought your aunt was your boss.

RubyMars: She is.

RubyMars: Was. You know what I mean.

RubyMars: She fired me.

A Hall80: Why? Because you got sick?

A Hall80: I thought it was the other aunt you have beef with?

RubyMars: Sort of. Remember how I told you I was worried about being far behind on work, how she'd gotten someone else to do alterations while I'd been sick . . . and then how she hadn't given me as much as she usually does recently? I thought I was being crazy, but it turns out she ended up finding someone else to "help" and this person is cheaper than me . . .

A Hall80: So she fired you.

RubyMars: And that other aunt still wants me to work for her, but she's being so mean. She's worse than the jackass boyfriends my friends have dated in the past who try to do messed-up reverse psychology on them to get what they want. I'm trying not to even think about her right now. It's making me really upset.

RubyMars: I cried. Again.

RubyMars: How does my own aunt fire me?? She said she felt bad but that "it's business." My mom is pretty pissed. She called her brother (that aunt's husband) and ripped him a new one over the "she-monster" he married.

A Hall80: Rubes. That sucks. I'm sorry.

RubyMars: I'm sorry too. It's the only job I've ever had. Plus, it really hurt my feelings she just kicked me to the curb like that as soon as I delivered the last of the garments she'd left me to alter. It was like she thought I wouldn't finish my work or I'd do a crappy job if she'd told me before. I wouldn't ever do that.

RubyMars: I get it's a business decision, but :(:(:(

A Hall80: Nah. She's your aunt, and you said you've worked for her since you were what? 16? Seems harsh to me too. It's not like you chose to get sick.

A Hall80: You need to do something about your other aunt too.

RubyMars: Yeah. My whole family is boycotting ever seeing her family again. That makes me feel a little better, but not much.

A Hall80: They should. I would.

A Hall80: Don't think I didn't notice you ignored my comment about your wedding aunt. You need to tell her something. Or tell your mom or your dad, whoever is the one related to her, to tell her to cut it out if you don't want to be the one to say anything. But you should.

RubyMars: I know I should, but . . .

RubyMars: I really hate confrontations.

RubyMars: My whole body starts to shake, my stomach hurts, I get nauseous, things start to feel funny.

A Hall80: You're going to make yourself sick trying to make her happy when she doesn't seem to deserve you being loyal to her with that attitude. What'll be worse? Pissing her off or you sweating over making her happy for the rest of your life?

RubyMars: . . .

A Hall80: . . .

A Hall80: Think about it, all right?

RubyMars: All right. :)

A Hall80: Any idea what you're gonna do now?

RubyMars: No clue.

RubyMars: My mom's husband says the company they work for is hiring entry-level positions. That's an option.

A Hall80: Where do they work?

RubyMars: An accounting firm.

A Hall80: . . .

RubyMars: . . .

A Hall80: . . .

RubyMars: . . . what?

A Hall80: You're just going to quit?

RubyMars: I don't want to.

A Hall80: Then why are you considering it?

RubyMars: Because it isn't like it's easy to find a job opening for what I do.

RubyMars: I sound like a whiney baby. I'm sorry. I'm only a baby, not a whiney one. I'm so frustrated right now. I don't want to give up what I do, and I'm mad at myself. I know I can do something that makes me more money. I wasn't making bank before, but I like what I do. I've looked through the paper and Craigslist for openings but haven't found anything that pays even a dollar more than minimum wage. I haven't made that little since I was sixteen.

A Hall80: You're not being a whiney baby.

A Hall80: Maybe a little :]

RubyMars: :)

A Hall80: You said you have money in savings?

RubyMars: Yeah, but not much.

A Hall80: For how long?

RubyMars: 2 months if I don't change any spending habits. I can make it stretch longer if I have to.

AHall80: So don't rush into a job we both know you're going to hate.

AHall80: Can you try and get more ice-skating work?

RubyMars: I can try. I was limiting myself on how much I take on because of the day job. I was thinking about starting to run ads with a faster turn-around time, but that'll cost me money to front. My brother's boyfriend asked me to make his dog a rain jacket and some bandanas in the meantime because he felt bad after he heard what happened. He was here when my mom was on the phone with my uncle.

AHall80: Have you made dog clothes before?

RubyMars: No, but I'm sure I can come up with something. It can't be any harder than that dress I made for my sister I sent you.

AHall80: Even I know you can do it.

AHall80: Hey, I gotta go. We'll talk soon.

AHall80: Don't give up and get a job yet, all right?

RubyMars: Fine. :) I won't.

RubyMars: Take care. Talk to you soon.

AHall80: Bye, Ruby Cube.

March 13, 2009

AHall80: Hey

RubyMars: Hey you

RubyMars: This is a miracle. It's 12 p.m. here.

AHall80: I know . . . It's a miracle you're awake.

RubyMars: Har har

AHall80: How you feeling?

RubyMars: Sleepy but good. :) You?

A Hall80: Rly tired

A Hall80: Long long day

RubyMars: Go to bed.

A Hall80: I will in a min. Just wanted to get on and check on you for a sec.

RubyMars: Go to sleep. I'm all right. I still haven't gotten another job, if that's what you're wondering.

A Hall80: It is, but good.

A Hall80: Back to normal? Feeling better?

RubyMars: Yeah, I'm good now. I'm back to eating normally too.

RubyMars: You okay?

A Hall80: Yeah, everything's as good as it can be.

A Hall80: Your mom doing all right?

RubyMars: She's good. We're all still kind of spoiling her and she's eating it up, saying she should have gone to the doctor sooner if we were all going to be so nice to her afterward.

A Hall80: That's . . .

RubyMars: Awful. I know, she's out of her mind.

A Hall80: Heh

RubyMars: Are you ready to come back to the States?

A Hall80: More than ready.

A Hall80: Max has been sending over info on Scotland. I try not to look forward to things because shit happens, but it's getting harder.

RubyMars: :) That's sweet and terrible at the same time.

A Hall80: It's reality.

RubyMars: I know.

RubyMars: :)

A Hall80: I'm falling asleep. I'll try to get on soon.

RubyMars: Okay. Sleep good.

A Hall80: Night, Rube.

March 16, 2009

AHall80: Rubes
RubyMars: Hey.
RubyMars: How are you?
AHall80: All right. You?
RubyMars: Pretty good.
RubyMars: I have news. Guess what?
AHall80: You found a job?
RubyMars: No.
RubyMars: I appreciate the reminder.
RubyMars: :/
RubyMars: I have a date.
AHall80: With who?
RubyMars: My friends invited me over for a potluck last
night, and this guy I've known for a while was there
too. We weren't really friends before, but we got
along, and before I left, he asked if I'd go out with
him. I thought of you and said sure.
RubyMars: I'm kind of regretting it now, but I
don't want to say never mind. I think I'm being a
chicken.
AHall80: You are.
RubyMars: . . .
AHall80: You know him?
RubyMars: Well enough. He's really nice, but he's
younger than me.
AHall80: How much younger?
RubyMars: 2 years
AHall80: So he's what? 21?
RubyMars: Yeah.
AHall80: hmm
RubyMars: Hmm what?

AHall80: 21 year olds are shitheads. Don't let him get away with too much.

RubyMars: Jeez. What kind of girl do you think I am?

AHall80: A good girl. That's what I'm trying to say.

RubyMars: :) Okay good.

RubyMars: I have zero expectations, except hopefully having a free meal, lol.

RubyMars: If my older sister saw me write that, she'd kill me.

RubyMars: One time a few weeks ago, I made a joke about looking for a sugar daddy and she lectured me for half an hour.

AHall80: Let me know how it goes. Don't go back to his place.

AHall80: You don't need a sugar daddy.

RubyMars: I'm not. I swear. Just a meal.

RubyMars: I know. :)

RubyMars: Speaking of, were you a shithead when you were 21?

AHall80: Yeah, I was a complete shit back then. I'm telling you from experience.

AHall80: :]

AHall80: How's the job hunt going?

RubyMars: Bad, but I got more work doing ice-skating dresses for a few girls up in New York, and this one popular male figure skater's coach wrote me today, so we'll see what happens. My older sister is paying me to make her dog some bandanas. We'll see how that goes too. I won't say no to pity money.

AHall80: Good

RubyMars: I'll let you know what happens, but I promise I'm not jumping into anything random. I'm just trying.

AHall80: It's about time you did.

RubyMars: Hey, I got those pictures you e-mailed me yesterday of Ax with her collar on. If I thought it would get there before you leave, I'd send her a bandana.

AHall80: Make one for Aries. I'll pay you.

RubyMars: I'll make one for him, but you don't have to pay me. Just tell me where to ship it.

AHall80: I have a job, you don't. I can pay.

RubyMars: All I see is "Blah, blah, blah." Give me an address to ship it to.

AHall80: . . .

RubyMars: . . .

AHall80: Your mom isn't the only bossy one.

RubyMars: :)

RubyMars: Send me the address.

AHall80: I'll think about it.

AHall80: I gotta go.

AHall80: Talk soon.

RubyMars: Okay bye.

AHall80: Bye RC

March 19, 2009

AHall80: Hey

RubyMars: Hey.

AHall80: I got your box today. Thank you.

RubyMars: You're welcome. I hope you aren't getting bored I'm always sending the same kind of stuff, but why mess up a good thing?

AHall80: It's all great. I've told you before you don't have to send me anything, but I'm not going to say no to books and food.

RubyMars: I forgot to ask. Did you end up trading for *The Hobbit*?

AHall80: Yeah. Already finished it and traded 2 Dan Brown books for the first *LotR* book.

RubyMars: That's a fair trade. Tell me what you think.

AHall80: I will.

RubyMars: Have any of your other Help a Soldier people sent you things recently?

AHall80: A couple weeks ago I got a big box of socks, baby wipes, and snacks.

RubyMars: Sounds like fun.

AHall80: It was. I already ate everything. :]

RubyMars: Party animal. :)

RubyMars: Have you heard anything else about when you're leaving for good?

AHall80: Not yet, but everything seems to be on schedule. Should be about 8 weeks. The longest 8 weeks of my life.

RubyMars: I'm sure.

AHall80: I want a shitty, greasy, deep dish pizza like you can't imagine. I can already taste it.

AHall80: A hot shower . . . a real bed . . . AC everywhere . . .

RubyMars: Clean clothes?

AHall80: Clean clothes. Clean socks. No sand.

RubyMars: Clean underwear.

RubyMars: No sand? I thought you were planning on going to the beach?

AHall80: The beach is different. There's water. It isn't just desert and more desert.

RubyMars: I guess that makes sense.

RubyMars: My brother said once that his goal is to never see sand in his life again.

AHall80: For real.

RubyMars: What I didn't finish saying was that he said that, but he's gone to Cancun twice with his boyfriend, LOL.

AHall80: It's different. I'm over this sand shit.

AHall80: Never again

RubyMars: Does that mean you're dead set on not re-enlisting?

AHall80: . . .

RubyMars: Whatever you want. I'm not judging. We don't have to talk about it.

AHall80: It's not that I don't want to talk about it . . .

RubyMars: But you don't want to talk about it.

AHall80: :] Basically.

RubyMars: I'll change the subject then.

RubyMars: Have you gone #2 lately?

AHall80: Three days ago.

RubyMars: Are you joking?

AHall80: I wish.

RubyMars: AARON

AHall80: I know. I KNOW.

RubyMars: Does it hurt?

AHall80: Uh, when it comes out?

RubyMars: Omg

RubyMars: Aaron

RubyMars: I meant your stomach.

RubyMars: Does your stomach hurt?

RubyMars: I can't breathe

RubyMars: Or type

RubyMars: I didn't mean your . . . rectum.

RubyMars: Aaron?

RubyMars: Aaron?

RubyMars: Are you there?

RubyMars: AARON?

AHall80: You're not the only one who couldn't breathe or type.

RubyMars: LMAO I'm crying.

AHall80: me too

AHall80: me too

RubyMars: I mean . . . you can tell me if your butt hurts too, I guess.

AHall80: Ruby, stop

RubyMars: Seriously. You can tell me. I won't judge.

RubyMars: It happens.

RubyMars: I think.

AHall80: Stop

RubyMars: I can't breathe

AHall80: I don't know when the last time I laughed so hard was.

AHall80: Everyone is looking at me wondering wtf happened.

RubyMars: Your rectum happened

AHall80: BYE

RubyMars: I can't stop laughing

AHall80: You're never hearing from me again

RubyMars: There are tears coming out of my eyes.

AHall80: Bye. I'll write you again when I find my balls.

RubyMars: It was nice knowing you.

AHall80: BYE

March 22, 2009

AHall80: Hey

RubyMars: Hey

RubyMars: How are you?

RubyMars: And by 'you' I mean you as a whole, not any specific body part.

AHall80: . . .

AHall80: . . .

AHall80: Never living that down, am I?

RubyMars: What do you think?

AHall80: I'm thinking that's a negative

RubyMars: :)

RubyMars: I'm still laughing about it.

AHall80: I bet you are

AHall80: Miss I-Walk-Into-Closed-Doors

RubyMars: Har har

RubyMars: I'm guessing you found your balls somewhere?

AHall80: . . .

RubyMars: I'll take that as a yes.

RubyMars: Guess what?

AHall80: You're not constipated?

RubyMars: Yes because I eat enough broccoli (covered in cheese), but besides that.

AHall80: What is it?

RubyMars: I went on a date with that guy.

AHall80: The 21 year old?

RubyMars: Yep, and it was only awkward about half the time.

AHall80: What'd you do?

RubyMars: We went to this comic book store and then went for coffee.

AHall80: A comic book store?

RubyMars: He's into comics. I like graphic novels more. The stories are better and they're longer.

AHall80: Hmm.

AHall80: Did you have a good time?

RubyMars: Yes. He's a little shy, but it was nice.

AHall80: Did he pick you up?

RubyMars: And tell him where I live? You nuts?

AHall80: Smart girl

RubyMars: Duh. We met up by the comic book store and the coffee shop was in the same shopping center. He had to wake up early for school, so we weren't out all night or anything.

RubyMars: He texted me an hour afterward to see if I'd like to go out with him after his midterms in a couple weeks.

AHall80: Did you say yes?

RubyMars: Yeah. What do you think? I'm not in love with him or anything like that, but I didn't mind spending time with him. I figured I'd give it another shot and see how it goes.

AHall80: "didn't mind spending time with him . . ."

AHall80: Hmm

AHall80: Go with him

AHall80: I've done worse with girls I did mind spending time with.

AHall80: And here I am

RubyMars: Yeah, I'm sure.

RubyMars: I'm still going to finish my dating profile though. Why not?

RubyMars: "and here you are," damn it, Aaron. You're just picking the wrong ones is all.

AHall80: Good girl

AHall80: I never said I was picking good ones, more like "good for now."

RubyMars: "Good for now"

RubyMars: . . .

RubyMars: All I'm going to say is, maybe you just need to find the right girl. Not at a bar.

RubyMars: Maybe she's waiting for you at a church or a shelter.

AHall80: You're a pain in the ass, Ru

RubyMars: Yeah, you don't like that idea so much when someone turns it around on you, huh?

AHall80: . . .

AHall80: How's your little sister?

RubyMars: Fine, we'll change the subject.

RubyMars: She's being a pain in the butt. She still hasn't gone to the rink. I don't know what to do.

AHall80: Drag her.

RubyMars: She's bigger than I am, and stronger.

AHall80: How tall are you? I looked up a video of her and she looks small.

RubyMars: You did?

RubyMars: I'm five one. She's five three.

RubyMars: She's freakishly strong, don't let her deceive you.

AHall80: You can take her

AHall80: Why didn't I know you were short?

RubyMars: Honestly, I'm scared of her. You just have to know her to get it.

RubyMars: My mom is five feet tall. It isn't a big deal in my family. We're all short. I don't even think about it half the time.

AHall80: Why are you scared of her?

AHall80: Your brothers are short?

RubyMars: Because she's a crazy person. She doesn't care about anything right now. When things are going her way, she might give two craps in a day, max. She can be the meanest person I know on a good day. I caught her eating ice cream straight from the gallon while watching *Glee*. She's relapsing.

RubyMars: One of my brothers is like five six and the other one claims he's five eight, but he's full of it.

AHall80: Isn't *Glee* the show about the kids in choir?

RubyMars: Close enough, and yeah, that show. It's a bad combination. It's the beginning of the end. I know I need to do something, but no one else wants to say anything to her. They're all letting her sulk. If it wasn't for her going to work, I doubt she'd leave the house.

AHall80: Do something

RubyMars: I will, but I'm not forcing her to the rink. Actually, I think I have an idea . . .

AHall80: What is it?

RubyMars: I think I'm going to make her the nicest ice-skating dress I've ever made, since it's not like I'm swamped or anything. She's a sucker for the good ones.

AHall80: Do it

RubyMars: You think so?

AHall80: Yeah

AHall80: Have you talked to your aunt, the wedding one?

RubyMars: Yes.

AHall80: What did she say?

RubyMars: I talked to her about a new dress she wanted me to start working on.

AHall80: Ruby

RubyMars: I know, I know.

AHall80: You can do it. I believe in you.

RubyMars: You're a good friend to me, Aaron Not-An-Asswipe.

AHall80: I'd be a better friend to you if I got you to stand up for yourself.

A Hall80: I have this feeling she doesn't pay you as much as you deserve.

RubyMars: :)

RubyMars: Probably not. I don't look at what she charges anymore.

A Hall80: Ask her for a raise at least.

RubyMars: She was just complaining about how she's broke.

A Hall80: I'm going to drop it for now, but I know you know she's taking advantage of you.

RubyMars: I know . . .

A Hall80: I gotta go, but think about saying something. For real.

RubyMars: I will.

A Hall80: I'll msg you soon. Bye

RubyMars: Bye, Aaron.

March 24, 2009

A Hall80: Rubes

RubyMars: Hey you.

RubyMars: How is everything?

A Hall80: Good. About to go play some *Halo*.

A Hall80: Check your e-mail

RubyMars: If you sent me a chain letter . . .

A Hall80: Just check your e-mail.

RubyMars: Okay, one second.

RubyMars: He's so handsome!!!

A Hall80: I told you you didn't have to send Aries anything.

RubyMars: I know you said I didn't, but you did give me your dad's PO box, and I had leftover material. It looks perfect on him.

AHall80: Max saw him and asked if you could make three more. He has two huskies and a lab mix.

RubyMars: Of course I can.

AHall80: How much should I tell him to send you?

AHall80: You better not tell me you'll do it for free.

RubyMars: Why?

AHall80: Why what? Why you can't make them for free?

RubyMars: Yes.

AHall80: Because you should sell them

AHall80: And we both have jobs and you don't.

RubyMars: . . .

AHall80: :] Let him pay you. I'll tell him $20 each, or more?

AHall80: You can say more.

RubyMars: $20? Are you crazy?

AHall80: 15

RubyMars: No!

AHall80: 14.99

RubyMars: When did you become a pest?

AHall80: You've rubbed off on me.

AHall80: 10

RubyMars: $10 is too much. It's from an old bolt I had and the bandanas aren't even reversible, and it's you.

AHall80: $9?

RubyMars: Stop. $5 each. That's my final offer.

AHall80: You sure?

RubyMars: Positive

AHall80: K. To the address you sent them from?

RubyMars: Yes, stalker

AHall80: . . .

RubyMars: . . .

AHall80: How's the job hunt going?

RubyMars: Terrible, but I've picked up a few more dress jobs and my brother's boyfriend ordered dog bandanas and so did his mom. Something is something. As long as my mom doesn't kick me out, I'll be fine. No going out to eat for me unless someone treats, but that's okay.

AHall80: You're still fine besides that?

RubyMars: Yeah, I'm okay. I'm really grateful I didn't move out right about now. :)

AHall80: What's that you tell me? Everything happens for a reason?

RubyMars: Yeah.

AHall80: See?

RubyMars: Yeah, I see, pita.

AHall80: Pita?

RubyMars: Pain in the ass. :)

AHall80: Heh

AHall80: I gotta go. I'll msg you soon.

RubyMars: Okay bye!

AHall80: Bye RC.

March 27, 2009

AHall80: You okay?

AHall80: I just saw your e-mail to IM you.

RubyMars: Physically I'm fine. But I got cash from Max for his bandanas, and I also got four bolts of fabric in the mail that I know I didn't order.

AHall80: Oh?

RubyMars: Don't "oh" me. Did you send them?

AHall80: You're welcome, Rubes.

RubyMars: Aaron. You didn't have to do that!!!!!

AHall80: I wanted to. Happy early birthday.

RubyMars: How did you know my birthday was coming up?

AHall80: Stalker, remember? :]

AHall80: I told Max to look you up on Facebook.

AHall80: You shouldn't have your birthday on there. People can steal your identity.

RubyMars: Apparently.

RubyMars: . . .

RubyMars: You didn't have to do anything for me.

AHall80: Okay.

AHall80: It wasn't shit fabric, right? Max picked it out.

AHall80: I saw him wear a Hawaiian print shirt one day . . . I should've gotten Des to pick it out instead.

RubyMars: No, it was great. I'll e-mail you pictures in a second. I was so surprised. Thank you so much, Aaron. Really.

AHall80: I figured you could make more bandanas with it . . . or dog sweaters or something to make you money. Thought you'd like that more than a birthday card.

RubyMars: I like that so much more.

RubyMars: It's way too much. I don't know what to say.

AHall80: Thank you, Aaron?

RubyMars: Har har har

RubyMars: Thank you, Aaron! :)

RubyMars: Really, thank you. I'll make Aries something out of what you sent.

AHall80: That's not why I sent it to you.

RubyMars: I know it isn't, but you sent a lot of material. It must have cost an arm and a leg to ship them.

RubyMars: I'm going to send it regardless of whether you want me to or not.

AHall80: . . .

AHall80: Fine

RubyMars: They're going to be reversible. I can see them already.

RubyMars: Thank you!!!

RubyMars: Thank you. I really don't know what to say. It made my month.

AHall80: Yeah, you're welcome.

AHall80: I can only get on for a sec, but happy birthday, stalker girl.

RubyMars: Thank you, stalker boy. You made my day.

AHall80: :] I'll write you soon.

RubyMars: Okay, be safe. :)

March 30, 2009

AHall80: Rubes

RubyMars: Hey stalker

AHall80: . . .

AHall80: I got your e-mail about going on date #2. How'd it go?

RubyMars: Really good. He had tickets to a hockey game and dinner.

AHall80: Houston has a hockey team?

RubyMars: It wasn't pro hockey, just some local rec league.

AHall80: He knows about your sister?

RubyMars: No. I don't usually tell anyone about that lazy fart. His friend is on the team.

AHall80: She still hasn't gone skating again?

RubyMars: No . . .

AHall80: Shit.

AHall80: What happened to the dress you were going to make her?

RubyMars: I'm almost done with it, but I'm having second thoughts now.

A Hall80: What's the worse that'll happen?

RubyMars: She yells at me and throws the dress on the floor?

A Hall80: You yell back at her and sell the dress if she acts like that.

RubyMars: :)

A Hall80: It's not like you have anything else to do.

RubyMars: I take back ever telling you you're sweet.

A Hall80: Lol

A Hall80: Have you ever called me that before?

RubyMars: No, lol.

A Hall80: Remember that time I sent you cloth?

RubyMars: Fabric and yeah, I do.

RubyMars: Remember that time I sent you socks?

A Hall80: I'm wearing them right now

RubyMars: No you're not.

A Hall80: Nah, I'm not. They're dirty. :]

RubyMars: Remember that time you thought I was talking about your butthole, but I was talking about your stomach?

A Hall80: BYE

RubyMars: Lol

RubyMars: Lmao

RubyMars: I can't stop laughing.

A Hall80: Happy birthday, girl.

A Hall80: Wishing you nothing but the best, Rubes.

RubyMars: Thank you, Aaron.

A Hall80: I gotta go, but I'll msg you soon.

A Hall80: Happy Birthday again

A Hall80: Bye, Ruby Cube

RubyMars: Bye. Thank you!

Chapter Eleven

April

April 2, 2009

AHall80: Hey

RubyMars: Hey yourself.

AHall80: How was your bday?

RubyMars: Great. Everyone came over and we went out to eat. The restaurant brought me out a slice of cake and sang happy birthday while I stared at each of my family members, cursing them out in my head for doing that to me.

AHall80: They do that to you every year?

RubyMars: No. They know I hate it, so they switch it up. I never know when they'll do it and when they won't, because if they always did, I'd stop going out to dinner on that day.

AHall80: Poor Ruby

RubyMars: Poor me. :)

RubyMars: It was a good day.

AHall80: Did you get any presents?

RubyMars: Yes. :) Let's see, my mom and #4 got me clothes and a season 1 DVD of *Buffy the Vampire*

Slayer with the cover signed. My dad sent me a gift certificate for an airline to buy a flight out to visit him. My oldest brother, Seb, gave me $50. Jonathan gave me $50 too and a gift card for makeup. His boyfriend gave me a really pretty scarf that I'm scared to wear because I'm pretty sure it cost two hundred dollars. Tali, my older sister, gave me $50 and a gift card to this fabric store, and my little sister gave me some really neat custom business cards. And my friends just gave me random things like bags of Fritos, some DVDs and gift cards. It was great.

AHall80: Happy to hear that

AHall80: Doing okay?

RubyMars: Yeah, I'm really good. You?

AHall80: Really good? What'd you do today?

AHall80: I'm all right.

RubyMars: I worked on a bunch of bandanas, almost finished up some details on my sister's new dress. I'm going to kickboxing later. How was your day?

AHall80: Same old shit every day. :] The days feel even longer knowing I'm leaving soon.

AHall80: Is kickboxing a monthly membership?

RubyMars: I bet.

RubyMars: No. It was cheaper to buy a year pass for X amount of classes.

AHall80: You don't care if I give some of the soldiers staying here the books you sent me? Not all of them, just some.

RubyMars: Of course not. They were a gift . . . and they were all used copies. Do whatever you want.

AHall80: That's what I thought, just wanted to check. I need something to read on the flight back in case I don't fall asleep.

RubyMars: I bet you'll be asleep in the first twenty minutes.

AHall80: Not betting against you lol

RubyMars: Are you dead set on having pizza first thing you can when you get back?

AHall80: Pizza and a beer.

AHall80: A real beer.

RubyMars: I forgot they don't have real beer over there . . . and you did mention having a beer before.

AHall80: Yeah. They have the nonalcoholic stuff, but no. Some guys get it when they're desperate, but I'd rather not waste my money. That and cigarettes are what everybody starts missing the most over here.

RubyMars: You never told me, do you smoke?

AHall80: Nah

AHall80: Not really. Sometimes if I'm really stressed.

RubyMars: Have you smoked that cigar someone gave you?

AHall80: Not yet. Saving it for the day I leave

AHall80: What happened with that guy you went on a date with?

RubyMars: He's been texting me. He asked when we could go out again.

AHall80: What did you say?

RubyMars: I said maybe soon. I like him, but . . . I don't know. I feel like I should like him more. Our texts are still awkward, and I feel like maybe they shouldn't be that way. I don't know.

AHall80: Awkward how?

RubyMars: Like neither one of us knows what to talk to each other about.

AHall80: Oh

RubyMars: Is that normal?

A Hall80: I guess.

A Hall80: I only texted my girl if I had something to tell her.

RubyMars: That's romantic.

A Hall80: I know, that's why I'm single.

RubyMars: I meant it as a joke, I'm sorry.

A Hall80: I know you did. It's fine.

A Hall80: It is what it is.

RubyMars: :)

RubyMars: Anywho, I keep thinking if I'm not crazy about him by now, it's a waste of both of our times. Do you know what I mean? My mom says she knew the same day she met my dad, she knew she was crazy about him.

RubyMars: Not that they stayed together, but you know what I mean.

RubyMars: She said the same thing about every man she's been married to. You either hit it off or you don't, even if it isn't romantic.

RubyMars: I've hit it off with each of my best friends from the start.

A Hall80: Huh

A Hall80: I never thought about it like that. You got a point. I guess you should know there's something special there.

RubyMars: My sister is telling me I'm making things up in my head and expecting too much.

A Hall80: What does she think you're expecting?

RubyMars: Someone perfect.

A Hall80: That doesn't exist.

RubyMars: I know it doesn't. I'm not. I just figure I should feel something more than a little bit of weird friendship, but I just feel . . . I don't know. Not enough. Like I don't miss him if I don't hear from him. I don't go out of my way to text him. I don't find myself telling him things. I don't sit around thinking about him.

AHall80: I don't think I've ever met anybody who I was crazy about first thing, Rube. Least not as more than a friend.

RubyMars: Never?

AHall80: Nah.

AHall80: But you should wait. I'm not saying it doesn't happen, I just haven't experienced it.

RubyMars: Maybe I should give him another shot.

AHall80: Or not

RubyMars: . . .

RubyMars: You think I shouldn't bother then?

AHall80: I'm thinking about it, and I think you got it right the first time. It's basically wasting your time and their time if you aren't interested like that. There has to be at least a little something there if you want it to last longer than a day.

AHall80: I wish I'd known that. It would've saved me a lot of crazy girlfriends.

RubyMars: Lessons with Ruby at 1 p.m. central time. Stay tuned.

AHall80: No

RubyMars: :)

AHall80: What happened with your dating profile?

RubyMars: I haven't finished it yet. I keep putting it off and haven't felt like doing it. I might get back to it soon. I have more important things to worry about than dating.

RubyMars: If you say something again about me going to church or volunteering at a dog shelter . . .

A Hall80: I'm not.

RubyMars: You were thinking about it, weren't you?

A Hall80: Maybe :]

RubyMars: Are you going to join a church when you decide to start dating again?

A Hall80: . . .

RubyMars: . . .

A Hall80: Bye

RubyMars: Lol, that's what I thought.

A Hall80: I'm going to volunteer at a shelter.

RubyMars: You're a freaking liar.

A Hall80: :]

A Hall80: Nah, I'm good, for real. I've had enough drama and bullshit for the rest of my life.

RubyMars: You're over your ex though, right?

A Hall80: Yeah I haven't thought about her since the last time I msged you about her.

A Hall80: I gotta go. Message you soon?

RubyMars: That works for me. Be careful.

A Hall80: You too. Bye, Ru

April 6, 2009

A Hall80: Hey you

RubyMars: Hey stalker

RubyMars: How are you doing?

A Hall80: All right. You?

RubyMars: Good. :)

A Hall80: I started packing today. I wanted to figure out what else I'm going to leave here.

A Hall80: It's too soon, but it isn't like I have anything better to do.

RubyMars: What are you considering?

A Hall80: Some books, cards, my shower bag.

A Hall80: My worst underwear

RubyMars: Would anyone want your old undies?

A Hall80: Not willingly

RubyMars: Lol, did you take a lot with you?

A Hall80: Yeah

A Hall80: Learned my lesson the hard way that it's better to have too many than not enough.

RubyMars: Might as well leave the ones with skid marks while you're at it too.

A Hall80: Skid marks??

RubyMars: Are you crying or am I the only one?

A Hall80: You're the only one.

A Hall80: I can promise you there's 0 skid marks on my underwear.

RubyMars: Zero, really?

A Hall80: Maybe not 0 . . . maybe 2.

RubyMars: That sounds more like it.

RubyMars: Lol

RubyMars: How did we even get to this point?

A Hall80: You telling me about peeing in public

RubyMars: . . .

A Hall80: You talk about skid marks with all your friends?

RubyMars: Only with the ones I like the best. :)

A Hall80: Lucky me. :]

A Hall80: I had a few old whities that aren't so white anymore.

RubyMars: They're brown now?

A Hall80: . . .

A Hall80: Yeah, but not for the reason you think. They're dirty because I don't get to shower every day. I know better than to buy white ones.

RubyMars: Eww. Yeah, leave those.

RubyMars: Do you have to do anything right before you leave?

AHall80: Nah, not usually. Our replacements will start showing up soon, and then it'll just be us sitting around, waiting for our turn to fly out.

RubyMars: I want to ask how long your flight is, but maybe you can tell me afterward.

AHall80: Yeah. If I disappear randomly, it's because I'm gone, but I'll try to let you know so you aren't expecting the worst.

RubyMars: You'll let me know at least when you get back to base? Just so I know you're okay?

RubyMars: You don't have to or anything.

AHall80: Yeah, but we still have time till then

AHall80: I'll tell you

RubyMars: What are you doing after you get there?

AHall80: I got about a week of reintegration before I get 30 days of leave. I left my truck with Max, so I'm going to fly to Louisiana, then go to Scotland for a week, then Florida another week and back home for a couple days before I drive back to base.

RubyMars: I'm so happy for you going to Scotland. I think you're going to have a great time with your friends. I'll live through you.

AHall80: :]

AHall80: We got the beach house situation sorted too.

RubyMars: Where are you staying? South Florida?

AHall80: Nah. We just want to fish and stuff. We're staying at a place in this town called San Blas.

RubyMars: I've never heard of it.

AHall80: I've been there a few times

AHall80: I gotta go, but I'll msg you soon.

RubyMars: Okay, bye!

April 9, 2009

AHall80: Hey

RubyMars: Hey. How are you?

AHall80: Just got an e-mail from my brother that's
stressing me out

RubyMars: Everything okay?

AHall80: Some asshole was picking on my sister and she
hadn't told anyone

RubyMars: Picking on her how?

AHall80: He works for my dad. From what my brother
knew, he'd been coming on to my sister . . . touching
her even though he knew she doesn't like to be
touched

AHall80: I'm shaking from how fucking pissed I am

AHall80: I'm all the way over here and I can't do
anything, you know

RubyMars: This is going to sound stupid and
presumptuous, but I'm getting pissed off and she isn't
related to me. How did he find out?

AHall80: My dad was looking through security film
after someone fell and saw it. He asked my sister
about it and she admitted he'd been doing it for a
while. It wasn't anything . . . inappropriate because
he'd be dead by now if that was the case, just her arms
and shoulders, stuff like that. Not a big deal for most
people, but it is for her. I've gotten two hugs from her
her whole life. She doesn't . . . know how to react to
people . . . what to say, how to interact, so she gets
pretty quiet and doesn't make eye contact . . . that
kind of thing.

AHall80: That's my little sister, Ruby.

AHall80: I'm shaking

AHall80: I can barely type

RubyMars: If that was my little sister, I'd feel the same way.

RubyMars: What did your dad or brother do?

AHall80: He fired him, but that doesn't change much. Everyone knows she's autistic and this asshole took advantage of her.

AHall80: I'm sorry

RubyMars: For what?

RubyMars: What can I do?

RubyMars: I've been taking kickboxing for almost a year now. I know how to booby trap an airbag, you know.

RubyMars: You tell me and I'll do it.

RubyMars: No one will ever know it was me.

RubyMars: *Strangers on a Train,* Ruby and Aaron style.

RubyMars: Are you there?

AHall80: Yeah, I'm here

AHall80: Just busy

AHall80: Shaking my head

AHall80: How you can make me laugh even when I want to kill someone is beyond me

AHall80: Thank you

RubyMars: :) I wasn't trying to make light of the situation, just offering up my limited skill set for revenge since it couldn't come back to me.

AHall80: I know you weren't, Rubes, but thank you

AHall80: For real

AHall80: "limited skill set"

RubyMars: :)

RubyMars: I stole part of it from a movie I watched a few months ago.

RubyMars: Joking aside, is there anything I can do? I really will booby trap an airbag. You can look up a

video on how to do anything nowadays. I'll do it for
you. Because if that was Jazz, I'd kill someone.

AHall80: Thanks, but I already feel better. I don't need
you getting into trouble for me.

RubyMars: I wouldn't get in trouble because no one
would find out.

AHall80: . . .

RubyMars: I really am sorry, stalker. Between my
brothers, my sisters, and me, I'm confident we can do
just about anything. You don't mess with someone's
family. They'd help.

AHall80: :] I'll tell you if I think of anything.

RubyMars: Don't forget I took aikido for a while.

RubyMars: I said that to make you laugh.

AHall80: You did.

AHall80: I need to go, but I'll msg you soon.

AHall80: Thanks, Rubes

RubyMars: You're welcome.

RubyMars: You're a good brother for being upset.

AHall80: I could be a better one.

AHall80: :] bye

RubyMars: Bye

April 11, 2009

AHall80: Hey

RubyMars: Hey.

AHall80: We had another blackout.

RubyMars: I figured. You okay?

AHall80: Tired and the days are too long

RubyMars: Just think, in four weeks you'll be touring
Scotland and it's going to be great. In five weeks,
you'll be lying out on a beach somewhere.

AHall80: That's why my days are seeming longer I bet

AHall80: I'm ready to get the hell out of here. I keep thinking about that. I try not to because you never know what'll happen in an hour, but it's the only thing getting me through the days.

RubyMars: I get it.

RubyMars: Want a distraction?

AHall80: Yes

RubyMars: I got asked out on a date.

AHall80: With the 21-year-old?

RubyMars: No, with my brother's friend.

AHall80: . . .

AHall80: The one who led you on?

RubyMars: No. Not that one. My marine brother's friend. My brother suggested it.

AHall80: Your brother was okay with it?

RubyMars: Yeah. I've known that guy for a while. They were roommates before he moved in with his boyfriend. He's nice.

AHall80: You said the other guy was nice

RubyMars: I think you're nice, too.

AHall80: You know what I mean

RubyMars: I do. But this guy really is nice. Like you. He was always pretty sweet to me but never said or did anything about it. I was over at my brother's place for his boyfriend's birthday and that guy asked me out.

RubyMars: He's really hot and that makes me nervous, but if I wait around to meet someone who doesn't make me feel awkward, I'm going to be in adult diapers.

RubyMars: I don't know why I told you he's hot. I'm sorry. Like you care or want to hear that.

AHall80: You can tell me whatever

A Hall80: Where's he taking you?

RubyMars: I don't know. He said he'd call me on Thursday so we can go out Friday.

A Hall80: Why is he waiting to call you all week?

RubyMars: . . .

RubyMars: He's going on dates with other people, isn't he?

A Hall80: I don't know, but . . .

RubyMars: It's fine. I don't have any expectations. It's not like I'm in love with him or anything. I'm just trying to get out there and get some experience.

A Hall80: I shouldn't have said that, Ruby. I'm sorry. Maybe he's busy.

RubyMars: Maybe.

A Hall80: Look, I got to go, but I'm sorry for saying that.

RubyMars: You didn't do anything. It's okay. Be safe.

April 18, 2009

A Hall80: Hey

RubyMars: Hey stalker.

A Hall80: How was your date?

RubyMars: Awful.

A Hall80: Awful how?

A Hall80: Did he do something?

RubyMars: No. He brought up the other guy.

A Hall80: The one who led you on?

RubyMars: Yes. We were in the middle of eating at this place that was way too fancy and made me uncomfortable when he said, "I was waiting to ask you out." No biggie, right? I said, "Really?" He goes, "Yes. I wanted to give you some time to get over Hunter."

RubyMars: I wanted to throw up, Aaron. I lost my appetite, and I don't ever lose my appetite unless I'm dying from pneumonia.

AHall80: Hunter is the guy?

RubyMars: Yes.

AHall80: Shit

RubyMars: Yeah. My thoughts exactly.

RubyMars: Everyone knew! Everyone!

RubyMars: It was one thing to know my family was aware of it, but for my brother's friends to know too . . . I'm such an idiot. I could tell he knew I wanted to throw up because he immediately started backpedaling. I told him it was fine, but I wasn't fine. I was mad at myself.

RubyMars: I'm so stupid.

AHall80: You didn't do anything wrong.

RubyMars: I did. I could've handled that different. I could've gotten over him years ago and moved on with my life, but no . . . not me.

RubyMars: I'm an idiot.

AHall80: You're not an idiot

AHall80: Everyone has liked someone who didn't like them back at some point, Ruby.

AHall80: You know that. Everybody.

RubyMars: But not for years like a complete moron.

RubyMars: I . . .

RubyMars: UGH

RubyMars: Here was this guy who liked me and I had no idea because I'd been goo goo gaa gaa for someone who wasn't interested in me for half my life like a jackass.

AHall80: You're not a jackass.

AHall80: You like this guy?

RubyMars: I wouldn't say I "like" him. I've never really thought about it much. He's nice and he's not hard to look at.

RubyMars: I tried not to act different the rest of the date, but I know he could tell I was pissed off and embarrassed.

AHall80: You didn't do anything wrong, remember that.

RubyMars: I'll try . . .

RubyMars: Still. Did everyone in the entire world know I was hung up on him? I wanted to crawl into a hole of pathetic and never come out.

AHall80: You aren't pathetic.

AHall80: You're over him now and you can move on, right?

RubyMars: Right.

AHall80: Chill.

RubyMars: Easier said than done. I never really thought I was this prideful, but I guess I am.

AHall80: You're good. It's one guy.

AHall80: Relax

RubyMars: Fine.

AHall80: I thought your sister was the sore loser in the family?

RubyMars: Har har har

RubyMars: I don't want to talk about it anymore.

RubyMars: Anyway, how are you?

AHall80: Fine

AHall80: I'm dropping it too

AHall80: The stress is high. Everyone's itching to get out of here. Same old shit.

RubyMars: :)

RubyMars: That's better than crazy stuff happening, right?

AHall80: Yes and no.

AHall80: I don't need to be complaining.

RubyMars: I'll change the subject.

RubyMars: Have you heard anything else about your sister and that piece of crap?

AHall80: My dad e-mailed me and said Paige is fine and acting more like herself than she had been. He said he hadn't noticed she'd been acting strange until now that she's not.

AHall80: Knowing my dad, he feels like he failed her, but he won't say anything about it.

RubyMars: I'm sorry, Aaron.

RubyMars: If there's something I can do or say, tell me.

AHall80: I will.

AHall80: Tell me something

AHall80: Anything

RubyMars: That's not broad. :)

RubyMars: I gave my sister her dress.

AHall80: Send a picture.

AHall80: What'd she say or do?

RubyMars: I took it to her room when we were home alone and gave it to her. She stared at it for a long time, and I really thought she was going to cry, but then she hugged me and told me thank you.

RubyMars: Today I walked by her room and found her sitting on the edge of her bed, kind of staring off into space. Hopefully she's thinking about going to skate, but who knows.

RubyMars: I'll send you a picture right now. I think it's my best one yet.

RubyMars: But . . .

RubyMars: I don't know if she'll actually fit into it if she tries putting it on. I used her measurements from when she was training regularly.

AHall80: Maybe it'll motivate her to get back into it.

AHall80: Wow. I just opened the attachment. Did you do a rainbow pattern?

RubyMars: Yes :). I thought about doing more of a red theme, like a phoenix coming back from its ashes, but the rainbow just popped out at me. It's not as depressing either. She lost, she didn't die. I wanted it to look like she was rising up, or evolving. Like it's more about living your life than death.

RubyMars: I don't know if that makes sense, but . . . maybe I overthought it.

AHall80: I get it. A phoenix is more about the rebirth. You were thinking more of the life afterward.

RubyMars: Yes! Exactly!

AHall80: I can see the little wing-like things you did. Wow. Really, Ruby. Wow.

AHall80: If she doesn't wear that, you should give it to someone who will. That doesn't deserve to go into a closet.

RubyMars: Thank you.

AHall80: Have you heard from that guy?

RubyMars: Which one?

RubyMars: ^^ the first and only time I've ever sounded like a player.

AHall80: The younger one

RubyMars: He sent me a message a few weeks ago, but I'd already kind of snuck in that I didn't want to waste his time anymore.

AHall80: Good girl

RubyMars: :)

AHall80: I need to go. I'll msg you soon.

RubyMars: Okay. Bye bye. Be safe.

AHall80: You too, RC.

April 21, 2009

AHall80: Tell me something good that happened to you.
RubyMars: Hello to you.
RubyMars: I quit my job today.
AHall80: . . .
AHall80: For real?
RubyMars: For real.
AHall80: What happened?
RubyMars: I snapped. I went into the shop to talk to my aunt about a change she wanted to make to a dress, and she started saying some really mean things to me . . . I stood there wanting to cry. I didn't, which I deserve an award for, but I wanted to. Then she said something about how she could find someone as good as me for less money and it got me thinking about you, and I just told her I quit.
AHall80: What did she say?
RubyMars: She said I was lucky I was related to her or she would've fired me a long time ago, how my work was substandard, that my family had babied me for too long, and that I wasn't sixteen anymore and I needed to grow up . . . just a bunch of crap.
AHall80: . . .
RubyMars: No one has ever talked to me like that before. It really hurt my feelings.
RubyMars: I probably sound like a baby saying that, but who cares. I don't want to lie to you and make it seem like I laughed in her face or anything. I wish I would have.
AHall80: You don't sound like a baby, Rubes. Your aunt sounds like a witch, and I don't mean that with a W. She sounds like an unhappy person.

RubyMars: She is mean and unhappy. Her husband cheats on her all the time. I feel bad for her, but I don't get why she takes it out on me and everyone else.

AHall80: Cheating on her or not, that pisses me off.

AHall80: A lot

AHall80: You quit for sure?

RubyMars: Yeah. My hands started getting sweaty and I wanted to throw up and my heart started beating really fast, but I quit. That's how I told her, "I quit."

RubyMars: Part of me regrets not making more of a spectacle of it. Like flicking her off or saying something really good like "You'll never find someone better than me" or "You'll regret this" or shoving a mannequin over when I walked out.

RubyMars: Oh well.

RubyMars: I'm trying to make a joke about this so I don't throw up.

RubyMars: It's not helping that much.

AHall80: Oh Ruby.

AHall80: I'm laughing at you and I feel for you at the same time.

AHall80: Don't throw up.

RubyMars: I don't have a job anymore, Aaron.

AHall80: You have a job. Your stuff you do on your own.

AHall80: You had to quit. You know that.

RubyMars: I know.

AHall80: You couldn't work there forever. You didn't even like making those dresses, did you?

RubyMars: No . . .

AHall80: And she paid you shitty, didn't she?

RubyMars: Yes . . .

AHall80: Then what's the problem?

RubyMars: I'm just scared. I've never not had a job, and now in less than two months, I've lost both of them.

RubyMars: I'm going to throw up. I really am.

AHall80: You're not going to throw up.

AHall80: Breathe.

AHall80: You've got it. You're going to be fine.

AHall80: I got to say I'm really damn proud of you for quitting.

RubyMars: :)

RubyMars: Now you make me want to cry in a different way.

RubyMars: Thank you for saying that.

AHall80: It isn't like I'm not telling you the truth.

AHall80: I'm sure it's scary as hell to quit.

RubyMars: It really is.

RubyMars: I think I might have to go break into #4's liquor stash to calm down. My heart is still racing.

AHall80: . . .

RubyMars: Not like that. It isn't palpitations.

AHall80: You sure?

AHall80: Be serious.

RubyMars: I'm sure. I'm sorry for saying it like that. Don't worry. I'm okay.

AHall80: . . .

RubyMars: Really.

AHall80: I need to go, but I'm real proud of you, Ruby. Don't be scared. You did the right thing. You'll figure everything out. Maybe it's time you focused on doing your own thing full time.

RubyMars: Maybe. :)

AHall80: Don't go running out getting the first job that pops up either if you freak out more later.

RubyMars: It scares me how well you've gotten to know me.

AHall80: Heh

AHall80: I gotta go. You'll be good.

AHall80: Talk soon. Bye.

RubyMars: Bye you.

April 23, 2009

AHall80: So?

RubyMars: You're getting straight to the point lately.

RubyMars: I want to ask what, but I know what you're asking already.

AHall80: ?

RubyMars: I haven't gotten another job.

AHall80: Good.

RubyMars: :)

RubyMars: I told my mom what happened and she lost it. I haven't seen her face get that red since she ripped her pants getting out of the car.

RubyMars: She grabbed the phone, ready to call my aunt and rip her one for the ages, but I stopped her. I told her to let it go and that I'd handled it. She looked so impressed. She hugged me.

AHall80: She should. I don't know anybody that's quit their job just like that.

RubyMars: . . .

RubyMars: You haven't?

AHall80: No. Who quits their job without having another one lined up?

RubyMars: You're not joking.

AHall80: I'm not joking.

AHall80: :] You did the right thing.

RubyMars: I'm going to pretend you didn't just tell me that, but thank you again.

RubyMars: All I knew was that I didn't want to keep getting chewed out. I was tired of my stomach hurting every time she would call or text me.

AHall80: You've got this.

RubyMars: I've got this.

RubyMars: Maybe if I say it enough I'll start believing it.

AHall80: Lol

AHall80: You've got this.

RubyMars: :)

RubyMars: How are things over there?

AHall80: Fine. We got Ax's paperwork together. I already know who I'm leaving things with. My bag is packed. I'm ready to go.

RubyMars: I'm so happy for you.

AHall80: Me too. Ready to go to Scotland too. Max sent me some itinerary stuff through the mail I've been looking through.

RubyMars: What's on the list?

AHall80: Edinburgh, some small towns, a castle, three days in Skye.

RubyMars: What's Skye?

AHall80: An island. Look it up right now. They film movies there.

RubyMars: Okay hold on.

AHall80: Are you looking?

RubyMars: I shouldn't have looked. I'm so jealous it's a sin. Now I need to get a job so I can save money to go one day.

AHall80: I can find out if there's room for you to come.

RubyMars: No money, remember?

RubyMars: :) Thanks anyway. I'll make it someday.

AHall80: I'm sorry, Ruby.

RubyMars: For what? You deserve a vacation. I don't want to take the excitement away from you.

AHall80: You're not. I know you didn't mean it that way.

AHall80: I just remembered you were supposed to go see your dad this month.

RubyMars: Something came up with his stepkids. The good thing is the gift card he gave me is enough to cover a round trip ticket, so I can go whenever. Maybe July.

RubyMars: It worked out anyway. I shouldn't be spending that money right now.

RubyMars: My mom and #4 are going to Hawaii. Have you been there?

AHall80: Hawaii? No. Want to though.

AHall80: Can't really handle the big tourist places anymore. Too many people, too much noise . . . nah.

RubyMars: I get it. My brother is the same way. There are a lot of places to go that aren't theme parks and tourist traps.

AHall80: You're right.

AHall80: I need to go, but I'll msg you soon.

RubyMars: Okay. Be safe.

AHall80: You too. Bye, RC

April 25, 2009

AHall80: Hey Rubes

RubyMars: Hey.

RubyMars: Everything good?

AHall80: For the most part.

RubyMars: Bad day?

AHall80: It hasn't been the best.

RubyMars: I'm sorry.

RubyMars: Anything I can do?

AHall80: Take my mind off it?

RubyMars: Okay.

RubyMars: Let me think. Nothing stupid has happened to me lately, or anyone I know . . .

AHall80: You were going to tell me about how your mom taught you how to ride a bike a long time ago.

RubyMars: I forgot about that! Okay. I'll tell you.

RubyMars: It isn't a long story.

RubyMars: It's kind of stupid, actually. I don't know why I was even going to tell you about it.

AHall80: Tell me anyway

RubyMars: You're sure?

AHall80: Tell me.

RubyMars: Okay.

RubyMars: Remember how I told you she's always talked a bunch of crap to us but won't let other people do that? Keep that in mind.

RubyMars: I was probably like 6 and my dad had been on my case about taking my training wheels off for a long time (they were still together back then.) But my dad has always been the softie of the two, and every time he failed with me learning, when the bike would tip over or if I'd crash into something, etc., he would drop it and put the wheels back on. No biggie, right?

RubyMars: My mom finally got tired of me not learning and came outside one day after I'd fallen while I was telling my dad I didn't want to try again . . . pretty sure I was crying. Anywho, she comes up to us, points at me, and says "Get on the bike. I'm going to teach you since somebody can't." So I get on the bike, because by that age, I already know not to mess around with my mom. She holds the back of the seat while I get on and gives me some instructions . . . the same thing my dad would say every time. Balance, keep your hands on the handles, that type of thing.

RubyMars: Before she starts walking the bike and me forward, she leans into my ear and says "If you don't do this right the first time, Rubella, you're on bathroom and kitchen cleanup for the next month, okay, honey? You can do it. I believe in you."

RubyMars: Yeah, I learned how to ride that freaking bike that time LOL.

AHall80: That's not at all what I thought was going to go down.

RubyMars: She did the same thing to Jazz when it was time. I heard her. You've never seen two little five-year-old's legs pump pedals that fast in your life.

RubyMars: When it was time for me to learn how to drive, I begged my older sister to teach me instead of my mom because I was worried about what kind of threats she'd make me live with once she got tired of my BS.

AHall80: LOL

AHall80: My dad taught me how to drive

RubyMars: How'd that go?

AHall80: Fine. I'm a good driver.

RubyMars: That's not cocky at all.

AHall80: I am. It's the truth.

RubyMars: So modest. What kind of car did you learn on?

AHall80: His white sedan. He's always had white cars. Says they don't get as hot as black cars do.

RubyMars: My mom says the same thing!

AHall80: :]

AHall80: How old were you?

RubyMars: 17. I had to have a job first to pay my insurance. You?

AHall80: Got my permit at 15 and was driving at 16.

RubyMars: Show off.

AHall80: It seems like forever ago. Sometimes I can't believe I'm going to be 30. I still think I'm 16 or 18 most of the time.

RubyMars: I know. I can't believe I've been out of high school almost 7 years already. Like what have I done with my life since then? You know?

AHall80: Me too.

AHall80: I never knew what I was going to do, but it wasn't being in the military.

AHall80: Still don't know what I want to do.

RubyMars: You still have your whole life ahead of you. You can do whatever you want with it. You're smart, responsible, and you have a good head on your shoulders.

AHall80: I don't know about all that.

RubyMars: It's true. I wouldn't say that if it wasn't.

RubyMars: I read somewhere you're your happiest in your thirties anyway.

AHall80: For real?

RubyMars: Yeah, I guess by that point you know who you are better and have more of your life on track by then.

RubyMars: If that's the case, I have six years to get my crap together, lol. I'm going to need every minute.

AHall80: You'll figure it out.

RubyMars: Everything can always be worse. That's what I tell myself when I'm not crying into a gallon of Blue Bell.

AHall80: What's Blue Bell?

RubyMars: . . .

RubyMars: You're joking.

AHall80: No what is it?

RubyMars: . . .

AHall80: Yes, I'm joking. They have it in Louisiana.

RubyMars: Bless your heart, I was about to have to try
and figure out how to freeze-dry ice cream to send it
to you across the world.

AHall80: LOL

AHall80: You're something else

RubyMars: :) I've been told I'm very loveable.

AHall80: Who said that? Your mom?

RubyMars: . . . .

AHall80: . . . .

RubyMars: . . . . . .

AHall80: :]

RubyMars: I take back that one time I called you nice.

AHall80: LOL

AHall80: I thought we were friends?

RubyMars: You're basically my closest friend now.

RubyMars: I don't know why I just told you that. No
pressure. I don't mean it to be weird. I have other
friends too. It's just different with you.

RubyMars: I like you more than just about everyone else
I know. You get me.

RubyMars: I keep making it worse.

RubyMars: I'm going to stop typing now.

AHall80: I get what you mean. You're pretty much my
closest friend too

RubyMars: :)

AHall80: You can start typing again

RubyMars: I'm worried I'll say something I'll regret.

AHall80: Like what?

RubyMars: I don't know. Something I'll regret.

AHall80: Like?

RubyMars: I'm not digging this hole of shame any deeper, lol.

AHall80: You already dug one deep hole, what's another one?

RubyMars: You stepped in human crap too!

AHall80: I was talking about the peeing in public, Ruby

RubyMars: Oh.

RubyMars: About that

RubyMars: Lol

AHall80: Yeah, about that

AHall80: :]

RubyMars: I'll own it.

AHall80: I gotta go, but I'll message you soon.

RubyMars: Okay, bye and be safe.

AHall80: You too

April 26, 2009

AHall80: Hey

RubyMars: Hey.

AHall80: Peanut butter or jelly?

RubyMars: Is this a trick question?

AHall80: No.

RubyMars: Jelly.

AHall80: Thank God

AHall80: Just listened to five people argue peanut butter over jelly for the last hour at dinner. I was too tired to tell them they were all out of their minds.

RubyMars: You're Team Jelly too?

AHall80: All the way

RubyMars: Good. I wouldn't have wanted to stop being your friend over something stupid like liking peanut butter more, but I would've looked back on our friendship fondly.

AHall80: Heh

AHall80: Aaron and Ruby RIP 2008–2009

RubyMars: There are tears in my eyes

RubyMars: "Ruron Forever"

AHall80: Ruron? Ruby+Aaron? That's clever.

RubyMars: It's our ship name

AHall80: Like a battleship?

RubyMars: You poor, sweet, innocent child

RubyMars: Ship. Shipping. I ship _____.

AHall80: I don't know what you're talking about

RubyMars: Today is the day our friendship dies.

RubyMars: You've never heard that term before?

AHall80: No

AHall80: For real.

AHall80: "Today is the day our friendship dies"

AHall80: Ruby . . .

RubyMars: I'll forgive you then. I forget the dork doesn't run strong in you.

RubyMars: Shipping is . . . "relationSHIP" like, liking two characters and thinking they should be in a relationship together in a fandom.

RubyMars: Do you know what a fandom is?

AHall80: I know what a fandom is.

RubyMars: Okay. You watched *Buffy*. Remember Angel? The vampire? Buffy + Angel = Bangel.

AHall80: Got it.

AHall80: I liked the other guy more

RubyMars: . . . . .

RubyMars: Spike?

A Hall80: Yeah

RubyMars: Marry me.

RubyMars: I think I might love you.

A Hall80: Lol

A Hall80: OK

RubyMars: I'm not even joking. Marry me. The offer stands.

RubyMars: Kidding, I am joking. :)

RubyMars: How much of the show did you watch . . .?

A Hall80: . . . . .

A Hall80: 7 seasons?

RubyMars: There was only 7 seasons.

RubyMars: Aaron

RubyMars: That's tears in my eyes twice today

A Hall80: Max sent me tapes of every season about 4 or 5 years ago when I was deployed. He watched it too, but he'll never admit it

RubyMars: I take back what I said. Today is the day our friendship turned into a forever thing lol

A Hall80: :]

A Hall80: Works for me

RubyMars: Good lol.

A Hall80: I gotta go, but I'll msg you soon, Ruron

RubyMars: Okay, bye, Ruron.

April 28, 2009

A Hall80: You ever feel like beating the shit out of someone?

RubyMars: Hello to you

RubyMars: Only once or twice.

RubyMars: Why?

A Hall80: Who?

AHall80: Just some new guy that's driving me up the wall. He's so damn naïve and stupid.

RubyMars: Who did I want to beat up?

RubyMars: I'm sorry. Did you get into a fight with him?

AHall80: Yeah

AHall80: I didn't, but I wanted to. I know he's a dumbass private who hasn't seen or done anything before, and I know he doesn't know anything . . . but it's hard to keep my mouth closed when he's rattling nonsense out of his mouth.

RubyMars: I wanted to beat up this girl in high school who used to talk about me behind my back. I also wanted to beat the crap out of the random stranger who hit my car in the parking lot a year ago. That's all.

RubyMars: Those kind of people are the worst.

AHall80: Somebody bullied you in high school?

RubyMars: I wouldn't call it bullying. All she ever did was make stupid comments under her breath when I could hear her. It only upset me the first ten times she did it.

AHall80: Did you do anything to make her stop?

RubyMars: No.

AHall80: . . . . .

RubyMars: I told you it didn't bother me so much. She was just a hateful person in general. No biggie. But for a while, I did want to kick her ass if I could have.

RubyMars: She had these giant boobs, and one time she must have bent over and the whole shebang came out of her bra because her nipple was really obviously out of her bra. You could see it. I saw it and didn't tell her anything.

RubyMars: I also saw her boyfriend back then cheating on her when I went to the movies and never said anything either.

RubyMars: I feel guilty thinking about it now.

RubyMars: I'm stealing the conversation with my random crap. I'm sorry. Tell me about the idiot private.

AHall80: No, you're not. I'm not even that pissed off about him anymore.

AHall80: Do you know what happened to her?

RubyMars: The mean girl?

AHall80: Yeah

RubyMars: No. Now I want to look her up, lol.

RubyMars: Have you ever beat up anyone?

AHall80: Beat up? No. Gotten into a fight? Yeah

RubyMars: Over what?

AHall80: Nothing. Just drunk and dumb in high school.

RubyMars: Lame. I wanted something juicy.

AHall80: Heh no. Nothing like that.

RubyMars: Not even over one of your million girlfriends?

AHall80: I didn't have a million

AHall80: And hell no. Not ever over a girl.

RubyMars: Only 999,999 girlfriends

AHall80: . . . . .

AHall80: Bye

RubyMars: :)

RubyMars: You're still here.

AHall80: 20 something max. Most of them were girls I dated for a month.

RubyMars: Mister Commitment right here.

AHall80: . . . . .

AHall80: Swear on my life, I've lost so much face with other soldiers since I started e-mailing and IMing you, I don't know if I'll ever recover it. People can't take me seriously when I laugh out loud at you.

RubyMars: First world problems.

AHall80: Damn it, Ruby

RubyMars: Lol

RubyMars: I respect you, if that means anything.

RubyMars: Mostly.

AHall80: "Mostly"

AHall80: BYE

RubyMars: :) :) :)

AHall80: Moving on, you doing okay?

RubyMars: Yes. You?

AHall80: Yeah, I'm all right.

AHall80: I heard this joke that made me think of you

RubyMars: Share it.

AHall80: What do cows like to read?

RubyMars: There are already tears in my eyes

AHall80: Cattle logs

RubyMars: You are a treasure I will value every day for the rest of my life.

AHall80: :] I knew you'd like it. I had to tell you.

AHall80: I gotta go, but I'll write you soon, RC

RubyMars: Bye, Ruron

RubyMars: Be safe.

April 30, 2009

AHall80: Hey

RubyMars: Hey you.

AHall80: What are you up to?

RubyMars: Nothing. On the couch, eating my troubles away while I watch TV.

AHall80: Want me to let you go?

RubyMars: No.

AHall80: What are you watching?

AHall80: Someone put on the first *X-Men* movie today and I thought of you

RubyMars: I feel so pleased with myself.

RubyMars: I'm watching a *Project Runway* marathon . . .

AHall80: What's that?

RubyMars: A show about designers competing to kick off their careers.

AHall80: I should've known that. :]

RubyMars: I'm on my second cup of ramen. I thought of you.

AHall80: LOL.

AHall80: It's good. I don't eat it when I'm not here, but I get used to it.

RubyMars: Guess what?

AHall80: What?

RubyMars: I went on another date yesterday.

AHall80: With?

RubyMars: My brother's friend.

RubyMars: Not the one you don't like, the one who didn't lead me on.

AHall80: I thought he pissed you off?

RubyMars: He did, but he called and asked if I wanted to go to a special exhibit at the science museum. I was going to tell him no because of what happened last time, but not going because I was embarrassed about what happened . . . I figured you would tell me to go too.

AHall80: Yeah

RubyMars: So I went. It was nice.

AHall80: He didn't try to come on to you?

RubyMars: He kissed me.

RubyMars: That was all. It was nice.

RubyMars: Are you there?

A Hall80: Yeah

RubyMars: Everything okay?

A Hall80: Yeah

A Hall80: Are you going to see him again?

RubyMars: He invited me to go to the movies with him tomorrow. They have a morning showing at a theater that serves pancakes.

A Hall80: You're going to wake up early?

RubyMars: Yes. You're not the first person to ask that. :)

A Hall80: OK

RubyMars: I think it'll be fun as long as I don't fall asleep during the movie.

A Hall80: Don't do that.

RubyMars: I won't. I hope.

RubyMars: He really is nice. He wouldn't do anything to me.

A Hall80: If you say so

RubyMars: I told you I've known him for years. He's good people.

A Hall80: OK

RubyMars: . . .

RubyMars: Are you okay?

A Hall80: Yeah

RubyMars: Was today a bad day?

RubyMars: Want me to let you go?

A Hall80: No.

A Hall80: Nah, it's ok

RubyMars: Okay.

RubyMars: Good.

RubyMars: I sold a bunch of bandanas to this dog groomer my sister knows through her job.

A Hall80: That's good.

RubyMars: I thought so.

A Hall80: Yeah

RubyMars: Have you heard anything else about Scotland or Florida?

A Hall80: No

RubyMars: Are you sure you're okay?

A Hall80: I'm fine.

A Hall80: I gotta go. I'll write you soon.

RubyMars: Okay.

RubyMars: I'm here if you need to talk about anything.

A Hall80: I know. Bye.

RubyMars: Bye, Ruron.

Chapter Twelve

May

May 16, 2009

AHall80: Hi
RubyMars: Hey.
AHall80: You good?
RubyMars: Yes. You?
AHall80: Yeah
AHall80: How's the job hunt going?
RubyMars: Fine. I got more commission work.
AHall80: Ice-skating costumes?
RubyMars: Yes and some dog clothes.
RubyMars: Thank you for asking.
AHall80: What's wrong?
RubyMars: Nothing.
AHall80: Something's wrong. What is it?
RubyMars: Nothing.
RubyMars: Everything is fine.
AHall80: Ruby
RubyMars: Aaron.
AHall80: Ruby
RubyMars: Aaron.

RubyMars: I'm fine.

AHall80: I can tell something is wrong.

AHall80: You're barely responding

AHall80: And when you are it's not like you

RubyMars: . . .

AHall80: . . .

AHall80: What is it?

RubyMars: Nothing.

AHall80: Would you tell me?

RubyMars: I'm just trying not to say anything that's going to piss you off.

AHall80: Piss me off?

RubyMars: Yes.

AHall80: What are you talking about?

RubyMars: You were being all weird on our last IMs and you didn't write me back for almost two weeks. I e-mailed you twice and nothing. You were pissed off. I don't have to see your face to know. You aren't the only one who can tell when something is up.

AHall80: I wasn't pissed

RubyMars: You're going to insist you weren't pissed at something?

AHall80: . . .

RubyMars: Was it something with your ex?

AHall80: No. Not at all.

RubyMars: . . .

RubyMars: Okay, fine.

RubyMars: If something was bothering you that has nothing to do with me, that's okay. You can talk to me about it if you want to, you know. But you were being weird and you know it.

AHall80: I wasn't being weird.

RubyMars: Whatever you say.

RubyMars: You only disappeared for two weeks for no reason. I watched the news. I know there wasn't a reason for a blackout. I was worried something had happened to you.

RubyMars: We're friends. You don't owe me anything. All I wanted was to not do whatever it was that I said or did last time.

A Hall80: You didn't do anything, RC

RubyMars: . . .

A Hall80: Serious

RubyMars: All right.

RubyMars: I missed talking to you.

RubyMars: That's all.

A Hall80: I was busy

RubyMars: Okay.

A Hall80: I missed talking to you too, all right?

RubyMars: Okay.

A Hall80: . . .

RubyMars: . . .

A Hall80: I'm leaving pretty soon from the looks of it, but I'll make sure to try and let you know before we ship out so you don't worry.

RubyMars: Okay.

A Hall80: . . .

RubyMars: Be safe.

A Hall80: You too. Bye, Rubes.

RubyMars: Bye.

May 21, 2009

A Hall80: Hey

RubyMars: Hi.

A Hall80: You still mad at me?

RubyMars: I was never mad at you.

AHall80: I was never mad at you either

RubyMars: Okay.

AHall80: Serious

RubyMars: Are you sure?

RubyMars: I know I'm always complaining about people being mean to me, but I can handle the truth.

AHall80: Yes I'm sure

RubyMars: Okay then.

AHall80: For real?

RubyMars: What?

AHall80: That's all you need and you're like "okay"?

RubyMars: . . .

RubyMars: Yeah. Why wouldn't I? You're not lying to me, are you?

RubyMars: I already asked you a bunch of times if anything was wrong, you had your chance.

AHall80: No

RubyMars: Okay.

RubyMars: That's what I figured. If you were upset about me doing something, I'd hope you would tell me. If there's something you want to talk about, you can tell me anything too.

AHall80: Yeah

AHall80: I know

RubyMars: Then we're good.

RubyMars: I didn't mean to flip out on you last time. I'm sorry.

AHall80: You didn't flip out

AHall80: Much

RubyMars: :)

RubyMars: We're all right then?

AHall80: Yeah

AHall80: I've had a lot on my mind lately. I didn't mean to put anything on you. Sorry for scaring you. I hadn't thought about it.

RubyMars: I get it. I'm sure you do. It's okay.

RubyMars: How's everything?

AHall80: Good. Ready to get the hell out of here

RubyMars: I bet.

AHall80: Hey, what's happened with your sister?

RubyMars: Nothing at first, but her coach called my mom a few days ago and said that one of the younger skaters told her that they'd seen Jasmine at the rink busting her butt, trying to do some jumps before people started showing up. It's too early to say victory, but I think it's a good sign. Yesterday I heard her running on the treadmill in the garage.

AHall80: Good, that's great

RubyMars: I think so. :)

RubyMars: I'll let you know what happens.

RubyMars: I thought about e-mailing you, but I didn't.

AHall80: I noticed.

RubyMars: Har har har

RubyMars: I didn't get any e-mails from you either, buster.

AHall80: :]

AHall80: You're the only one I'm still messaging. I already said bye to my two other HaS matches, and my family and friends know I'll let them know as soon as my flight is off.

RubyMars: You're making me feel special.

RubyMars: If you're trying to suck up to me for ignoring me for two weeks, it's working.

AHall80: None of them make me laugh like you do

AHall80: I'm not trying to suck up. :]

RubyMars: Sure you aren't. :)

RubyMars: Speaking of . . . I'll tell you something funny that happened a couple of days ago.

RubyMars: My allergies have been really bad lately, and I haven't been taking any medication. I was at my older brother's condo helping him paint and we had the windows open. I'd been holding in my pee because he was busy doing the bathroom. I sneezed so hard I peed myself. A lot. So much. There was no way for me to hide it. He laid down on the floor when I told him what happened, covering his face with his hands.

AHall80: . . .

RubyMars: Funny, huh?

AHall80: Yes

AHall80: Yes

RubyMars: :) Luckily he has a washer and a dryer in his condo. He promised not to tell anyone, and luckily he still hasn't, so I'm holding out hope he doesn't blurt it out one day while he's drunk.

AHall80: I wouldn't do that to my sister.

RubyMars: He would, lol.

AHall80: You're not worried I'll tell somebody?

RubyMars: No. You wouldn't do that to me.

RubyMars: How is your sister anyway?

AHall80: She's good from what I heard last e-mail. My brother said she's back to acting like normal.

RubyMars: I'm happy to hear that.

AHall80: Me too

AHall80: Have you gotten more work?

RubyMars: Only a little, but one is a big job. One of the local theaters reached out to me two days ago about doing costumes for their play. Their usual costume designer quit unexpectedly and hasn't finished them,

and I said I could finish her work. I have three days
before costume rehearsals, but I'll trade sleep for
money.

AHall80: How'd they get your number?

RubyMars: One of the actors is friends with my big
sister. :)

AHall80: Whatever works

RubyMars: That's what I said.

RubyMars: Anywho, have you heard anything else about
Scotland?

AHall80: Nothing new yet

AHall80: Ready to go

AHall80: The new unit showed up already. I'll be
heading out any day now

RubyMars: Air conditioning everywhere!

AHall80: Plumbing

RubyMars: Beer!

AHall80: Pizza

RubyMars: Clean clothes!

AHall80: No sand

RubyMars: No mice!

AHall80: No mosquitoes

RubyMars: Smaller chances of dehydration!

AHall80: :]

AHall80: You're something else

RubyMars: Something good?

AHall80: Very good

RubyMars: :)

AHall80: My bad on the last few weeks.

AHall80: I missed talking to you too

RubyMars: Nobody told you you couldn't talk to me.

AHall80: Way to lay down the guilt trip

RubyMars: It's the truth, isn't it? :)

RubyMars: I'm just messing with you.

AHall80: Nah, you got a point. It is the truth.

AHall80: My bad

RubyMars: I know, it's fine. I forgive you.

AHall80: You forgive everyone, don't you?

RubyMars: For the most part. Holding grudges takes too much energy and time.

RubyMars: I don't want to live my life pissed off, you know?

AHall80: I know.

AHall80: Huh

RubyMars: We're still the platonic version of Ruron.

RubyMars: If you want.

AHall80: . . . yeah

AHall80: I gotta go, but I'll write you before I head out. I've got this feeling it's any day now.

RubyMars: Okay. Be safe. If I don't hear from you before you leave, have a good flight and make sure you take a book with you to read when you aren't snoring away.

AHall80: Har har

AHall80: I missed talking to you.

AHall80: Bye, Ruby Cube

RubyMars: Bye, stalker

May 25, 2009

AHall80: Tell me something

RubyMars: I fell down the stairs today. I was wearing socks and my heel just slipped on the edge. It's a miracle I didn't break my arm.

RubyMars: My butt was like a stack of dominos on each step going down.

AHall80: Ruby

RubyMars: It wasn't my most graceful moment. No one was home, so there's that.

AHall80: No video?

RubyMars: No video. Sorry for bursting your dreams.

AHall80: That's on my list of things I'd like to see after a pizza with double pepperoni.

RubyMars: I'm so honored busting my butt is on your list after pizza, lol.

AHall80: :]

AHall80: Before mac and cheese too

RubyMars: Lol

RubyMars: You never tell me if embarrassing, dumb stuff happens to you.

AHall80: Because it doesn't

RubyMars: Liar.

AHall80: Heh

AHall80: I put my underwear on inside out once.

RubyMars: Once.

RubyMars: Get out.

AHall80: :]

RubyMars: Want a new joke? It's been a while.

AHall80: Sure

RubyMars: What has four wheels and flies?

RubyMars: A garbage truck.

AHall80: They're so bad they're good.

RubyMars: I know!

AHall80: :]

RubyMars: I bought my plane ticket to go see my dad.

AHall80: Yeah? When?

RubyMars: July 8th, I'm going for a week.

AHall80: Nice

AHall80: I gotta go. I just wanted to get on real quick and say hi.

RubyMars: Sure. :)
RubyMars: Be safe.
AHall80: Bye.
RubyMars: Bye.

May 27, 2009

AHall80: I'm leaving really soon.
RubyMars: Really?
AHall80: Really for real.
RubyMars: !!!!!
AHall80: :]
RubyMars: Okay. Have a safe flight.
AHall80: It's going to suck, but it'll be worth it.
RubyMars: Is Ax travelling back with you guys?
AHall80: Yeah, my CO . . . commanding officer . . . is
    taking her home.
RubyMars: I'm so happy.
RubyMars: Really, have a safe flight, and just in case I
    don't talk to you again, I really enjoyed getting to
    know you. Give Aries a big hug from me and enjoy
    your trip to Scotland and Florida. If you ever decide
    to open a Facebook account, post pictures on it some
    day, and if I send you a request, accept it. Or don't. :)
AHall80: I'll e-mail you soon.
RubyMars: Good luck :) Have a safe flight.
AHall80: Thanks, Rubes.
AHall80: Hold up a sec
AHall80: I hope you know you're the best person I've
    ever been paired with. This tour would've been a
    whole lot shittier without you.
AHall80: I'm sorry for what happened at the
    beginning . . .

RubyMars: Don't worry about it. It's in the past and I understand.

AHall80: Still feel like shit about it.

RubyMars: You made up for it already. Don't think twice about it. I get it.

RubyMars: We worked it out.

RubyMars: For whatever it matters, I'm glad you ended up writing me back in the end. These last few months would've sucked without you too. Thanks for being there for me with everything.

RubyMars: You really did become my favorite friend.

RubyMars: I'll always remember you.

AHall80: Don't think twice about it.

RubyMars: I won't.

AHall80: I will write you when I get back to base in Kentucky. I'm not going to fall off the face of the planet.

AHall80: Promise

RubyMars: If you say so, but don't feel obligated if you don't want to. You don't owe me anything.

AHall80: I owe you a lot more than you think.

AHall80: Not just going to forget you, come on.

AHall80: Hey, what happened with that guy you went on a date with? Your brother's friend? Not the one I don't like.

RubyMars: Nothing. We went to the movies. Then he invited me over to his house another day for a barbecue. He's been out of town for about two weeks now. He's supposed to get back in a few days, but we've only texted.

AHall80: I see

RubyMars: :) I like him, but it isn't love at first sight or anything.

RubyMars: I know you need to go but have a good flight and enjoy your plumbing.

RubyMars: One last thing

A Hall80: Okay

RubyMars: Make sure to eat plenty of fiber so you can finally poop

A Hall80: BYE RUBY

RubyMars: Xoxo

Chapter Thirteen

May

"You did *what*?"

I hung my head in shame and—for one more freaking time—let the humiliation roll over my face, neck, chest, and *my entire soul*.

Stupid, stupid, stupid, *stupid, stupid.*

I was so stupid.

"Squirt," my sister cackled, her shoulders shaking as she sank deep into the cushioned seat of the booth the hostess of the diner had led us to fifteen minutes ago. The clinging and clacking of plates and silverware swallowed most of her laughs, but I'd heard her crack up enough over the course of my life to know exactly what it sounded like from memory. Except usually she laughed at Jonathan or Sebastian, not me.

The problem was, there was laughing your butt off so much you made a spectacle of yourself, and then there was laughing so hard no sound came out of your mouth.

And Anatalia, or Ana or Tali as we all called her, was exactly right smack in the middle of both. It was like her body couldn't decide what it wanted to do. Laugh or not laugh.

"*You didn't*," she basically gasped.

I stared at her as I dragged the glass of iced water toward me by the coaster. My face went red, red, red as I remembered for about the hundredth time the unforgiveable, unforgettable crap I'd typed as my last message to Aaron.

Xoxo.

X-freaking-oxo.

Ugh. Ugh, ugh, ugh.

For the rest of my life. For the rest of the universe's existence. *Forever.*

Tali's eyes bulged and her face turned a shade of red that bordered on maroon. Her hands went up to her chest and the entire upper half of her body molded to the booth's back cushion like she was attempting to melt into it. Like she was reliving what I'd done in her head and wanted to disappear. I knew that expression. I'd tried to do the same thing after I'd hit Enter on the keyboard. I'd wanted a black hole to suck me in and make me disappear.

"Ruby," she inhaled my name, wildly.

Unfortunately, I hadn't been able to pull a *Back to the Future.* My random black hole hadn't appeared either. I'd shut the screen of my laptop as if that would magically make the letters disappear.

But I knew the truth.

And Aaron knew the truth.

I'd sent him that xoxo.

Closing the screen hadn't done a single freaking thing.

When I'd opened my laptop again, those letters had still been there on the screen, mocking me.

"Why would you do that?" Tali busted out, her hands still going up to cup her nearly maroon cheeks. Her dark blue eyes, which were the only thing we had in common, were glassy like she wasn't pulling enough oxygen into her brain from how hard she'd been, and still was, cracking up.

She was going to make me relive it even more than I already

had. Why was I surprised? "I didn't do it on purpose. One second, we were messaging each other, joking around, then the next thing he types 'bye,' and before I realized what I was doing, I wrote that." I thought about raising my hands directly in front of me where we could both see them, so I could shake them and shame them for what they'd done. They'd betrayed me. They'd gone rogue on me.

After all we'd been through . . .

My sister threw her head back and laughed, loud, finally, her entire body vibrating. Even while she was cracking up, she was one of the most beautiful people I'd ever seen. I didn't miss her fingers wiping at the tears I was sure pooled at her eyes. I'd known that was going to be her exact reaction. I'd known it. I'd expected it. That was why it had taken me days to fess up. Because if it had been the other way around and she'd been the idiot who wrote a friend "xoxo," I would have been the same way.

"And he didn't say anything afterward?" she somehow managed to ask even as she cracked up.

I shook my head as I watched her pinched face, scowling. "I closed my computer screen and he'd logged off."

I shrugged and let my shoulders drop in defeat, in total freaking failure. At this point, half my life seemed like a failure. What was one more?

I was starting to sound like Jasmine with her "the world is working against me" crap.

"Oh, Ruby," Tali half sighed and half choked like she could feel my pain but also thought it was hilarious. "Did you e-mail him after?"

I waited until after I took another sip of water before telling her the truth. "No, I thought it would make it worse." What I didn't tell her was that I'd stayed in bed for two hours going over that sequence of two letters like a broken record, wishing I could go back in time and relive those three seconds again so I could stop myself from possibly ruining a friendship that I'd really started to care about for over the last nine months.

That was an understatement I was still lying to myself over, and probably would keep lying to myself over for the rest of my life.

Friendship.

Like that was all I felt for this man whose face I had never seen. *That's* how I knew I had it bad. I didn't even know what he looked like and I had such a huge attraction to him it didn't matter.

He was nice, but not too nice. Funny. Honest. Spiteful enough to be real. And he wasn't a creep. He understood me and still liked me.

So it wasn't a surprise that I liked Aaron Hall. I liked him a lot. A lot, a lot. More than a lot. If I really let myself think about it, I wouldn't even call what I felt for him being along the lines of "like."

Even though I knew there were a thousand and a half things he wasn't willing to share with me.

But that thought only lasted until I reminded myself that I was dumb and had no business having feelings for anyone, especially him. I'd already spent more than half my life pining away for someone who didn't see me as anything more than his best friend's little sister even after we'd ... done something. I'd learned my lesson. At least you'd figure I would have learned my lesson. I wasn't about to go down that road of unrequited love again. I was fully aware of the castle I'd built and what it was made of, and it was friendship.

Case closed. The door was locked and deadbolted. I wasn't going there, not today, not tomorrow, not ever. No, thank you. My castle lived in Denial's city limits, and it was and would have to be perfectly fine there.

"What are you going to do if he messages you again?" Tali

asked as the server approached our table. Neither one of us said anything as he dropped off three plates of food with a sleek smile aimed at my sister that went unnoticed because he wasn't a woman with at least a D-cup breast size.

I dragged my Reuben and fries toward me as I smiled at the server still looking at Tali's pale skin, dark red hair, and blue eyes, with so much hope. Poor guy had no idea he never could or would stand a chance with my sister. Been there, done that. I knew what that was like. I told her, "Either pretend like nothing happened, or say I'm sorry and that I don't know why I wrote that and I regret it big time."

My sister snickered as she picked up her own Reuben with both hands, oblivious to the server still hanging around, arranging the silverware around the plate he'd set next to mine. "You want to keep being friends with him, don't you?" she asked.

It wasn't like I didn't talk about Aaron. I did. My whole family knew about him. There wasn't a whole lot I kept from them, except this whole giant-crush-on-a-practical-stranger thing. All I'd told them was that we were friendly. "Yeah . . ." I said, watching the neglected server shoot Tali one last look before finally huffing and walking off.

"Then just say 'my bad' and hopefully he'll understand you were joking around." There was a pause and a second later, her lips pinched together. Her chin wobbled.

I knew what she was going to do before she did it, but I still made a face when she started laughing her butt off all over again, loud, loud, loud.

"*Why would you do that, Squirt?*"

"*I don't know!*" I hissed back at her, trying not to laugh and feel mortified at the same time and failing. Like usual. "It just happened. It was like I was talking to you or something."

"You've never written that to me!"

I groaned and felt my entire body flame up all over again in shame. "I know! I've never sent that to anyone." Because I hadn't. Not even at my most desperate with Hunter did I ever write him that.

"What haven't you sent to anyone?" came the other female voice a split second before Jasmine slid into the spot on the bench seat beside me, her hands already dragging the Cuban sandwich with sweet potato fries she would never eat on a regular basis closer to her.

Dragging my hand across my throat, I shook my head at Tali, trying to tell her not to say anything.

She either didn't see me or didn't care, because the next thing I knew, she blurted out, "Squirt wrote XOXO on an IM to her army friend."

Jasmine snorted a second before she bit into her sandwich. With a mouthful of pork, she said something that sounded like, "The one you like?"

"I don't like him like that," I tried to lie.

The eighteen-year-old who treated me like the younger one, snickered in what I knew was disbelief.

I rolled my eyes and sighed, training my gaze on the wall behind Tali's chair, ignoring the way my little sister was brushing this all off and how my older one was pretty much dying of embarrassment for me. "Shut up."

"Before you were a dumbass, did he tell you if he was going to keep in touch?" Tali asked as she tried to reach toward Jasmine's plate to snag a fry. It was either my imagination or our little sister growled loud enough for Tali to snatch her hand back on her own.

"He said he would, but . . ." I shrugged and cleared my throat. "We'll see." Things would be different once he got back to the States and his life didn't revolve around the same old people and the same old base. I understood.

"You haven't kept in touch with any of the rest of the soldiers you've written before, have you?" Jasmine asked between bites, making it really apparent that she was usually so focused on her own life that she didn't pay that much attention to anyone else's.

"No." Then again, most of my conversations with my other Help a Soldier pairings had consisted of the weather, their kids, and if they liked this-or-that more. I'd never told anyone else things about my family or my lack of relationships or . . . anything really that personal. I was a moron. A giant moron who knew better. Another sigh that probably gave too much away slipped right out of me. "Who knows, maybe he won't write me again. He doesn't have to."

Because he didn't. He didn't owe me anything.

I didn't miss the look my sisters gave each other. Neither one of them thought he'd write me. Or maybe they both saw through my façade. Honestly, I would rather not know.

If there was one thing I'd learned over the last few years, it was that just because you cared about someone, and just because they made it seem like they cared about you too, didn't really mean a single thing at the end of the day.

I'd take what I'd been given and be happy with it.

Chapter Fourteen

June

I was in the middle of cutting fabric when my phone beeped. I'd been tracing the pattern for the reversible style of bandanas I was working on for the last hour, and wanted to start on the other fabric I was planning on using for the other side. I never got used to how excited the little things in life made me, but knowing I'd see a finished product soon . . . it made me smile, even if it was dog bandanas I was making, because they were *my* dog bandanas. Not anyone else's.

I didn't even bother rushing to look at my cell phone screen. Anyone texting me knew that after six o'clock, I was usually in work mode. If it was something important, they could call. It wasn't for another half hour, until I was done cutting out giant triangle-like shapes on the second fabric I was using, that I dragged my cell over the worktable toward me.

And then I saw it.

AHALL80 SENT YOU A MESSAGE

My heart leapt.

And as quickly as it leapt, it seemed to seize up in a way it hadn't in years.

It had been two weeks since the Skype app had been opened on my phone, much less on my computer. Two weeks in which I'd tried to stop thinking about this man I'd been forced into a friendship with through a foundation. Fourteen nights where every time I lay in bed—and every time I had a spare moment to think—I thought about those damn Xs and Os. Mostly though, I thought about the man I'd gotten to know, and I wondered if he had gotten home okay and tried not to miss his messages and e-mails.

I'd put my foot in my mouth plenty of times in my life, but what I'd done in our last conversation was at the top. So far at the top, I didn't know how something else would ever beat it.

Knowing my luck, I'd jinxed myself by just thinking about it, but I shoved that possibility to the back of my mind for later.

I had more important things to think about. Like Aaron messaging me after weeks. Like he'd said he would. After I pretty much told him I was sending him hugs and kisses like a stalker.

Since talking to my sisters about it, I'd wondered if I was overthinking it. Maybe he hadn't even read it? Or if he had read it, he didn't take it to mean I was ready to have his babies or was secretly in love with him and playing it cool. I told myself not to linger over not hearing from him for weeks; I'd heard about the layovers the soldiers faced when they were flying back from overseas deployments. It wasn't like they had nonstop flights. When I wasn't telling myself not to overthink our last IM session and worry I'd never hear from him again, I told myself that if I never heard from him again, I would be fine.

But every time I thought of never hearing from him, it made my heart ache a little. More than a little. It made me feel like I had indigestion, and I've never had indigestion.

But I'd understand if he never contacted me again.

I would.

My sister Jasmine was a different person when she was in the middle of training for a competition coming up. Every aspect of her life changed during those periods. If he didn't have time to be my friend once his life was back to normal on base in the States, I couldn't hold it against him. Time was something you couldn't just give out freely. It was precious.

So when **AHALL80** flashed across my cell phone screen again with **(2)** next to his name, my heart practically did a shimmy I hadn't felt since . . .

I wasn't going to think about it.

I'd been worried about him. He'd been flying across an ocean. There was nothing off about being happy your friend was okay.

And that was what I was going to keep telling myself.

Forever.

Because that was all I was ever going to have, and I just needed to live with it like I'd been doing.

Setting aside my scissors and the pile of banana print I'd just finished with, I unlocked the screen and tapped on the notification icon, ignoring the spike of excitement and relief at his name on my screen.

I had this. *I had this.* He wouldn't be writing me if I'd done irreparable damage to our friendship.

And that was another thing I was going to keep telling myself.

June 10, 2009

7:49 p.m.
A Hall80: Hey
A Hall80: I'm alive
RubyMars: Is it really you?
A Hall80: Heh. Yeah.
A Hall80: Hey
RubyMars: You hey.

AHall80: I made it back.

RubyMars: I'd hoped so. :) How was the flight and everything?

AHall80: Shit, but the thirteen hours I was stuck in Baghdad was worth it. I'm here, I don't care.

RubyMars: That's the spirit.

RubyMars: Did you have your beer and pizza already?

AHall80: Yeah, a few of us went out to eat right after the ceremony.

RubyMars: There's a ceremony? I don't remember that.

RubyMars: How many beers did you have?

RubyMars: Judgment-free zone, remember?

AHall80: After the plane landed. I only had two beers . . . didn't want to go too crazy after so long.

RubyMars: Did you have a pepperoni pizza?

AHall80: Megaroni

AHall80: Deep dish

RubyMars: Party animal

AHall80: Baller

RubyMars: Lol.

RubyMars: Please tell me you had a hot shower already.

AHall80: . . .

AHall80: Ruby

AHall80: Yes.

AHall80: Finished reintegration today and my friend took me to get a new phone since my truck isn't here.

RubyMars: What did you do to the phone you had before you left?

AHall80: Canceled the service since I was leaving. No point in keeping it. Sold my phone too.

AHall80: I don't care about having a new number. Nobody's calling me anyway.

RubyMars: Are you messaging me on it right now?

A Hall80: Nah, just got a cheapo phone. Don't need anything fancy. I bought a new laptop. That's what I'm on.

RubyMars: You sold your laptop too?

A Hall80: Mine broke before I even deployed. Didn't bother getting another one because the sand gets into everything. That's why I'd message you from a computer on base.

A Hall80: Got some clothes and other shit while we were out. I'm leaving for Shreveport tomorrow.

RubyMars: Are you excited?

A Hall80: Yeah

RubyMars: I'm so happy for you. I'm glad you're back.

A Hall80: Me too

A Hall80: How you been?

A Hall80: I wanted to msg you sooner, but couldn't because of the phone and laptop situation.

RubyMars: Good. Fine. Everything is good.

A Hall80: Got more work?

RubyMars: Some. I'm doing okay on money, but I need more work. I'm not freaking out yet. You'd be proud of how well I'm handling it.

A Hall80: You'll be all right, Rube

RubyMars: :)

A Hall80: Gone on another date?

RubyMars: Yeah

A Hall80: So?

RubyMars: It was okay.

A Hall80: With?

RubyMars: Someone else. This other guy I went on a date with like a year ago.

RubyMars: Before we became friends.

A Hall80: How'd that work?

RubyMars: He's another friend of a friend. I was at that friend's house for her birthday and he was there and asked. I guess he'd been dating someone for about a year, but they broke up. I said yes. Went on it.

AHall80: What happened?

RubyMars: What do you mean?

AHall80: Did something happen on the date?

RubyMars: . . .

RubyMars: Am I that obvious?

AHall80: You've been messaging me for months. Yeah.

AHall80: What happened?

RubyMars: Nothing bad.

RubyMars: He kissed me and tried to take it further than I'd intended.

RubyMars: Did you know some guys think after one date it's time to get down?

AHall80: Get down?

AHall80: Ruby

AHall80: Did he try to force you?

RubyMars: Force me, no. He just . . . expected it. Like taking me to the movies and a cute Italian restaurant meant I owed him something. It pissed me off is all. More at me than him.

AHall80: You didn't do anything wrong

RubyMars: I know I didn't. I just felt like a little kid. I didn't even have the girls coming out of my top trying to entice him or anything.

RubyMars: I don't know why I used the word entice.

RubyMars: Sorry for the "girls" comment. I forget you're a guy sometimes.

AHall80: . . .

RubyMars: You know what I mean.

AHall80: Yeah, yeah I know.

RubyMars: Am I the only one who didn't know one date is the new thing? I thought it was a three-date thing before the sex was expected?

AHall80: "the sex"

AHall80: Damn it, Ruby

RubyMars: Lol, you know what I mean!

AHall80: Yeah

AHall80: And yeah, that's the new norm. You're the only one who didn't know.

RubyMars: Great. Thanks.

AHall80: You sure he didn't do anything to you?

RubyMars: You're sweet. And no, I promise. He's still alive. He kissed me when I wasn't expecting it and started trying to touch my little boobies (spoiler alert). I told him to stop and he did.

RubyMars: I could tell he was frustrated, but it was fine. I'm sure he's never calling again. Not that I even want him to. He was kind of a pig.

AHall80: Good.

AHall80: You're not missing out on anything. Fuck that guy.

RubyMars: Yeah, fuck him.

AHall80: Did you finish your profile?

RubyMars: No. I think I'm done for a while. I don't think I'm missing out on anything awesome.

AHall80: Have you gone out again with the other guy? Your brother's friend?

RubyMars: Him. Once. Last week.

RubyMars: Another failure.

RubyMars: I went over to his place for dinner and a movie and guess what I found?

AHall80: You went over to his place for dinner and a movie? Do you know what that means?

RubyMars: Dinner and a movie . . .?

AHall80: . . .

AHall80: No.

AHall80: The same as the three-date thing or the new one-date thing.

RubyMars: I was wondering why my mom was eyeing #4 so much when I told them where I was going.

RubyMars: That makes me feel worse that they knew what that meant. I remember my mom going to Ben's house for dinner almost every night before they got married.

RubyMars: I could have gone without that mental picture.

AHall80: Ruby

RubyMars: I digress. I'll brain bleach later. Guess what I found at his house?

AHall80: If you say condoms . . .

RubyMars: Not condoms. WTF.

RubyMars: I found women's underwear shoved into the cushions of his couch. I was looking for the remote and ta-da! Lacey black underwear. It was straight out of a bad date movie. I couldn't wash my hands fast enough afterward.

RubyMars: What I really want to know is, how does someone leave somewhere without their underwear on? Is that a thing? That really happens?

AHall80: . . .

AHall80: RC, the joy you bring to my life . . . I can never pay you back.

RubyMars: I'm being serious!

AHall80: I know you are :]

AHall80: I've never had girls' panties lying around my place.

AHall80: . . . I did find some at Max's place a few times. That is a good question though. If I couldn't find my boxers, I'd look for them.

RubyMars: That's what I'm saying. Underwear isn't cheap.

AHall80: Lol

AHall80: What'd you do? Leave?

RubyMars: No. When he came back from the kitchen, I showed them to him.

AHall80: You didn't

RubyMars: I did. I wasn't a jerk about it, I just said "I think someone you know is missing something." He started apologizing. He basically turned purple, stuttered for a minute straight and said they were probably his ex-girlfriend's, blah, blah, blah.

RubyMars: "Probably his ex-girlfriend's." Am I that naïve?

AHall80: You're sweet

AHall80: But a little. Not that naïve though.

RubyMars: That's what I thought.

AHall80: And then?

RubyMars: Then it was awkward, but we ate dinner, watched the movie, and I went back to my house. He's texted me a few times saying he's sorry and things like that, but I'm not going out with him again.

AHall80: Didn't like him enough to forgive him?

RubyMars: More like it's nasty he hasn't vacuumed his cushions since he broke up with his ex. I'm a slob. I can't date another slob.

AHall80: . . .

RubyMars: :)

RubyMars: Anyway, enough about me. What about you? Any dates since you got back?

A Hall80: Nah. I got other things to spend my money on right now than buying some overpriced drinks at a bar to pick somebody up.

RubyMars: Remember that time you told me it was a bad idea to pick up women at a bar?

A Hall80: Har har

RubyMars: Har har, lol

A Hall80: I only got one girl I'm interested in right now.

RubyMars: Oh?

A Hall80: Lady Liberty

RubyMars: And you think I'm cheesy.

A Hall80: I've never said you were cheesy

RubyMars: . . .

A Hall80: All right maybe once, but it was your joke that was cheesy. Not you.

RubyMars: Yeah yeah.

RubyMars: Are you getting any sleep?

A Hall80: Not much, my times are screwed up.

RubyMars: Melatonin, ever heard of it?

A Hall80: It's only 7 p.m., it's too early for sassy time.

RubyMars: :)

RubyMars: It's never too early for sassy time.

RubyMars: I'm really glad you made it back okay.

A Hall80: Me too, Rubes.

A Hall80: I'll msg you soon.

10:03 p.m. (the next day)

A Hall80: Made it to Shreveport

RubyMars: Finally.

A Hall80: What are you doing?

RubyMars: Watching some movie with my little sister.

RubyMars: What are you doing? I thought you'd be hanging out with your friends.

AHall80: They're playing *Need for Speed* next to me.

AHall80: We went out to eat right after they picked me up.

AHall80: What movie are you watching?

RubyMars: Do they live together?

RubyMars: *Killer Klowns from Outer Space*

AHall80: Max and Des? No. Des is staying here tonight though. He's already drank half a bottle of vodka.

AHall80: What the hell is that?

RubyMars: How much have you drank?

RubyMars: It's a movie . . . about killer clowns from outer space, lol.

AHall80: Two beers and 1/8 of the vodka.

AHall80: I'm good.

AHall80: I guess it's late enough for the sassy to come out?

AHall80: Is the movie like what I'm thinking it's like?

RubyMars: I bet you're good, lol.

RubyMars: The sass is out.

RubyMars: Are you asking if the movie is so over the top it's hilarious with some really interesting costumes? Yes.

AHall80: Lol

RubyMars: Have fun with Max and Des. :)

2:14 a.m.

AHall80: Ruby

AHall80: U there?

RubyMars: Hey

AHall80: What do you look like?

RubyMars: Like a girl . . .?

AHall80: I think u shud come visit

RubyMars: Are you drunk?

A Hall80: No
A Hall80: Maybe
A Hall80: A litl
RubyMars: Okay
A Hall80: Youll come visit?
RubyMars: No, I mean, okay you're drunk, lol.
A Hall80: U wont come visit?
RubyMars: Ask me tomorrow when you aren't plastered.
A Hall80: Ur not saying no
RubyMars: I'm not saying yes either. :)
A Hall80: Think about it
RubyMars: Okay
A Hall80: Ur like my little sister
RubyMars: Okay
A Hall80: I'm wearing the socks you sent me
RubyMars: You are?
A Hall80: Yeah
A Hall80: I'm gonna go to sleep
RubyMars: Good idea :)
RubyMars: Night night. Sleep on your stomach.
A Hall80: K nite

12:16 p.m.
A Hall80: I am so damn sorry about last night
RubyMars: What are you talking about?
A Hall80: The messages I sent
RubyMars: What messages?
A Hall80: The drunk ones
RubyMars: What drunk ones?
A Hall80: . . .
A Hall80: You responded to them
RubyMars: I KNOW
RubyMars: LOL

RubyMars: Just wanted to mess with you.

AHall80: . . .

AHall80: I drank too much

RubyMars: I could tell :)

AHall80: Sorry

RubyMars: You don't have anything to be sorry about. You aren't the first person to text me drunk.

RubyMars: You know who else texted me drunk last night?

AHall80: Who?

RubyMars: That guy I went on a date with. Panties-in-the-couch guy.

RubyMars: He was all "sory bout the othe nite. Ur just rly pretty."

AHall80: What'd you tell him?

RubyMars: I didn't respond, lol.

AHall80: Who else drunk texts you?

RubyMars: Everyone. My brothers, my sister, my friends. They know I'm awake so they do it.

RubyMars: What are you doing today?

AHall80: Nothing. They're all hungover.

RubyMars: And you're not?

AHall80: Nah

RubyMars: Liar.

AHall80: :]

AHall80: Yeah, I'm lying. I got a headache.

AHall80: I don't think I'll ever be able to smell vodka the same way again

RubyMars: Lol

RubyMars: I'm not going to say that's what you get, but . . .

AHall80: That's what I get.

AHall80: Har har

A Hall80: I read what I wrote you a minute ago, sorry for being weird.

RubyMars: It's okay. I know you didn't mean anything by it.

A Hall80: Not that I don't want to meet you

RubyMars: I get it. People say stuff when they're drunk.

A Hall80: Yeah they do

A Hall80: But I wouldn't mind meeting you.

RubyMars: . . . are you still drunk?

A Hall80: No

A Hall80: For real

RubyMars: Maybe one day. :)

RubyMars: When are you leaving for Scotland?

A Hall80: In a few days. On the 18th.

RubyMars: I meant to e-mail you. You should look into getting waterproof shoes or boots for your trip. I watched this episode on one of the travel channels that they filmed there and they talked about how unpredictable the weather was. Rainy one minute, blue skies the next.

A Hall80: Huh

A Hall80: That's not a bad idea.

RubyMars: Maybe take a rain jacket too.

A Hall80: Yeah, good idea. I'll see if I can buy some boots today to give me some time to break them in.

RubyMars: Yeah, you don't want to end up with blisters while you're over there. :)

A Hall80: Yeah.

A Hall80: I'm going to head out. I'll msg you later.

9:22 p.m.

A Hall80: Hey

RubyMars: Hey

RubyMars: How was your day?

A Hall80: Fine

A Hall80: Just got back from a run to the store, glad to be done with that

RubyMars: What store?

A Hall80: The big store

RubyMars: "The big store." That narrows it down.

RubyMars: Why do I feel like there's more to this story?

A Hall80: Heh

A Hall80: Nothing happened. It just made me realize how many things I don't miss after a year away.

RubyMars: What else haven't you missed?

A Hall80: Traffic

A Hall80: People with problems that aren't really problems

RubyMars: :)

RubyMars: I wanted to ask but didn't want to ask, are you handling being back fine so far?

A Hall80: Yeah

A Hall80: Mostly

A Hall80: My first two tours, not really, but I've gotten better. When we get back, we have to go through reintegration and they take it seriously. We have to take a class on identifying signs of depression and PTSD. I'm lucky and haven't had either happen yet. Worst thing for me is big crowds. I can't handle them anymore. Loud noises don't do me any good either.

RubyMars: Who really likes being squished in with a ton of people willingly anyway?

A Hall80: :]

RubyMars: Are you doing anything tomorrow?

A Hall80: My brother was asking if I wanted to go to NOLA with him for a couple days.

A Hall80: It isn't mardi gras, so I should be good to not step in any shit.

RubyMars: You think you're so funny, don't you?

A Hall80: Are you laughing?

RubyMars: No

A Hall80: Liar.

RubyMars: BYE

June 16, 2009

2:21 p.m.

A Hall80: Hey

RubyMars: Hey you

A Hall80: Sorry I went MIA

RubyMars: It's okay. I assumed you were busy.

A Hall80: I went to Max's parents' lake house. Didn't realize there was no service until I got there.

RubyMars: I thought you were going to go to New Orleans and not step in crap with your brother?

A Hall80: I like my brother, but two days with him? Nah.

RubyMars: Did you have fun at the lake house at least?

A Hall80: It was nice, quiet and there was AC. It was good.

RubyMars: It's the little things in life. :)

A Hall80: Now I'm rushing to get my stuff together for my trip.

RubyMars: Did you end up buying boots?

A Hall80: I did, so did Des. Max didn't. Don't know about everyone else.

RubyMars: . . .

A Hall80: I know. When he starts complaining, I get to say I told you so.

RubyMars: Lol. Yeah you do.

RubyMars: Hopefully the weather is great the entire time you're there, but . . . :)

AHall80: If I don't talk to you before I leave in two days, I'll e-mail you when I can.

RubyMars: Okay. Have fun!

RubyMars: Enjoy your vacation for the both of us.

AHall80: I will. :]

AHall80: Bye, RC.

12:33 a.m.

AHall80: Hey

RubyMars: Hey.

RubyMars: What are you doing awake?

AHall80: I'm pissed

RubyMars: Want to talk about it?

AHall80: There's nothing to talk about.

AHall80: I'm sorry

AHall80: You didn't do anything.

AHall80: Max's sister broke her arm and her friend broke her leg.

RubyMars: Max's sister's friend . . .

AHall80: They were both going to Scotland with us as a graduation present.

RubyMars: When did it happen? We just talked like 6 hours ago.

AHall80: An hour after I messaged you.

RubyMars: Oh crap. Are they all right?

AHall80: They're alive and fine besides the broken elbow and leg . . .

RubyMars: What happened?

AHall80: Someone T-boned them in a car wreck.

RubyMars: That's terrible.

RubyMars: Wait

RubyMars: Does that mean they can't go?

AHall80: Yeah

AHall80: That's why I'm so . . .

AHall80: The friend can't walk, and they said Max's sister might need surgery. If she doesn't go, Max won't either.

AHall80: I know it's selfish to be so mad about some girl breaking her leg and Max's little sister, who I've known forever, getting hurt in an accident, but I'm not happy.

RubyMars: Maybe it's a little selfish but you're entitled to feel that way. You deserve your vacation.

RubyMars: I'm sorry, Aaron. That really sucks.

RubyMars: Your other friends are still going with you, right? Either way, plenty of people travel alone. I have a friend my age who's always going places by herself and she's five foot four, maybe one forty, not a big, strapping soldier like you.

AHall80: :]

AHall80: I'll msg you later. I got a pounding headache.

RubyMars: Okay. Hope you feel better. Sorry about everything.

1:45 a.m.

AHall80: I'm not really pissed

RubyMars: Of course you're not.

RubyMars: And you're still awake.

AHall80: . . .

AHall80: Can't sleep.

AHall80: I'm disappointed. There's worse shit in the world than not being able to go on vacation.

AHall80: You'd figure I'd be used to things not working out.

RubyMars: There's nothing wrong with being disappointed. I'd be disappointed too.

RubyMars: I'd probably cry.

RubyMars: Okay, that last comment of yours makes me want to cry.

RubyMars: You can still go on vacation though, even if Max doesn't.

AHall80: :]

AHall80: Don't cry. I'm feeling sorry for myself and not handling this like I should. It's a sorry-ass excuse, but I'm tired.

AHall80: What are you doing?

RubyMars: Watching TV

RubyMars: Eating donuts.

RubyMars: It's been a long day.

AHall80: You too?

AHall80: Bad day?

RubyMars: No. Not really. I went to my brother's place to pick up my mom's carpet cleaner earlier for her and his best friend was there.

AHall80: The asshole you were hung up on?

RubyMars: That one. I hadn't seen him in a while, and I guess you must have planted some bugs in my head because I saw him and just got pissed off.

AHall80: At him or yourself?

RubyMars: Both. Mostly him. It's your fault. All I can think now is that he was the older one and he should've let me off the hook instead of letting me . . . forget it. It's over. It's stupid to be mad about it.

AHall80: No it's not.

RubyMars: :)

AHall80: It isn't. He was a dick. You have a reason to be mad at him for leading you on. How much older is he?

RubyMars: 6 years

RubyMars: He's the same age as you I guess.

AHall80: Maybe, but I grew up by the time I was 22

AHall80: For the most part

AHall80: Did you say anything to him?

RubyMars: Only hi. I was too busy going back and forth between calling myself an idiot and calling him an idiot in my head, and trying to count all the things about him I don't like.

AHall80: He's got a lazy eye or something?

RubyMars: Lol, no. His clothes are too tight. There's that.

AHall80: You don't want to date anybody who wears clothes tighter than yours.

RubyMars: I know!

RubyMars: His hair is too long too. :) And he has crappy taste in movies.

AHall80: :]

RubyMars: I got out of there as quick as I could. My brother texted me while I was driving home asking what had been my deal. I told him I was fine, but I'm still a little mad just thinking about it all.

RubyMars: Now I'm really ready to move on with my life. I've wasted enough time being dumb over people who don't deserve my time.

AHall80: That's what I said.

RubyMars: . . . you also told me to go to church to find a boyfriend, lol.

AHall80: I don't get what your deal with that is. It could work.

RubyMars: In your dreams.

RubyMars: Then there was you telling me to volunteer at a shelter.

AHall80: Heh

AHall80: Good thing you ignored me

RubyMars: You made me feel better, thank you.

AHall80: I owe you, stalker girl.

RubyMars: I'm keeping tabs, don't worry.

RubyMars: We can be here for each other.

AHall80: :]

AHall80: Gotta go. Msg you soon.

12:02 p.m.

AHall80: You there?

RubyMars: Yeah, hey.

RubyMars: I just woke up a little while ago.

RubyMars: So . . .

AHall80: ?

RubyMars: Did you hear anything else about Max or his sister?

AHall80: No.

RubyMars: No you didn't hear anything about either of them or no he isn't going?

AHall80: No I haven't heard anything about her or from him.

RubyMars: :(I'm sorry

AHall80: Not your fault

RubyMars: I told you, you can go by yourself if Des and the other guy flake. Scottish people are supposed to be really friendly. I'm sure Max wouldn't want you to not go because he can't.

AHall80: That's what I heard.

AHall80: You'd be surprised. He's petty.

RubyMars: Go anyway.

RubyMars: Have you gone to see your dad?

RubyMars: Why don't you ask your brother or your sister to go? I'm not sure if that's possible since it's so last minute . . .

AHall80: I did go see them, but no. We don't get along that well.

RubyMars: I see.

AHall80: It was good seeing them. I told them I'd come by again when I get back.

RubyMars: I've got my fingers crossed for you. You'll figure something out.

AHall80: :]

AHall80: Msg you soon

6:09 p.m.

AHall80: Guess we're going without Max.

RubyMars: I'm sorry.

AHall80: It's all right. I'm not going to not go just because he can't. I can't just take time off whenever.

RubyMars: I agree.

RubyMars: Still sorry though. I'm sure you'll have a great time with Des and your other friend.

AHall80: Yeah, it'll work.

RubyMars: :)

8:08 p.m.

AHall80: Leaving for the airport in a minute

AHall80: Got a long drive

AHall80: I've been trying not to be in a shit mood but failing at it

RubyMars: It's okay. It isn't uncalled for.

RubyMars: Have fun though and relax.

RubyMars: Send me pictures.

AHall80: All right I will
AHall80: Be safe, RC
RubyMars: You too.

June 19, 2009

2:01 p.m.
AHall80: Hey
AHall80: I made it
RubyMars: Hey.
RubyMars: Did you have a decent flight?
AHall80: Two flights.
AHall80: They were good. We got to stretch out a little in economy since Max and his sister/friend couldn't go.
RubyMars: That's good. :)
RubyMars: Did you get any sightseeing done today?
AHall80: A little. We saw something called Scott's Monument and walked around this park. Went to some place called the Royal Mile and saw the castle from outside.
AHall80: The line to get in was too long, so we didn't go.
RubyMars: Boo.
RubyMars: Besides that, everything sounds fun.
AHall80: The Internet at this hotel is too slow. I'll send you pictures another day.
RubyMars: Your tour thing starts tomorrow?
AHall80: Yeah. 5 days.
RubyMars: Lucky.
AHall80: You all right?
RubyMars: Yes. Working.
RubyMars: Trying to work, you know what I mean. Making things I can't sell yet. Trying to finish the jobs I have before I leave in a few weeks.

AHall80: You'll sell them.

RubyMars: I like your optimism.

RubyMars: I'm acting like my sister, I'm sorry.

AHall80: What's going on with your sister anyway?

RubyMars: She's still hiding that she's training. I don't get why, but whatever. My mom is still paying her dues so she can skate even though "she isn't" and we all know she's a big, fat liar.

RubyMars: I don't get it. I really don't. But I still love her anyway.

AHall80: What don't you get? Why she isn't skating?

RubyMars: Yes. She doesn't get it. She doesn't remember how tight money was for a while with the rest of us. My mom wouldn't have been able to afford putting the rest of us into any kind of lessons, but by the time Jazz wanted to skate, my older brother and sister were already out of the house, that's the only reason why she could. She doesn't get how lucky she is. I tried telling her once a couple years ago, but she didn't get it.

RubyMars: One Christmas, I asked my mom for roller skates and she couldn't buy them for me because she didn't have the money and didn't want to ask my dad to buy them.

RubyMars: Jazz doesn't know about any of that.

RubyMars: After my heart thing, there was a while where my mom wouldn't let me participate in my school's field day. I was the only kid who couldn't. She doesn't get how lucky she is. I love her so much, and usually we get along really well when she has time to hang out, but sometimes she drives me crazy with how self-centered she can be.

RubyMars: That was longer than I thought. I guess it bothers me more than I think it does. Sorry.

AHall80: I'm sorry, Ru.

AHall80: I get why that would piss you off.

AHall80: Tell her.

RubyMars: Maybe.

RubyMars: :)

RubyMars: Changing the subject. Have you gotten any sleep?

AHall80: Yeah, it's been easier than when I was back home. The time zones aren't so different.

RubyMars: Good. Are you sharing a room with someone?

AHall80: Nah. I was supposed to with Des, but since Max isn't here, I got my own and Des gets the room the girls were supposed to share.

RubyMars: I know it sucks, but that is nice.

AHall80: Yeah

AHall80: Trying not to be a shit about it

RubyMars: Too late. :)

AHall80: Har har

AHall80: I'm going to bed. Msg you again when I can.

RubyMars: Okay, have fun, stalker.

AHall80: Night, Rubes.

June 20, 2009

3:15 p.m.

AHall80: What are you up to?

RubyMars: Hi stranger.

RubyMars: Just finished arguing with my sister.

RubyMars: No biggie.

AHall80: With your little sister?

RubyMars: Yes.

RubyMars: My big sister is sane.

A Hall80: What happened?

RubyMars: We were eating lunch when she started complaining about how much she hates her job and is so tired of everything. Literally, everything. She complained about how hard her mattress is and how she's hoping to talk my mom into buying her a new one. I think that's what drove me the most crazy.

A Hall80: Keep going

RubyMars: So I told her that her mattress is newer than mine and how if she wants a new one she should just save up money at her "shitty job that pays her $10.50 an hour" and buy another one because it isn't like she pays rent or insurance or anything.

RubyMars: It was like another person was using my mouth to talk to her, Aaron. I've never talked to my sister like that. I don't think I've ever talked to anyone like that.

A Hall80: For real?

RubyMars: For real. She got so pissed after the shock wore off. She said I don't understand what she goes through and how her life isn't as easy as everyone thinks it is. I don't think her life is easy. I know how hard she works. So then we started arguing about that.

RubyMars: Then, I told her she needed to quit acting like a brat and either get back on the ice or not so Mom wouldn't keep paying for her coach if she didn't have to. I know I got to her because all she did was look at me and storm out.

RubyMars: I feel bad for saying all that, but not really.

RubyMars: My stomach hurt and I sweated a whole bunch the entire time. That was the meanest thing I've ever done.

AHall80: That wasn't mean. That was tough love. She needed to hear it from somebody.

RubyMars: Thank you for telling me that. I still feel bad.

AHall80: Don't.

AHall80: I'm proud of you. That took guts.

RubyMars: It did.

RubyMars: :)

AHall80: When I first started getting promoted, it was hard for me to be tough on these guys that I'd known who weren't moving up. I didn't know how to treat them or act because I didn't want to step on their toes. At the end of the day, you know you got to get things done even if you're pissing somebody off. You just figure it out with time. Sometimes you have to stop and finally make your point . . . like you did with your aunt.

RubyMars: What you're trying to say is that you're bossy now?

AHall80: I'm used to people listening to me.

RubyMars: That sounds about right. :)

AHall80: . . .

RubyMars: Have you always been bossy?

AHall80: When I know what I want and think I can do it better than someone else.

RubyMars: I'll take that as a yes.

RubyMars: I'm not. We balance each other out. It isn't a bad thing.

AHall80: You're bossy when you want to be.

RubyMars: Sometimes, but it's rare.

AHall80: Sure

RubyMars: Like you said, when I know what I want.

AHall80: And in the middle of the night when you're in a mood.

RubyMars: I don't know what you're talking about.

AHall80: Sure

RubyMars: . . .

RubyMars: I'm logging off now.

AHall80: Lol

RubyMars: How was your day? What'd you do?

AHall80: Got picked up early for the tour. We stopped in a town called Dunkeld, I think it was called, stopped in an old pine forest, walked around a loch . . . that's what they call a lake . . . with some old castle in the middle of it. Checked out Loch Ness, and we're staying in this town called Ullapool for two nights.

RubyMars: You went to Loch Ness????

AHall80: Yeah, the water is so dark, it looks like coffee.

RubyMars: Jealous.

AHall80: You'd love it.

RubyMars: :) Now you have to live your life for me too, mister.

RubyMars: I wouldn't be doing my own thing if it wasn't for you, so I'm doing my part living my life for you too.

AHall80: :]

RubyMars: Thank you for being such a good friend to me.

AHall80: :]

RubyMars: You there?

AHall80: Yeah

AHall80: I'm taking pictures while I'm here. I'll send them to you when I can.

RubyMars: Deal.

AHall80: Gonna hit the sack. We're getting picked up at 8.

A Hall80: Night, Ru.
RubyMars: Goodnight, have fun.

June 21, 2009

2:57 p.m.
A Hall80: Hey
RubyMars: Hey.
RubyMars: How was your day?
A Hall80: All right. Saw some castle ruins and checked out a bay and a village.
RubyMars: Was it pretty?
A Hall80: Yeah
A Hall80: Just got back from dinner.
RubyMars: Was it good?
A Hall80: Yeah, Des and Ian stayed at a pub by the hotel. I wasn't in the mood to drink.
A Hall80: I'd rather be in my room
RubyMars: Are you okay?
A Hall80: Just got a lot on my mind lately.
RubyMars: You know you can always talk to me about anything.
A Hall80: I know, Ru
A Hall80: Being in the van all day here just gave me a lot of time to think about things
A Hall80: I'll sort it out.
RubyMars: Yes you will.
RubyMars: Everything will work out.
A Hall80: :]
A Hall80: I'm going to hit the sack.
A Hall80: Have a good rest of your day, Ruron.
RubyMars: Night, stalker.

June 23, 2009

12:11 p.m.
A Hall80: Hey
RubyMars: Hi.
RubyMars: How's the vacay going?
A Hall80: :]
A Hall80: Good
A Hall80: The hotel we're staying at doesn't have Wi-Fi. We're eating dinner right now
A Hall80: This town is called Portree
RubyMars: Eat your dinner then.
RubyMars: Wait, how are you messaging me?
A Hall80: Eating as I type
A Hall80: Borrowed Des's phone. He's using mine to call his girl. I got an international plan for calls before I left.
RubyMars: To call all your girlfriends while you're over there?
A Hall80: . . .
A Hall80: No. In case Max called.
RubyMars: I see.
RubyMars: What'd you see today?
A Hall80: You'd be in heaven.
RubyMars: Tell me every detail.
A Hall80: We're in Skye today. We stopped at this place called the . . . I can't spell it . . . Quiraing . . . Ian says that's how it's spelled . . . most beautiful place I've ever seen. Got to hike about half the trail. It was rainy and really cloudy, but the longer we walked the more the clouds went away and you could see these lakes, lochs whatever they're called . . . Never seen anything

so amazing in my life. Like I was on a different planet. Saw a waterfall, had a walk through another place called the fairy pools, another castle ruin, a cemetery . . .

A Hall80: Wish you could have seen it.

RubyMars: :) As long as you had fun, that's good enough for me.

A Hall80: Had to do most of the fairy pools walk by myself because these lazy asses didn't want to.

A Hall80: I jumped into one of the pools and froze my ass off. Got tons of pictures.

RubyMars: Good. Send them to me.

A Hall80: Des is off the phone.

A Hall80: I'll msg you when I can.

RubyMars: Okay. Have fun.

A Hall80: Bye, Ruron

June 24, 2009

12:09 p.m.

A Hall80: Hey

RubyMars: Hey you.

RubyMars: How was your day?

A Hall80: Good

A Hall80: Saw this castle called . . . I wrote it down . . . Eilean Donan castle, stopped in a town called Fort William and checked out this place called Glencoe.

RubyMars: You had fun?

A Hall80: I wouldn't say fun, but it was good.

RubyMars: What's wrong?

A Hall80: Just wishing things would have worked out better for this trip.

A Hall80: Hate thinking like that.

RubyMars: I'm sorry, Aaron.

RubyMars: Hopefully you can go on another trip with Max sometime in the future.

A Hall80: It's not even that.

A Hall80: About to head out for dinner. I'll msg you before bed.

RubyMars: Okay, have a good dinner.

A Hall80: :]

4:33 p.m.

A Hall80: You there?

RubyMars: I'm always here.

RubyMars: Unless it's the butt crack of dawn.

RubyMars: What did you have for dinner?

A Hall80: Fish n chips

A Hall80: I've been thinking

RubyMars: What brought this miracle on?

A Hall80: I wish you could've come with me

A Hall80: You there?

RubyMars: I'm here, sorry.

RubyMars: I didn't mean to give you a guilt trip about going to Scotland.

A Hall80: You didn't.

A Hall80: Just wish you could've come too.

RubyMars: :) That's really nice of you. I wish I could have too.

A Hall80: I've been thinking about it a lot

RubyMars: When is your flight back?

A Hall80: Tomorrow

A Hall80: You gone on another date?

RubyMars: No.

RubyMars: You?

AHall80: Nah

AHall80: I'm sleepy

RubyMars: Then go to bed. :)

RubyMars: Did you drink too much tonight?

AHall80: Yeah

RubyMars: Lol

AHall80: :)

RubyMars: That's the first real smiley face you've given me.

AHall80: Nah

AHall80: You haven't seen the rest

RubyMars: Go to bed.

AHall80: Ok

AHall80: Night

RubyMars: Goodnight, Ruron.

AHall80: Bye

June 25, 2009

1:23 a.m.

AHall80: About to check out of the hotel, just wanted to say bye.

RubyMars: Good morning to you.

RubyMars: Okay. Have a safe flight home. Enjoy your extra space on the plane.

AHall80: I will

AHall80: Hey

RubyMars: Hey

AHall80: Never mind I'll msg you when I get home.

AHall80: Go to bed

RubyMars: Yes, Mommy Aaron.

RubyMars: :) Be safe.

AHall80: You too.

June 27, 2009

1:54 a.m.

AHall80: I figured it out

RubyMars: Hi to you.

RubyMars: Glad you made it home safely, lol.

RubyMars: What did you figure out?

AHall80: Why don't you come with me?

AHall80: Ruby?

AHall80: You there?

RubyMars: I'm here.

AHall80: . . .

RubyMars: I dropped my phone sorry.

AHall80: Did you see my message?

RubyMars: That's why I dropped my phone. You want me to go with you . . . where?

AHall80: To Florida

RubyMars: . . .

RubyMars: You want me to go with you to Florida?

AHall80: Yeah

RubyMars: I'm just trying to understand. Why do you want me to go with you?

AHall80: I want to meet you. You said you wanted to meet me . . .

AHall80: Unless you don't

RubyMars: I do

RubyMars: I do!

RubyMars: You just caught me totally off guard is all.

AHall80: Come with us.

RubyMars: You keep saying that.

AHall80: Because I want you to

RubyMars: I thought Max was going with you to Florida?

AHall80: He is

AHall80: He doesn't feel bad going there

RubyMars: But you want me to go too?

AHall80: Yeah

RubyMars: Why? Because you want to meet up?

AHall80: Yeah . . .

RubyMars: But why?

AHall80: Because what's the point in waiting? It'll be a while before I get more time off.

AHall80: Come with

RubyMars: Maybe you aren't thinking about this clearly.

AHall80: I am.

RubyMars: Mmm-hmm . . . I don't think you are.

AHall80: Why?

RubyMars: Because.

AHall80: Why?

RubyMars: Because!

RubyMars: You can't just decide overnight you want to meet me all of a sudden.

RubyMars: I'm leaving in less than two weeks to visit my dad.

AHall80: There's no "all of a sudden."

AHall80: And I didn't decide that overnight

AHall80: I've been thinking about it a lot

AHall80: What's the problem?

AHall80: You're leaving after I have to be back from Florida.

AHall80: You there?

RubyMars: I'm here.

RubyMars: I just . . . what if I get on your nerves? Maybe you won't like me in person.

RubyMars: You're not exactly asking me to have dinner with you and your friends. You're inviting me to go to

a beach house with you and people you've known for
a long time for multiple days, right?

A Hall80: Your argument right now is that you might get
on my nerves?

RubyMars: We've never met!

A Hall80: So

A Hall80: You said you love Florida.

A Hall80: And you know I'd like to meet you. I'd
thought next time I came down to Louisiana, we
could meet up . . . all it is is sooner. We've known
each other for almost a year.

A Hall80: I don't see a point in waiting

RubyMars: Yeah, but . . .

RubyMars: This isn't us meeting up at a coffee shop or
something.

A Hall80: We wouldn't have met at a coffee shop

RubyMars: Why not? We could before you went back to
base.

A Hall80: No.

RubyMars: . . .

A Hall80: We could've met at a comic con if there was
one going on

RubyMars: You're killing me.

A Hall80: Why?

RubyMars: Because you know me too well.

A Hall80: That's a problem?

RubyMars: . . . no

RubyMars: I want to meet you. I really do, but going to a
beach house with you is a big step.

A Hall80: Why?

RubyMars: I already told you. We've never met.

A Hall80: In person

AHall80: I don't think we're strangers. You know more
about me than just about anyone I spent a year with in
Iraq. More than most people I know in general, Rubes.

AHall80: I like you. You like me. What's the problem?

RubyMars: I didn't even know for sure you'd been in
Iraq, Aaron.

RubyMars: I hadn't even known until right before you
flew back that you were even based in Kentucky.

RubyMars: I get why you didn't tell me until now.
I would've done the same, but . . .

AHall80: You know now.

RubyMars: This is crazy.

AHall80: Do you think it is?

AHall80: Maybe a little.

AHall80: It's fine

RubyMars: Maybe a little?

RubyMars: The sad part is that I don't think it's as crazy
as I should. My mom would kill me for not
immediately telling you no.

RubyMars: This giant part of me wants to tell you yeah,
I'll go. But . . . we barely know each other.

RubyMars: You know what I mean.

AHall80: We know each other.

RubyMars: You know we know each other. I know we
know each other, but nobody else knows or gets that.

RubyMars: We've never met.

RubyMars: It would be like . . . an arranged marriage
where we meet on the day of the wedding.

RubyMars: I thought . . .

AHall80: So?

AHall80: I'm asking you, not anybody else. I wouldn't
ask anybody else. Only you.

AHall80: Who says we don't know each other?

RubyMars: I don't know . . . society?

RubyMars: But what if I get on your nerves?

RubyMars: We've never even talked on the phone.

RubyMars: I don't even know what you look like.

RubyMars: I think I'm freaking out.

A Hall80: I doubt you'll get on my nerves more than anybody else I've ever known.

A Hall80: . . . I can send you a picture. You never asked for one.

A Hall80: Stop freaking out. You know me.

RubyMars: !!!!!!

RubyMars: I know I know you.

A Hall80: Call me

RubyMars: Wut

A Hall80: Call me. I'll know the instant I talk to you if I can put up with you for a week.

RubyMars: Put up with me . . .

A Hall80: You know what I mean

RubyMars: . . .

RubyMars: I think you should think about this more.

A Hall80: I have thought about it.

A Hall80: The entire flight back from Scotland

A Hall80: Most of the time I was in the bus

A Hall80: I've thought about it, Ruby.

RubyMars: Maybe you should sleep on it.

RubyMars: This is crazy. This is really crazy.

A Hall80: I already did.

A Hall80: You keep saying that.

A Hall80: You want to come to Florida.

RubyMars: You're stealing my words.

RubyMars: You're a pain.

RubyMars: Why am I not telling you no?

A Hall80: Because you want to meet me too

A Hall80: Because we're friends and we were going to meet one day.

RubyMars: !!!!!

RubyMars: Sleep on it tonight, and if tomorrow you wake up and you still want to talk on the phone and see if we'd get along, I'll call you.

RubyMars: I can't believe I just typed that.

RubyMars: My hands are shaking.

RubyMars: I should feel like the stupid girl in a horror movie who goes on a date with a serial killer right now because I'm not telling you no.

A Hall80: It's just me, Rubes.

A Hall80: But fine. I'll sleep on it

A Hall80: I gotta know ASAP. We start driving there the day after tomorrow.

A Hall80: You could just fly and I could get you from the airport.

RubyMars: You're already making plans . . .

RubyMars: No hard feelings at all if you change your mind.

A Hall80: All right. Deal.

RubyMars: Deal.

11:58 a.m.

A Hall80: Hey

RubyMars: Hey

A Hall80: 270-555-5025

RubyMars: . . .

A Hall80: That's my number. Call me.

RubyMars: Did you even think about it??

A Hall80: That's why I'm giving you my number.

A Hall80: You said sometimes you know immediately if you hit it off with somebody. We get along already on messenger. I'm not worried.

RubyMars: . . .

RubyMars: Are you serious?

AHall80: Yeah. Call me right now.

RubyMars: Do you know what you're asking of me?

RubyMars: I'm still asleep, aren't I?

AHall80: For sure.

AHall80: You're awake. Call me.

RubyMars: You're sure?

AHall80: Yes. Call.

RubyMars: Fine, but if there's awkward silence and we never recover from this, I'll never forgive you. We had a good thing, you and me.

AHall80: It's too early for the sass to be out.

RubyMars: . . . . .

RubyMars: I barely slept thanks to you.

RubyMars: You better answer the phone and that better not be one of those numbers you give strangers when you don't want them to know your real number. I'll never get over it.

AHall80: Just call, Rubes.

Chapter Fifteen

Aaron wanted me to call him.

Aaron wanted me to call him.

Aaron wanted me to freaking call him.

Because he was inviting me to go to Florida.

Because all of a sudden, he'd decided he wanted to meet me. Spend time with me. And he didn't want to wait until the next time he had leave.

No pressure.

I gulped as I sat there at the kitchen counter, picking at a bowl of Fruity Pebbles with my heart in my throat and my stomach attempting to do somersaults. I should have been freaking out at the idea of traveling with someone who, in a tiny way, was a stranger, but I wasn't. Not really.

It would be the first time I met someone in a different place for a purpose that didn't revolve around fittings for dresses or costumes. I wouldn't be Ruby in work mode. It would just be . . . me.

That was the terrifying part. Just me and my poor heart that seemed to pick the worst people to have feelings for. People who didn't see me as anything other than someone's little sister and a friend.

Then there was the whole "we had never met in person" aspect of it.

Not like that had stopped me from pretty much falling in love with him or anything, so there was that. At some point, after a few months, I'd started going on dates with other guys to get my mind off him because I understood my feelings were pointless. He didn't feel the same way. Plus, *he'd told me to date*. How much more obvious did I need our situation to be?

And if none of that was reason enough to convince myself that going was a stupid idea, I knew what I would tell anyone who was going to meet a stranger they'd met online.

I'd tell them they were out of their minds. And if I told any of my family members what I was thinking about doing, they would think the same thing.

The thing was, for once in my life, my gut wasn't telling me not to go do this crazy thing. It was telling me the exact opposite. *Go, go, go.* Despite being scared and worried about my safety. Hadn't I just told him a couple of days ago that women traveled by themselves all the time?

Then again, I couldn't afford to buy a plane ticket. It would also be really irresponsible of me to charge something that expensive on my credit card when I didn't exactly have a steady income coming in. I hadn't been rich when I had two steady jobs; now, I was even further away from that point.

Yet, even knowing all of this, I flexed my tingling fingers and typed in the phone number Aaron had given me.

I ran up the stairs just as I hit the call icon, which in hindsight, wasn't exactly the smartest decision I'd ever made because by the time my legs got me to the second floor, I was out of breath and still hadn't made it to my room. My mom and Ben were at work, so they weren't going to be looking at me like I was crazy for running up the stairs for the first time in my life.

The phone kept on ringing as I dashed into my bedroom, and just as I thought a voice mail recording was going to pick up, I closed my door.

The familiar clicking sound of someone answering the call had me freezing as I turned the lock, and then I heard it. My name. "Ruby?"

I was panting and trying not to pant at the same time, as the baritone voice on the phone seemed to steamroll my entire soul to the carpet floor. I wasn't sure what I'd been expecting from Aaron, but I hadn't been expecting the not-too-soft but just-deep-enough voice on the other end of the line. It was just in the middle. Friendly. Deep but not too deep. A little raspy. Perfect.

It was right then that it sank in.

He'd answered. I'd called Aaron and he'd answered.

I was on the phone with Aaron.

"Rubes?" the male voice came over the phone again, still that beautiful pitch, a natural narrator, sounding . . . amused? What was he amused over? "You there? I hear you breathing."

I stopped breathing. Through my mouth at least. And I swallowed even though I was fairly certain it sounded more like a gulp.

Then the man on the line chuckled, easygoing and almost sweet. "What are you doing?" he asked like he'd asked me the same question a thousand times before. Like we hadn't been pen pals for almost a year and instead had been friends for the last ten.

This was Aaron. *Aaron.* The only person other than my best friend who knew I'd stepped in human crap once. And just like that . . . "I ran up the stairs and I'm out of breath," I told him, holding my phone away from my mouth at the end so he couldn't hear me panting.

His—Aaron's—relaxed chuckle lengthened and somehow, someway, relaxed me. It reminded me of our IMs when we were messing with each other. Normal. Playful. Friendly. *Like always. Like my friend.* "Just from running up the stairs?" he asked, and for some reason I could picture him raising an eyebrow of a color I wasn't sure of, like he was teasing me. Like normal.

"It's a lot of stairs." I didn't even realize I'd started smiling into the phone until I laughed. This was Aaron. No big deal. "I'm so out of shape." And there it was. What in the world was coming out of *mouth*? "That's embarrassing, I'm sorry. You can probably run ten miles at a time. The only time I run is . . . never. I never run. I don't want to lie to you. I'm rambling, I'm sorry. I get nervous and I ramble."

"What are you nervous over? It's me," he drawled, steady and consistent, that slight Louisiana accent tinting his words just enough. *It's me*, he'd told me a few times before, and each time, just like this one, shot an arrow straight into my heart that seemed to cripple every excuse I gave myself for why being more than a little in love with him was a stupid idea.

Because it was a stupid idea.

A really stupid idea.

And you would figure with my track record of stupid ideas, I would know when to get rid of them.

But I hadn't. Knowing me, I wouldn't because I was an idiot like that. Weak. I was so weak. That term "wearing your heart on your sleeve" had been written with me in mind.

Oblivious to the fact he'd taken an imaginary baseball bat to my kneecaps with his tone and his words, he kept going in that smooth voice that I would listen to read the dictionary. "You sound . . ." He made a noise of hesitation.

"Like an idiot?" came out of my mouth before I could stop it.

Aaron laughed that time, clear and loud, sweeping my legs out from under me one more time, because it wasn't like he could be awkward and graceless and unlikeable and laugh like a donkey. That would just be too easy. And fair. This was the guy who'd had two dozen crazy girlfriends for a reason. It all suddenly made sense. "No. Your voice is different than I thought it'd be."

Taking another deep breath to try and not sound like I was

as out of shape cardio-wise as I was, I finally took a step away from my door, ignoring the clothes hanging off two chairs and the pile of dirty clothes that was way too close to the pile of clean clothes I'd pulled out of the dryer and dumped on the floor three days ago. *This is Aaron*, I reminded myself. I could do this. "What do you mean?" I asked him, sounding more like myself than I would've expected while on the verge of flipping the heck out.

It wasn't my imagination he made another hesitating noise.

I got this sinking feeling . . . "What? Did you think I was going to sound like Minnie Mouse?"

His "Uh" didn't even take a second. I burst out laughing, forgetting I was out of breath and that I'd been nervous all of ten seconds ago.

"*You did?*"

He started chuckling, like he was trying his best not to and failing. "I don't know! I thought you were going to sound younger, not—"

"You're wounding me, Aaron. You're wounding my pride here." I snorted into my cell as I plopped down on the edge of my messy full-sized bed, feeling too at ease.

It was his turn to laugh again, louder than his chuckle, the sound fuller and from the belly. "You don't sound like you're twenty-four," he tried to argue, his words getting broken up by his steady laugh.

"That's not what you mean. You thought I was going to sound like a fifteen-year-old cheerleader from the Valley or something. Didn't you?" There was no response, just a hint of a sound that was suspiciously distant . . . like he was laughing with his face away from the receiver . . . That was it, wasn't it? "I cannot believe you."

"I'm sorry!" he tried to say, but he started laughing harder, that time directly into the phone, the sound making me smile so wide, I was glad no one was around to see it, otherwise they'd ask questions I didn't want to answer.

"It's because I told you about the cosplay, isn't it?"

There was a pause by the man I'd been e-mailing for over a year. "No—"

"You're a liar."

Aaron's laughter suddenly got lower in volume, and I knew he'd pulled the phone away from his face again, for sure. My best friend did the same thing when she was laughing as hard as she could.

"And the no-boyfriend thing," I added.

Even with the phone not being close to his mouth, I could tell he'd started cracking up all over again. I shouldn't have loved the sound as much as I did, but . . . *guilty*.

"I can't believe you."

"You sound like you work for those phone sex lines," he finally managed to get out, sometime ten minutes later.

What? "No, I don't." Had he not ever listened to his own voice before?

"Have you heard yourself? I was watching TV last night after I messaged you and the commercials for those chat lines came on. You sound just like those girls . . ." He trailed off for a moment, his voice changing. "Are you sick?"

I had no right to smile as wide as I was, but I did it anyway. "No, I'm not sick anymore. This is my normal voice, thanks."

There was another pause over the line and then, "Are you really Ruby?"

"What do you think?" I snorted. "Do I need to ask about your butthole for you to believe me?"

Aaron choked. I didn't need to see him to know he'd done it. He didn't try to hide it or pull the phone away from his mouth. "Now I know it's you for sure."

I was a fool, and it didn't matter. "Are you sure? Because I can," I offered him before I could shut myself up.

"I'm sure."

"If you change your mind . . ."

Aaron shot out another laugh. "No, I know it's you. We've been on the phone . . . four minutes and you've got me laughing more than I have in weeks. It couldn't be anybody else but you, Ru."

I couldn't count the number of times he'd said something to me like that in written word, but just like every other time he had, I felt like . . . I felt like I'd done something amazing. And I needed to get it together and control myself. I needed to act normal. *Normal, Ruby.*

"You could've warned me before I called," he said quietly before I could get my normal game together, but somehow I could tell he was smiling as he said the sentence.

I pulled my knees up toward my chest, heels on the mattress side by side. I tried not to wonder what he was doing right then, what he looked like, what he was thinking . . . and I failed. Like usual. "What would you need a warning for?" I asked, almost hesitantly but definitely a little distracted.

There was another soft chuckle. "For that voice. Jesus, Ru. You told me you were worried I wasn't going to like you, so I had this plan in my head for how I'd get you to talk to me in case things got awkward. And you start giving me shit thirty seconds in," he argued. "You threw my game off."

Act normal. Act normal. Don't ask what his plan was. Don't tell him you love his voice too. "You? I was nervous. I am nervous. My hands started sweating, then they started tingling, and then it took you half a year to answer the phone—"

He choked again. "I thought I had enough time to use the bathroom—"

"How long does it take you to use the bathroom?"

Aaron shouted out a laugh that pulled at the corners of my mouth.

"I ran up the stairs to call, and I was dying, then *you* start messing with me—"

"I told you I thought it was going to take a minute for you to warm up talking to me."

"—and then I learn my friend Aaron, who is basically my best friend, thought I was going to sound like Malibu Barbie, and I forgot I was nervous."

"You didn't have anything to be nervous about. It's just me."

Just him. Why did he have to keep saying that to me? Like he wasn't aware . . .

"I know everything I need to know now," he stated evenly.

"What's that?" I asked.

"We get along fine."

"We've been on the phone—" I pulled it away from my face and watched the counter on the screen. "Five minutes."

"I know and you made me laugh more in five minutes than I have with everybody else in the last year combined." He had no idea how those words affected me. No idea at all, and I could never tell him. I squeezed my eyes closed without thinking about it. There was a pause on his end, and then totally seriously, he said, "Come with me." He cleared that throat of his and added, "Us."

"Where?" I regretted it. Like there was somewhere else he'd invited me to.

He let out this huffing noise that was pretty close to a groan and had me wondering what face belonged to that voice and personality. It wouldn't be the first time that thought had crossed my mind. "Florida, Ruby," he said a lot more patiently than anyone else would have.

It was my turn to groan as I rolled onto my back on the bed.

Something on the mattress dug into my shoulder, but I ignored it. He really was inviting me out. For real.

"I've been thinking about it for a while. Since before we left for Scotland. I wanted to invite you, but . . ." He trailed off. There was a sound I couldn't figure out before he said in a totally confident tone, "I want to meet you." Just like that. *I want to meet you.* He let out a soft breath over the phone. "I'm not going to kill you in your sleep."

That made me snort. "I wasn't thinking that."

"You could have your own room. I'm sure there's a lock on it."

Anxiety and stress and nerves and vomit all rolled around in my belly. Go with him. To Florida. By myself. When I didn't technically know him or his friends.

Meet him. Meet Aaron.

Meet this person I thought the world of who had basically called me his little sister.

What if he didn't like me in person? What if I liked him even more once I met him in person? What if I liked him even more and he decided he didn't like me for some reason once he met me? What if—

"Yes, then?"

Yes? My heart rate sped up, excitement and nausea and something I couldn't completely identify filling my veins. "Aaron, do you understand what you're asking me?"

"Yeah," he said, but it really came out more like "duh."

"We've never met in person."

"So? We e-mailed each other back and forth for nine months. I talk to you more than I do my family and friends." There was a rustling sound in the background, and I swear I heard a door close. "It's only weird if you make it weird, and we wouldn't make it weird. We already hit it off." Neither one of us said anything for a moment, but when he finally spoke again, it made the hairs on my arms stand up. "You don't think so?"

Did I not think so? Was he insane? I groaned and brought up a closed fist to my eye socket. "Look, I want to go with you. I really do, but—"

His voice was soft and determined. "I would never do anything to you, or let anyone do anything to you."

"It's not even that—"

"I know I'm coming on strong, but the more I think about it, the more I want you to come with us. The entire time I was in Scotland, I regretted not inviting you to come when Max bailed. I wish I would've invited you even if he hadn't bailed."

He had?

I blew out a breath and curled my toes together once more. Why did every single cell in my body get excited at the idea of going to Florida with someone I didn't know that well and other people I didn't know at all? If my best friend were to tell me she was going to meet up with her online friend at a café by herself, I would tell her she was out of her mind and that her body was going to show up on the nine o'clock news for being a total idiot.

But my brain rebelled against that completely.

Completely.

Some part of me deep down knew that Aaron wouldn't hurt me. I didn't know how I knew that, but I did. I really, really did. And I did love going to Florida . . .

"Look, I don't have any money. I have a lot of coins saved I can go get cashed and I have some money, but I shouldn't be blowing it on a ticket that's probably going to be crazy expensive because it's so last minute—"

That calming voice cut me off. "I got your ticket."

I felt myself scrunch up my nose and groaned. "You can't pay for it."

"You just said you don't have any money. I'm the one who wants you to come . . ." He trailed off. "If it makes you feel any better, I can afford it."

"I have to leave next week for California—"

"I'll make sure you're back before you have to leave."

I was making a terrible mistake, wasn't I? Who the heck goes to a beach house with strangers, one stranger I was pretty much totally in love with who had no idea because I'd never even seen his face—

I'd thought about it. He could basically look like a troll and chances were, if he was as wonderful in person as he was online, I would still be in love with him. Beauty fades, a good personality and chemistry doesn't.

"I can afford it, Ruby, and I'll make sure your flight gets you back home before you need to leave. You've sent me hundreds of dollars' worth of stuff while I was deployed—no, don't say you didn't because we both know you did. I can cover your ticket. You're the one doing me a favor."

"How am I doing you a favor?" I asked him in a mumble.

"Because I could've had a better time in Scotland, and I'm being selfish inviting you to come to Florida because I want to be around someone . . ." He trailed off again. "I want to meet you, and I'm not giving you any time to think about it. You're telling me you're worried, and I'm pushing you into it. That's selfish, and you know what, Rube? I don't give much of a shit."

Was I dead? Was this a dream? Had my mom baked mushrooms into dinner last night and I was still on some sort of weird trip?

I moaned. This was crazy, and I told him exactly that.

"So what? It's crazier for me to think about a girl your age going places by herself," he said. "I've got you, Ruby Cube."

Ruby Cube. It had killed me the first time I read it and killed me every time since then when I saw the RC he wrote me. I was so dumb. So damn dumb to fall into this position again. Even knowing I was dumb didn't change anything.

"I want to tell you yes." How could I explain this to him? "I really do. I've only gone places by myself for work without my family. They're going to think I've lost my mind if I tell them I'm going with you."

"You're twenty-four not ten."

Those words hit my chest with the force of a thousand of Thor's hammers. Hadn't I told him all this before? How much I hated getting treated like a little kid? It was my fault, I knew it. I let them all boss me around. I'd let them all clip my wings, and then I'd finished off the job myself.

"I know we'd get along. I know it. You know it. I'll send you my social if you promise not to post it on the Internet or pull out a bunch of credit cards under my name. You can have my dad's address and all the beach house information where we'll be staying. It's a big house. You can have your own room." There was another pause, but it was his calm, steady breaths that I couldn't help but pay attention to. He breathed like my sister. Like someone who didn't get out of breath running up stairs. "I know you'll get along with all of us."

My heart thought it was a downhill skier going for the gold. How I could be so excited and so scared at the same time, blew my freaking mind.

Why wasn't I telling him this was crazy?

Why?

Because it was crazy freaking stupid, but not in a bad way. I wanted to go so badly I could taste it. That part of me that wasn't scared of what he would think of me, of what could happen if we didn't get along in person, wanted to go so badly it made the rest of my brain shut up.

How could I tell Aaron I didn't usually even get to choose my seat when I flew with my family? Just thinking that made me feel so young and—

"Ruby, don't worry about the money. We can figure it out. I'm not expecting anything from you. I told you the truth when I said you're my closest friend. You are. I tell you more than I tell any-one else. How the hell could I let anything happen to the one person who's made me laugh when it was the last thing I wanted to do?"

My whole world seemed to stop.

And he kept going, oblivious. "If you really don't want to go, I don't want to force you or give you a guilt trip. Come because you want to. If not, we'll make it work some other time. All right?"

Chapter Sixteen

"We are just about to begin our descent into Panama City . . ."

If I hadn't had so much one-on-one time with heart palpitations when I was younger, I would have thought for sure I'd started having them when the pilot's voice came over the air.

Because *holy crap.*

I was here. About to be here. In Panama City. Where Aaron was going to be.

I was a chicken. This was my truth. I wasn't afraid to admit it. It was me. Ruby Marisol Santos was a certified, grade-A chicken. Not even the good kind of chicken that was grass fed and antibiotic-free because I'd been on antibiotics a few months ago. I was the worst kind of freaking chicken.

The human kind.

I wasn't prepared for this. It wasn't every day, or every month, year, or decade that I stepped out of my comfort zone. Flying solo to vacation with people I'd never physically met wasn't something I did or even thought about doing. I'd been verging on freaking out for the last twelve hours. I'd sweated, chewed most my fingernails down, sweated some more, panted so hard you'd figure I'd run a mile in heels, and had my heart racing so fast I could never tell anyone that knew me, otherwise they would send me to a cardiologist.

Yet here I was. Trying my best to not be what came so naturally to me: a chickenshit.

After spending an entire lifetime trying to tell myself I wasn't scared of things while also actively avoiding those things that might terrify me, I usually didn't find myself in situations that had me wondering what in the world I'd been thinking, because I wouldn't put myself into that position. That just wasn't what I did, and it shamed me.

But someone I trusted had told me I needed to live my life to the fullest. I wasn't brave or ballsy like a lot of people who went after the things they wanted all the time. Maybe because there wasn't a whole lot I wanted, but I wasn't sure. Quitting my job and coming here were the two bravest things I had ever done in my life, hands down. I'd tried being that resilient, go-getter type person once, and only once, and it had backfired on me like no one's business. But, I'd watched my little sister fall enough times and watched her get right back up to know that you needed to do that, every single time. You needed to pick yourself right back up, even if you were bruised and hurt and just wanted to lie on the ground and stay there forever because it wasn't as uncomfortable as you thought it'd be.

Or because you were scared of falling again as you tried to pick yourself back up.

Not that I knew from experience or anything.

Which was why and how I found myself stuck in the middle seat of an airplane, smashed between one stranger trying to hog my armrest and another stranger using my shoulder as a pillow. Not surprisingly, when you try to buy a ticket the day before you want to leave somewhere, you aren't exactly going to find a nonstop flight at a decent price, much less score a window seat. But I'd been okay with that. All that had mattered was that I was on my way.

Nonstop from Houston to Panama City Beach, Florida.

I still couldn't believe I was about to touch down, and my family definitely hadn't been able to believe what I was doing either.

Yesterday, my mom and Jasmine had both taken turns yelling at me.

What is wrong with you? You're already leaving next week!

Have you lost your fucking mind, Squirt?

"You've never done crazy stuff," my mom had argued, not knowing that those words alone had backfired on her so much. It only egged me on to insist on doing what I wanted to do. And that was go.

"I'm going to" and "No" hadn't been the right thing to answer back with because that was when they'd started yelling over each other for half an hour, give or take. At that point, I did the exact same thing I had done hours later when the older man sitting beside me in the plane had slumped over midsnore and rested his head on my shoulder: I had let it happen. Except, I had let my little sister and mom yell all the reasons I shouldn't go.

What if something happens? my little sister had asked, one hand flailing around her face while her other hand held a chocolate chip cookie clutched in it. I didn't need to answer because my mom had rattled off a dozen things that could happen, including but not limited to me getting kidnapped, sold into slavery, and being used as a drug mule.

But I managed to keep my mouth closed and let them keep going and venting and turning red.

Until finally, I said as calmly as possible, loving them so much even though they blew my mind, "I get that you're worried . . . but I'm going."

It had set them off all over again, but after a few minutes, I turned around and walked out on them for the first time in my life instead of breaking down and agreeing that going across the gulf was freaking insane.

It was. I knew it was, but as much as it scared me, their words only made me want to go so much more. Whether it was to prove it to myself, prove it to them, or neither one, I had no clue. All I knew was that I wanted to go, even more because I was nervous.

But mostly because I wanted to meet Aaron, though it scared the heck out of me.

I wanted to meet him so I could get it over with and move on with my life, or so I told myself. I could see him and know that all I felt was friendship. I figured it would be like meeting a celebrity in person and seeing they were human instead of this imaginary, perfect person you had built up in your head.

And when my mom and sister showed up at my bedroom door after I walked out on them to start packing, I stood my ground as they still attempted to talk me out of going.

I wasn't going to budge. And I hadn't, despite my stomach hurting and how unnatural it felt to not do whatever was in my power to please them. Because that was what I usually did. That was what came naturally to me.

Somehow, someway, I made it to the flight that Aaron had e-mailed me the details of not even two hours after I'd agreed to go to Florida, before I'd told anyone I lived with. Even leaving on bad terms with my mom, with her husband being the one to drive me to the airport because the two I was related to by blood were too pissed off to want to take me, I hadn't been able to *stop* being excited. And scared. Mostly scared. Maybe fifty–fifty.

I was about to land in Florida, a place I'd been to a dozen times before.

To vacation with my pen pal I was a little in love with and his friends.

There was no need to freak out.

According to his last IMs, he and his friends were driving overnight and should have arrived at the beach house they were renting four hours ago. After that, he was driving back to Panama City to pick me up, and then we were going back to the house. **I'll meet you outside Arrivals**, he'd messaged me. So we were meeting outside of Arrivals.

Hopefully.

I hoped.

I really hoped.

This tiny part of my brain kept warning me to expect the worst. That maybe he wouldn't show up. That maybe Aaron Hall didn't exist. That I should be prepared for him not being there, and if he wasn't, it wasn't the end of the world. I could figure something out. I had a credit card. Maybe I didn't have a lot of money in my bank account, but I had my credit card, and I'd gone to swap my coins for cash the day before and come out with almost two hundred dollars.

I was good. *I was good.*

That's exactly what I kept chanting to myself as the plane landed and everyone filed off. I lugged my weekend bag through the airport, so much smaller than the one back home, and stopped at the first bathroom I could find. I used it, but while I was washing my hands, I made the mistake of looking at myself in the mirror.

I was a wreck.

The light brown hair I'd been dyeing since I was fifteen had decided it was done being straight and wanted to resemble something out of a frizzy hair product commercial. The color I usually carried from lack of sleep under the blue eyes I'd inherited from my mom had decided to darken to an almost purple. And my mascara . . . I almost shuddered. Beauty was on the inside, I knew that, but a little makeup never hurt anyone.

After putting on a little more foundation, blush, and lipstick, and giving my hair a brush with my fingers, which had it looking decent again, I reminded myself that I was here for my friend and not for any other reason. I'd already told him I didn't look like my mom or Tali. If he was disappointed in my appearance . . . I could get over it. I really could. I would. It wouldn't be the first time that happened.

I didn't even believe that myself, but I needed to.

Friends didn't care what other friends looked like, unless this was *Mean Girls*, and it wasn't. As long as we got along, that was all that mattered. Our friendship had been built on our personalities. Everything could be fine.

Unless he wasn't outside waiting for me . . . If that was the case, I wasn't sure I'd ever recover.

A few minutes later, in baggage claim, my suitcase finally came around the conveyer and I picked it up, straining under the weight of 48.8 pounds of bathing suits and more clothes than I'd realistically need. Wheeling my bag behind me in one hand and clutching my weekend bag over my opposite shoulder, my heart rate started going crazy, so much I let out a deep exhale to try and calm it, but failed. Like usual. A knot formed in my throat anyway.

It wasn't until that exact moment that I remembered Aaron had never sent me a picture of himself even though he had mentioned it.

It was fine. Totally fine. I knew he was six foot two and that he'd have a hint of a Louisiana accent in his voice. I would figure it out. Two automatic glass doors went wide as I approached them, dumping me directly outside the building and at a curb.

And . . . there was no one waiting.

At least there was no one waiting there that looked like a twenty-something man who had just spent the last year in Iraq. The only people hanging around were other passengers on my flight and two men dressed in black suits holding signs with names that weren't Santos on them.

I looked right, I looked left, then I took a deep breath. There was no need to panic.

Maybe he was running late.

Maybe he was at the departure entrance by accident and making his way over right that second.

Maybe . . .

I looked around again and tried swallowing around the lump in my throat.

Maybe, I could grab one of the taxis parked along the curb. This wasn't a foreign country with a language I didn't understand. I had an app on my phone for booking hotel rooms. This wasn't 1940.

My hand shook as I reached into my purse and pulled out my cell, taking it off airplane mode for the first time. That was how pathetic and nervous I was. I hadn't even bothered taking it off because I'd been dreading getting a message that said plans had changed and I was on my own. It didn't even take a minute before the icon that showed I had seventeen unread messages flashed on the display, only slightly making my stomach churn.

But none of them were from the newest number on my phone. Eight were from my mom and the other nine were from Jasmine according to my notifications.

At the sound of the doors behind me opening, I dragged my bag to the side and took another look around, hoping to see a man standing by himself in a corner I hadn't seen, looking expectant, or maybe holding up a sign with SANTOS or RUBY on it. Or something. *Something.*

I could wait a little while. He said he'd gotten a crappy phone. Maybe he didn't have service, or he was still driving and couldn't reach his phone to let me know he was running behind.

I took a sniff. And I blinked. And then I did both all over again, glancing from side to side, standing on one foot and then the other.

One minute turned to five.

Five minutes turned to ten.

And ten minutes became fifteen.

My eyes started to sting because I hadn't slept, I assured myself as I checked the time on my phone one more time. They weren't itchy all of a sudden because I was feeling abandoned and sick to my stomach at the thought Aaron was going to leave me here.

Once, before Jasmine had started kindergarten, when I'd been the only Santos left at that elementary school, my mom had forgotten to pick me up. Four o'clock had come and gone, and she still hadn't shown up. It wasn't until closer to five, after I'd been sitting on the front steps for close to two hours that the vice principal had come out and spotted me. She'd known my mom for years thanks to my older brothers and sister basically being demons that didn't shut up, and after asking me why I hadn't been picked up yet, she'd tried calling my house and there hadn't been an answer. So she'd offered to drive me home.

I'd cried on the way, feeling so betrayed that my own mom had forgotten about me. My dad had moved out by that point, and looking back on it now, I understood that that's why I'd freaked out so hard. Of course my mom had a million other things on her mind and wouldn't willingly forget to pick me up from school, but it had happened.

She never forgot about it and neither had I from the looks of it.

Now, standing there outside the Panama City Beach airport without a single familiar face to reassure me, that forgotten but familiar feeling settled on my lungs and my heart.

I'd been left behind.

I sniffed. I blinked. I swallowed.

More people came out of the building and more cars pulled up along the curb, but not a single one of them was there for me. Not one single car. Not a soul.

I sniffed, blinked, and swallowed some more. My mouth went dry.

He'd left me here, hadn't he?

A family of four walked past me, smiling, laughing and joking as they crossed the street, so happy, so freaking happy.

What had I been thinking? Why hadn't I stayed home? I was an idiot, wasn't I?

But why would Aaron buy me a ticket and then not show up to pick me up? Hadn't I told him I wasn't sure about coming? It wasn't like this had been my idea. He'd invited me. I hadn't invited myself.

Tears prickled my eyes, and I honestly felt like something sharp jabbed me in the stomach.

This is what you get for taking a chance, Rube, my brain egged my heart on.

He wasn't here. He wasn't coming. He'd left me.

He'd left me here. He wasn't coming to get me.

I was so, so, so *stupid.* I *knew* better. *I freaking knew better.*

It wasn't until something cool slid down my cheek that I realized my eyes hadn't just started prickling, they'd gone for it all. The breath that came out of me was hiccupped and choked. Strangled.

It isn't the end of the world, I tried to tell myself even as two more tears streaked down my cheek. Stop. I needed to stop and get it together. I wasn't going to waste tears over being left. I wasn't.

I had my credit card.

Plenty of people traveled by themselves.

I had a cell phone.

There had to be a hundred hotels I could stay at close by.

There were worse places to get stranded at. At least there was a beach. It was summer. I had a bathing suit and plenty of sunscreen.

I could do this.

I could—

Two more tears slipped out of my eyeballs, and I heard more than felt myself suck in a choppy breath.

I had to get it together. I couldn't cry. It was fine. I was fine. It wasn't a big deal that Aaron hadn't shown up. I should have known better than to let myself get disappointed. When had I ever had good luck with guys to begin with?

Never. That's when.

Aaron not showing up . . . being stranded alone in a city I'd never been with limited money . . . none of it was the end of the world. I wasn't going to cry over being ditched. We were friends—had been friends—and he didn't owe me a thing. It was fine.

I wasn't going to dwell.

Not me.

I had my credit card, my good health, and plenty of people back home who loved me. This didn't reflect on me. Aaron letting me down had nothing to do with me. He was the one who had chickened out, not me for once, and that was supposed to be a victory I could celebrate when my organs didn't feel like they were getting stabbed repeatedly with an ice pick.

He'd left me, but it was going to be okay. It was.

This small part of my brain tried to tell me that maybe something had happened to him. That he wouldn't have left me here at the airport for no reason. Part of me vouched for the man I'd gotten to know over the last few months, telling me he wouldn't do something like this . . .

But the biggest part of me said I was being naïve.

Three more tears came out of my eyes, and I wiped at my cheeks with the back of my fingers, fighting the urge to cry more because my body sure wanted to do that. *Get it together, Ruby. Figure it out and stop standing here crying in public. You're better than this. It's fine.*

I was getting a headache.

I had to wipe at my face twice more, and when I looked at my fingers, I found black marks from my runny mascara smeared on them, and it just made me even more upset. It made my head hurt worse, instantly.

All right. *I could do this*. First thing, I needed a taxi, and I could ask him to drop me off somewhere close to everything. I could find a hotel.

I had just taken a deep breath as a group of six that had been on the same flight as me walked by, when I heard distantly, "Rubes?"

I stopped breathing.

I almost didn't look up, my vision bleary, but I made myself do it.

Standing not even five feet away, with a torn-out piece of notebook paper in his hands that said RC SANTOS in thick, scribbly red letters, was a man. Not a boy. Not a man-boy. A man I could have looked at all day for the rest of my life. With neat, short, golden blond hair on his head that I noticed first thing, and a deep tan covering every inch of his exposed skin, I stopped breathing. Deep-set eyes, high cheekbones and a mouth that was pretty darn full for any gender, seemed to tie in together to shape a face that was too good-looking.

Way too good-looking.

He looked like a model. If this was him, it was no wonder he'd had so many girlfriends and they'd all been nuts. Nobody gave up this kind of guy without a fight. But it couldn't be him.

There was no way . . .

No freaking way.

Was this a joke?

I turned my head to glance over my shoulder, and then turned to look over my other shoulder like there was some other Ruby or person in the world that could go by RC Santos that this man could be asking for. Because the name was common and all that.

But when I faced forward again, the tall, very six-foot-two-ish blond man with the paper that said RC SANTOS on it raised his light-colored eyebrows gradually. I saw his Adam's apple bob. Gulp. And in the slowest motion possible, hesitant, hesitant, hesitant, one of his hands let go of one side of the sign and both his fists dropped, paper and all. The man blinked, and I took in what seemed like dark brown eyes staring at me beneath that heavily constructed bone structure. I took in the way his lips slightly parted, and the way his whole face went slack as he swallowed again.

Then that mouth, *that mouth*, seemed to curve up, his smooth shaved cheeks went pink . . . and I realized he was smiling. At me. Brown eyes lit up as they scanned me from my face down to my gold flats and back up again.

"Ruby?" the man asked in that voice I fully, totally recognized from the one and only conversation we had on the phone in the months we'd known each other.

But I still blinked at him.

This was a joke.

It had to be.

This could've been straight out of a movie where I got kidnapped and taken, sold into human trafficking and my family would never see me again unless one of my brothers vowed vengeance and went to search for me. Like that would happen.

But it was the smile on the blond man's face that seemed to just . . . click. To say maybe this wasn't a prank. That I wasn't imagining this.

"Aaron?" His name out of my mouth sounded as wary as it seemed in my head.

"Yeah," the man my gut was 99 percent sure was the person I'd spent a year e-mailing, said.

I didn't miss the way he looked me over one more time, or how his smile wavered. Hesitated. Flickered. Before coming back to life, lips together with only the corners arching upward.

Maybe it had been a bad idea to not send him a picture of myself after so many months.

Was he disappointed? If he'd genuinely thought I'd resemble my sister or my mom, it was his own fault for setting up those expectations. I'd told him I looked like a mix of both my parents. I wasn't the pretty one in the family or the funny one or the talented one or the outgoing one or the smart one . . .

I was just Ruby.

Just Ruby. And that had to be enough. I'd come too far for it not to be.

I blinked at those brown eyes staring a hole into me. I swallowed just as hard as he'd swallowed a minute ago. Then I told him before even processing the whispered words coming out of my mouth, "Can I see your ID?"

He blinked, and just as quickly as he blinked, he smiled almost, *almost* tenderly and nodded. One of his hands went behind his back as his gaze bounced all over me. Something small and brown filled his hand, and he finally moved his gaze to the wallet he held. His hand was steady as he passed me two plastic cards, one was a Kentucky driver's license and the other was a military ID with the name I knew well: Aaron Tanner Hall.

It was him. Crap on a stick, it was really him. My hands were shaking just a little as I looked at his driver's license one more time before handing it over, *thisishimthisishimthisishim* going around and around my head, stealing the power from my lungs as I told him the one thing I hadn't exactly been planning on admitting as my voice practically shook, "I thought you weren't coming."

Aaron—not some faker who had hacked into his account and decided to come kidnap me out of all the other people in the world that he could find—shook his blond head, still frozen in place even though his features seemed to be bouncing back and forth between a smile and an expression that might have been a surprised one or a confused one, but I didn't know him well enough to be sure.

"I thought—" He cleared his throat, making me drag my eyes toward his bobbing, very tan Adam's apple. "I was standing over by the lot, waiting. I didn't know . . ."

He was disappointed. He was disappointed, wasn't he?

"You don't look like I thought you would," were the words he used to break the silence. His pronunciation was slow, calm. He blinked in the middle of his sentence as his chest went wide with an inhale and just as quickly deflated with an exhale. I stopped breathing as those dark brown eyes of his roamed over my face and down my front all over again. His mouth did that wavering thing again, fluctuating, indecisive before settling into a weak smile as his eyes bounced all over me one last time. His voice was as wary as his smile as he said the five words we'd said to each other so many times over the last few months, a reminder of our friendship, a reminder that he'd invited me to come here. "You know what I mean."

He was disappointed. That's what he meant. What was new? I should have known. Should have expected . . .

I didn't fight the urge to blink or suck in a breath through my nose that sounded choppy and broken into syllables that it wasn't capable of. My heart started beating faster, nervous, more nervous than I thought I'd probably ever been before, and that had been really nervous. Tears prickled in my eyes like they had moments ago, but I didn't let them fall. I wouldn't. Somehow, someway I managed to clear my own throat and tell him more softly than I would have liked, "I told you I don't look like my mom or my sister."

The man I was sure was named Aaron made a sound that resembled a huff, almost like a laugh, but the next six words out of his mouth made me flinch. "No. You don't look like them."

And then, while I was pinching my lips together again at the brutality of his honesty, telling myself not to cry because he'd done this to himself by thinking I was lying, he really did laugh as he took a step forward, his eyes suddenly so bright and focused, that face of his I'd just been shocked with, lit up. "You hungry?"

He asked it like it was nothing. Like he hadn't just confirmed something I'd accepted a long time ago but never got that much easier to accept. Like I didn't have one little tear I desperately wiped at in the corner of my eye.

"What's wrong?" Aaron asked immediately as his eyebrows knit together, by some miracle making his gorgeous face look even more handsome, even after he'd basically admitted he'd thought I was something or someone else and was trying to process it.

I was such an idiot.

My vision went blurry, and I could sense the anxiety in my sternum and belly. "This feels weird," I told him honestly, nervous, nervous, nervous. More nervous by the second. By the millisecond. I tried sucking in a breath that wasn't there.

"Ruby, what's wrong?" came his concerned question as I looked down at the ground, fisting my hands at my sides.

I swallowed. I told myself to keep it together. Reminded myself that I'd known this was going to happen and that I wasn't going to be disappointed. So I lied as I wiped at my face again, forcing myself to look at him as I spoke. "I thought you changed your mind and I was deciding what to do . . ."

Those dark eyes, so at odds with his coloring and hair, widened. There was no hesitation on his face when Aaron took another step forward, a frown growing across his mouth and practically radiating throughout his entire body. "I wasn't going to change my mind," he claimed, steadily. His irises bounced back and forth between one of my eyes and the next, the line of his jaw going tight. "Are you all right?"

I sucked in a breath through my nose, shrugging, and gulped, reaching up to rub my palm over my breastbone. I couldn't be having a panic attack. I couldn't. But I tried to take another breath and there was nothing there. There was nothing there and my hands had begun sweating at some point and feeling like they were covered with ants, and my heart was beating like crazy and—"I feel like I can't catch my breath . . ."

Aaron's head jerked, and I'd swear his face paled. The four steps he took forward were immediate, leading him to stop directly in front of me before I even realized it. Aaron Hall, who was even more gorgeous than I ever could have imagined, was in front of me and I was freaking the hell out.

I was freaking the hell out.

Because I was frustrated and let down and trying so hard not to be. I wasn't good at this crap. I should never have come.

When his hand reached for my arm, he didn't hesitate for a second as his fingers wrapped around the delicate skin on the inside of my elbow, and before I knew what was happening, he was steering me toward a bench I hadn't seen, one arm going over my shoulders like it was the most natural thing in the world. And the entire time he did that, he said, "You're fine, Ruby, you're fine. Breathe, breathe . . ." over and over again until my butt hit the bench and he was stooping in front of me.

And I was still losing it.

I made a circle over my heart, swallowing, feeling like an idiot but at the same time like not an idiot because this guy who said he was Aaron, and acted like Aaron and sounded like Aaron, was crouching by my knees after making me think I was on my own in a city I'd never been before because he'd changed his mind.

Hands I hadn't even realized were cupping my knees, gave them a squeeze. "Hold on, okay? I'll be right back." Another squeeze. "Right, right back," he promised me as I sat there.

I blinked and felt a third squeeze, and then he was up on his feet and gone, jogging somewhere I wasn't sure of because I didn't keep watching him.

I rubbed the skin over my heart, my fingers clammy over the exposed skin above my shirt. My hands weren't shaking, but it sure felt like the rest of me was. A part of me wanted to decide I'd changed my mind, go back inside the terminal, buy another ticket, go home and pretend this hadn't happened. I could just tell everyone—

I just barely thought of "everyone" before the word fell like a wet blanket over my entire nervous system.

I couldn't go back home. No way. My family would never let me live this trip down. They'd think something bad happened or think that I couldn't handle going somewhere by myself and that would be it. No one would ever let me forget it. Most importantly, I would never, ever do anything that made me squirm ever again. That was the whole purpose of this trip. I wanted to do this. I'd wanted to come. I wanted to be here, and it had nothing to do with them.

I didn't want to go back.

If I did . . .

Everything was fine. It was okay. I hadn't been left. Maybe I wasn't what he was hoping for, but he was here. Aaron was here.

Aaron who was so good-looking my eyeballs could have started hurting in the three minutes we'd been face to face if I hadn't been flipping out internally. And it wasn't a big deal that he didn't look like what I'd pictured. That if I'd known he looked the way he did, maybe I wouldn't have been making jokes about his butthole.

And then I wondered why I didn't have boyfriends. Why I couldn't get one person to love me like more than a friend. Why I'd given my virginity to some guy I'd thought I would marry one day and all it had done was make him apologize and blush and beg me not to tell my brother because it had been a mistake. I had been a mistake.

Aaron was my friend. I'd always known this, and I'd liked him before I'd seen him. I'd known nothing more would come of this friendship. Mostly though, I knew that none of this had anything to do with Hunter. Aaron was as different from that idiot as one could get.

I saw green Nikes and light brown hair on a pair of male legs first. Aaron's steps were fast as he jogged slowly over to me before dropping back into a crouch. The next thing I knew, he was shoving a bottle of water at me, one hand going to the spot right above my knee where it met my thigh. He cupped it. Me. Squeezing over the tights I'd put on under my brown skirt in case I got cold on the plane.

"Drink some," he told me in a low, insistent voice, as he shoved the bottle closer to my chest.

I raised my eyes to meet his. His face was right by mine, maybe six inches away. I hadn't noticed that I was leaning forward, that my elbows were on the middle of my thighs even as one hand rested between my boobs. Aaron's face, this face I'd never seen before five minutes ago, was open and worried. That mouth that was almost too full for a man's mouth was strained, and he looked like . . . well, he looked like he didn't think of me as a stranger he'd felt bad for and invited on this trip. He didn't look let down. Because you couldn't look at someone you didn't care for the way he was watching me, eyebrows knitted together, lines at the corners of his eyes, and a pursed mouth.

Those eyes of his, which were a warm mahogany color, were on me. "Drink some. Take a deep breath," he repeated, as his palm came off my thigh and he reached forward with two big palms. I didn't need to look down to know one set of his fingers was on the lid, the other set suddenly covering mine as he turned and twisted the lid off before nudging it at me again.

All I could do was watch him as I lifted the bottle to my mouth.

It was the most self-conscious drink of my life having Aaron balancing on the tips of his toes in front of me almost eye level. He watched me so closely, with all that golden skin and that amazing bone structure I had rarely seen anywhere other than a high-fashion magazine, that I expected to choke on the water and spit it all over him or something stupid like that. I watched him, and he watched me. And I wondered what he was thinking.

Mostly, I thought *he's here.*

I smiled at him, anxious and nervous, as I took him in, and he took me in too. He smiled in return, not at all anxious or awkward, just . . . worried. I knew that look well enough from my own brothers. I could see it for what it was.

This was Aaron. My friend. And something told me I had nothing to worry about. I didn't need to freak out any longer. I'd known what I was getting into coming here, and I couldn't let that ruin my weekend. I could make the best out of this. I could be the best female friend he'd ever had. I could be the little sister figure he already looked at me as.

I could, I thought as he put a hand on my shoulder and slid it down the length of my upper arm.

But it would be unbelievably hard.

"You all right?" he whispered. He still had that smile on his face that honestly made my heart start beating a little weird again, but in a way that had nothing to do with a panic attack or palpitations.

I nodded at him, sensing my unease slowly going away as I took him in, this guy who knew more about me than a lot of other people I'd known for years. This guy who brought me water and squeezed my leg when I told him I was on the verge of losing it. This was the man I'd become friends with. The man I'd tried talking myself out of having a crush on and failing, all because of e-mails and messages.

This was Aaron. My friend. The person who had invited me to Florida because he wanted to meet me, and he was smiling at me, looking more worried than he should have.

"You sure? Your heart is okay?" he asked so earnestly I had to stop breathing for a second.

I plucked the bottle cap from his fingers and looked down as I screwed it on. "It's okay. I was nervous."

"You're not anymore?" he asked, and it took everything in me to not glance up as he spoke.

I lifted up a shoulder and let out another breath from my mouth to calm down even more. "No." My mouth twisted, and that time I couldn't stop myself from glancing up at him. He was still watching me so closely, I had to glance down for a second before looking up again. "I lied. I am. Just a little."

That pretty mouth twisted, his eyes going nowhere. "I thought I could watch the doors better if I was on the side of the lot, but this van was blocking right where you were standing," he explained. His mouth formed a soft smile that my entire body wasn't sure how to handle. At the same time, he put his hand back on my knee like it had always been there. His voice was slow and still so low only I could hear. "I wasn't going to leave you."

There went my heart once more.

He blinked, and it was like he could read my mind. "You really thought I wasn't coming?"

I shrugged all over again.

"I—" He shook his head, and I finally noticed his hair wasn't just neat, he'd combed it a little. There might have even been gel in it. It was short but just long enough to be able to be parted. "I don't know what to say, Rubes." It was the reluctant smile that crept over his face that was so unexpected, so much like the sun coming out over a cloudy day, I forgot about his hair. If that smile wasn't enough, he squeezed my knee one more time. "Maybe we should text for a minute first. Break the ice."

It was me who laughed, all awkward and choppy and still sounding like there were tears hanging around the back of my throat. "Maybe." I laughed again, and that time it was watery and a bit broken, and luckily I hadn't tried to act like I was tough because he'd know right then that I'd been on the verge of crying because I thought he wasn't coming.

That handsome, model-like, slightly sun-weathered face flashed me a grin before tipping toward the bottle of water I was holding between my hands. "Take another drink."

I undid the cap and took another drink. He was still watching me. Why was he watching me so much?

That pink mouth went tight as his eyes scanned over my face with a slowness that made me want to fidget and ask him to stop. "Why didn't you say anything?" he asked, still being so quiet.

Dragging the rim of the bottle from my mouth down to my chin and leaving it there, suspended in the air, I blinked, taking him in one more time and eating up the lines of his bones and the clear skin of his face and thinking he was the most beautiful man I'd ever seen. Of course he was. "I've told you everything." Did he have a dimple too or was I imagining it? "I promise," I assured him, trying to think of what I could have deliberately missed.

Aaron's golden eyebrows rose just a little, just a little, that smirk-ish smile still playing at the corners of his mouth. "Almost everything."

I lowered the bottle to my lap and frowned. "What do you think I didn't tell you?"

Those brown eyes swept over my face, and he squeezed my knees again before planting his feet flat. He started straightening, his face pausing while he was still eye level with me when he said way too evenly, "You could've told me your mom and sister are the ugly ones in the family."

I didn't even get a chance to throw my head back before I laughed, laughed like I hadn't just been on the verge of crying and then on the edge of having a panic attack. I just laughed my butt off. Loud and dorky and big.

When I managed to open an eye to see what he was doing, what that was, was him crouched all over again in front of me like he'd been, with his cheeks and neck colored.

He was blushing.

And that only made me blush.

Leaning forward, his words and his pink cheeks and his smile with a dent in it still fresh on my mind, I asked him, still practically whispering, "Are you drunk again?"

That dimple that was for sure a dimple went even deeper and his smile went full-powered on my heart, almost knocking the wind and every thought out of me when he snickered.

"Are you going to hug me or are you just going to stand there?" I asked him.

I had no idea right then that, for as long as my soul resided in my body and I could reminisce on the best parts of my life, I'd remember how Aaron Hall leaned forward and wrapped those long, tan arms around my back and pulled me into his chest. Me who was still on the bench. The way he hugged the hell out of me would be something that sickness and death could never take away. And in the time it took me to suck in a breath, I put my own arms around him. I'd hugged dozens of men before. Dozens and dozens, hundreds of times. And Aaron's upper body was just as wide and solid in front of mine like the best of them.

But better. So much better. Because his hug was the greatest. He smelled like a hint of cologne with cedar in it. And I would remember it forever.

My friend had come. This man whose beauty had nothing to

do with what was on the outside. I only tightened my arms around him and felt him do the same thing to me. He hugged me and kept on hugging me, one hand going to the back of my head and sliding its way back down again. Affection. That was exactly what he was giving me, and I drank every sip of it up.

When he pulled back after a few moments, those tan hands went to my shoulders and stayed there. His face couldn't have been more than a foot away as he asked one more time with that expression that I couldn't properly process, "You didn't say. Are you hungry?"

I couldn't help but do anything other than nod, taking in his features and filing them away for later. *Who would have known?*

Aaron smiled again as he reached out to take the handle of my suitcase from where it was propped against the wall. Who or when it had been moved, I had no idea, but later on, when I could think about it, I'd be happy no one had stolen it while I'd been having a mini-meltdown. "Let's go. I was waiting to eat in case you were hungry too."

I nodded and watched as he pulled my suitcase to his side, then tipped his head across the street toward the giant parking lot. Without another word, I followed just to the right of him, the suitcase on his left, finally taking him in fully. In a V-neck, olive green T-shirt that fit the width of his shoulders perfectly, brown cargo shorts that showed off tan, muscular calves, and running shoes, he looked so . . . normal.

But better.

Aaron must have sensed being eyeballed because he glanced over his shoulder and raised those sun-lightened eyebrows. "Do I have something on my face?"

I could feel my cheeks get red; that's how bad it was getting caught. "No. It's just . . . weird to see you in person." I hesitated for a second and told him the truth, because I'd promised not to lie, and something in my gut said if he'd known when I was full of crap online, he could tell the same thing in person. "You're just . . . not as hard on the eyes as I thought you were going to be."

His mouth did that hesitating grin again that fluctuated between a grin and a controlled smile before he winked.

He winked. At me.

Then he said the most perfect words that could have come out of his mouth. "If it makes you feel better, we can talk about my . . ." He waved the hand closest to me behind his butt. A butt I'd have to totally catalogue later when it wasn't so obvious.

I pressed my lips together and tried not to smile.

And I totally failed at it.

Chapter Seventeen

Aaron was smiling at me.

This could-be runway model, with cheekbones that could cut glass if they wanted to, a jaw that was so defined it would give a sculptor a hard-on, and a mouth that must have given hundreds of women over the years countless raunchy dreams, was smiling at me from across the table. Me. And he wasn't looking anywhere else.

The most important place this not-looking-anywhere-else part included was the waitress who had been playfully pouting and trying her absolute best to make eye contact with him when she'd come by to take our drink orders a few minutes ago. She'd struck out. Then she'd struck out again when she'd brought them over and taken our food order. Her squeezing her boobs together with her upper arms hadn't been enough to get him to look elsewhere, and she had girls even I had glanced at twice. But Aaron? He'd been constantly sneaking looks and smiles at me while we'd been in the car, and hadn't stopped doing so since we'd been seated at the café he'd pulled over at.

I'd be fooling myself if I tried to deny that on the first leg of the drive, I'd taken some sneaky glances to my left. Neither one of us had said much yet. When I hadn't been busy looking at Aaron, I'd been focused on the scenery outside the window, eating up the darkening landscape that was so different from what I was used to back in Houston.

Most importantly, as we sat facing one another, I was smiling at him cautiously and he was giving me that smirking little smile that seemed like it had secrets stitched in some compartment below his practically flawless skin. If he had pores or blemishes, I hadn't been able to see a single one . . . and I'd looked.

Luckily, Aaron wasn't as quiet as I was, because it was him who finally broke our silence with his elbows on the table we shared. He had his chin on his hand, not looking at all like he'd driven hours on end to get to the beach house and then had to drive to get me.

"You look really tired," was what he decided to start off with.

I blinked and bit down on my bottom lip as I struggled not to take that as an insult. "Do I?"

The corners of his mouth flexed upward just a bit, a smirk hiding in plain sight. "You know what I mean."

Uh.

His mouth lost the battle when that quiet laugh of his came out. "*You know what I mean.*"

Raising an eyebrow, I nodded enthusiastically, trying not to smile and mostly failing at it. "You're saying I look like hell."

One of those hands that had been on my knees less than an hour ago palmed a lean cheek. "That's not what I'm saying."

I squinted at him that time and tipped my head to the side. "Pretty sure that's what it seems like you're saying."

"It's not," he argued, his gaze still totally focused on me.

I wrinkled my nose. "It's okay. I haven't slept much the last two nights thanks to someone I know. I'm sure I do look like hell."

That had him groaning as he seemed to push his chair closer to the table from the scrape of wood on tile. "I didn't say you look like hell. You just look tired."

I'm not going to smile. I'm not going to smile. "There's a difference?"

He cocked his head to the side and made his eyes go wide as he nodded. Apparently it was his turn to bring out the sass. "Yeah."

Aaron stared at me and I stared back at him.

"Hmm."

"Hmm," he repeated.

I smirked and he smirked right back.

This really was just like our conversations online. It relaxed me. Made me feel better about . . . everything. "If you say so." I held back a grin, snickering before letting out a yawn I tried my best to muffle but failed at. Wanting things to be as normal as they could be, I fidgeted with my hands, trying to think of what to ask him. Of all the things I could have brought up, I went with, "How was your drive?"

Those muscular shoulders I hadn't gotten to ogle much yet both went up casually. "Fine." The hand, the one he wasn't using to cup the side of his face, reached blindly toward his beer. Those brown, brown eyes still hadn't left my direction. "Your flight was okay?"

"Besides having an old man use my shoulder as a pillow, and having my mom yell at me before I walked out of the house, everything was good."

He groaned and it made me think of all the times he'd typed out something that conveyed the same emotion, making this all seem so much more real by the second. More safe. "She was pissed?" he asked.

I wouldn't say she was pissed, but . . . "You can call it that."

The corners of his eyes wrinkled, and I wondered if the lines were from all the time he spent outside or if it was from him smiling. "She doesn't know me. I'd be surprised if she wasn't worried I'd kidnap you and sell you on the black market." Those irises raked over me for what seemed like the hundredth time since he picked me up, making me feel just a hair self-conscious and grateful I'd hit the airport bathroom before I'd gone outside to wait for him. "She loves you. You're lucky."

How the hell he managed to say the same exact thing I thought was beyond me, but I let it go.

"Did you tell them you made it?"

I reached for my phone inside of my front pocket as I told him the truth. "Not yet. I forgot until now. Hold on." It took two swipes, but I unlocked the screen once I had my cell out. The icon that said I had nineteen unread messages now, instantly made me cringe. They were thousands of miles away. It wasn't like they were going to pop out of the display and holler at me when I read their messages. They were just being loving and worried, like a good family would. Like I would have done if it were any of them in my position, more than likely. This was what I got for never going through the rebel, hormonal teenager, jerk stage. I'd been the quiet one. The one who didn't like getting into trouble, never got home late, never talked back, and spent most weekends LARPing or sneaking into the movie theater my friends had jobs at, when I wasn't doing work for my aunt.

I'd always been the one who listened and tried to make everyone happy.

Until now.

I opened the first message and groaned.

"What does it say?" Aaron asked.

"*Why are you doing this to me?*" I told him. "These are all from my mom right now."

I went on to the next one.

"*If you get kidnapped, I'm not paying your ransom.*"

That one had Aaron snickering. I snuck a glance at him with a smile, before picking back up on the rest of the messages on my phone.

The next one had me snorting. "*They're going to harvest your organs and throw you in the ocean. Tell Shamu I said hi. We'll remember you.*"

He snickered even louder than I did before taking a sip of his beer. "That's pretty messed up."

"I told you she's crazy. Okay. Wait, listen to this one. *I'll name our next goldfish after you.*" I had to lower my face to my hand to laugh, and heard Aaron doing the same thing. My mom. My freaking mom.

"What do the rest of them say?"

I was still cracking up as I read the remaining texts to him. "*You're going to give me a heart attack. Why are you trying to kill me? You were supposed to be my good girl, not like these other dipshits. Do you not care about my health? I'm too young to die from a heart attack. Do you even love me?*" It was one thing to know I was related to drama queens, but it was another thing to be faced with it via text messaging. "These are from my sister. *You're a dumbass. I should've gone with you. I'm not joining any search parties going to look for you. I'm never going to wear the dress you made me if you don't come back.* There's a few repeats ... *Squirt, you shit, tell me you made it.*"

That last one had my heart hurting, and there was no hesitation in me as I typed out a reply to my mom and another to my sister.

I love you too. Made it to Panama City safe. Aaron already picked me up. Everything's good. Text you soon.

You can borrow my clothes but touch the ones I have folded on the floor and I'll put Nair in your shampoo. P.S. I love you too.

"Did you tell them you made it?" Aaron asked.

"Yeah, and that I'd message them soon. My sister threatened to borrow my clothes, and I told her if she took the ones I set aside to take with me to visit our dad, I'd put hair removal cream in her shampoo."

He raised one of those blond eyebrows of his, a slight smile playing at his pink mouth. "Is she skating again?"

"She's going early in the morning just by herself still, but she hasn't worked out with her coach since her last competition. She's been skating longer each day from what I overheard her coach tell my mom on speakerphone the other day. They've been watching her on security footage, but no one has the guts to confront her about it."

"She's still mad at you?"

"She was."

He nodded, his hand still propping up his chin, his other one still resting loosely around his bottle. Those brown irises continued lingering on me. What in the world was he thinking?

I fought the urge to fidget and cleared my throat, trying to be a lot more casual and easygoing than I really felt. "So, you left your friends at the beach house?"

Out of the corner of my eye, I could see Aaron caress the beer bottle with the tips of his fingers. "Yeah, but knowing them, they're probably sleeping, even though I'm the one who drove all night."

"You didn't trust them driving your truck?"

The blond man smirked. "No." He paused and took another sip of his beer before setting it down on the wood surface of the table, loudly, peering up at me in this way that made me even more self-conscious. "I didn't want to overwhelm you bringing a bunch of people you don't know to the airport," he explained at the same time the pads of his fingers made a trail up the neck of the bottle. His gaze was on me as he said, "And I wanted to hang out with you first. Just us two."

Of all the responses I could have come up with after that, I said, "Oh."

Oh.

When in reality it was more like, *are you trying to kill me?* That he knew me well enough to understand I'd feel overwhelmed . . . I wasn't going to overthink it. I couldn't. I wasn't about to stew on him wanting to hang out with me first either.

Either my tone or blah response must have unsettled him because, for one brief second, a flash of hurt crossed his eyes, but it was gone before the next blink. He smiled at me tightly. "If you're not comfortable, there's a couple motels on the way to the house instead—"

He thought . . .

"No, no," I stammered. "That's not it. You've done—you're—" Why couldn't I get my words straight? "I'm still a little nervous. You're just—" *Too surreal. Too perfect. So much more than I ever could have imagined.*

But I said none of that.

"What?" he asked, cautiously, like he didn't know his billboard-belonging face could reduce anyone with a pulse to a mess of blood and bones.

I mean, I'd grown this giant crush on him just through e-mails. Having him face to face was almost too much to handle when he looked the way he did. But I couldn't tell him any of that. I knew why I was here. Because he'd connected with me too, because he'd liked me.

As a friend.

Like a little sister, he'd told me that one time recently when he'd been drunk.

That was all . . . Even if the T-shirt he had on showed off pecs that demonstrated he'd definitely been hitting the gym regularly while he'd been stationed in the desert and had biceps and fore-arms that were lined with lean muscles. I could see, but I couldn't touch as anything more than a friend could or would.

The Friend Zone: The Life of Ruby Santos.

I cleared my throat and glanced at his styled hair again, something about it niggling at me. I swallowed and dragged my eyes up to the ceiling for a second before flicking them back down to him, regretting even starting to say something. I blinked at him.

And he blinked right back at me, expectantly.

When I slid my gaze to the side for a moment and then returned it to him, he just sat there, like he was trying his best to look innocent and curious.

"I already told you when we were leaving the airport."

He blinked innocently one more time but said nothing.

I groaned deep inside of myself. "You're going to make me say it?"

He nodded, and I thought for sure he knew exactly what I was thinking.

My face flamed up for the hundredth time, and I was tempted to glance at the ceiling so I wouldn't have to make contact with those eyes of his. I scratched at my neck and peeked at him again, feeling the words scrape against my throat. I needed to quit being a chicken. "I mean this in a totally platonic way, okay?" I warned him.

Out of the corner of my eye, I saw him dip his chin once more, and I wasn't going to pay attention to the way his mouth was doing that fluctuating thing again. Amused, happy, mocking, and back all over again. Why? Why couldn't he just be plain-looking or be so good-looking and not be so direct with his stare?

Because that wasn't my luck, and I knew it. I coughed. Then I did it. "You're gorgeous," I said to him almost painfully, prying the words out. "Like . . . the army should put you on their recruitment ads or put you as the face on their website. I feel like I can't look you in the eye or I'll turn into stone, and they'll need to add my statue to a garden of other women who have made eye contact with you before and lost their lives."

Aaron just stared at me for a moment, just a moment, and

slowly that wavering smile turned into a full-fledged one, one with straight white teeth and warmth to it that couldn't be faked, that could have had angels singing and playing harps in the background.

"You smile a lot more than I thought you would," I kept going. "You said you never really smiled while you were over there."

"I don't usually smile so much," was his cryptic answer.

I scratched at my neck again and watched him, nerves making a nest in my belly. Anxiety prickled at the center of my chest, and so, so hesitantly I said, "I was worried you were going to be disappointed meeting me."

Those brown eyes seemed to twinkle a little, his eyebrows shaping, his mouth doing that turning thing like he was trying to stop smiling.

My hands were starting to get itchy.

But then he said the words that made a dozen more butterflies explode into existence. "I'm really damn happy to see you, Ruby." His voice was quiet, not hesitant but more cautious. "I look at you and I can't stop smiling. That's all. You're adorable."

I couldn't in a million years envision Jasmine or Tali turning red at someone calling them adorable, but I did. Scarlet, red, garnet. I was covered in invisible lava all of a sudden.

And then with my dignity swimming out of my grasp, I hacked out an, "It took me an hour to decide what to wear before I left the house. I almost brought my Ghost Rider costume with me, but I thought I'd be too hot."

Aaron shook his head again, brown eyes trained on me, hands folded. "I like you just the way you are, stalker."

Looking back on it, it's weird thinking about the moments you *don't* realize are important. The sentences, the touches, the actions that seem so innocent in that second, you take them for granted. The words that make water into wine in the course of your life. But I would never forget the way his words made me feel. The way *he* made me feel right then.

I had no idea.

"I'm really happy you came, you know that, right?" he asked.

I nodded again, too quickly, the emotions and words and gestures and Aaron in general too much, stealing the words right out of my mouth until I had to scarf them back down inside me. "I know. I'm happy I'm here too," I said, pretty much whispering, definitely blushing. "Thank you for inviting me and paying for my ticket and coming to pick me up. As soon as I get steady work again—"

Something nudged at my foot, and I didn't need to look down to know it was his foot. "I'm not hurting for money, Rubes. You don't owe me anything. I wanted you to come, remember?" he reminded me in that warm voice of his just as the waitress brought over two plates of food and slid them across the table in front of each of us, only standing there a second longer than she needed to before moving away because she saw it. She saw us staring at each other.

Neither one of us talked much as we ate; we were both that hungry and tired. It didn't take long to pretty much inhale everything, to the point where Aaron scraped every crumb off his plate, and the only thing left on mine was a single burned french fry. When the waiter brought the check, we both eyed each other as I pulled some cash out of my pocket and he pulled his wallet out. We silently each put down an appropriate amount of bills to cover our meals.

I kept my mouth shut when he pulled out more cash to leave a tip.

I tried to tell myself to quit being nervous and awkward, but the pep talk did nothing. We made our way back to his white truck and got in, with Aaron shooting me a closed-mouth smile as he started it up and backed out of the spot.

I was going to talk to him, I told myself as I buckled in the seat belt.

It was going to be just like when we messaged each other, I swore to the universe.

I was fine now. We were going to have a good time, get to know each other even more than we already had, and that was going to start right then . . . as soon as he was back on the road.

I told myself all of this over and over again as he pulled the truck back onto the highway to drive the rest of the way to the beach house.

I told myself all of this, really believing it, feeling pretty darn determined . . . and I still passed out almost immediately after he began driving. Because the next thing I was aware of was gasping awake, jolting in my seat, the air getting ripped out of my lungs when I felt my head droop so far forward it scared me badly enough that I jerked backward and hit my head on the rest behind me.

That's when I heard Aaron choke.

I watched him out of the corner of my eye as I raised the back of my hand to wipe at the area around my mouth in case I'd started drooling, because it wouldn't be the first time that happened. I fell asleep at my work table every other day, that was my norm. There were more than likely at least fifty pictures of me passed out with drool on my face floating around my family members' phones. One picture had been Jasmine's screensaver for six months, until Christmas had come and Tali had drawn that penis on Sebastian's face.

Aaron did that choke again, his whole face scrunched up, and I watched him press his lips together then tuck them in as his shoulders shook. I was pretty sure those were tears making his eyes glassy and not allergies.

"Laugh all you want," I mumbled, wiping at my mouth anyway because he'd already caught me. What was I going to do?

Pretend it hadn't happened? But I still said, "I wasn't joking when I told you I hadn't slept in a while."

To give him credit, he kept his lips tightly sealed. What he did do was reach toward his face with his right hand and press the tip of his index finger to those long, curling blond eyelashes of his, swiping upward as he choked back another laugh. And in a quiet voice that said how much control it was taking him to not burst out laughing, he gasped, "Your face was almost on your knees . . ."

"I thought I saw a stain on my tights . . ." I muttered, pinching my own lips together because the urge to laugh at him, with him, was right there as his hands squeezed the steering wheel so tight his knuckles went white and his shoulders shook even more.

He snickered deep in his throat and cocked his face away from mine just as his shoulders trembled even harder. "Is that what happened?"

"Yes. It was."

Aaron coughed, earning him a side-eye and a frown. "Sure. Whatever you say, Rubes."

I'd gotten what I wanted, hadn't I? Us being back to "normal"? "Do you know how much longer we have until we get there?" I asked, trying to change the subject. The scenery had started to change again. Beach houses clustered together on the left side, and even though I couldn't see it, I knew water had to be close by.

"Five minutes, ten minutes max," he informed me.

Ten minutes to meet more people. No biggie. I squeezed my left hand into a fist. "Do you mind if I use your mirror?"

He shook his head.

"Thanks," I told him as I flipped the visor down and then opened the panel for the lit-up mirror. I tried to ignore the nerves in my stomach as I swept my hair into a low ponytail and started wiping below my eyes with the side of my finger.

I could feel him glance at me. "You already look nice."

I blushed and flipped the visor closed like a little kid caught with her hand in the cookie jar. "You only get one first impression—"

"What?"

"You only get one first impression," I repeated myself, pretty sure I was still blushing. "I don't want them to not like me."

Aaron's mouth screwed up and his forehead furrowed as he shot me a glance out of the corner of his eye. "They're not going to not like you, Ru." Then he slid me a full look. "You don't have to be nervous. You meet your friends' friends all the time, I thought."

One explanation after another backed up inside my throat, and I couldn't pick one that made me sound less lame and self-conscious, but I had to. I tried to reason with myself that he already knew nearly all the worst things about me and I was still here. What was a little more embarrassment after I'd already called him gorgeous? "But these are *your* friends," I explained, hoping he'd understand what I meant.

Which was that he was special to me. More special than he should have been. But there was my newest truth out in the open.

And Aaron must have known what I was trying to tell him, because he smiled so tenderly, so freaking sweetly, like you'd look at a puppy being cute, that I felt like a nut cracked in half. "*You're* my friend. I want you to like them too. I told them not to make a mess before we got back."

He . . .

"Don't worry, all right?" he said in that gentle, calm voice that could have made him a Ruby Whisperer. When I didn't respond, he reached over and touched the side of my arm with the back of his hand briefly. "All right?"

"All right," I agreed, even though my stomach was still all knotty and uneasy, and it wasn't all because of his friends.

Luckily, he didn't say anything else as we drove for all of six minutes longer before he turned left into a neighborhood of massive, colorful beach houses, one right next to the other. We drove past aqua, blue, green, and white homes, but it was a bright purple house on stilts he headed toward. To one side was a small, fenced-in pool, and on the other side of where he parked was a silver Alero. Aaron shot me another calming smile as he opened his door and got out. I only felt a little nauseous as I got out too, hopping down. Aaron was already opening the back door as I pulled my bag out from the front and tossed it over my shoulder, looking around at the rest of the homes and listening for the waves that had to be close by.

"Come on," he said, snapping me out of looking around, as he stood there with his hand extended toward me.

Neither one of my sisters would have taken it. I knew that.

But they were them and I was me, and I didn't wait until he realized I had to think about it before I took the two steps I needed to get to him and slipped my fingers through his, like we'd done this a thousand times in the past. His fingers were cool and rough and his palm was broad, and somewhere my subconscious was aware that these hands might have done something that wasn't nice or tender, that Aaron had lived in dangerous places for a long time and might have done things he would never want to talk about.

But I took his hand anyway and wrapped my fingers around his, hoping mine didn't feel as warm and clammy as they would have with any other human being in this situation.

The tiny smile that came over that beautiful mouth made the lines at the corners of his eyes crinkle, and for one moment, I couldn't believe his crap about how he claimed he wasn't in the business of smiling. I couldn't see it. He seemed so good-natured and thoughtful and warm, I couldn't see him for anything else but the man who went out of his way to make me comfortable.

He didn't say a word as he tugged me toward a white door in the center of the carport area below the house, opening it with the hand he'd been using to drag my bag behind us. Aaron didn't let go of my hand as he led me into a mudroom and then reached back to drag my suitcase in and close the door behind us. He kept right on holding it while we walked up a flight of tiled white stairs that weren't really wide enough for two adults and a suitcase, but we made it work somehow as anxiety at meeting people who had been in Aaron's life for decades filled my thoughts and stomach even more than they already had.

He smiled at me lightly on the next landing when he dropped my bag off beside the stairs with a "Your room's on this floor. I'll show it to you after we find everyone." Then we were back going up the stairs, and it was subconscious when I squeezed the fingers still entwined with his, this man I'd barely just seen for the first time three hours ago.

Aaron didn't let go when we made it to the third floor, which opened into a huge living area painted in a bright blue with sea-themed frames and knickknacks highlighting white furniture. It was the sound of voices talking over each other that had me glancing to a big kitchen tucked to the right, further into the wide-open layout. I sensed Aaron perk up, his spine straightening, and something about him in general just changing. There were two men and two girls standing around the white kitchen island, arguing.

One of the men, the tallest of the two, who might have been stunning if I hadn't seen Aaron first, happened to glance up just as he finished saying, "I don't want pizza either, but it's the only thing open," and spotted us. A grin immediately crept across his sharp face. I almost paused, but when Aaron kept walking, so did I.

"Where have you been?" the man asked, almost immediately, looking back and forth between Aaron and me, not being very shy or sneaky about it.

My friend, who had been nothing but soft spoken with me, tightened his hold on my palm. "We stopped to eat. I texted you."

The handsome stranger opened his mouth for a moment before slamming it closed. He reached into his front pocket and pulled out a cell phone, then frowned down at it in the time it took us to stop a few feet shy of the island, where the rest of Aaron's friends were doing the same thing I would have done. Looking at the odd person out. Me.

"I had it on silent," the man admitted with a laugh.

If Aaron screwed up his mouth into a smirk, I wasn't positive. What I was positive of was how hard he smacked his friend on the shoulder. "Told you. You barely woke up?"

The second man, with light brown skin and bright green eyes, nodded as he gazed directly at the hand I was clutching, his eyes seeming to sharpen and narrow enough so that I started loosening the grip I had on Aaron's hand. He held my hand tighter. "Not all of us can run on three hours of sleep like it's no big deal," the green-eyed man commented, still watching that spot between Aaron and me.

My friend made a dismissive noise in his throat as his hand slipped out of mine all of a sudden, and before I had a chance to snatch for it again, he moved it . . . and settled his palm on my lower back. The next thing I knew, he was leading me forward as he shifted to the side, giving me room to stand beside him directly in front of the island. I hadn't even realized I was standing partially behind him.

"This is Ruby. Ruby, this is . . ."

I didn't mean to zone out as he pointed from one man to another and then moved on to the two girls, but I did. One of them was a younger girl in a cast, and the other was older than me. They were both smiling genuinely . . . at least I hoped it was genuine. All I could do was freeze there and breathe as I stood and listened to one name after another, going in one ear and out the other.

I think I blinked and I might have smiled, but my heart started beating so fast, fast, fast again, there was no way I could be sure.

What had to be Aaron's palm rubbed at my lower back and swept up my lower spine to the middle of it, landing right by where my bra strap lay. That big hand had outstretched fingers spanning what felt like most of my back, and I swear I heard him whisper, "It's fine."

And from one moment to the next, the hand on my back disappeared, and I sensed it move further up my spine before moving to cup my shoulder and gradually ease me in closer to his side. More than a little distracted and only slightly aware of what was happening, I reached out to shake each person's hand across the island, trying to rack my brain for their names and who was who but failing miserably. One of the fingers on my shoulder rubbed a circle there.

"We're going downstairs. Neither one of us got any sleep. See you in the morning," Aaron told them, the hand on the back of my neck sliding down to palm my lower back once more.

The guy with the darker skin and light eyes was still glancing back and forth between us as he said, "We need to go grocery shopping, but the store closed at eight."

"We'll go in the morning then. You good with going at ten?"

The tall, good-looking man almost blanched. "Ten? In the morning?"

The fingertips on my back did a little tap. "Nobody told you to nap."

The tall guy and the one with the green eyes made a noise that had Aaron making a noise in his throat.

"Go by yourselves then. I'm going at ten. I'll see you in the morning," Aaron said as he took a step back.

Nerves started to clog my throat, but I managed to mutter out a, "It was nice meeting you all. See you in the morning."

The four of them waved at me, two more nicely than the other two. With another bye, I followed after Aaron as we headed toward the stairs we'd just come up. He stopped to scoop up four bottles of water from a pack on the floor I hadn't seen on the way up when I'd been too busy looking around at everything.

Neither one of us said much as we headed down and turned off onto the second floor where he'd left my suitcase. He stopped almost immediately and frowned down at me. "You don't have to go to bed if you don't want to. I just figured you were tired." He paused. "We can stay up if you want."

Was I tired? Yes. It was only eight, and it wasn't even pitch-black outside, but for the first time since I was younger than ten, I was more than ready to pass out before midnight. Plus . . . "I can go to bed." Then I thought about it. "Unless you don't want to."

Aaron flashed me a lazy smile. "I'm tired."

I nodded at him and let out a breath that was supposed to be calming but really felt more embarrassed. "Will you tell me everyone's name again tomorrow?" I whispered.

That mouth smirked. "Yeah."

"Was the girl with the cast Max's sister?"

"Yeah."

I nodded. "And the other girl?"

"Brittany. That's Des's girl."

I wasn't sure which one was Des but hopefully tomorrow I would. Just standing there, I could feel my eyes getting droopy, and Aaron must have noticed too because he let out another tiny snicker. "Let me show you your room before you pass out."

With sweaty hands I had clenched at my sides, I nodded, almost relieved. "Thank you so much for inviting me again," I told him as he led me toward one of six doors I counted, stopping at the one furthest away from the stairway. "I'm sorry for being so awkward, but hopefully tomorrow—"

Aaron shook his head. "Stop saying you're sorry. Everything is all right, Rubes. Right? I'm just me. You're just you. We'll be fine. You'll be back to giving me hell in no time with everyone around."

That had me smiling.

Which must have made him smile.

Something brushed against the balled-up hands I had at my sides, and I didn't need to know it was his knuckles. "I'm in the room right next to yours," he said, gesturing to the door just behind his shoulder with the hand he'd just touched me with. "The bathroom is the door in front of mine. There's another one upstairs. If you need me, any hour, wake me, all right? Get some sleep."

I nodded at him for a moment before reaching forward to grab ahold of his wrist. His skin was warm and his wrist thick, and that focus on me was almost too much. Sliding my grip down the length of his fingers, I dropped my hand and swallowed, trying so hard to act like this was all normal. "Goodnight. Thank you for inviting me again."

He dipped his chin down and handed over two of the four bottles of water he'd been holding before taking a step back, toward his door. "Night," he whispered, that smile still playing at his lips. "I'm glad you're here."

I was screwed. Here I'd come, expecting and hoping that this weekend would help me get over him and . . . I was screwed. Even if I knew this road went one way and one way only.

A little sister. That's what he saw me as. I couldn't let myself forget it.

I flashed him a smile I only partially felt before turning around and pushing the door open, dragging my suitcase in behind me. More white walls and seashells and sea dragons stared back at me in the small room that was quickly going dark as all traces of the sun completely disappeared. Flicking on the light switch, I kicked off my flats and stumbled toward the bed, ripping my clothes off and dropped the bottles of water beside the frame. Too tired to shower after wiggling out of my tights, I crawled on top of the mattress after shutting the gauzy mint-colored curtains. I'd just tugged the sheets up to my neck when I thought twice about it and jumped back off, grabbing my computer and phone from my weekend bag and hooking the smaller device up to charge. I'd call my mom tomorrow, or at least text her. She hadn't responded to my last message and I wasn't surprised.

I opened my computer and found a Wi-Fi connection, thankful that whoever owned the house had a framed portrait with the password on it directly in front of the bed. I launched the Skype app without thinking. It had barely finished logging me in when it pinged with an incoming message.

AHall80: Night, Rubes.

AHall80: I'm glad you're here.

RubyMars: Me too :)

RubyMars: I promise to try my best and not be an awkward twat tomorrow.

AHall80: You're not an awkward twat.

AHall80: Goofy

AHall80: Cute

AHall80: Not a twat

RubyMars: Stop.

AHall80: Why?

RubyMars: Because you don't have to say that stuff. I know what I'm like.

AHall80: Me too

AHall80: I'm falling asleep. Go to bed, Ru.

RubyMars: Okay, I will.

AHall80: Text your mom.

RubyMars: Yes, ma'am.

AHall80: . . .

AHall80: I'm ready for the sassy whenever you're ready to bring it.

RubyMars: I don't know if you're ready for it in person all day.

AHall80: I'm ready.

AHall80: Night. Tell me if you need anything.

RubyMars: I will. :) Goodnight.

AHall80: Night, Rubes.

Chapter Eighteen

It was still dark outside when I woke up.

Only the palest hint of blue lit up the curtain covering the window. It didn't take but a minute as I lay there in bed, groggy and grumpy, to remember where I was and who was in the room right by mine. I'd stayed up for an hour after I'd logged off Skype, snuggled there under the covers beating myself up for how awkward and quiet things had gone with Aaron on-and-off since he'd picked me up. There had been these moments that seemed so right, so similar to the way we had been online . . . and then there were the other moments where I'd crawled back into myself and let my nerves get the best of me.

I wanted to blame it on the fact that Aaron could practically be considered spectacular by any mortal woman, but I knew it was more than that. It came back to him being everything and more than I'd thought he would be. I'd lain there and thought about how he'd brought me water while I'd basically flipped out, and hadn't brought his friends to the airport, and hugged me, and held my hand, and . . . it was all too much. Too freaking much. Him as a person was beyond my expectation.

Sometimes it was easy to let people who had disappointed you in the past make you think everyone was like that, but apparently that wasn't the case. At least not with him. I wanted to have a good time this weekend. I wanted things to be as normal as they could be. I wanted . . . I wanted a lot of things, but I'd take what I could get.

Knowing there was no way I could go back to sleep after lying there for who knows how long, I got up and started going through my suitcase. In no time, I found clothes, underwear and my toiletry bag. I hadn't showered the night before and I'd regretted it, but I hadn't wanted to walk out of my room and chance running into someone.

Sure enough, the house was totally quiet when I opened my door and snuck into the bathroom. It didn't take long to shower, shave, and scrub off the makeup I'd left on from the day before, which was gross. I tried to be as quiet as possible as I headed back into my room to drop off my things.

For a second, I thought about staying in there until someone else got up but decided that's what normal Ruby would have done, so instead, I went right back out. Up the stairs, the oversized kitchen and living area were empty. Blue and lavender colors filled what I could see of the sky through the giant windows, and I knew it was only a matter of time before the sun took its throne. I grabbed a bottle of water from the pack on the floor that Aaron had picked at yesterday and headed toward the sliding doors connected to the living area. On the deck outside were a handful of colorful chairs and patio furniture. I closed the door and plopped down into the one furthest down the deck.

It was a lot cooler than I'd imagined it would be as I set the bottle on the floor beside the leg of the chair and brought my legs up, knees to my chest, heels close to my butt. Wrapping my arms around my bare shins, I shoved aside the idea of going back inside for a jacket and pants and simply sat there, sucking it up, watching the horizon just behind the row of houses facing the one we were at.

The silence and fresh air were wonderful. I wondered how long it would take for everyone else to get up, and then I wondered what we'd do that day besides go to the beach and grocery shopping. When I was done wondering about that, I thought about Aaron for about the hundredth time over the last twelve hours.

Coming here had been a mistake. I realized that. A giant mistake. The worst kind of mistake. Because I'd come to hopefully get over him, or at least cement our platonic relationship and move him into the friend zone, and in less than four hours, he'd pretty much built himself a house in I Will Never Look at Him as Just a Friend land, and that was worse.

But it wasn't like I had another choice.

I could talk to Aaron like he was the man I'd gotten to know online, I tried to tell myself for only the thousandth time. It would be the same thing as having a friend who was really, really unattractive. You had to see and focus on what was on the inside. Because really, that was all that mattered at the end of the day. Beauty faded . . . unless you were my mom and somehow managed to stay attractive every year.

And Aaron had proven himself to be a good friend plenty of times over the past few months. I didn't want to screw this up. I could keep it together and be a friendly, normal friend who wasn't making moony eyes at a guy who was so far out of her league, he saw her as a little sister. Me.

That thought was a lot more miserable than I would have liked it to be.

There was no way I'd been out there longer than half an hour when I heard the door slide open and found Aaron standing there, balancing a tray in his hands. When I went to stand up and help him, he shook his head. It took him a second to balance everything, but he slid the door mostly closed behind him and walked toward where I was sitting with a groggy, rough, "Morning" in that wonderful timbre that was almost hoarse so early in the day.

I whispered back, "Good morning," as I dropped my feet to the floor and sat up straight as he set the tray down on one of the small tables and took a seat on the chair closest to the one I was on. His blond hair was damp and his skin still held a hint of pink beneath the golden color. In a faded, old gray T-shirt that said HALL AUTO and aqua blue swim trunks that nearly reached his knees, he was barefoot.

"Did I wake you up?" I asked him as he started moving things I couldn't see around on the tray.

Aaron peeked over at me with a small smile that could have been a reserved one or a tired one, and shook his head a second before picking up something off the tray and holding out a plate in my direction. On it were two slices of toast, each topped with a perfect little square of butter.

I snorted and glanced at him, catching his smile cracking into a wider one.

"It's all we have until we go to the store, swear," he claimed, his expression telling me that might be the truth, but he was still enjoying messing with me.

Taking the plate from his hands, I tried pinching my lips together to keep from telling him he was the first person who had ever brought me breakfast unless I was sick, but I kept the words in my mouth. I locked them up and threw away the key. Settling the plate on my lap, I held back a gulp and smiled, feeling a little shy. "Thank you."

He winked as he leaned forward and angled the chair he was in to face mine more, before pulling another plate off the tray to his left and settling it on his bare knee. "Somebody needs to make sure you're eating."

I picked up a slice and held it an inch away from the plate, watching him out of the corner of my eye. "Remind me to buy some cream cheese or jelly when we go to the store."

He grinned this sleepy, tired grin.

"Really, thank you though," I repeated myself, just in case he couldn't tell I was just messing with him.

"You're welcome," he replied easily, almost lazily, his eyes flicking to mine quickly before lowering back to the plate. "I told you that I'd make sure you were good. We'll get something better later."

"It's perfect. This was really nice of you."

Aaron shrugged off my gratitude and leaned back as he took a bite out of one of the three pieces of toast on his plate. I did the same, taking turns between looking at him and glancing at the sliver of beach visible behind the house we were facing.

I zeroed in on the coloring under his eyes. "Did you sleep okay?" I asked him after I finished off the first piece of toast.

He lifted a shoulder a little more casually than I was comfortable with, but I was on to him and his vagueness already. "You?"

"Yeah." *Act normal, Ruby.* "This is really pretty," I said to him, gesturing forward with my chin. "This house is amazing."

Half of Aaron's mouth tipped its way up, but he changed the subject. "Do you want to go to the store with us to buy groceries? We're going to take turns cooking most nights."

Cook? "Sure. Tell me how I can pitch in."

He waved me off.

"I'm being serious. Make it easy on yourself and tell me how I can help. Otherwise I'll just do it anyway."

The other side of his mouth tipped upward too, and those brown eyes flicked my way. "I thought you weren't bossy?"

I could play the side-eye game if he wanted to. "Only when you're being stubborn."

That had him laughing as he plucked at another piece of toast and brought it up to his mouth, taking a big bite out of it. "I have this to look forward to every day while we're here then?"

My heart beat a little faster, but I ignored it. "I guess you do."

Aaron smirked as he wolfed down the rest of his bread, and I didn't take too long with what I had left. The moment I finished swallowing the last piece, he stood up and took the plate from me. "Want to watch the sunrise on the beach?" he asked. "If we go now, we'll probably make it."

I nodded.

I followed him back into the house, watching as he dropped our plates off in the sink, before turning to me with that easy-going expression that somehow looked like he knew something I didn't. He looked really tired. We headed down the stairs, skipping the second landing and continued on down. If he wasn't going to stop for shoes, neither was I.

When we made it to the bottom floor, Aaron stepped forward first, unlocking the door and swinging it open with a, "Rubies first" that had me holding back a smile that would for sure tell him how much I liked him.

I hadn't noticed the day before, but the driveway outside of the door was graveled, not paved, and the small rocks nipped at my bare feet. Aaron didn't comment as he closed the door behind us, slipping his long fingers through mine, and casually said, "Let's run for it."

Run for where, I had no clue, but when his hand tugged, I took off running beside him, dashing into the street between the houses and going slightly to the right where there was a path of wooden planks between an aqua blue home and a cream-colored monstrosity. I didn't notice what temperature the wood was, or worry about splinters, all I felt was the sand that had been spread over the path over time and the feel of Aaron's warm fingers.

It wasn't the Caribbean, but the water was beautiful, especially in the oncoming sunrise. White sand snuck up between my toes and over the tops of my feet as Aaron led us to the right. There were probably twenty umbrellas anchored into the sand within a fifty-foot stretch of beach, all of them spaced apart with beach chairs settled beneath them.

We didn't go to any of those. Instead, Aaron led us almost to the edge of the water, just before the sand became thick, damp and cool. Almost gracefully, he lowered himself until his butt hit the ground, his hand letting go of mine as he did it. He raised those brown eyes to me and made them wide as he propped his hands behind him. "You want to sit down, or are you going to keep panting standing up?"

I scoffed and fought the urge to kick sand at him before I flopped down just like he had. "We don't all run ten miles a day."

"Or one mile," he muttered, angling his hips just enough so that he was facing me and the water at the same time, the side of his foot moving just enough so that it brushed my own.

"Ha, ha."

He grinned. "I thought it's good for people with heart problems to do cardio?"

"I don't have a heart problem anymore," I reminded him. "And I like to go for walks—"

He coughed.

"—long walks, thank you very much."

"Long walks," he repeated. "And kickboxing."

I nodded at him. "I took a Zumba class three times a week for three months once."

He blinked. "What's Zumba?"

It was my turn to blink at him. "You dance to exercise."

The way he stared at me blankly made me snort.

"It was harder than you think," I said, earning a smirk from that mouth that I purposely hadn't thought about.

"I'll take your word for it."

I snickered, and before I knew what I was doing, I moved my foot to the side until it bumped with the side of his. "Are you still going to run now that you're back?" I asked.

He shrugged as his eyes swung toward the water. "Not as much. It relaxes me, but I don't love it."

What he meant too was that he had better things to occupy his time with than running just to make the day go by faster. That was one of the things I tried not to worry about with our friendship once his life got back to normal. About how he'd forget about me. Make less time to sit on his computer and chat . . . and then, eventually, he'd be gone, living his life. And if I was lucky, he might think of me once a month or once every other month and shoot me an e-mail. As time went on—

I was being a selfish jerk, wasn't I? Worrying about things I couldn't control? Expecting everyone to be like everyone else that had used me for something and then forgotten I existed?

"I like going for bike rides more," he admitted, breaking my thoughts when he nudged my toes with his sand-covered ones.

That had me perking up. "Mountain biking?"

"Yeah." He smiled. "You mountain bike?"

I shook my head. "No, but it's always sounded like fun. There aren't any mountains or hills in Houston. There are two trails that I know of, but they're usually packed with people because there's nowhere else for them to go. I'd be too scared to start there."

"There are lots of trails in Kentucky," he told me, giving me a little smile that sent my heart doing pit-pats it had no business doing.

"What kind of bike do you have?"

"A Yeti."

"Never heard of it. I still have my Huffy from when I was a kid."

I could tell by the creases at the corners of his eyes that Aaron was biting back a smile. "I bet you'd still fit on your kid-sized Huffy."

That got me side-eyeing him. "I know a lot of people shorter than me, thank you."

"Oh yeah?" He raised an eyebrow like he didn't believe me, which chances were, he didn't.

I nodded sarcastically. "Yeah."

"Where do you know them from?" he asked, those eyebrows still up. "From the Shire?"

The laugh that busted out of me had me tipping my head back and literally setting my foot totally on top of his as I reached over to poke him hard in the side. Aaron captured my hand as he laughed too. "I'm going back to the house," I whined when I could finally catch my breath.

"No you're not," he quipped, squeezing my fingers before slowly letting them go.

He smiled at me and I smiled at him, and I felt . . . I felt something. In my heart. On my skin. On my fingers and toes. Along my spine. It wasn't a tingling. It wasn't some earth-shattering sensation. It was something I wasn't totally sure of, but it was enough for my smile to grow wider.

Then he said, "I'm really glad you came, Ruby," and I didn't know my mouth could go so wide.

"I'm glad too." Sliding my foot off his, I didn't stop smiling. "I'm sorry for freaking out yesterday and then being so hot and cold."

"I told you. Don't apologize. It was fine."

Clasping my hands on my lap in front of me, I shrugged. "It could've been better. I feel bad not talking to your friends more. I don't want them to think I'm stuck-up or anything."

It was the tightening at his jaw that told me he didn't like something about what I'd said. "Somebody thought you were stuck-up before?"

"Once or twice, but I'm just quiet until I feel comfortable around complete strangers, you know? That's all."

His eyes bounced from one of mine to the next, his features still taut, and I could tell he was processing my words before he slowly let out a breath. His words were low again, understanding, so freaking Aaron. "I know, Ru. You're not. They won't think you're stuck-up."

"I hope not."

His smile was so soft I genuinely felt like it didn't matter what they thought as long as he liked me. But I couldn't think like that. "Don't worry." He gestured toward the rolling waves lapping close to our feet. "Look, it's about to come up any second now. Watch."

We sat there on the edge of the water, with his foot directly beside mine, that long upper body lined with lean muscles within touching distance if I really stretched to the side, and we watched the sun rise directly in front of us. Blue, purple, lavender, orange, red, and so, so yellow in a few places it made my heart hurt. I'd been a lot of places, but watching the sun rise that morning—because I'd never been awake early enough to watch it before—was something I couldn't forget. It felt like an awakening. Like nothing I had ever seen and everything I had, all rolled into one single, unforgettable event.

And when Aaron asked, "It's beautiful, huh?" I told him the one and only truth I had.

"It's really beautiful." And then I told him the second truth in my long list of things I couldn't deny. "I'm going to owe you forever for inviting me and showing this to me."

He didn't say another word and neither did I as the sun kept creeping upward, unrushed. I know at one point I held my breath at the same time the sound of two new voices from somewhere behind us broke the silence. I didn't look back, all I did was keep my eyes forward and swallow the rays entirely.

"I think I want to wake up every day and watch this," I whispered to him, pulling my knees into my chest so I could settle my chin on top of them. "It would be worth waking up early for."

And all Aaron said, in his low, soft-spoken voice that he'd been using on me since yesterday, with something in the notes I couldn't classify that sounded almost like hope, if hope had a sound and if a promise could be made without vocalizing it, was, "Any morning you want, Rube. I'll watch it with you."

"So, Ruby . . . I have an important question to ask you."

Scrunched into the middle in the back of Aaron's double cab pickup truck, I slipped my hands between my thighs and accepted that I'd gotten off easy on the way to the grocery store. I'd helped Aaron make a list that mainly consisted of salt and vinegar chips, Fritos, macaroni and cheese, and frozen pizzas while we'd waited around in the kitchen for everyone to wake up. Aaron, Des, Max's sister whose name I learned was Mindy, and Brittany, Des's girlfriend, and I had all climbed into the truck at exactly 10:05 a.m. Aaron had invited me to take the front seat, but I had waved him off because obviously Des's legs were longer than mine. Then, noticing that Brittany was five inches taller than me and that Mindy had a broken arm that probably shouldn't get jostled around, I'd offered to take the seat on the bench in the middle.

Mindy and Brittany had both been busy on their phones before we'd even gotten into the car and had stayed on them the entire trip to the grocery store. I'd only caught bits and pieces of each of their conversations over the music that Des had started playing in the truck, but I knew Brittany was on the phone with someone she worked with and Mindy was arguing with who I'm pretty sure was the other girl who had been in the accident with her because they'd been talking about pain medication and how it was affecting them differently.

Not that I was paying that close attention. I'd already texted my mom to let her know I was alive and kicking; there was no one else for me to message.

Half an hour later, with the groceries in the bed of the truck, we'd all climbed back in, no one on their phone. So I wasn't surprised when Mindy finally spoke up.

"Okay," I told her, taking in her light brown hair and a face whose youth and angles reminded me of Jasmine . . . if my little sister didn't have the crazy person glint in her eye.

The younger, very pretty girl had her broken arm propped against the car door. Her expression was serious. "Where did you get those tights from?"

Tights?

"The ones you had on yesterday with the cats on them. Where'd you get them?" she asked, like she'd read my mind.

I blinked, taking a second to process what she was saying. "Oh. Online. There's a store that I order things from that's cheap. I'll write down the link for you if you want," I answered her, only sounding a little awkward.

The side of Brittany's thigh touched mine as she asked, "And the skirt?"

My face definitely turned a little pink at the attention they were both giving me. "I got it from a thrift store and redid a lot of it, I'm sorry."

She blinked. "You redid it, how?"

"She makes costumes and dresses," Aaron piped in from the front, his brown eyes visible in the rearview mirror.

Brittany leaned further into me, narrowing her eyes a little in a way that didn't make me feel like it was judgmental, more just . . . curious. "Where do you live?"

"In Houston," I told her, cocking my head to the side just enough to make eye contact with the pretty black-haired woman that had been watching me closely on and off with a friendly expression on her face every time I'd caught her. I could do this. Everyone had been nice so far. "Are you in Shreveport?" I asked her, trying to make conversation.

"I live in Haughton. It's outside Shreveport," she explained, giving me an easygoing smile that relaxed me.

I nodded and tried to think of something else to ask her. "Have you been here before?"

"Yeah, we came last spring before Hall shipped out," she said.

I hadn't known that. Had I? I couldn't remember him mentioning if this was his first time in Port St. Joe, the town closest to the strip of peninsula called Cape San Blas, where we were staying, or not. Either way, it wasn't like it was any of my business to know where he'd gone before we'd met.

Even though I might have wanted to know everything.

"Do you have a boyfriend?"

I froze at the random question that came from my right, from the younger girl whose face was suddenly red like she couldn't believe she'd asked that. I guess I was too, a little. I'd never heard anyone just . . . ask that kind of question like that before.

"Ahh . . ." I trailed off, knowing the answer but . . .

She must have realized what the heck had come out of her mouth because she started stuttering, "I'm sorry. I'm so sorry. I don't have a filter—"

"It's okay—"

Mindy waved me off. "That's so rude. I've just been wondering because Max said that Aaron said you weren't his girlfriend—"

Why that felt like a sock to my stomach, I had no idea. It wasn't like I didn't know that. It wasn't like he didn't know I wasn't his girlfriend either.

"—and my mom always says guys and girls can't be friends, and I'm just trying to figure out why you would come if you aren't together, and oh my God, I'm still talking. I'm sorry," the girl, who couldn't have been older than eighteen, rambled on in the same breath.

I could only look at her.

"Jesus Christ, Mindy," that was Aaron from the front seat, glancing over his shoulder with a shake of his head.

"It's okay," I tried to butt in, even though I was positive my face was red. "I would probably wonder too." I just wouldn't ask outright something like that. It was one thing for everyone I knew and had known for years to know my miss after miss in the relationship business, but for this girl I barely knew to ask, was a little bit depressing. The whole world was aware that there was something strange about Aaron inviting me to come. There was no hiding it. There was no pretending like he saw me as something more than a . . . than a . . . *relative*. Ugh. But I told her the truth—"No"—and my face definitely turned red, if it hadn't already been.

"You just broke up with one?"

"No," I repeated myself. "I just haven't had one . . . in a while. Aaron is just my," I almost choked on the word but managed to get it out with a little bit of fake nonchalance behind it, "friend. One of my favorite friends."

And there were my two lies before I even knew I was going there.

I was not going to look at Aaron. Nope. Not then.

I forced a smile on my face and asked the girl another question before she could throw a new one out that I didn't know what to do with, "Do you have a boyfriend?"

The way she shook her head quickly, like she was disgusted. "Oh no. I don't have time for dumbasses."

I couldn't help but grin even as I faced forward again.

And it was Brittany beside me who chimed in with, "It takes a while to find one that isn't a dumbass, but there're a few out there."

I'm not sure why I glanced up at the rearview mirror again but I couldn't help but smile, especially not when Aaron's gaze flicked to mine. The way his eyebrows moved said he was probably smiling.

"How long did it take you, Brit?" the younger girl asked.

The woman beside me made a thoughtful noise as Des turned

in his seat to shoot her a look that wasn't meant for me to see. I wondered how long they'd been together. "Twenty-eight years."

From up front, I heard Des, the man with the green eyes, mutter, "Damn right" under his breath.

"Don't rush it, Mindy. He—whoever—you want is out there somewhere. You're still a baby, have fun and don't worry about relationships. I wish I could go back and skip some of the guys I dated when I was your age, believe me," was Brittany's advice.

If her words reassured Mindy too, I had no idea, but they did me. Wasn't that what I'd told Aaron before? How I hadn't missed out on anything? Not really.

Okay, maybe in a way I had.

The sigh that came out of Mindy had me glancing at her, but her attention was focused through the window. "One day. Who knows how long that'll be?"

Maybe it was because I saw so much of myself in her while she had a face like my little sister's, but maybe it was because I didn't want her to feel like she was alone, but I told her a tiny part of something I hadn't really ever admitted out loud to anyone. "I'm twenty-four and I still haven't found anyone who likes me enough as more than a friend. It's okay."

I didn't acknowledge until after the words were out of my mouth how sad and woe-is-me they sounded, but . . . they were the truth. I'd been my brothers' little sister, and now Aaron only held platonic feelings for me. It was one strike after another that I couldn't let myself forget no matter how badly I wanted to.

And it must have been a good thing to admit because I could see the seventeen-year-old smile a little at the window in her reflection.

But when I glanced forward again and just happened to look at the rearview mirror, I could see Aaron's eyes on me.

And I just smiled at him, hoping I wasn't coming off as pathetic as I thought I would after that comment.

Chances were, I did.

"You okay?" I asked Aaron the second we finished carrying all the groceries up the two flights of stairs, with everyone except him cursing over them.

With the upper half of his body mostly in the fridge as he put up four cartons of eggs and three gallons of milk, I could tell something was bothering him even though he lifted his shoulders almost casually. But it was too casual. He'd been quiet on the remainder of the trip home, letting Brittany and Des argue about who was the better cook between them. I'd let it go, but now everyone had disappeared when Aaron had offered to put up the groceries, I wanted to take the opportunity we had to be alone together again and ask.

"Are you sure?" I asked him as he took a step back and shut the white door.

Those dark brown eyes landed on mine and he nodded, his face too serious, too . . . distracted? I didn't know his body language well enough to be sure yet. When he changed the subject, it pretty much confirmed that he had something else going on in his head he didn't want to talk about. Just like when we messaged online. "Want to go to the beach?"

What I wanted was to know what he was thinking. What I could realistically get was a trip to the beach. "Yeah, sure," I agreed, watching his face closely. He'd looked tired that morning, but now that six hours had passed, there was something in his eyes that made him seem even more exhausted. Was he not sleeping well?

"I just have a few more groceries to put up and I'll meet you outside your room to go," he offered with a funky smile that seemed like a poor imitation of the ones he'd given me before.

What was going on with him?

I nodded, keeping the question buried deep in the back of my throat, and headed down the stairs toward the room I was staying in. It didn't take me too long to find my bathing suits, but what took the longest was deciding which one to wear. I put all three of them on before picking the most modest, this red one-piece with thin straps and a back that tapered into a V-shape halfway down my spine. There weren't a lot of benefits of having small boobs, but a non-supportive bathing suit was one of the pluses. Throwing a cover-up over it and shoving my towel, sunblock, sunglasses and the bottle of water I hadn't drank the night before into a canvas bag I'd brought with me, I put on my shoes and left my room, expecting Aaron to be changing or still be upstairs.

He wasn't.

He was already waiting in the hallway, leaning against his door like a model in a denim commercial, with a towel under one arm, a gallon of water that we'd bought at the store in hand, and that faint, unreadable smile on his mouth. "Ready?" he asked, straightening off the door.

"Yes."

Not sure how to act or what I should say, if there even was anything to begin with, we walked side by side in silence, down and out. The sky was bright and blue, and the wind was strong as we made our way toward the beach, weaving between the houses and onto the boardwalk leading to it. I spotted Brittany and Des to the right, Des under an orange umbrella with Brittany laid out on a towel, face down sunbathing.

"Is Max still not awake?" I asked Aaron in a whisper. He had already explained to me that Mindy had mainly just tagged along to San Blas to get out of the house; it wasn't like she could swim with her cast on.

Aaron made a snickering noise in his throat. "No. He works

a graveyard shift. It'll probably be closer to the end of the week before he's waking up before two."

"He's the one who works at the refinery?"

"Yeah."

I nodded as we headed closer to his friends, and took a deep breath at what I'd have to do next. I'd never really been too self-conscious about being in a bathing suit before, but that was mostly because I'd given up comparing myself to others. When you have one sister who works out all day and you have another sister and mom who are both slim and perfectly proportioned no matter how much they ate, you kind of had to. I was pretty small all around, except for my thighs and butt, but it was nothing to note when I'd seen Jasmine's buns of steel every day for years. There was nothing worse than comparing yourself to another woman because there was always going to be something that they had that you didn't. Always. It helped that my mom had always told me I was pretty just the way I was, even if I didn't always completely believe her. That's the kind of thing moms said. She'd even told my brothers they were handsome and those two looked like gremlins.

What might have also helped, as Aaron and I dropped our towels close to where Des was stationed on a lounger, with two arms crossed behind his head and sunglasses over his face, was that Aaron didn't see me as . . . more than a friend. I didn't have anything to prove to him . . . even if I would have wanted to. With my towel extended long-wise, I dropped the rest of my things on top of it and faced the direction of the water as I pulled my cover-up over my head and let it fall too.

I didn't bother looking behind me as I lowered myself onto my towel and settled on my butt, snatching the bottle of sun-block I'd brought and pouring a handful into my palm so I could start applying it to my legs. Out of the corner of my eye, I spotted Des sitting up and going to pick on a sleeping Brittany before they both stumbled toward the water. I managed to get both my legs saturated before I glanced to the side to find Aaron sitting there with his own towel maybe three inches away from mine. His gaze was so focused on the beach break, I frowned. I hadn't thought too much of how quiet he'd been, but . . . What was going through his head? Something bad? I could remember how quiet my brother had been for a while after he'd gotten back from his tour following his injury, and I didn't like Aaron doing the same thing, especially when I didn't know him well enough to have a solution . . . if there even was one.

Feeling something pretty close to panic, or maybe it was desperation, filling my belly, I reached over to poke him, not knowing what else to say or do to get him to stop making that distant face.

Luckily that was enough to get him out of his trance because he blinked once and turned to face me, an easygoing expression on his face finally, not the strange one that had been on there right before. "You okay?" he asked, looking at me like it was the first time he'd seen me in a long time, his gaze going from my face down, being totally obvious about checking out my bathing suit.

I wasn't going to think about it.

"Yes," I said to him, noticing he still hadn't taken his shirt off. "Are you?"

He did that quick nod again that made my stomach clench. What was going on with him?

"Sure?"

"Yeah," he said, his gaze finally swinging slightly lower, a dimple prickling at his cheek. "That's cute."

My face turned as red as my bathing suit. At the rate I was going, I needed to get a sunburn all over so it wouldn't be so obvious every day.

His index finger touched my right strap so lightly, I almost didn't feel it. "Did you make it?"

I fought the urge to squirm. "My bathing suit?"

"Uh-huh," he said, now checking out the little gold clasp right between where my barely B-cup boobs were.

No one had ever looked anywhere below my neck before. "No. It was Jasmine's, but she gave it to me." I picked at the strap he'd just finished touching, giving it a pop. "It looks better on her, but I like it."

The smile that came over Aaron's mouth was the most gradual, slowest thing I'd ever seen. It was almost pitying, but something about it cut that corner and made it so sweet, it confused me even more. And of all the words he could've said to me, he went with, "I doubt it, RC." And with that expression still on his face, he lifted his chin and frowned down at my skin. "You don't have a scar."

I made a noise in my throat loud enough for him to glance up at. "From my surgery?" I basically croaked, even though I knew that had to be what he was talking about.

Aaron nodded, his gaze flicking back down at the triangle of exposed skin on my chest.

"They didn't . . . the catheters were by my . . ." I waved my hand around my groin. "Hips."

That had him glancing back at me, one eyebrow up. "Yeah?"

"Yeah." I smiled.

Another slow smile crawled across that mouth I'd probably be daydreaming over for the rest of my life. "All right. Hurry up and finish putting sunblock on then, would you?"

I wrinkled my nose but reached for the tube, part of me glad he was letting the surgery talk go. I put more sunblock on my palm as I bounced my gaze from my palm to Aaron and back again, attempting to move the conversation along before he changed his mind. "Did you not bring any?"

Like every other man I'd ever known, he didn't "need" any.

I tipped my head to the side and gave him a flat look that had him cracking into a grin like he hadn't just been staring off into space minutes ago and then staring at my bathing suit and chest. "Fine," he finally groaned, taking the sunblock from where I'd left it balanced on my thigh.

Trying my best not to be obvious as I spread the cream over my forearms before moving up to my biceps and shoulders, I watched as he rubbed the barest amount into his legs, the white getting stuck in the light brown hairs and over the tops of his big, almost pale feet. There was a line somewhere a few inches above his ankle bone where the color of his legs changed almost dramatically to the shade of light tan his feet were. From his boots, I figured.

"Hey, don't be stingy. Get some more sunblock if you need it," I told him.

He let out this little snicker in his nose. But that was all. I smiled at him and he smiled back at me, before he dropped his hand and went back to applying sunscreen, his hands dipping beneath the hem of his shirt to rub at his chest without exposing more than a sliver of a lean hip and an inch of skin above his swim trunks.

I finished putting sunscreen on my face when Aaron rolled up to his knees on his own towel, his body facing mine. He didn't move for a second, and I didn't want to look at his face to see what he was focused on, until finally he said, "You missed a spot."

When his thumb went to the shell of my ear, smoothing sunblock on it before swiping down to rub at my earlobe, moving the small star-shaped studs there, I let him. I shouldn't have, but I did. Keeping my gaze on the center of my chest so he couldn't see the struggle going on inside of me was harder than I'd ever imagined, especially when he did the same thing to my other ear, and I had to hold in my breath to keep from panting.

He was touching my ears for freaking sakes. If I didn't know how sad my experiences with men were, I would have been more surprised at how pathetic I felt getting excited at him touching my earlobes of all things. Lame.

I swallowed and waited until Aaron moved his hand to the center of my face, his thumb swiping across my chin slowly before pulling back and saying, "There."

All I could do was manage to grind out a "thank you" that sounded like I was out of breath.

Aaron got to his feet and I did the same, rubbing some more cream under the seam of the bathing suit on my bottom. I was doing that when Aaron's shirt fluttered to the sand. *He was shirtless.* It shouldn't have been a big deal, because how many times had I seen a shirtless guy? A thousand? *Thank you, Internet.* I could be calm. Be cool.

I made sure not to suddenly look up and ogle him or make him self-conscious as I kept rubbing sunblock into my skin. When it had been long enough, and I couldn't think of anything else to stall with, I let out a breath and had a smile already on my face when I raised my eyes all casual and friendly. Standing under the sun, the difference between the almost bronze color on his face, neck, and arms, and the lighter, slightly tan shade on his chest, legs, and feet, was pretty apparent. I would never call it a farmer's tan though. There was no hint of red or pink on his skin, like my mom or Tali would get if they were under the sun for too long. No matter how much those two tried, they never got tan. They were either white or red, there was no in-between.

Aaron was not one of those people. He was light gold and he was gold, there was no hiding it. But the main thing that there was no hiding from was that body under the three different shades of his skin tone.

Stick a needle in me, I was *done*.

I saw the rest of my life in that split second.

There was never going to be any getting over Aaron. Ever. I was going to die alone. I accepted that as I gave up trying to be sneaky, taking in the way he was built. He wasn't big and bulky, or barrel-chested in any way. Aaron was slightly thicker than a swimmer but had their physique, all abs and shoulders and long biceps. He was perfect. Absolutely perfect. That saying about God breaking the mold when they made someone had been written with Aaron's birth in mind. Each muscle looked like it had been chiseled, each bone perfectly sculpted. Even his nipples were perfect. How? *How?*

How was I supposed to look at this for nearly an entire week and know *he was just my freaking friend?*

The answer was: I had no idea how that was supposed to happen. I really didn't. I'd lied to myself and tried to convince myself it was possible, but it wasn't, was it?

I swallowed and looked away, reminding myself not to be that person. I could do this. I could survive this week. I had to.

"Ready?" he asked, making me glance back at him, but that time, keeping my gaze on his face.

There was a knot in my throat as I nodded. "Yeah. But if you want to go ahead of me and hang out with your friends, it's fine. I don't mean to take up all your time." His mouth did that turn thing. "I can be alone."

His Adam's apple bobbed. "Ru," he said in that calm way. "I'd rather hang out with you." And then, as if that body on display hadn't been enough to remind me of how shitty of an idea coming here had been, he went on to add, "You don't have to be alone."

If my smile was tight and said *"you're killing me,"* it didn't reflect on his face. All I could do was make a sound in my throat that could have meant anything.

We were wordless as we made our way forward. The stretch of beach to the right and left was packed with people, but not so many that it felt crowded. Mostly, it was family after family in groups of every size, with kids running, sand castles in the process of being built, and cooler after scattered cooler.

The water was warmer than I expected when I stepped into it. "Drag your feet through the sand, so you don't accidentally step on a stingray," Aaron warned over his shoulder.

A stingray? In the water? That I could step on?

I'd been too busy trying not to stare at the smooth expanse of Aaron's back and his small waist with two tiny dimples settled right at the base; I hadn't really thought about anything swimming around in the water around us. I'd been to the Caribbean three times in the past with my family on vacation, and my mom, who wasn't a fan of snorkeling, had always booked us at hotels with crystal clear water nowhere close to reefs. I'd never been snorkeling before. The water here was pretty darn clear, but . . .

It was fine. No big deal. There were probably hundreds of families just on the few miles of beach stretch by here. What were the chances that—

I shrieked.

I could be woman enough to admit that I shouted at the top of my lungs the second something brushed my leg in the water.

I could also be woman enough to admit that when whatever it was touched me, and I yelled in this high-pitched voice that could have made a dog howl, I jumped.

I jumped in the air.

I projected myself at the closest thing to me despite being hip-deep in the water. That closest thing being six feet two inches of man named Aaron. Except at that point, Aaron hadn't been facing me or had his back to me, we had been practically beside each other, and it was only thanks to his lightning-quick reflexes at hearing me shout that he managed to catch me right before I barreled into him.

"Are you okay?" he asked quickly, his right arm winding around my waist instantly as he tipped that handsome face down to look into the mostly clear water below us. I wasn't imagining the protective, worried expression that had taken over his features the moment I'd shrieked. It had been there, for sure.

"Yeah, yeah," I gasped, looking down too, suddenly embarrassed that I'd . . . done that.

"What happened?" he asked, still sounding worried as he turned us in a half circle to look at another area. "Did you step on a ray? Are you all right?"

I swallowed and tapped his shoulder so he could let me down.

He didn't. He was still looking around at the water. Still holding me against him.

Of all the things . . . "Something touched me," I admitted, sounding just as sheepish as I should have.

He got it.

He stopped, his head rolling up slowly while I was there, for all intents and purposes, on top of him. One of his eyebrows went up and he asked, taking his time with every word, "Something touched you?"

Way to go, Rubes. I fought the urge not to cough and almost lost. I wanted to look away too, but I'd done this to myself. I had to own up to it. "I think it might have been a fish . . ." I mumbled just loud enough so chances were in my favor that he didn't actually hear me.

He did. It was the way he swallowed that told me he'd heard. I could see a brown iris move in my direction. I could feel the tension in his upper body as he kept talking slowly, "There's no fish around here."

"It's the ocean. Of course there are fish around here. He might have just swam off really fast."

I didn't need to look directly at his eyes to know he was blinking. His voice was a little hoarse. "You think so?"

He was so full of crap.

"Maybe."

Those lips went tight together, so tight there was a line of white where they met. His throat bobbed and I knew, *I knew* he was trying not to laugh. "Ruby," he practically whispered my name. "Honey, how many times have you been in the ocean?"

I felt myself deflate just a little even though he'd called me honey. *Honey*. What you'd call a sweet little kid who'd fallen off her bike and eaten asphalt. "A lot." I cleared my throat and gave him a strong side-eye, seeing him just well enough. "But I'm more of a pool person usually. You know, Houston. You don't exactly go to Galveston to swim for hours."

He was pinching his lips together tighter as he nodded, his grip still firm. He'd stopped blinking at some point. The fingers on my hip tightened.

I could tell. *I could tell* he was about to make a joke about it, so I beat him to it with a "Shut up" that had him swallowing even harder than any time before.

His eyes were closed and he was smiling like an idiot when he said, "The only fish I've seen were minnows by the edge of the water."

"Sure," I agreed, not hiding my frown of shame as I extended my legs, wanting to get down, and he slowly, finally lowered me until my feet dipped back into the water.

He was still grinning and trying so hard not to laugh when he pointed toward Des and Brittany further ahead of us, already deeper in the water, dog-paddling. He snickered, his voice shaky, "Safety in numbers."

All I did was give him a dirty look, deciding I deserved that, but walked beside him further into the water until we met up with his friends, my paranoia right there. Brittany smiled brightly at me, her head slightly propped out of the water, from where she was now partially floating on her back. "Did you get stung?"

"Excuse me?" I asked like an idiot.

"Did you get stung by a jellyfish? We heard you yell," she explained.

My face turned red; without a doubt in my mind, it had to have. There was no way it hadn't. Where was a big wave when I needed one? "Oh, uh, no. I stepped on something," I gradually managed to get out, looking straight forward and not at the man at my side.

"It was sharp," Aaron breathed out from where he stood not even a foot away. "Really sharp."

If Des or Brittany saw me kick him from the side, neither one of them said a word.

"I know, Mom. I love you too."

The sigh that came over the receiver had me shaking my head. "If you loved me," she started to say for about the tenth time in the last fifteen minutes we'd been on the phone.

"I do love you. I'm fine, I promise," I assured her from my spot sitting cross-legged on the bed of the room that I'd be sleeping in for the rest of the week. "I'm having a good time and you'd like everyone I'm with."

My mom made a noise that said she didn't want to believe me, but . . . "Fine. Okay. I know you're not a liar, Rubella. Not like these other kids who only call me when they want something." She muttered something under her breath that sounded suspiciously like Jasmine's name. "Be careful and text me at least once an hour."

I snorted.

"Okay, okay," she countered, and I could hear the smile in her voice. "Text me at least and let me know Jaws hasn't come and eaten you."

And then I wondered why I was such a chicken. I couldn't trip without my mom claiming I was "*this* close to breaking my leg."

"With my luck, it'll be Shamu that gets me, but okay, I'll text you and let you know everything is okay," I assured her.

"Love you, Squirt."

"Love you, Mom. Goodnight."

"Goodnight," she said before hanging up. It was already way past her usual bedtime.

I'd been surprised when my phone had started ringing at nearly midnight that Sunday night and I'd seen her name flashing across the screen. I'd been in bed on my computer after a long day at the beach that had given me a hint of a sunburn on my neck and shoulders. Des and Brittany had made dinner that night, some kind of wedding meatball soup that had been so delicious everyone had gone for seconds and thirds. Afterward, we'd all gathered around the television in the living room and watched the first *Star Wars* movie. Aaron had caught my smile while he'd loaded it into the DVD player, and I'd known he'd suggested it just for me. I knew it.

I had started falling asleep on the couch toward the end, and by the time the credits were rolling, I'd told everyone goodnight and headed downstairs while they all stayed up there doing . . . whatever it was they were doing.

But now, getting off the phone with my mom after a fifteen-minute-long conversation . . . I wasn't so sleepy. I knew there was no way I could fall asleep. Besides, I'd taken a nap beneath the beach umbrella for an hour at some point after we'd eaten a lunch of sandwiches and chips, before heading back to the water for more.

For a few moments, I debated staying in my room, just fooling around on my computer since I didn't have anything to work on, but decided I didn't want to. Opening the door, I could hear the sound of a television on in one of the rooms, but couldn't tell which one it was. The lights seemed to be off beneath the door of each one.

Up the stairs, I found all the lights on, even the television. Sitting in front of it, on the big couch with his feet propped up on the white wicker coffee table, with his arms crossed over his chest, was the only person in the house I would have really wanted to see. He must have heard someone coming up the stairs because his head rolled to the side, his expression calm and almost blank, and when it must have registered to him that it was me, a small smile covered his mouth.

He gestured me over with a tilt of his head.

I went. Of course I went. "Hi," I said as I crossed in front of the coffee table and plopped down on the couch cushion beside him.

"Hey," he whispered, his head lolled to the side to watch me as lazily as possible. "Woke up?"

"No, my mom called. I just got off the phone with her," I explained.

"Everything all right?"

The fact that he'd worry something wasn't right as the first thing, made my chest ache. "Yeah, she just wanted to make sure I was still alive," I tried to joke, watching for a hint of a smile or some kind of pleased expression on his face.

And there it was. "You told her we're treating you good?"

"Yes. I told her she'd like all of you a lot," I said. "You can't sleep?"

He shook his head, so lazy his neck didn't even support it so he could do it properly. "I'm tired, but I can't wind down." Unlike me, he hadn't napped on the beach. I hadn't asked why he didn't, but I could guess.

"You don't want to lie in bed and see if that helps?"

He didn't say anything for a second, and I was just starting to think he was going to ignore my question when he said, "That room makes me claustrophobic. I can sleep in there, but I can't . . . hang out in there."

I wasn't sure I understood, but I smiled and nodded at him anyway. "Want me to grab you a pillow and a blanket so you can try to sleep out here?"

"No, Rubes, I'm all right," he replied. "I'll get over it. I just need to wait it out."

"It's not the same thing, but I have a hard time falling asleep most nights too. I can't get out of my head, I think about all these things, and it keeps me up."

Those brown eyes blinked lazily. "Like what?"

I hesitated and lifted my shoulders, remembering that this was him. "Everything. I nitpick little things I did or said throughout the day. I think about things I can't control. I used to think about what I would do the day I quit my jobs, and if I could do my own business, or at least find something or someone with work that appreciates me more . . . That's how you know I was pretty much fantasizing. I know that would never happen. I just . . . I'd lie there and think about everything. Even other people's problems. My dumb problems. It's kind of lame."

"That's not lame."

I shrugged.

Aaron watched me for a second before letting out a long breath, his eyes going up to the high ceiling of the living room before flicking back down to meet mine. "I think about stuff too."

"Like what?" I asked, figuring the worst he'd give me was a vague answer.

But he didn't. "Like you said, shit I can't control. Could never control. I go back and replay things from years ago and wonder what I could have done differently."

I didn't want to interrupt him, but at the same time I had a dozen questions I wanted to ask him. The problem was, I'd realized that while I wouldn't call him secretive, there were a lot of things he didn't want to talk about. Things he actively avoided. As much as I might want to know, I didn't want to force him to do something he didn't want to do. I hated when people did that to me, so I kept my mouth shut as he kept going.

"I think about what the hell I want to do and then think about how I don't know what that is."

"What do you mean?" I couldn't help but ask.

His chest rose and fell, and he glanced back at the ceiling, his body language trying to tell me this was casual, but I knew it wasn't. "I don't know what I want to do when I get out, or even if I want to get out," he explained, and I figured he was talking about the army. "The idea of . . . failing . . . of not figuring things out really messes with me."

I must have reared back at his comment. "If you're a failure, I am too. But we're not." Maybe I was, but I couldn't admit that right then.

He shook his head in this way that seemed a little too resigned for me, and when he went back to his tactic of changing the subject, it made my skin ache. "I've stopped trying to look forward to things too, and I don't know when that started."

Was that the sound of my heart breaking?

Aaron still wasn't looking in my direction as he continued. "I want to, you know? I want to be excited about things, but it's hard. I expect the worst all the time. I know I've told you before I don't like to focus too much on the future, but sometimes when all you can focus on is what's going on right now . . . it's tough. It's all kind of one giant thing. Not knowing what I want to do, not being able to look forward to what's to come. I just need to figure it out. I will, I'm just tired I guess," he tried to explain, his tone a little tired, a little glum. That blond head of hair rolled to the side and Aaron widened his eyes, shaking his head like he could just shake off his thoughts and mood. "I'm a blast to be around, huh?"

His words were sarcastic, but I knew he didn't mean them to be rude. So I told him, trying to stay broad with my statement because his words weighed down on me so much, "I wouldn't call you a party. You'd be more like the bartender at the party, making sure everyone else was having a good time," I tried to joke. "I'm not the best person to give you life advice or anything, but I get it, to a certain point, what you mean. Everyone needs something to look forward to. You don't have to live your life anticipating the future or dreading it, but you can have these little things you look forward to every day. I know you'll figure everything out. You don't have to do it right now.

"I hated high school," I confessed. "The only way I got through it was because of my friends. I'd look forward to eating lunch with them and planning what we'd do that weekend. I hated college too, and the only reason I finished it was because I kept telling myself that the faster I passed my classes, the faster I'd get out of there and do what I really wanted to do. There's nothing wrong with that."

Mahogany eyes lingered on me for a moment, looking too thoughtful.

"Anything can happen any time, Aaron. You have to take what you can get when you can get it," I said to him, giving him a smile that I hoped he appreciated.

There was something about his nod that made me feel like there was so much about him I still didn't completely understand, and maybe I never would. And it wasn't my place or my responsibility, and it sure wasn't a good idea, but I reached across the sofa and covered the top of his hand, which had been resting on his chest, with mine. And I squeezed it.

And I told him, "You can start small. Look forward to . . . the smell of fresh coffee. The smell of a pizza you'll have for dinner. The way nice, clean, cool sheets feel when you crawl into them." I squeezed his hand and made sure those brown eyes were on me when I told him, "Plumbing."

The smile that came over his face at my last word was worth . . . everything. Everything in my kingdom for that smile. I'd never felt more powerful in my life than I did in that moment.

And then, like he hadn't just slayed me, Aaron murmured, "Have I told you today that I'm glad you're here?"

"Not today."

He spread his fingers and laced them through mine, still smiling. "In that case, I'm really glad you're here, Ru."

It shouldn't ever surprise me why I was so caught up with him. It really shouldn't. Who else would ever be half as warm and kind and funny as this man beside me? I should be grateful he treated me the way that he did when all that was between us was friendship. How would he be with a girlfriend?

The brush of his thumb along the side of my hand had me snapping out of my daydreaming. "You never told me you finished college or what you went to school for."

"Oh." I scrunched up my nose. "I did. Accounting."

He blinked. "Accounting?"

"Yeah. It's what my mom and dad both went to school for. I didn't know what else to study, and I'm not too horrible with numbers."

He made an amused sound of disbelief. "I can't see you being an accountant."

I laughed. "Yeah, me neither. I hated it. But by the time I realized how much I hated it, it was too late and I wasn't about to waste my mom's money and the partial scholarship I'd gotten and start over. That's why my mom and her husband are always trying to get me to join the company they work for. I have a degree in it. It would make sense."

"Why didn't you go to school for fashion design?" he asked, catching me totally off guard, because how the heck did he even know you could go to school for that?

It took me a second to get my thoughts together because I was so thrown off. "Ah, because everyone told me I needed to get a 'real' degree." Was that disappointment I was feeling in myself or something else? "Both my parents said I needed to finish school so I could have a 'backup,' and I always figured I could do whatever I wanted to do afterward. I told you I did my alteration work and the dresses on the side the entire time."

Aaron nodded, but I could tell he didn't agree with what I'd done.

Honestly, a part of me understood. It had been a waste for me to go to school for something I wasn't passionate about. Here I had this degree, and I would still rather make a fraction of what I could and do what I wanted instead. But I'd done what my parents wanted, like I always had.

"I know it's stupid," I reasoned, taking my turn to be way more nonchalant about something that wasn't. "But I can't take it back now. I'm trying not to always do what everyone else wants me to out of guilt and just wanting to make them happy. Anymore at least. That's why I'm here."

His mouth twisted to the side and he nodded, giving my fingers a squeeze where they were, not having moved even a little bit off his chest. "I want that for you too, Ru. You're a lot braver and self-reliant than you give yourself credit for, you know that?"

My face flushed at the compliment, and I wasn't sure whether to nod like I agreed, because I really didn't, or shrug and play it off. So I didn't do either. I just sat there like a lump of coal.

Luckily Aaron grinned. "All right. I'll drop it. You want to watch a movie or a show?"

Chapter Nineteen

Mom: Did you become fish bait?

Me: No, I'm still alive.

Mom: OK have fun

Mom: Not too much fun.

Mom: Don't show up on those girls gone crazy videos and embarrass us all

Me: LOVE YOU

Mom: I'm serious, Squirt. They show those girls on commercials. Jonathan would have a heart attack

Me: I would never do that and you know it. I'll text you later.

Mom: I never thought you would go on vacation without my permission

Me: Mom, I'm 24.

Mom: You're still my baby

Me: Jasmine is your baby.

Mom: Jasmine came out an old woman.

Mom: Need to get up. Ben says hi.

Me: Okay, text you later. I really am okay. Everyone is being nice to me. Love you.

Mom: Love you 2

"Good morning."

Setting my phone on the floor beside the leg of the deck chair,

I turned my upper body to face Aaron at the sliding doors and smiled at him sleepily. We'd only gone to bed four hours ago, after we'd both started dozing off watching infomercial after infomercial, running commentary on them the entire time. I couldn't remember the last time I'd laughed so much, and that was saying something because I almost always had a good time around my friends and family.

"Morning," I said to him in a low voice. "You couldn't sleep either?"

He shook his head as he closed the door behind him, balancing a tray in his one free hand as he came toward me. His face held all the signs of how tired he was, and I was positive I looked the exact same. "Yeah, I couldn't go back to sleep," he replied, setting the tray down on the small table and taking the same seat he'd used the morning before.

A girl could get used to this, I thought, as I took it from him with a "thank you" that hopefully didn't sound like *I love you* or *you're amazing*. "You really don't have to do this," I let him know, giving him a smile at the same time.

He had his back to me as he picked up his own bowl from the tray. "I know," was all he said as he faced me again with his breakfast held against his chest. "Texting your mom?" he asked with a raise of an eyebrow.

"Yeah," I told him with a smirk. "She's making sure I'm alive, basically telling me not to flash my boobs at a camera and trying to convince me to text her every hour."

"Every hour?"

"Yes."

He laughed.

"I know. She's lucky if any of my other siblings call or text her once while they're on vacation. She's nuts."

"You can give her my number if you want," he offered.

Give my mom his number. Why? *Why?* Why did he have to

be so damn near perfect? It wasn't fair. It really wasn't. What also wasn't fair was that I now needed to tell him the truth about what I'd done. "I did give her your cell phone number last night in case of an emergency. I hope that's okay," I said to him.

He blinked. "Yeah, it's fine." Aaron stirred his spoon into the oatmeal, giving me a side look I couldn't miss. "Did you give her my social too?"

My face flamed up for what must have been the thousandth time since I'd met him two days ago. I wanted to lie, I really did. But I had promised him I wouldn't, and I didn't want to go back on my word. So I told him the truth, even though I pretended my oatmeal was the most interesting thing on the planet. "I wrote it down on a piece of paper and stuck it under my bed."

There was a pause. Then, "How would anyone know to look there for it?"

I gave him another side look and pretended I cleared my throat because there was something there and not because I was ashamed I'd done what any other sensible woman would have done. "I left a note with my stepdad with instructions, just in case something happened," I practically whispered. "He's the most trustworthy one in the whole house."

Aaron didn't say anything.

He didn't say anything for so long I slid a look at him.

But when I did, his pinched eyes and equally pinched mouth were the first things that I focused on. Followed by that was the fact that his shoulders and upper body were shaking just a little, just a little, little, little, so little that I hadn't been able to sense it sitting next to him. After a moment, his right hand reached up toward his face and he slapped the palm of his hand over his eyes as he said very, very slowly, "What did the instructions say?"

Blushing for the fifty-first time, I admitted it. "That if I go missing to try and contact you first. I put your name and number on there, and your dad's PO box. I also wrote where they can find your social and Max's address," I muttered, feeling so ashamed with myself but also proud that I expected the worst and that's what a smart girl would do. "Then I wrote that no one better take my things until I've been missing at least two years, after that they're allowed to give up hope finding me."

He said nothing. Not a single thing, and it only made me want to go searching for my black hole again.

"I'm sorry. It wasn't like I was expecting you to be a serial killer or a sex trafficker or anything, but you can't be too careful, you know what I mean? Imagine—" I had to clear my throat again before I could get the words out "—imagine if I was your sister. You'd tell me to do the same thing, wouldn't you?"

One deep brown eye opened and looked at me, his beautiful, handsome face slightly pink. Aaron nodded, just a little, just enough to notice. But it was his dimple that caught my eye. "I'm not giving you shit over it. That's good you did that," he managed to get out with that cute dent still out and about.

"Okay," I mumbled back at him, still embarrassed that I'd practically admitted that I didn't trust him enough, like those wives who thought their husbands were going to kill them and left letters behind pointing fingers at them. "I do trust you though. I think if someone tried to take me, you'd at least fight them for me a little . . ." I watched his face for a moment before narrowing my eyes. "Wouldn't you?"

That had his other eye popping open, his cheeks still slightly pink, but everything else about him completely alert. "You know I would."

Why that pleased me so much, I wasn't going to overanalyze.

"If someone tried to take you, I know aikido, some jiu-jitsu, and kickboxing," I offered him up. "But my dentist says I have really strong teeth, so I'd be better off trying to bite someone's finger or ear off instead."

Aaron's eyebrows climbed up his forehead almost comically. "Like a little Chihuahua," he suggested, the spoon going into his mouth with a sly grin.

I winked at him, immediately regretting it. I didn't want it to come across like I was flirting. "I was thinking more of a piranha. I've only had one filling in my entire life," I told him, wishing each word coming out of my mouth wasn't coming out of it.

If he thought I was being awkward or a flirt, he didn't make it known. "Or a raptor."

"A lion."

"A tiger."

"Did you know a jaguar has twice the strength in its bite than a tiger does?"

Aaron frowned as he took another bite of his oatmeal. "No shit?"

"No. Two thousand pounds per square inch. They're the only big cat that kills their prey by biting its head, through bone and everything. A tiger bites the neck of whatever animal they're eating to cut their air and blood flow off. Crazy, huh?"

He looked impressed. "I had no idea."

I nodded. "Not a lot of people do."

"Is there anything that bites harder than they do?"

"Crocodiles. The really big ones. I'm pretty sure they have about 4000 or 5000 psi bites." For the fifty-second time, I shrugged. "I like watching the Animal Channel and Discovery," I said, making it sound like an apology.

Aaron gave me that soft smile that made me feel like my insides were on fire. Then he winked. "I don't know much about crocodiles, but I know all about alligators," he offered. "Did you know there are only two species left in the world?"

"There are?"

"American alligator and the Asian alligator. More than a fifth of all of them live in Florida."

"We have some gators in Texas. There's a state park by Houston where you can go and you can usually see a bunch. I went camping there one time."

One corner of his mouth tilted up as he chewed. "Look at you, Rebel Without a Cause."

With anyone else, I'd probably think they were picking on me, but I could see the affection on Aaron's face. I could feel the kindness that just came off him in waves, so I winked back at him. "I live life on the edge. I should start teaching a class on how to be bad."

"Right? Quitting your job, coming to Florida even though you were worried . . ." He trailed off with a grin and a look out of the corner of his eye.

"I pretty much have my masters and license to practice. I'll teach people everything I know."

I didn't miss the other quick look he shot my way. "As long as they don't ask about boyfriends."

I shoved at his shoulder before I realized what I was doing and laughed, loud, so much louder than I had so far. "I'm just waiting for the right one. I thought you were on board with me waiting now?"

Those deep brown eyes met mine, and he flashed those white teeth at me. "I am. What are you rushing for?"

That was pretty much the complete opposite of what he'd been drilling into my head since he'd found out about my lack of relationships, but he was right. What was the rush? It wasn't like any other guy I'd meet anytime soon—or ever—would or could compare to this one. I could feel it. Clearing my throat, I looked down at my bowl of oatmeal again as I said, "The good thing is, now I can quit going to church trying to pick up all the divorced and widowed dads."

His snicker had me glancing at him out of the corner of my eye. "You're never going to let that go, are you?"

"Nope." I smirked, taking in that handsome face that had me sighing on the inside. "Is that okay?"

The spoon was on the way to his mouth when he said, "I wouldn't expect anything else from you." Then he winked again. "Eat your food so we can go," he ordered right before taking another bite, his eyes on me, his cheeks showing he was smiling even as he chewed.

Why? What had I done in another lifetime to deserve this?

I did what he said and managed to get about three bites in before his words really clicked. "Where are we going?" I asked him the second I'd swallowed my food.

"Fishing," he said casually.

I said the words slowly to make sure I'd heard him correctly. "Did you say fishing or swimming?"

That time he did slide me a sneaky look. "Fishing," he enunciated.

"Swimming?"

Aaron finally turned to look at me with a smile on his beautifully sculpted face. "F-i-s-h-i-n-g."

I hummed in my throat and ate two bites before I said, just low enough for him to barely hear me, "I don't really want to."

He had the nerve to wink at me again. "I figured. That's why we should go."

"I don't have a rod."

"There are some here you can borrow."

Setting the plate on my lap, I started to reach for my left wrist with my right hand, "My wrist is a little sore . . ."

He snorted, seeing straight through my crap.

I'd asked for this, hadn't I? It didn't mean I had to be graceful about it the entire time. With a groan, I pretty much made a crying face and slowly nodded. Basically whining out a "Fine" that had him grinning in triumph. "I'm not touching it while it's still alive though."

Aaron had a big grin on his face when he agreed, "Deal."

"How have you never been fishing before?"

He hadn't been lying when he said there were extra fishing rods at the house. Part of me had been hoping that he'd change his mind . . . or that it would rain, but neither thing had happened. After we'd gone to get four fishing licenses—one for him, one for me, another for Des and Brittany, who had overheard us arguing about going fishing and decided they should get one too—I'd started to accept that it was going to happen regardless of whether I wanted it to or not.

I could have done without it.

Standing beside the truck, with both poles in my hands, I shrugged as he pulled out the minnows he'd bought at the same store we'd gotten our licenses at. Fresh minnows that I wasn't going to touch. Nope.

"My dad took my brothers a few times from what I remember, just off the pier at the beach closest to us," I explained, watching him. "After he moved back to California, there was never enough time when he'd come down to visit to just . . . take us fishing, you know?" I eyed the bucket he had the minnows in and grimaced. "Not that it's ever really interested me to begin with."

Aaron snickered with his back to me. "It's pretty relaxing if you give it a chance."

I highly doubted that.

"It won't be that bad. If you hate it, you don't ever have to do it again," he told me, making it seem like that would be the case for the rest of my life. Just like that. I'd never have to do it again.

While I appreciated what he was implying, I accepted that

I needed to quit being a chicken and just . . . do things. Even if it meant touching a minnow to put it on the hook or whatever it was called. Even if I screamed while I did it and maybe cried during and after. "Did your dad take you fishing when you were younger?"

His head bobbed in a nod. "Almost every Sunday. He worked a lot, but Sundays were our days, after church, to go do things as a family. When we'd go on summer vacation, we'd always go somewhere where we could fish."

"That sounds nice."

"Yeah. I still remember it. That's the whole point about doing family things together. I remember most of them, especially after our mom left." He'd been speaking so easily before he dropped the "M" word that I almost missed the way his entire body tensed up in reaction.

He'd rarely mentioned his mom before to me. I'd wondered what the deal with her was, but now that I knew, and now that I'd seen his reaction . . . I wished I hadn't. It didn't take a genius to know it was a sensitive spot for him.

And it also made a ton of sense how he'd react to my mom being overprotective and his views on marriage. My dad had left too, but he'd still been an active member of my life even afterward. I would never call my dad my "biological father" or anything like that. He was my dad, my father figure through thick and thin. I'd never doubted he loved me.

As much as I wanted to contemplate what he'd just said, I knew I only had a matter of time to change the subject and act like his mention was no big deal. He didn't want to talk about it, and I understood. So I changed the subject. "Our family bonding time in my family was on Sunday with everyone cleaning the house. My mom would make us all chip in making dinner. Then we'd all sit around and watch a movie. Every Sunday. My brothers wouldn't even bother asking to go out with their friends on that day because it didn't matter if they were seventeen, *that* was family day for whoever was still living with her."

He chuckled and it only sounded partially forced. "Does she still do that?"

I snorted and watched as he rolled his shoulders back, as if willing them to relax. "No. She stopped after she married husband number three. By that point, I was already a sophomore in high school, Jasmine had her ice-skating going on, and my brothers and Tali were older. But now, everyone still comes over at least once every other week for dinner at the same time or breakfast or whatever. I don't actually know how they schedule that to make it work. I guess I never thought about it. They just show up."

"Have you talked to any of them beside your mom since you got here?"

"No. I don't bother them when they go somewhere without me. None of them have messaged me except my little sister. I'm a little worried Jasmine hasn't sent me any more texts, but I'm hoping it's just because she's mad and my mom has been relaying my messages to her," I explained. "Either that or she's taken all my stuff and she's being sneaky." I smiled. "Have you talked to your dad?"

"No." He slammed the tailgate closed and faced me. "He knows I'm here. I told you, we're not all that close."

That just sounded sad as hell to my ears. "Because of you going into the military?"

Aaron shrugged, and in this case, it didn't seem to be an upset one. "We've always been like that. He'd . . . give and would do anything I needed financially, you know? The basics. More than the basics, I guess. He was there as much as he let himself. My dad doesn't show a whole bunch of emotion. That's just the way he is. He didn't coddle or tuck us into bed every night or anything like that. He spent time with us. But after I told him

I was going to enlist, things got strained between us." I must have been making a face because Aaron winked. "It's not that bad, Ruby. He loves me in his own way. He just wanted more from me."

"I'm not trying to criticize him. Nobody's parents are perfect. But it just makes me a little sad that you aren't closer to him, is all. But . . . I don't know. Everyone deserves hugs and to know that someone in the world still worries about them, no matter what they're doing, or even if they're mad at one another. I'd never do that to anyone." I made sure to meet his gaze when I said, "You're great the way you are, military or not. I'd be proud of you regardless of what you did with your life."

The smile had gradually crept off Aaron's face the longer I talked, and I started to worry I'd said something wrong. I'd overstepped my boundaries, hadn't I?

"I'm sorry, I don't mean to criticize your family—"

"That's not it," he said almost cryptically, still standing there, watching me with that careful expression on his face. His Adam's apple bobbed, and in three long strides he was standing in front of me, the hand not holding what he'd called our bait bucket, was cupping my cheek. As he pretty much towered over me, with his head tilted down, I could feel the hint of Aaron's breath on my chin, just a little puff. Almost nonexistent like he was holding his breath.

Then his thumb moved, just a small swipe that might have only covered an inch of my cheekbone.

What was happening?

Something almost cool brushed across one small spot on my forehead the second before what was obviously his thumb made another tiny path over my skin.

Aaron had kissed me on the forehead.

I was naïve but not that naïve, and it confused the heck out of me.

But as quickly as he'd come to stand in front of me, he took a step back. His words were that soft, commanding thing he'd given me in the past. "All right, enough talking. Let me teach you what to do."

"Then he made me throw it back in," I told them all with a sideways glance to Aaron, who was sitting beside me at the restaurant we were at.

He smiled, and beneath the table, the side of his shoe bumped into mine. "I told you we were releasing them."

"Yeah, but those had all been *tiny*. We were out there for what? Six hours before I caught the big one?" I'd gotten fried out in the surf with him and had the sunburn on my neck to prove it. It had taken about an hour for him to teach me how to use the spin casting rig, and even then, my technique had been pretty iffy. But we'd wandered out into the water and cast line after line out for hours, whispering jokes to one another as we tried to stand as still as possible, failing at being quiet at least five times when I'd feel something brush my leg and I'd shout.

Aaron had only made about four shark jokes the entire time we'd been out there.

I hadn't touched the first two fish I'd caught that had been too small, but by the third one, Aaron had made me poke it. When he'd caught one, he made me hold it for a second and I might have wailed. By the time I caught one so big I'd figured he would prepare it and make for dinner . . . I'd held it in my hands—wiggling, thrashing—at least until he'd unhooked it and then tossed it back into the water to live another day.

Honestly, I wasn't sure if I'd ever be able to eat fish again after holding a live one in my hands, but the day had been a lot more fun than I ever could have imagined. Fishing. Me. Who would have thought?

A gentle hand came up to cup the back of my neck then,

conscious of the swollen pink skin that had taken a beating under the sun's rays, and I could sense Aaron leaning closer to me as he said, loud enough for everyone at the table in the pub to hear, "I'm really proud of you."

I did know he was proud of me. He'd kissed my forehead once more after I'd caught the fish and told me those same exact words, and when I'd gone to hug him for the first time since the day he'd picked me up at the airport, he'd hugged me back. Squeezed me. Needy, needy, needy. All warm and solid and affectionate and perfect.

"We were going to meet up with you, but someone suddenly started feeling bad," Des chipped in with a smirk.

Brittany rolled her eyes from her spot across the table from me. "My stomach was hurting. It's not like there's a bathroom out there for me to use. What was I supposed to do? Go in the water?"

Des shrugged and had her mumbling "nasty."

"You did great for it being your first time," Aaron repeated.

It was sad how much I ate up his attention and praise, like I'd never gotten it before.

"Need more time to decide?" came a voice from my left that had already become familiar to me. It was the waitress. The very attractive waitress. One of the handfuls of women I'd already spotted eyeballing the heck out of Aaron.

It had taken all of two minutes after we'd gotten out of his truck for the looks to begin. I wasn't sure if I'd just been too overwhelmed the first day to notice all the attention Aaron got or if I was just that oblivious, but the truth was: there was no ignoring it now. The teenage hostess at the restaurant had taken one look at Aaron and Max and turned redder than I ever had. She'd stuttered her way through a greeting before leading us to a table, only turning around every two steps to look at both of them.

And then the waitress had appeared.

"You're back!" the woman had basically shouted before we'd gotten to the table.

Everyone except Mindy and me apparently knew who she was because they had immediately greeted her. From the bits and pieces I picked up as the four of them greeted her, they knew her from the last trip they'd taken to Port St. Joe. All I could gather was that they had gone out drinking together, or something like that. It wouldn't have meant anything.

Until she'd turned to Aaron and Max with a smile on her face and asked, just *asked*, "You both still have girls?"

Like that. Just like that.

To give him credit, it was Max that answered with a "Not anymore" that had me looking away and, at the same time, reminding myself that it was true. At least Aaron was single now. And if he'd been here before he'd shipped out, he hadn't been back then. He was now.

The woman had taken everyone's drink order in between playful touches of shoulders and more than one wink I hadn't been sure who it had been aimed at, but while she'd been gone, Aaron had jumped into our fishing story, distracting me with the way he told it, sounding so pleased. But the waitress was back, and I didn't like the way my stomach felt in reaction to her presence.

"What do you recommend on the menu?" Max asked, still holding the menu in his hands.

The friendly, pretty waitress didn't even think about her answer as she stood at the foot of the table, directly between Aaron and Max. It wasn't that I didn't like her because she was so attractive; no one held a flame to the women in my family. Also, I wasn't that kind of person. Mostly, the ache in my intestines came from the blatant attention she was showing Max and Aaron. Realistically, I knew I couldn't blame her. I did. They were both too good-looking for their own good.

But . . . she'd touched Aaron's shoulder twice since we'd sat down. I'd counted.

"The chicken and waffles is one of our bestsellers," the woman answered Max's question, her eyes settling on Aaron for a moment as her flirting smile turned into a coy one highlighted by her bubble gum pink lipstick.

Friends don't get jealous when other friends get hit on, I reminded myself.

"Lots of folks like the frog legs, too," she added.

Frog legs?

"Frog legs?" I heard Mindy echo beneath her breath from her spot beside me, sounding just as horrified as I felt.

"It's a local favorite," the waitress threw in, like that would make it sound more appetizing, with a bright smile aimed at the younger girl.

"I'll take the chicken and waffles," Des basically muttered with Brittany echoing that order, followed by me. Mindy and Aaron chose something with a sandwich.

"I'll take an order of frog legs," Max piped up, grinning.

"Oh, gross, Max," Mindy muttered.

"What?" He shrugged as he handed over the menu to the waitress with a wink before she backed away.

"That's disgusting."

"I'm sure it'll taste like chicken. Everything tastes like chicken."

Even Brittany shook her head with an "Ugh."

Max's eyes met mine and I smiled at him shyly. "Everything does taste like chicken. I had gator once, tastes just like it."

Mindy turned in her chair to look at me. "You've had alligator?"

I nodded. "I had sheep's head once."

"*You what?*"

"In Iceland. Our tour guide didn't tell me what it was and I tried it. I'd never eat it again, but it wasn't the worst thing I'd ever had," I explained.

Mindy was looking at me with a horrified expression on her face, her fingers picking at the napkin she had rolled up. "What was the worst?" she asked hesitantly, like she didn't really want to know the answer but couldn't help herself.

Fidgeting with my hands on my lap, I smiled and looked over at Aaron who was watching me. "I've had cow tongue a few times. That was good actually—"

"*Cow tongue?*" that was Brittany.

"Yeah. They sell it all over the place in Houston. I've had dinuguan—"

"What's that?" Max asked.

I scrunched up my nose, remembering eating that way too clearly. "It's a Filipino dish that my dad made me try. It's pig intestines, kidneys, lungs, heart, and the snout cooked in its blood—"

At least four of them said a variation of "eww" that made me grin.

"I know. My dad claimed it was dessert, like pudding. He loves it. I can't eat pudding anymore because of that, no matter what color it is."

"I'm not going to be able to eat pudding anymore after that . . ." Mindy trailed off.

"That's not the worst," I started to say before I shut my mouth. "Never mind. I'm just going to stop now. I don't want to ruin anyone's food."

"There's something more gross than that?" Brittany asked.

I lifted my shoulders, not wanting to say more.

"Now you need to tell us," she insisted.

"We can handle it," Max kept going.

"No, seriously, you don't want me to tell you," I tried to explain.

"Come on, Rubes," Aaron chimed in, making me glance at him.

"I'll just close my ears," Mindy offered. "I don't want to know."

I watched them and asked, slowly, "Are you sure?"

Four nods around the table confirmed they were sure. Even Mindy raised her hands to the side of her head, middle fingers already going to her ears to plug them in.

"Don't say I didn't warn you, okay?" I reminded them. They all looked so confident . . . it almost made me laugh. "I've never tried it, but my dad has a bunch of times—"

"What is it?" Max asked.

"It's called balut. I've watched him eat it and I didn't gag, and I'm pretty proud of myself for it—"

"What is it?"

"Jesus, Max, give her a second," Aaron chimed in, his big hands resting on the table.

I squeezed my fingers between my thighs and just got it over with. "It's a duck embryo in its shell."

Four sets of eyeballs blinked. But it was Des that slowly asked, "Excuse me?"

"It's a—"

"No, no, I heard you." He cut me off, still taking his time with his words. He blinked, lowered his voice, and squinted his eyes. "How?"

"How what?"

"How do you . . .?" he stammered.

I knew what he was trying to ask and I cringed, regretting bringing this up. "The baby duck is boiled . . . alive."

Four different people made dry-heaving and gagging sounds.

"*And they eat that?*" I'm pretty positive that was Brittany.

I nodded.

"I'm sweating thinking about it," Brittany definitely whispered, visibly letting out a shudder.

"I know, I'm sorry. I shouldn't have said anything," I apologized.

Des's face was definitely a little green. "You've eaten it?"

"She said she hasn't," Aaron said. "Your dad did, right?"

I nodded. "Nothing grosses him out food wise. I try to be as brave as he is, but I can't."

"Has one of your brothers or sisters tried it?" my friend asked.

That had me laughing out loud. "No way. That's the only thing they aren't willing to take risks with." And trying new food was one of the only things I wasn't too afraid to try.

"I'm never going to look at a duck the same way again . . ." Des mumbled.

"Can I take my fingers off my ears now?" Mindy asked a little too loudly, her eyes sweeping around the table.

I smiled and nodded.

The younger girl looked around the circle and frowned as she lowered her hands. "I'm going to guess I should be happy I missed that conversation. You guys look like you're going to be sick."

Max made a coughing sound, turning in his chair. "Is it too late to change my order?"

It wasn't.

We must have all been thinking about ducks and/or pretty waitresses that came by every few minutes to check on us more than any other table, because no one really spoke much after our food was dropped off. We ate silently, and every once in a while, I'd meet Aaron's gaze as I chewed.

"I want to go check out some of the shops around here before they close. Text me when you're ready to go," Mindy said, pushing her chair back. "Anyone want to come?"

When no one immediately said anything, it made me feel bad, so I pointed at the food I still had left on my plate. "I'm going to finish eating, but I'll go look for you when I'm done."

She gave me a little smile and flicked her brother on the ear on her way out of the restaurant, apparently assuming he'd pay for her meal. That made me miss my own brothers and sisters.

"I'm going to get a beer. Any of you want anything?" Aaron asked a moment later, standing up. His hand squeezed my shoulder. "Ruby?"

"I'm fine," I told him, perfectly okay with my glass of water.

He gave me a faint smile just as Max said, "Get me a beer. You know what I like."

"Get me one too," Des piped in.

Aaron snickered, releasing the hold on my shoulder. "I'm not buying either of you shit, come with me or give me cash."

"So you can forget to give me my change? Nah," came Max's response as he pushed away from the table too. Des groaned but got up too, following his friends to the bar. I only watched him for a second before looking back down at my plate.

Brittany made a noise, her elbows on the table, as the three men walked away. "You know, I was at a friend's house once, and her parents are Filipino. They had this crispy pork thing out that I thought was amazing—"

"Crispy pata?" I asked, grinning.

She nodded, dipping a french fry into a giant pile of ketchup she'd squirted on her plate. "I was eating the shit out of it until her mom told me it was knuckles. If I would've been anywhere else, I would've thrown up."

"It is good, but yeah, it is a little gross when you think about it."

She tipped her head to the side and looked at me. "You can't really tell you're Filipino, except for the shape of your eyes." She blinked. "That sounds really racist. I'm sorry. Mindy's been rubbing off on me this week."

I snorted. "I get it. My mom has really red hair and she's super pale. I got a mix of both of them. No one can ever tell what I am."

"No shit?"

"It's true. One of my sisters has red hair and the other one has black hair like our dad," I told her, casually glancing at the bar where Max, Aaron, and Des had just headed.

My eyes froze there for a moment.

Leaning forward across the counter of the bar was the waitress, and she was smiling and laughing, talking to the three of them who were all smiling and laughing at her too.

Was that indigestion or . . .

No. That wasn't indigestion making my upper chest feel tacky. It was me being jealous like crazy in the blink of an eye.

I had no right to be jealous. No right at all. Zero. Zilch. She was pretty and outgoing. She could do whatever she wanted.

Stop freaking looking, Ruby. You wouldn't be looking if it was anyone else. Which was the truth.

I glanced back at Brittany, hoping she hadn't noticed where my attention had been, even as everything north of my chest went hot. "Where's your family from?" I got out, trying to distract her.

She lifted a shoulder. "My dad's from Ethiopia. My mom's Creole. They've been in Louisiana forever," she explained.

"Was Des the one who moved to Shreveport in elementary school or was that Max?" I asked at the same time a cute laugh from the direction of the bar reached my ears. I tried, *I tried* my hardest not to look at the bar again.

I failed.

I peeked, just out of the corner of my eye.

Aaron was still laughing at something the waitress was saying. That handsome face had a pleasant, easy expression on it, his body language was forward . . . and he wasn't looking at her the way he looked at me. Affectionately. Or like a puppy. He was just . . . looking.

I'm not sure why that made me want to throw up, but it did. Realistically, I should have been happy he didn't give everyone the faces he gave me. And it wasn't like he was taking her in like he was interested either. I'd witnessed that face enough in person to recognize it for what it was.

He was just looking at her. And it still felt like a knife blade into my belly. Because I knew what it meant, what it reminded me of.

One day, regardless of what he said about relationships and marriage, he was going to have another girlfriend. It could be a month from now, it could be a year from now, but it was going to happen.

And there was nothing I could do about it.

He wasn't my boyfriend or my lover, and I needed to be grateful I even had that much, I told myself as I squeezed my hands into fists beneath the table. He was my friend who cared about me. He was a man who didn't want to get married. He was a man who only wanted to share part of himself with me. I had no business looking or caring. None.

And yet . . .

"Des is the one who's known him his whole life. Max moved to Shreveport when they were in high school," Brittany explained, her words helping me focus on her and not anyone or anything else.

I nodded, swallowing down a ball of what I wasn't going to consider being agony. "That's cool."

Brittany nodded, her own eyes flicking in the direction where mine really, really wanted to go to again. But I wouldn't. I wouldn't. The cute, high-chiming laugh belonging to the waitress seemed to carry across the freaking restaurant one more time, and it was so cute and sweet it made me feel like mine sounded like a donkey, loud and abrasive, uncultured and just . . . me. Awkward. This was why I didn't compare myself to other people.

My traitorous eyes slid toward the bar even though I knew better. And I saw that the waitress had her hand really close to Aaron's on the bar counter. I glanced back as fast as I could, luckily beating out Brittany's gaze. I was too strung out to notice the frown on her mouth.

"She's a real fucking flirt, isn't she?" she stated under her breath, her eyes narrowing.

Pressing my lips together, I tried to act stupid. "Who?"

"The waitress," she said, still looking in that direction. "Every time we came in here last time we visited, she was just a little too friendly even to Des, seeing me sitting next to him. I don't like it."

I couldn't tell her I didn't like it either, but I smiled like I could understand where she was coming from. "Des is really cute."

That had Brittany instantly grinning over at me. "He is, huh?"

I nodded.

"Aaron's not too hard on the eyes either if you like that kind of Captain America thing," she joked.

Yeah, me playing it cool ended there. I didn't trust myself not to say something stupid and instead giggled. *Giggled*. How much more fake could I get? I hadn't giggled since I was seventeen and around Hunter.

It must have been obvious I was full of crap because she laughed. "I've tried asking Des what's going on between you two and he says he doesn't know."

"Oh, there's nothing—"

She rolled her eyes.

"Really, there's nothing. He called me his little sister one day," I explained, reaching up to scratch at my neck.

Brittany's mouth twisted to the side for a second, like she thought I was full of crap, but she didn't say anything else, settling for just taking a sip of her iced tea.

There was another laugh from the bar that had my throat knotting up, and I knew what I needed to do. Pushing my plate forward, I took another sip of my water and shoved my chair back. "I was thinking about taking a walk around and see if I can find Mindy."

She nodded, her expression focused on the bar again until her eyes flicked to mine briefly. "Want me to go with you since Prince Charming over there is busy?" she asked.

I shook my head. "I'll be fine, unless you want to come."

"I'm saving to buy a house. I shouldn't be doing any shopping right now. I don't have any self-control," she explained.

"Okay," I told her a little too quickly, my smile a little too brittle as another cute laugh made its way to our mostly empty table.

My hands were not shaking as I pulled out the approximate amount of money my bill was going to be plus tip and left it in the center of the table. I was not about to cry. No. No. No. When I forced my eyes not to blink, I reasoned that they needed some ventilation, not because I was worried one bad blink would lead me to burst out crying.

"I'll see you in a minute then."

On my feet, with my purse going over my head, I told myself not to look at the bar again.

And I failed. Like usual. Like I did at most things.

This time, the three men were all sitting at the counter, listening to the waitress talk openly about who knows what. And they were all smiling. Who was I to get mad about someone making Aaron happy when all I'd heard was how unusual it was for him to have those kind of reactions?

I wanted to be jealous and petty, but I couldn't be.

That was a lie. I could. But I wouldn't let myself.

And so, even though my hands shook and sweated, I shot Brittany another smile and wormed my way through the crowd of tourists, heading toward the door. The cool air was more than welcome on my nostrils even if it did nothing for the ugly, bitter feeling bubbling around in the pit of my stomach at the stupid image in my head of Aaron smiling and laughing at another woman. God, I was acting worse than a crazy girlfriend.

Of all the men in the world I could be nuts about, I had to be in love with the one who saw me as something I didn't want to be. What was wrong with me? It was like I was asking for the heartbreak since I knew darn well what I was getting myself into. I did this to myself every freaking time, didn't I? Always. Always falling for the one guy who couldn't and didn't see me as more than a friend.

What was wrong with me? Who kept doing this kind of crap to themselves willingly? Knowing how this would end?

Way to go, I told myself. *Way to freaking go.*

No wonder. No freaking wonder I was where I was.

Maybe I'd been looking at this relationship business the wrong way all along. Maybe I shouldn't expect fireworks and heart eyes straight from the beginning. Maybe falling in love or liking someone was gradual and it took a few dates. Maybe.

After all, I was listening to my mom who had been married four times.

Maybe I really was expecting too much.

Shoving my hands into the pockets of my shorts, I looked up and down the nearly deserted street and went left, my heart feeling so heavy it was hanging around my belly button. There was hardly anyone out and about as I speed-walked toward the shops I'd seen on the way over, literally fifty feet away from the pub's entrance.

I'd barely made it halfway down the block when my phone vibrated against my hip, where the body of my purse was resting. Stopping on the corner, I pulled it out and forced a shaky breath out of my mouth that was immediately followed by a tear that rolled out of my eye. I wiped it before it made it far, and stared at the **NEW MESSAGE AARON HALL** on the screen. Swiping my finger across the screen to unlock it, I told myself the same thing I had from the moment I became aware I had feelings for him. He didn't see me the way I wanted him to, and even if he did, did I want to be with someone who kept so much to himself?

Not really, my head said, but my heart said it could deal.

I opened the message.

Aaron: Where are you?

Standing there on the street, I typed back my reply.

Ruby: Going to look for Mindy.

I had possibly taken five steps forward after sending the text when my phone vibrated again.

Aaron: What way did you go?

I squeezed the phone in my hand and took a deep breath, reaching up to wipe at my face the second I thought I felt another tear in my eye. I was such a loser. Why was I tearing up?

Ruby: Left.

I answered him honestly even though I didn't want to. I typed out another message.

Ruby: You don't have to come. I'm fine. I won't get lost. Text me when you're done.

I sent it and then added :) because that wasn't passive-aggressive enough.

Aaron: Ruby

That was all his response said.

Ruby: It's okay. You need to hang out with your friends too and not spend all day babysitting me. I typed up *I'm used to being alone*, but deleted it because that didn't sound all melodramatic and pathetic at all. Instead, I settled for **I'll be with Mindy. Have fun.**

Putting my phone back into my bag, I reached up to my face and pressed my fingers against my brow bone, my thumb on my cheekbone, and let out a shaky breath. I needed to get over this crap, or at least learn how to deal with it better, ASAP. I couldn't be a jerk to him because of the things going on in my head that he had no part of. I couldn't be mad at him for flirting with a pretty woman.

. . . Even if it felt like everything inside of me had gotten beaten up, and I felt defeated and more than a little alone.

My phone didn't vibrate again as I slipped into the first shop I found open. Mindy wasn't in it, but I walked around the glass-blowing store, taking in all the knickknacks there. Then I went into a souvenir shop and spent some time in there, buying a small magnet for my mom and Ben that was on sale. After that there was a T-shirt store, an art gallery . . . I must have spent an hour going from one business to the other, never coming across Mindy. It wasn't until my phone started ringing that I finally pulled it out again. Aaron's name flashed across the screen.

I held back a sigh as I went to answer it. "Hello?"

"Where are you?"

I smiled at the man behind the register as I walked out of the shop, trying to remember what direction I'd come from. "At a store. I couldn't find Mindy. Are you all done?"

"She just got back here a minute ago. I thought you were going to be with her?"

I knew I was in one of my rare crappy moods when his worry irritated me. "I was going to, but I couldn't find her. I'll head back if you're ready to go."

There was definitely a sigh over the receiver followed by a, "We'll see you here. Be careful."

Squeezing my hands at my sides, I shook off the emotions I could and started walking back in the direction I'd come. It didn't take me more than ten minutes to make it back to the restaurant after I'd taken a wrong turn a block too early. By the time I made it, I could see the group standing on the street right by the two cars. Brittany was by her white Alero, keys twirling in her hand. The one blond in the group, the one I could probably recognize from a mile away stood beside the passenger door of his pickup, his head swinging left to right, up and down the street.

It was Mindy who spotted me first.

"I had no idea you were looking for me, I'm sorry," she said immediately once I was close enough.

"It's okay," I assured her, making sure to keep my gaze on her face and her face alone.

"I'll give you my number for next time," she offered, already rattling off numbers before I even had my phone out.

"I'm sorry for taking so long," I apologized to the other four, the second Mindy stepped aside. Brittany looked fine, but the three men . . . not so much. Even with more than five feet between us, I could see the red in Max and Des's eyes. I still hadn't glanced at Aaron because, what was the point?

How much had they had to drink?

"Yeah, you're going to need to drive," Brittany said, as if reading my mind.

Thankfully, Aaron wasn't an idiot because he asked, "Ruby, can you drive?"

I nodded, finally glancing in his direction but setting my gaze on his mouth. I started to say that maybe I wasn't the best person to drive a big pickup around, but with Mindy's arm in a cast, who else would do it? So I settled for a crusty, "Sure." I only had to drive. I could do it. I knew enough people with trucks. If they could do it, I could too.

He didn't toss the keys, and I was thankful for it. Walking toward him, I took them from his hand, noticing he held them a moment longer than he needed to, and walked around to the driver side of the door. The doors were already unlocked as I lunged up onto the first step and then swung inside the cab as Aaron took the passenger seat and Max and Mindy took the bench in the back. I didn't look at him as I adjusted the seat so I could reach the pedals, and I didn't look at him as I messed with the mirrors either. I also definitely didn't look at him as I pulled his truck onto the street.

"Want me to navigate you back?" Mindy asked from the back seat.

"Yes, please," I told her, fully aware I only knew the basics on where we were supposed to be going.

It wasn't until we were basically on the straight shot back to the beach house that Aaron's question came at me, like he was trying to be quiet, but it wasn't happening. "Did you buy anything?"

He was my friend and I had no reason to get weird. With my hands tight on the steering wheel, I glanced at him quickly and gave him a smile that was totally tight. "Just a magnet for my mom and her husband."

"Nothing for you?"

In a grumpier tone than I intended, I told him, "No."

"You didn't find anything you liked?" he asked.

"There were a few stores with really nice things in them," I told him, trying to sound normal. Nonchalant. Fine. "I just can't . . . you know, be spending money on things I don't need right now."

"I would have spotted you if you wanted something."

Flexing my fingers around the steering wheel, I reminded myself that none of this was his fault. He was just trying to be nice to me. He was always trying to be nice to me. And it made me feel guilty because why did I deserve it? I hadn't done anything special for it to be called for.

He had no idea how I felt about him. He didn't deserve my pissy attitude. If I was Jasmine right now, I'd tell her to stop being a brat.

Torn between feeling bad and still holding on to that residual anger simmering in my veins while I flashbacked to the pretty waitress he'd been talking to, I swallowed the golf ball in my throat and really, *really* tried to be normal. To be kind. To be fair. "That's okay, but thank you," I said, only sounding about half as ungrateful as I needed to, my voice higher and squeakier than normal, betraying me. "I already owe you enough."

Maybe I hadn't needed to add that part to the end.

"You don't owe me anything," Aaron practically whispered.

"If you say so," I responded just as quietly, my fingers squeezing the steering wheel.

"Ruby—"

I shook my head and shot him a wary smile quickly before glancing forward again, the lie on my lips, the ache in my heart. "You're a really good friend to me, stalker. Thank you."

I might have been fine the rest of the night if he'd responded, if he'd said *anything*, but he didn't. He just turned his attention toward the window and didn't say hardly another word to me the rest of the night.

Chapter Twenty

I woke up early the next morning again all on my own. Whether it was because I was somewhere my body subconsciously knew wasn't my bed back in Houston, or if it was because I had *Aaron, Aaron, Aaron* so imprinted on my brain that I didn't want to sleep longer than I absolutely needed to, I had no idea. All I knew was that it was thirty minutes after six when I reached for my phone and sent my mom a message telling her I was alive.

It was three minutes later I got a response from her that said **Good. Keep it that way.**

I'd showered the night before once we got back from the restaurant, but the idea of being in a bathing suit all day, even knowing that there was no one other than me who would notice or care if my legs were shaved smooth, made me head back into the bathroom and take a quick one. After getting dressed, the house was quiet like it had been every other morning. I headed upstairs to see the sun already rising. I grabbed a bottle of water from the kitchen, and instead of heading out to the balcony like I'd been doing, I leaned against the kitchen counter and sipped at my water, looking around the kitchen and living area, trying to get my thoughts together in a place that wasn't where Aaron had been surprising me every morning with breakfast.

If that didn't make me sound like a bitter jerk, I didn't know what would.

I was disappointed in myself, honestly—especially the more I thought about our situation, the situation I found myself in with Aaron. The part of my brain that wasn't ruled by hormones and emotions, that had watched people around me struggle with relationships and friendships and judged them for their actions, knew I was being crazy. It knew it. It realized and accepted that I had zero claim on this man I was in love with who brought me breakfast and fixed my sunscreen for me and taught me to fish and made me feel special.

The part of me that didn't want to hear any of this BS about how any relationship between Aaron and me was never, ever going to happen, wanted to call time-out and rage over it.

He may or may not have flirted with another woman.

He didn't want a relationship.

I was his friend Ruby.

These were the most important facts of all the things I knew.

After those were: there were things he hadn't wanted to tell me about his past, and there were things he didn't want to tell me in general. I'd put all that together. What I could or would do about it was yet to be determined. I wasn't the pushy type, and the last thing I wanted to do was force him to tell me something that he didn't want to, for whatever reason he had. At no point had he given me a reason not to trust him, I knew that for a fact.

But . . . I really wanted him to trust me. And if I was going to be real honest with myself, it hurt my feelings that he hadn't and didn't. And I could live with it or I couldn't, the choice was up to me.

No biggie.

Right.

Maybe I had been better off not caring about dating and men and relationships. This crap was way too complicated. I wasn't built for this. At the rate I was going, everything was going to make me cry silently into a pint of ice cream.

With a sigh, and with the remainder of my water bottle in hand, I headed out to the balcony, hugging my legs to my chest once I'd sat down.

There were only four full days left until I flew back to Houston, and the notion made a lump fill my belly . . . but I tried my best to ignore it and just clear my head and enjoy the moment. I didn't have to dread whatever came, or didn't come, in the future. Sometimes things worked out and other times they didn't. I'd go to San Francisco to visit my dad for a while, and then I'd head back home and keep on trying to expand my business. Somehow. If not . . . well, I wasn't sure what Plan B was exactly.

Plenty of people didn't figure out their lives for a long, long time. It wasn't a big deal if I still hadn't sorted out what I was supposed to do. Maybe it was a good thing that Aaron was just my friend. Who was I to be in a relationship with someone when my life was all over the place?

I'd survived having feelings for someone who didn't share them in return with me before. I could survive it again. I would have to.

I needed to—

It was the sliding of the deck door that had me glancing over my shoulder to find Aaron there, one shoulder coming through the door first before another one followed. His hands were awkwardly up at his sides as he held a plate in each one. How long had I been outside already? Long enough for him to make food? He didn't bother closing the door behind him as he came out, giving me something that was supposed to look like a smile but didn't quite.

"Morning," he said in a restrained voice as he walked over to where I was sitting.

"Morning." My eyes bounced back and forth between him

and the plate in each hand that I still couldn't see well. "I thought you'd sleep in longer," I told him.

He shook his head and stopped right beside my chair, extending the plate toward me. "Couldn't sleep. Eat."

"Thank you," I told him a lot more quietly than I had over the last two days, taking the plate from his hands with that strange, uncertain emotion filling my chest. There were two pieces of toast, each topped with scrambled eggs, something that looked like pico de gallo, cheese, avocado, and bacon. I held my breath and watched as he lowered himself to his chair, already picking up a piece of toast with his left hand and taking a bite out of it. I watched him eat it.

We hadn't said more than fifteen words to each other after we'd gotten back to the house the night before, and yet, he'd still made me breakfast. I didn't know whether to cry or hug him, I really didn't.

Who made food for a friend anyway? I loved my friends, and I loved my sisters, but unless they asked, I wouldn't make them breakfast. Did he not know I wasn't mentally stable enough for this? That my heart wasn't in the right place? That it didn't know Aaron was my friend and would only ever be my friend, no matter how much I told it otherwise?

You would have figured no one in my life had ever been kind to me by the way I sat there.

He'd probably gotten through half of it when he realized I was staring at him instead of eating, and he started chewing slower. "I know you like eggs, and you have to like bacon, what is it?" he asked, hoarsely, swallowing what he had left in his mouth. His eyes went round and he spoke slowly, "If you say you don't like avocado, I'm going to need to rethink this whole thing we have going on."

This thing we had going on? Friendship?

We were back to acting like everything was fine and that I

hadn't started being crazy and cool the night before and he hadn't gotten lost in his mysterious thoughts and stopped talking to me?

I'd worry about it later. Instead, I shook my head, as every cell in my body cried out for this man who always made sure I ate and had made me something to eat for breakfast again. I wanted him. I wanted him so badly I could barely breathe. And . . .

I couldn't have him.

Was this a test? My mom always mumbled about how she was being tested: her patience, her wallet, her mental health. Then she'd start mumbling about how God never gave you more than you could handle.

So was that what this was?

Was I being tested by this beautiful man so if I passed, I could hopefully find one just like him that did like me the way I wanted to be liked?

"Is it the avocado, Ruby?" Aaron asked slowly, taking another bite and frowning as he did it.

Swallowing the questions and the frustrations inside of me, I tried to remember I had to be fair. I had to. So I told him, weak, weak, weak, "No, I like avocado."

Even with his cheeks stuffed full of toast, tomatoes, cheese, avocado, and bacon, he blinked. "You sure?"

Why? Why? Why couldn't he have been normal? Handsome but not stunning. Nice but not kind. Understanding but not so patient. Thoughtful but not so much.

I should have gone home. I really should have gone home so I could have had a fighting chance of moving on with my life once this week was over. I didn't need to add a person to my obsessive personality.

But I didn't do any of that.

"I'm sure," I promised him, forcing myself to pick up my toast and take a bite.

Maybe this was my test. Maybe I just needed to get through this week as best as I could, and then I'd know I could handle anything. I could be his favorite friend and eventually, at some point, move on and find someone else who might not be so handsome or sweet, but he could be honest and share things with me. And that would be enough. He could still be normal handsome. Who said he couldn't?

"Ruby—" he started to say before the sound of a phone ringing inside the house cut him off.

There was a home phone in the house? I wondered, knowing I hadn't seen one.

Aaron cursed, setting his plate on the side table and getting to his feet. "I'll be right back," he said to me, giving me a tight expression before practically jogging back inside.

I hadn't really planned on being nosey and eavesdropping on whatever conversation was about to take place on a phone I hadn't even known existed, but curiosity got the best of me. Mostly because I wanted to see where the heck the phone had been the entire time. But something bothered me as Aaron headed straight to a cabinet directly beside the refrigerator that I had never opened before, like he knew exactly where it was, and pulled out a corded white handset, bringing it up to his ear.

I guess that shouldn't have been surprising considering he'd been the one to put up the groceries the second day we'd been there. Maybe he'd looked around the house, or maybe this was the same place that they had all stayed at when they'd come to San Blas last year. That would make sense.

The thing was, I kept watching him as he answered, in a voice that was intentionally low, "Hello?"

I might not be as athletic as Jasmine or as smart and outgoing and pretty as my mom and sister, but I'd inherited my dad's excellent hearing, vision, and teeth. I wore earplugs every single time I went to a concert and I could usually hear just about everything. So even though Aaron was basically whispering as he reclined against the kitchen counter with the phone to his ear, I heard him and I watched his facial expression, and the tone of his voice change instantly. I mean, *instantly*.

We'd had our beef the night before, but it was nothing like the tension that strummed through his body, and I definitely hadn't thought it was possible for him to scowl and frown as he said to whoever was talking to him, "What do you want?"

If that wasn't abrasive, I didn't know what was.

His features didn't change even a little bit as he replied to the voice on the other end, "I'm fine. I'm sure Colin told you I was fine when you talked to him."

Who was Colin?

"Look," he basically growled after a moment, making me lean toward the glass panel separating the deck from the living area like that would get me closer to the action going on inside. "If I had wanted to see you while I was home, I would have. Sorry."

I'd already known Aaron had sarcasm down stat, but he'd never sounded more insincere ever. Who was he talking to? Who would have the home's phone number anyway?

"I'm at the beach house—"

The beach house. Not *a* beach house. Wait a second . . .

"—I need to go. If you want to talk, call Colin or Paige—"

I knew that name. Paige was his sister's name. Was Colin his older brother? It had to be. So who—

"I'm going now. Bye," he ended the call abruptly, still talking and sounding like a totally different person from the warm man I'd gotten to know.

He stood there. All long and lean, his body strung completely tight. It wasn't until his head drooped forward and his hands went up to lace behind his head that I turned around, my heart beating quickly.

I tried to process everything. A phone call. Aaron's entire

personality changing like Jekyll and Hyde. Him mentioning his sister and who I could only imagine was his brother. The beach house.

He'd never once mentioned renting the house, had he?

He'd brought up several times having a decent relationship with his dad, so there was no way that could have been him on the phone, but . . . had it been the woman he'd repeatedly called his "birth mom" who had "left"?

My mind was running a mile a minute as I tried to *think*. Think, think, think.

A brief memory of the T-shirt he'd worn the first morning flicked through my thoughts. Hall Auto. He'd never mentioned what his dad did exactly, only that he had employees and that his brother and sister worked for him.

I knew it was none of my business, but the need to know lingered in my brain as my stomach turned at the not-lie but not-truth Aaron might have been hiding from me. Maybe not hiding exactly, but he hadn't been forthcoming either. With a glance into the house one more time to find Aaron in the same position he'd been, I brought my phone up to my face and launched the browser, quickly typing in "Hall Auto" and "Shreveport" into the search.

It didn't take more than two seconds for five different results to fill the screen. Five different results for five different auto dealerships in the state of Louisiana, all called some variation of HALL AUTO. This lump formed in my chest, and even though I knew I didn't deserve to feel like he'd lied to me, I couldn't help it. It took about a minute of searching before I found an "About Us" section on one of the dealership's websites. Keywords like "family owned business since 1954" and "family values" caught my eye. But it was the three pictures at the bottom that made me not move.

One was an old picture that had to have been taken in the 50s with a gentleman and a woman beside a car that would have been vintage today. That one was no big deal.

The second image was a recent one of a man in his late fifties standing beside a white car.

The third was a clearly dated picture of a man standing in between two males and a younger girl. The older man was obviously the one who had been standing solo in the second photograph, but the male beside him was almost a mirror image of Aaron just a little younger than what he was now. Standing a few inches away was the younger girl, not touching the man. And on the far end was a face I knew well. A face much younger than the one I'd been seeing constantly.

It was a seventeen- maybe eighteen-year-old Aaron standing there beside who I was sure had to be his brother.

If the physical proof hadn't been enough, Aaron had told me his dad always owned white cars.

His dad owned car dealerships. Not just one or two, or the little, used car ones on the side of the freeway or took up space on corners of streets in certain neighborhoods. They were huge dealerships. And his dad—granddad, family, whatever—owned them.

Hadn't he told me he didn't want to join the family business and everyone thought he was dumb? Hadn't he said his dad would have supported him financially if he'd needed something? Hadn't he specifically told me *he was fine on money*? Always so vague.

Why hadn't he just . . . told me? Did he think I was a gold digger?

The answer to that question came to me immediately, making me feel foolish. No, he wouldn't think that. He had to have his reasons for not being up front with me about his family's businesses. He had to. I knew that.

The greatest question remained: who had he been on the

phone with? Did his dad own the beach house? I knew I could find out at least the second question, but going behind his back felt sleazy.

I needed to trust him. I needed to not take his silence personally. I needed—

"Sorry about that," Aaron said, stepping onto the porch with an expression that seemed a little too forced. He cleared his throat as he sat down and gave me a smile I knew he wasn't feeling. "What do you think about going fishing again?"

"Goodnight," Brittany and Des called out as they made their way toward the stairs.

Everyone else had already gone to bed, or at least headed to their rooms.

Aaron, who had been seated on the love seat while we'd been watching a DVD of *The Mummy* that he'd "found" in a binder full of other movies, sat up in his seat and looked over in my direction, his expression carefully blank, just like it had been the entire afternoon and evening since we'd gotten back from fishing. He'd been trying his best to act normal, sweet, like usual while we'd been out in the surf, but I could tell something was on his mind. I just didn't know what exactly. "You tired?"

We hadn't talked much while we'd been fishing, with Des coming along. I'd gone to the beach with Mindy and Brittany once we got back when Aaron had claimed he needed a nap and had stayed at the house. By the time we made it back after two hours of lying under the umbrella, we had found all three of the guys passed out throughout the house. Aaron on one recliner, Max on the big couch, and Des had apparently been sleeping in his room from what Brittany had said. I'd helped her make dinner, and by the time we were done, everyone had woken up.

It wasn't too much of a stretch to say that I had tried to give him his space when I could still tell there was something going on with him that he didn't want to share. I'd spent the last few hours, especially during the movie, reminding myself that he'd invited me to spend time with me. Because he cared about me. Not for me to act like a heartbroken twat who ignored him and got her feelings hurt for no reason.

You would figure I'd know by that point how complicated life could be, but apparently I didn't.

So his dad—his *family*—was rich and he hadn't said a word about it. So what?

So there was someone calling the house who made him mad enough for his entire demeanor to change and he didn't want to talk about it. So what?

I shook my head, trying to keep the expression on my face a clear, easygoing one that didn't have *you break my heart by keeping things from me* written all over it. It wasn't like I hadn't known that coming here. "I'm not tired, are you?"

"No," he answered, rubbing his hands over his khaki shorts.

I watched him, that beautiful face, the resigned-looking language printed all over his body, and honestly, it made me ache. What could I do?

"Want to take a walk on the beach?" I asked him before I thought it through.

To give him credit, he didn't hesitate. He nodded and stood up.

It didn't take us long to go down the stairs and out of the house, Aaron grabbing a flashlight from the mudroom on the first floor though he didn't bother turning it on during our walk down the moonlit street and through the homes in the neighborhood. I'd already done the walk enough to know exactly how many beach umbrellas we would find and how many chairs would be under each.

I wasn't surprised when Aaron headed straight to the same spot we'd gone to watch the sunrise that first morning. He lowered himself to the ground, the sound of him sighing the only noise other than the waves I could hear. It made me want to cry. I didn't want to see him like this; I didn't care who or what could have caused it. I just didn't want him with this . . . whatever it was, taking away so many of the things I loved about him. Knowing there was a line I needed to straddle, I tried to think of what I could say or do and simply went for the simplest option.

"Are you okay?" I asked as I took a seat a foot away from him, stretching my legs out. I didn't have the heart to punish him for being secretive. He was my friend, and most importantly, I cared about him.

He nodded, his gaze on the water, but it was this distracted kind of thing that only reiterated he was going through some-thing and not exactly winning.

I was sure he had his reasons, and if I hadn't already made it clear enough he could talk to me about anything, well, he was dumb and he should have known better by that point. "Are you having a good time so far?" I went with instead of pressuring him to talk to me about whatever or whoever was on his mind.

Aaron nodded, and I forced myself to quit wondering things that had nothing to do with me. "It's gone by faster than I thought it would."

"I know," I agreed with him, shifting my gaze toward the dark water. "I'm dreading going back home."

There was a pause and then a "You are?"

"Yeah. I wish I could stay here for another month or two." I sighed. "How perfect would that be?"

That had his head pivoting to look at me, a flicker of the man I'd started getting used to hiding in plain sight on the sharp bones of his cheeks and jaw. "What's wrong? You're stressed about work?"

I kept my gaze on the water as I nodded. "Yeah. I'm trying not to let it freak me out, but it is. My mom sent me a link to that job opening that's still available at her work while we were at the beach, and it's just got me thinking about what I'm going to do when I get back." I told him the truth. My mom had sent me a link with a smiley face at the end of it, but the problem was, I'd thought about it, only I'd thought more about what was going on with him.

"You're not going to do it, are you?" he asked, sounding more like himself than he had all day. Not totally like the Ron to my Ruron, but close enough.

I couldn't look at him then. "I don't know. They'll probably hire someone before I get back from my dad's. But . . . I can't keep going with my money situation the way it is, at least not for too much longer."

"But you don't want to get an office job," he reminded me.

"I know I don't." I swallowed and shifted my focus toward the midnight-colored gulf again, not wanting to look at him as I told him the truth. "I'm a chicken, Aaron. I've told you that already. I'm too scared things won't work out. I've already told you the craziest things I've ever done. I was freaked out to go *fishing*. Fishing. I think I've taken enough risks just these last few months since I quit the job I had with my aunt."

"You're not a chicken," he said, as what I could only assume was his foot slid across the sand to touch mine. I didn't let myself focus on his affection. What I did let myself zero in on was this gesture that was all my Aaron. It wasn't like I could bring attention to it though and tell him I noticed what was going on.

Instead, I told him, in a weird voice that almost sounded disappointed, "I hate to break it to you, but I am."

"No, you're not."

"Yes, I am. We talked about this."

"Yeah, we did, but you're still not."

"Aaron—"

"You're not," he insisted. "What are you scared of that you haven't done?" he asked, his voice rising.

I screwed up my nose and finally turned my head just enough to make eye contact with him for all of a second before glancing forward with a shrug. "A lot of things." Maybe I didn't want to talk about this, but I didn't want him going back to his morose, mopey crap again.

"Like?"

It was my turn to sigh. "I don't know. Lots of stuff. Jumping out of a plane. Getting a tattoo." I pointed at the water vaguely. "Heck, go swimming at night. There's a ton of stuff."

Aaron paused. "You're scared of going swimming at night?"

"You saw me jump on top of you when something touched my leg a couple of days ago. I almost cried when you made me hold that first fish, remember? The Loch Ness monster is probably swimming around in the water right now right beside Jaws, ready to get me if I go in."

Aaron snickered and I found myself smiling more at him sounding like himself than anything. I flicked my gaze to the side, finding him with his arms planted behind him, eyes on me. I looked back at the water. "Nessie isn't going to get you," he claimed.

I side-eyed him with a smirk. "You're on a first-name basis with her?"

"Yeah, what of it?" He nudged me again, and *again* I kept my attention forward. "Get in the water. Nothing will get you."

"No."

"Ruby."

"Aaron."

"Get in the water. You say you're scared, and I know you're braver than that, so do it."

I couldn't help but turn my head to look at him with a crazy expression on my face. "That's easy for you to say."

"Why?"

I blinked. "Because you're probably not *really* scared of anything."

Aaron's head jerked back and he frowned. "I'm scared of enough things."

It was my turn to raise an eyebrow. "Like?"

"I told you. Things I can't control. Being a failure," he said.

"You'll never be a failure, and I can't control if a giant sea creature swims up to me."

He sighed again and chose to ignore my first statement. "She's on the other side of the ocean, and Jaws is way up along the coast. You'll be fine."

I scoffed, but Aaron didn't make a sound. He was too busy looking at me expectantly, like he was waiting for me to see reason and decide that *yes* I would go in water so dark no one could see anything beneath the surface, because that was logical. But he just kept on staring.

And staring.

And staring a little more.

"Aaron," I mumbled, tipping my head back to look up at the sky because I couldn't handle his gaze anymore.

It wasn't until he swiftly got to his feet and stood up straight that I finally glanced up at him, finding that long body standing over me, his hands going to the hem of his shirt for a moment before he pulled it up over his head and dropped it to the sand without ceremony.

I jerked back, sputtered and glanced at his abs for all of one second before moving my eyeballs to his face. "What are you doing?"

He was watching me as his hands went to the front zipper of his shorts, and he was still watching me as he unbuttoned and unzipped them, tugging them down his legs with a shake of those narrow hips I'd been discreetly eyeing every time he'd been in a bathing suit around me. And just like the first time, and every time, his body was immaculate, even in the moonlight as he stood there in boxers that inadvertently highlighted his long, muscular legs and that spot right at the center of his body that made me feel like too much of a perv if I did more than glance at it quickly.

"Taking off my clothes so I don't get them wet," he replied casually, stepping out of his shorts before bending over to pick them up.

"Why would they get wet?" I asked him in a voice even I could tell sounded hysterical, something in me already telling me that I'd dug this grave for myself and knew exactly where he was going with this crap. I was beginning to have second thoughts about wanting to cheer him up if it was at this cost.

"Because I'm going in the water." He folded his shorts in half and dropped them on top of his T-shirt. "You coming?"

My heart was beating, beating, beating. "No."

Aaron winked. "Yes."

My throat clammed up. "Aaron—"

"Come on. We don't have to go in deep. You can hold my hand."

I coughed. Sputtered some more. Maybe even gagged a little. "I'd want to hold something more than your hand going into the water—"

Aaron choked. Literally choked. Gasping out, "Jesus, Ru."

Oh no.

The blood drained from my face. "You know that's not what I meant!"

His laugh was so rough and loud and happy it made something in me click. "Do I?"

"Yes!"

I didn't know it was possible for him to laugh louder, but he did.

"I'm going back to the house," I muttered, not moving.

He dropped his head back and kept on laughing, a hand coming up to rest on the six-pack I was not going to look at. "All right, all right. I'm just messing with you," he said, chuckling and sounding pretty much delighted, with a long sigh afterward. I narrowed my eyes when he reached up to swipe under his eye. "Come in the water with me and I'll never bring it up again. Promise."

I groaned.

"Ruby."

"Aaron."

"Come in the water with me," he insisted, sounding totally back to normal.

I stared at him. "I don't think so."

He stared back at me. "You're going to regret it later when you think about it," he egged on.

How could I have forgotten how well he knew me?

I scoffed again, ignoring the truth to his words.

"Come on, will you? Just you and me," he said gently. "Ruron forever."

Of all the things he could have said, he went with the one that I loved and wanted to hate at the same time. Ruron. Ugh.

What had to be his toes pressed to the side of my foot. "Ruby Cube. You can hold on to whatever you want if we go in. I won't let anything happen to you."

He had me. He had me big time. And I was pathetic.

Fisting my hands, I groaned in resignation and held back a whine. "Just for . . . two minutes. Two minutes is all."

I slid an eye in the direction of the waves gently rolling onto the beach, calm, black, black, black. No part of me wanted to go in there, but . . . I knew what he was trying to do. He knew what he was trying to do.

But . . .

I squeezed my hands into fists at my sides and told him the truth in a near croak. "I'm scared."

He blinked and the next thing I knew, he was dropping into a crouch directly in front of me, his face just above mine. Both his hands went to one of mine, enveloping it in between his. His words were soft and gentle as he brought our palms toward his chest. "I'll be with you the whole time. You know I wouldn't just leave you out there to be mean."

The worst part was, I knew he was telling me the truth. That was something my brothers would do, but not Aaron. Never Aaron. Not if he knew I was genuinely scared, which I was.

"Two minutes, that's all. I just want you to know there's nothing to be scared of. It's past feeding time—"

I stopped breathing.

"Ruby." His chuckle was low. "There's more scary shit in the world out there than in the water, but it's all about how you face the things that you're not sure about, understand?"

I groaned at his words and the truth in them.

"You understand," he answered his own question when I hadn't. "Come on. I won't leave you. You're braver than you think."

I was, wasn't I? Or at least . . . I could be. Hadn't I already shown myself that?

I didn't want to be that chicken Ruby anymore, even though I might always be. Maybe. I didn't want to be so scared of things that I actively avoided them. My mom, who had gotten her heart broken time after time, relationship after relationship, didn't stop being scared of falling in love because it hadn't worked out for her in the past. Besides losing, I couldn't think of a single thing Jasmine was scared of. They were the two most fearless people I had ever known. I could be like them. We had the same DNA after all.

I didn't even realize I was getting to my feet until I was on them. I definitely didn't notice I was pulling off my shirt until it was over my head and I was dropping it on top of Aaron's pile of clothes.

What I did realize, just as my hands went to the elastic band of my shorts, was that Aaron was now standing up once more.

He was watching me. His eyelids were a little hooded and his eyes might have been focused in a dozen different places, but I couldn't be sure because of the darkness. It was his turn to ask the same question. "What are you doing?"

I tugged my shorts down my legs and did the same shake he had before I stepped out of them. "Getting out of my clothes so I don't get them wet," I explained, using his exact same words. "I'm not getting naked."

Even in the darkness I could tell his throat bobbed. But he didn't say another word as I set my shorts down on top of the rest of the pile. Nerves and anticipation thrummed through my veins and arms, but screw it, I was going to do it. Two minutes. I could go in there for two minutes.

The breath that came out of my mouth was shaky and weak. "Are you sure I can hold on to anything that I want?"

Aaron raised an eyebrow in a way that had me thinking he was second-guessing his offer.

"All right, don't forget what you said," I warned him, taking a step closer to the water. "Let's get this over with then."

He kept his gaze on me a second longer before dipping his head just enough for it to be counted as a nod and then took a step forward. I waited until he was at my side to turn to face the water and wade in. His hand hung loosely at his side as we walked side by side, deeper into the cool but not cold water hitting my ankles, my shins, my knees. It wasn't until the water lapped just over my knee that I shivered and took a half step to the side, closer to him.

I was halfway up to my thigh when I reached over and grabbed his forearm.

"That's it?" he asked calmly the moment my fingers touched him.

I shook my head, looking down and trying not to freak out when the inky water started to lap at my hip. "Ah, nope."

"Then what—"

I moved behind him like a ninja, the palms of my hands going to his shoulder blades, absently noticing his skin was warm. The ridges of Aaron's spine rippled when I touched him, my palms sliding up to straddle each side of his neck. I knew what I was going to do, and I knew it wasn't exactly what platonic friends did, but he'd said it, hadn't he? I could grab whatever I wanted.

"Giddy up, cowboy," I told him all of two seconds before I jumped on his back.

Looking back on it, I should have given him a longer warning or at least a better one.

Because he hadn't been ready.

He hadn't been ready.

Otherwise, if he had, I'm sure neither one of us would have fallen face first into the water, me on top of him, flying over him, pretty much somersaulting into a roll that had me snorting water up my nose the second my head dunked into the surface. For one second, I thought I was about to drown, taking way too long to get to my feet before I could shove my upper body out of the water with a gasp like I really had been on the verge of death.

I heard him before I saw him spitting water. "What the hell was that?" he coughed, as I spit out the gulf water I'd just inhaled a gallon of.

Freaking soaked and with my nose and eyes burning, I shivered and crossed my arms over my chest. "I was going to make you give me a piggyback ride," I tried to explain, still blinking the water out of my eyes so I could see better.

"I could've if you'd given me a warning," he said, laughing easily as he swiped a hand down his face, so much like my Aaron

I couldn't find it in me to regret what had just happened. "My forehead hit the floor and my stomach scraped bottom."

I shivered again. "I'm sorry. This was a stupid idea. If that's not a sign I should get out before I get eaten alive, I don't know what would be."

Aaron's hand landed on my forearm before I could take a step toward the shore, and the next thing I knew, that smooth, muscular expanse of his back, with its two little dimples at the bottom, was in my vision. "We're already wet. Come on."

I hesitated and Aaron scooted back just a little more so that if I leaned forward just an inch, he'd be right there, pressed up against me.

I could see his profile under the moonlight as he glanced at me over his shoulder. "I can carry you in my arms if you want."

Aaron carrying me in his arms? Heck yes.

Realistically though, and for the sake of my sanity and feelings, *no*. Heck no. That was an awful idea.

"No, no, it's all right," I said, probably a little too quickly. "Are you ready this time?"

"I would've been ready last time if I'd known—"

I didn't wait after I put my hands on his shoulders and just *jumped*, again, knees going to the sides of his hips, my forearms locked around his neck so tightly I might have been choking him. Then his own hands were on my butt, and I squeaked as he gave me a boost just a little higher up him.

"Ru, I need to breathe before I pass out and we both become shark bait."

I tried wiggling one of my legs out from around where they were wrapped at his waist, but his palm slapped high up on my thigh.

"Stop. We'll just go in a little deeper," he assured me with a snicker.

"Fine," I mumbled behind him. "But I swear, if we become

a shark attack statistic, and it bites me in the face, and the surgeon can't repair the damage, you're marrying me so you can look at my face the rest of your life and remember it was your fault."

He chuckled so quietly as he moved deeper into the water I almost couldn't hear him. It didn't take long before we were chest deep in the gulf. The water was hitting me right at my breasts from how high up I was on his back. I could feel him breathing, and I was sure he could feel me breathing and feel my heart beating so fast it almost seemed at capacity.

But I ignored it all. I ignored it all except for the lights coming from the houses on shore when Aaron turned us in a circle. Except for the bright, nearly full moon in the sky illuminating the surface of the glassy water. Except for the feel of Aaron's solid build in front of me, his hands coming to rest on my calves.

"Nice, hmm?" he asked in a whisper like he was stuck in a trance too.

"Very nice," I agreed, my mouth just to the side of his ear. "I could get used to this."

"You'd come in the water by yourself next time?"

I snorted. "Heck no. But if you gave me a piggyback, I'd do it again," I said, letting my clutch of death go just enough so I could pinch his lean cheek. "Have I told you thank you today for inviting me?"

He made a thoughtful noise. "Not today."

With my arm back around his neck, I gave him another squeeze and whispered, "In that case, thank you for inviting me."

And Aaron squeezed my calves as he said right back, "Thank you for coming with me." And then, "And thank you for writing me for so long."

This man owned me entirely, and he had no idea. "Don't thank me for that."

He turned his head just a little, like he could see me out of the corner of his eye. "Why?"

"Because. Trust me, you helped me out a lot more than I helped you out."

"Nah."

"It's true."

"No, it's not," he argued. "You don't even know how much I needed your e-mails, Ruby." There was a pause. "I didn't even know how much I needed your e-mails."

I almost gushed sugar out of my mouth, and I definitely had to ignore the warm sensation in my stomach reminding me I was in love with him. I had no business thinking that, especially not when there were so many things he couldn't tell me. "You had like two other families, too. Don't give me all the credit. I know how it is."

Fingertips grazed my calves and I felt him sigh beneath me. "No, you don't, and I hope you never do," he said in a voice that sounded resigned or sad, or maybe both. "There are so many things you see and hear that you can never forget or get out of your head, no matter how much you try. It wasn't until you that I heard myself laugh, Ruby." That perfect profile tipped to the side and I saw the corner of his eye peeking at me. "You don't know what that means to me."

I sniffed, touched by his words, and so freaking in love with this guy I wanted to make a potion that would make him fall in love with me so I could keep him forever. I'd keep spiking him for the rest of my life if I could. All so I could have him.

But that wasn't the way these things worked, unfortunately.

Instead, I hoped he could tell the difference in the way I had my arms around him and that he could notice I was trying to hug him instead of cling to him for dear life, and I said with my mouth real close to his ear, "You're the best, Aaron Not-An-Asswipe."

I was pretty sure that if anyone had been standing out on their deck that night, they could have heard us both laughing.

Chapter Twenty-One

It was stupid to think it, but I woke up feeling different the next morning.

Maybe different wasn't the correct word to use, but I felt . . .

I don't know how the heck I felt exactly. After spending a lot more than two minutes out in the water, clinging on to Aaron like a spider monkey, something in me seemed changed. Maybe that was the thing about doing things you hadn't thought you could do, you realized that maybe you weren't who you'd always thought you were. There was more to me than even I'd thought there was. Despite everything I thought I'd learned the day before, I felt happier, more at peace, just . . . better, even though I was really tired after only sleeping five hours.

Dragging myself to the bathroom that morning, I showered quickly and headed upstairs, yawning nonstop. With my usual bottle of water in hand, I made my way to the balcony and tried to clear my mind as much as possible. I tried to think of the things that made me happy and the way the air smelled. I tried to think of anything but Aaron.

But like a high school girl with my first crush, almost every thought just went back to him in some way. How I was worried about him. How I was disappointed that he didn't trust me enough. How I shouldn't like him as much as I did, but I did.

When I wasn't thinking about him, I thought about what I was going to do when I got back home after visiting my dad.

The door of the deck slid open and there Aaron was, with his tray. There was some coloring beneath his eyes like there had been every other day, but he smiled at me warmer than he ever had before, and that was saying something in a language I didn't know.

"Morning," he said.

"Good morning," I called back to him, watching as he made his way toward where I sat.

He held out a plate toward me as he lowered himself into his same chair. On the white plate were two pancakes with what looked like chocolate chips in them. And they were shaped like Mickey Mouse's head.

I glanced up at him to see him smiling at me almost expectantly.

"You like?" he asked, pulling out two forks from the pocket of his swim trunks and handing one over.

I couldn't stop the stupid smile on my face. "How did you make these?"

"Skills."

I rolled my eyes even as I kept smiling. "No, really."

He winked. "There's a mold in the cupboard. I thought you'd get a kick out of it."

A mold in the cupboard of his father's beach house. I shoved the reminder away as I said, "I already told you, but you know you don't have to cook for me every morning. I can eat cereal."

His words were so simple, yet more powerful than anything. "I want to."

And like the needy idiot that I was, I asked him, "Why?"

With the side of his fork to the plate, he started cutting a piece of his plain, round pancake, his gaze flicking back and forth between the food and me, like the words coming out of his mouth were effortless. "Because I want to, Ru." Aaron's mouth twisted to the side as he chewed on the piece of pancake in his mouth, and he said, "Hurry up and eat so we can go."

"Fishing?" I asked him, sounding a lot more hopeful than I ever could have imagined.

His twisting mouth turned into a smile. "No. Scalloping."

"Scalloping?" I croaked.

"Yeah. Scalloping. Did you bring any water shoes with you?"

"I look like an idiot, don't I?"

"You don't look like an idiot." Aaron tipped his head to the side and smirked.

That grin said enough. I looked like an idiot. It was in the nineties, and I had on a giant straw hat and something Aaron called a buffer that really just looked like the neck part of a turtleneck. I blinked at him and sighed. "It looks like I was planning on going to the Kentucky Derby and then changed my mind and thought about going skiing, and finally decided to go to the beach."

He shook his head, but I couldn't miss the grin on his face. "Your neck is red enough. I told you to put more sunblock on yesterday, remember?" he reminded me for about the fifth time.

I was tempted to reach up and touch it, but I didn't. I'd already rubbed aloe vera gel into the skin twice before Aaron had come up to me with the buffer and smiled so sweetly, I hadn't realized what he was putting over my head until it was on there . . . and then he'd given me the hat.

He kept talking. "We could swim out further and dive, but we'll stick closer to shore. I've found a bunch here before."

Before. How had I missed all the signs he gave me that he'd been here more than once in the past? *It's no biggie*, I said to myself, trying not to let the reminder ruin our day.

"If the heat starts bothering you too much, just tell me and we can get out of the sun," he offered, stepping back to look at me.

I sighed, and that only made him grin more.

"Am I annoying you?"

Was he annoying me? It was the furthest from the truth in a way. And I told him so. "No. You're just—" I waved my hand a second before dropping it. "You're so nice to me." *Even though you don't tell me things.*

His laugh almost eased the ache away. "Am I supposed to be mean to you?"

"No." I snickered.

There was a smirk on his face as he turned his back to me to head into the water, when he threw over his shoulder, "If you decide you need to jump on my back today, give me a warning, will you?"

My mouth might have dropped open for a second before I blinked at him. "Has anybody else ever told you what a pain in the you-know-what you are?"

Aaron stopped walking and tossed that blond head back to laugh. "Yeah. Except you're the only one who's ever called it a 'you-know-what.'"

"Ha, ha," I joked, starting to follow his path. "It's something to work on, I'm just throwing that out there."

He snorted and glanced over his shoulder, a small smile on his face. "Lessons with Ruby at 8:00 a.m."

I was at his side when I nudged him with my hip. "Shut up and show me what we're looking for."

"Need a hand?"

I froze with my elbow in the air, my hand just barely touching the back of my neck as I sat on the edge of the couch in the living area of the beach house with a tube of aloe vera gel balanced on my thigh. Sitting on the recliner to the left of where I was, with the clanking of pots and pans in the background, was Max, leaning back against the seat with an amused smile on his good-looking face. On the love seat to the opposite side were Brittany and Des, who were busy snuggling adorably and watching television. Aaron was in the kitchen, washing the dishes that weren't going into the dishwasher, following a nice spaghetti meal the seventeen-year-old with only one good arm had managed to make, despite most of us offering to help her out. She'd gone to her room to talk on the phone.

I'd been trying to reapply aloe vera to the achy skin on the back of my neck, which hadn't gotten more burned after the three hours we'd spent scalloping . . . but it hadn't exactly helped either. The problem was, I couldn't exactly see what I was doing and my arms felt dead after hunting for clams and then following that up by going for a swim.

"Uh," I kind of muttered to myself for a second, taking in the man that had been sleeping most of his days away. I hadn't really spoken too much with him on this trip, but . . . it was fine. "Sure," I told him, with a shy smile, not wanting to tell him no when he'd offered assistance. I hated when I could tell someone needed help, and when it was offered, they denied it.

With a tip of his chin, the very handsome man that I'd learned through bits and pieces was thirty years old and worked graveyard shifts at a refinery, got up and took a seat on the cushion directly beside me. The side of his knee touched mine, but I didn't think anything of it as I handed him the tube of gel.

"Thanks," I said a little weakly, dipping my chin toward my throat to expose the back of my neck.

I heard the tube lid click open and followed by that was the almost farting sound of the gel coming out of the container and onto what I could only imagine was his palm. Seconds later, I felt the cool touch of his gel-covered fingers lightly grazing the nape of my neck and moving around. "I thought Aaron was going to make you wear a scarf or something?" he asked, spreading the gel.

Looking at my ultra-tan thighs from all the sun I'd taken in, I smiled. "He did. This is from two days ago. I think it's getting better."

"I guess," he said, his fingers still moving back and forth in circles and lines across my skin. "It looks painful."

"Only a little," I admitted, peeking at him over my shoulder.

Max leveled a smile at me that six months ago would have knocked me off the couch, or at least had me texting someone to tell them all about the hot guy touching me. But now . . . well, now I felt nothing but appreciation.

"You're good," he said, pulling his hand away.

"Thank you," I told him, taking the tube from him to set it on the side table beside me. Turning back around to face forward, I found a familiar pair of khaki cargo shorts standing nearly directly in front of me.

I didn't get a chance to say anything before he'd turned himself around and dropped that rounded butt into the sliver of space separating me from Max. Leaning to the arm rest, I lifted a thigh to give him room to sit as his best friend scooted over. *Way over.* What was he doing? I didn't need to look around the room to know there were other spots he could have taken instead. Not that I necessarily wanted him to sit somewhere far away, but . . .

I snickered when he leaned back against the back cushion, wedged so tightly in there that the only way he fit was because Max and I were both crowded into the sides. "What are you doing?" I asked him with a grin once he'd settled in and looked down at me.

He slipped an arm over the back of the couch behind my head. "Sitting down." I scrunched up my nose at him, and all he did was smile back. "Does your neck hurt?"

"Not really," I told him honestly. "It's fine. It was worth it."

"If you want to stay inside tomorrow to give your neck a

break, we can," he suggested, moving his leg just enough so that the entire length of his thigh was squished against mine.

"That's probably a good idea," I said. "I'm sorry. You don't have to stay inside with me if you don't want. I can just watch TV by myself or something."

His hand landed on my bare thigh, and I was really grateful that I'd showered and shaved after I'd come back inside following our swim.

"Ru, I don't care—"

The suggestion came out of my mouth so unexpectedly, I hadn't even realized it was still on my mind. "If you wanted to call your friend or hang out with her, I'd understand."

The lids covering those dark brown eyes hung low. "My friend?" he asked slowly.

Why had I brought this up? It was too late now, wasn't it? "The, uh, waitress."

"The waitress?"

Crap. "The one at the restaurant."

At the rate of a snail, the confused expression on Aaron's face slowly melted off, replaced by a smile at the same pace. Why did he look so smug? "RC, I know her, but she's not my friend."

I kept my mouth shut.

"She used to mess around with my brother. She's nice and all, but we're not friends."

Well. What could I say after that besides "Oh"?

The blond beside me grinned a little too smugly. "She's not my type."

"*Did she just stick her fingers in his ass?*"

What? Where? I wondered, forgetting all about what type Aaron had.

Across the room, Brittany let out a laugh in response. "She did!"

"What the hell are you watching?" came Max's second question as he sat up and looked around the room to make sure his little sister wasn't still in the kitchen.

She wasn't.

I could feel rather than see Aaron tense beside me. What I did see was him leaning forward, planting those impressive blond-hair dusted arms on his knees and saying in his controlled, even voice, "Would you change the channel? Ruby and Mindy don't need to see that shit, come on."

Me? Mindy I could understand. But *me*?

"Put it on something else," Aaron said with a finality I couldn't miss. "Ruby's right here."

And when three other sets of eyes all swung over to my direction, I blushed. Everywhere. Up to the roots of my hair.

While I wouldn't have been outraged at seeing a girl sticking her fingers in a guy's butt—and it wouldn't be the first time or the second or third I had—I cringed on the inside at Aaron basically comparing me to a seventeen-year-old. Because just like *that* I knew what he was saying and why he was being so defensive and overprotective.

He was hinting at what I thought he was hinting at, there was no doubt about it.

All I could do was give the other three a smile, which probably looked like a mixture of deranged and embarrassed, even as I looked down at my clean fingernails and stretched them wide on my lap, saying, "You can leave it on if you want." My voice was all whispered and funky and *I don't want to talk about this, but . . .*

But these friends of my friend, a lot nicer and kinder than I ever could have given them credit for, changed the channel. Immediately.

They all thought . . .

Yeah, they all thought I was a virgin now. Or maybe just really, really, really innocent. Basically: a virgin.

What was this? The 1860s? Was porn not a click away any-more? Did he not have any idea the kinds of things I'd seen on the Internet late at night when I had my door locked?

Not that there was anything wrong with being a virgin, but I wasn't one. I hadn't been one for a while. Where the hell could Aaron have gotten that impression from?

It took me all of a moment, sitting there embarrassed out of my mind, to figure it out.

It was the never-having-a-boyfriend thing. Being in love with the same guy for years. Not really even dating ever. That would be it. *I knew it.* It had to be.

Oh man.

I couldn't look at him as I blindly reached over the side table where I'd set the aloe vera gel and picked up my phone instead. I could sense Aaron's gaze on me as I brought the phone close to my face and opened my notepad app, typing the words that I didn't expect to ever tell anyone, much less Aaron. But I didn't know how else to get out of this conversation gracefully. I couldn't let him keep thinking . . . that. No wonder he thought of me like a little sister if he was comparing me to Mindy. This was my fault. Totally.

You know how much I love that you're so nice to me? I wrote him, before handing over the phone not very discreetly.

His eyebrows rose in my direction as he took it from me and read the screen, his eyebrows dropping back into place in an expression of confusion. **I know**, he replied before return-ing it to me.

How was I supposed to tell him this? I'd never told anyone this, never even thought it would come up and I'd have to have a game plan. Yet here we were, and I knew I needed to tell him.

I'm not THAT innocent, I typed.

Then I added, **But thank you for watching out for me**, and set the phone on top of the thigh he had lined up with mine. He lifted it up without hesitation and read the words. There was a moment between when he read it and then stared at the screen before typing, his thumbs looking too large for the touch screen.

He handed it back over.

I figured you . . . knew stuff was his response.

Knew stuff? What did he . . .? He was going to make me say it, wasn't he? He really was.

Flashing him a side look that he met with his dark brown eyes, I cleared my throat and typed a message back that had me cringing on the inside. Maybe I should have dropped it and let him keep believing what he'd been believing.

What do you mean by "stuff"? I've seen . . . penises. I've watched . . . stuff . . . online.

His face turned a shade of red I'd never seen on him before as he read my reply. He hesitated. Gulped. His thumbs flew across the screen in a blur before he handed me back the phone with his gaze trained forward.

OK.

I swallowed and decided I needed to just tell him. Get it over with. So I did.

I'm not a virgin.

It wasn't like he knew what I'd typed when he took his time picking the phone off his leg and reading what was on the screen. I didn't miss how his eyes flicked back up to the top as if he was rereading what I'd written. Then he did it again. Slowly, too slowly, he typed up another message and set the phone on my thigh.

I thought you said you'd never had a boyfriend before.

Really? *Really?* My heart was beating fast as I typed, **You've only had sex with people who were your girlfriends?** Did I write that more defensively than I probably needed to? Yes. Definitely yes. But I'd never told anyone this before, and . . . well,

I'd chosen him. It wasn't like admitting what I'd done was easy for me.

Aaron stared at the screen for a second before his Adam's apple bobbed once.

No, was his simple, basic response that I couldn't get even a remote feel on. His attention was still focused directly in front of him, and I didn't know what to think about him not wanting to make eye contact with me.

But what was I going to do? Lie? Let him do this double-standard crap? It was my fault for not being more upfront with him, but it wasn't like I was proud of what had happened, and if I could go back, I wouldn't have let it go down like that.

But you couldn't go back to change things that were already in the past.

It was only once and I was 21. He wasn't my boyfriend then or afterward. He regretted it almost immediately, and besides apologizing to me for it, we never talked about it again.

My face was red as I finished typing out the truth, but I kept holding the phone in my hand, trying to think of what else I could tell him.

I don't like talking about it because it's hard to think that I gave someone something I'd really wanted to, had them accept it and then pretty much reject it and make me feel like I was a giant mistake. He blamed it on "being caught up in the moment." Do you know what I mean? It wasn't what I had expected. I felt like an idiot.

Aaron took the phone from me slowly and read the message at least three times from the way his eyes moved down and across the screen several times. Then slowly, slowly, he typed out a message and set my phone back down on my thigh for me to take.

What happened?

Nerves caught up with me as I reminisced about that one thing I really tried hard not to think about ever.

Right after I turned 21, I told myself I was going to try and be more outgoing, that I'd go after the things I wanted more often, you know? I tried, I really tried to get out of my shell. My brother's birthday is a few months after mine, and he decided to have a party. I went. I'm a crappy drunk, and I had one too many margaritas at his house that night, so I wasn't exactly acting like myself. Which was what I wanted. I guess I was more outgoing and uninhibited. I never would've come on to him that hard or flirted so much if I hadn't drank so much . . . but I did. We ended up talking all night. He was being so nice to me and friendly . . . He acted like he liked me, but I think I made up more to it in my head, and when I wanted to go home, he offered to take me.

When he dropped me off, he asked if I wanted to go to a party with him the next day. I didn't want to, not really, but I wasn't going to tell him no. So I went. And I drank too much that night too because I'd been so nervous. I just wanted him to like me. And he was great. I thought that was it.

I cleared my throat and kept on typing away.

On the way home, I pretty much threw myself at him. Literally. It was the ballsiest thing I had ever done before I met you. He tried telling me it was a bad idea and that we shouldn't, but . . . we did. Once. He took me to his place and it happened. He wouldn't even look at me afterward. I got dropped off at home and he kissed my cheek without saying anything. The next day he came by and told me we shouldn't have done that. That he cared about me and thought of me like a little sister, and that he hoped I wouldn't tell anyone. I told him I wouldn't, but when he left, I cried for days. I thought there was more to "it," thought he'd come around one day and apologize because he'd changed his mind, but he never brought it up ever again, and I couldn't either.

I knew Aaron saw the way my hands were shaking as I typed

on the screen and then set the phone on his knee. I could see him flicking his gaze between my face and the phone as I put my hands in my lap and waited for him to read what I told him. He had to have read what was on the screen at least five times because it seriously took almost ten minutes before he finally wrote a reply. I didn't miss the way his hands trembled as he set my phone on his leg that time, not mine.

There were only three words on the screen, but they were the three words I'd hoped he wouldn't write.

It was him?

We both knew who "him" was.

But I couldn't actually type the words out and make it a reality. What I did manage to do was turn my head and meet those brown eyes even though I really, really didn't want to, those irises met mine so openly and evenly, and I nodded.

Aaron blinked.

His throat bobbed.

But his gaze didn't go anywhere else.

The breath that came out of his nose was strangled.

Those brown eyes moved over my face as his hands moved to his knees. He squeezed them. Once, twice.

And then he looked away and let out another deep breath that ripped the air right out of the room as it filled his lungs.

I was so stupid.

I'd been so stupid. Why? Why had I done that? I'd asked myself that a thousand times over the last three years, and I still didn't have an answer that made me feel any better. Chances were, I never would.

My heart started racing even faster, and tears pooled in the back of my eyes as I faced forward just like Aaron had done. For a second, I thought about getting up and going to my room, saying I had a headache or something. But I didn't want to be that person any more. Goose bumps rose on my arms and my stomach started cramping and a part of me wanted to throw up.

For all the world knew, Squirt was still a virgin. I'd never told anyone about that before. Not even my best friend. Not anyone.

Only Aaron.

And I'd kept my secret for this exact reason.

I lifted my left hand and ignored the way it shook as I swiped it along my lower lash line, holding back tears. I'd tried to justify my actions by telling myself I'd been young and dumb, but it hadn't helped at all. The only thing that had soothed me had been that no one except Hunter and I had known what happened. I could still remember the bright smile on my mom's face when I'd walked into the house after he dropped me off—after Hunter had sat inside his car and hadn't even bothered walking me to the door. She had asked me, looking expectant and happy, "How was it, Squirt? Did you have fun?"

And in one of the rare moments of my life, I'd lied to my mom and managed not to burst into tears even though I'd wanted more than anything to do that. I had told her, "It was fun. Hunter dropped me off."

I'd cried so hard in the shower, trying to get everything *off*. Off, off, off. When Hunter had shown up to the house the next morning, claiming I'd left my ID with him, I'd been hopeful, so freaking hopeful. But it had only taken him saying two words for me to know I'd misinterpreted why he'd come by.

The rest was history.

It had been my fault I'd been dumb enough to hold on to some blind faith that he'd somehow come back into my life in the end. It had been my fault I'd put my life on hold waiting for a love that would never present itself. Everything had been my fault.

Out of my peripheral vision, I saw both of Aaron's hands go up to his face, the fingertips pressing against his brow bone as he let out an uneven breath. I could see Max watching him with a frown, as if he couldn't understand what was his deal. It wasn't like I would tell him.

"Aaron," I whispered, touching the back of my hand to the section of thigh exposed from his shorts riding up.

He peeked at me from his left eye. And then he was up on his feet, maybe not intentionally shaking off my touch but basically doing the same thing as he strode toward the patio doors leading to the deck and disappearing through them, closing them with a lot more strength than was necessary.

Max looked at me with wide eyes, his forehead furrowed. "What's his deal?"

I wasn't about to give him a detailed explanation, but I could tell him part of it, even knowing this was his best friend and he might not like me afterward for making Aaron upset. "I think I made him mad."

Max's facial expression changed so quick I almost missed it. He rolled his eyes and let out a snort. "Ah. Don't worry about it. That just means he cares about you. That's the only reason he ever gets mad. I piss him off all the time."

What was that supposed to mean? I'd just watched him get mad yesterday at whoever he'd spoken to on the phone. Who could it have been then?

"Give him a minute. He'll be over it in a sec," Max assured me easily.

I hesitated. Did I want to go out there? Nope. But . . . I thought that maybe I did. Hadn't I already learned the hard way that when something was bothering him, he shut down and retreated until he was over it? My sister Jasmine was the same way, and even with her I'd learned that sometimes the people who instinctively went with that reaction, needed someone to say "screw it" and go after them anyway.

The last thing I wanted was for Aaron to think I didn't care about his feelings, even if I absolutely didn't want to confront him about anything related to Hunter.

I gave Max a weary smile as I got to my feet and let out a shaky breath through my mouth before heading toward the deck. I didn't open the doors quietly, I wanted him to know I was coming, and closed them behind me when I spotted him with his elbows on the deck railing, his fingers laced together. Even with only the light from the living room illuminating the space, I could see the tightness along his jaw and cheekbones. I could sense the rigidity in his body.

But I wasn't about to let any of that intimidate me. Not this time.

"Are you okay?" I asked, approaching him.

He didn't look at me. "I'm fine."

Everything in me screamed to just go back inside. *Go back inside.* I didn't want to do this. But . . . "I'm sure you are," I said to him. "But I'm not."

That had him cocking his head just enough to the side to look at me out of the corner of his eye. "Can we talk later?"

Chicken Ruby wanted to agree, but this new Ruby I wanted to be, she might have shaken and cried on the inside, but she said, "I would rather not."

"Ruby," he suddenly sounded exasperated. "I'm not in the mood, all right?"

"I get it. I'm not in the mood to talk about this either, but I think we should. I think I deserve to know why you're upset."

Aaron shook his head, his gaze straying back in the direction of the beach. "You know why I'm upset."

"No, actually I don't," I told him, my voice shaking.

"You . . . you—" He let out a grunt like maybe he didn't even know what he was mad about. "Everything you told me makes sense now. I told you I don't like feeling stupid."

Something inside of me reared up in indignation, in respect

for myself, and I got all defensive again. "No one does, Aaron. I don't like it either."

His jaw moved just enough for me to tell he was back to side-eyeing me. "What's that supposed to mean?"

"You know what that's supposed to mean. I don't like being kept in the dark about things either."

He could have lied. He really could have. He could have played dumb. He didn't. Instead, Aaron let out this deep breath that almost seemed like he'd been holding it for years and years and years. Some part of him seemed to deflate, but just as quickly as it had, he sucked in a fortifying breath. "Look, can we talk about this tomorrow?"

"No." Where the heck that had come from, I had no idea, but I kept going. "No. You don't get to push me away and choose when to talk to me about things. I care about you so much, and I'm not going back into the house so you can sit out here and stew and bottle things up. *I* told you something that I've never, ever told anyone, and I didn't want to. I know I did something stupid, okay? You don't need to remind me. I've lived with that almost every day for the last three years.

"You keep pushing me to be braver than I feel, and when I finally do, you're just going to storm out and not talk about it and try to turn this around? I don't think so, mister. Maybe other people will let you go and do your thing, but I'm not. Not with you," I said to him, my voice going in and out from normal volume to a whisper as my emotions got the best of me.

"I've gotten to know you, and I know there's a lot you still haven't told me, and that's fine. I figure one day, hopefully you'll trust me enough to. I know a lot of people haven't given you a reason to believe in them, but I'm not like that. I'm not one of your ex-girlfriends or anybody else. I promised you I wouldn't lie to you, and I'm sorry I kept that from you, but I hope you understand how humiliating that was. How much it still hurts me. I can't pretend like it doesn't, and it kills me that you might think differently about me because of it."

Aaron's head lowered until his forehead touched the hands he had hanging over the ledge of the balcony. I could hear him breathing. I could sense that his tension wasn't going anywhere, and I knew, *I knew* he wasn't going to break down now. Whatever he was thinking about and getting mad over, wasn't going to get resolved right then.

And that notion made a knot form in my throat in disappointment and resignation.

He didn't say anything, and I had no words left to give him. So I did the only thing I was capable of then, because I wasn't about to let myself cry. No way. I settled myself into one of the chairs closest to me and I sat there as Aaron kept standing against the rail of the balcony.

Neither one of us said another word.

Chapter Twenty-Two

I wasn't surprised at all when I woke up the next morning and realized I was already in a crappy mood that had nothing to do with being groggy and tired after only sleeping a handful of hours.

The night before had been exhausting, and that was keeping it simple. Aaron and I had stayed outside for over an hour, with everyone else eventually stumbling off to bed. It wasn't until he finally took a step away from the rail that he acknowledged I was there again. His fingertips had grazed my knee as he passed by me, his gaze not once meeting mine as he headed toward the doors and shoved one open. Aaron had stood there as I got to my own feet and headed back inside, while he closed it.

When he started flicking lights off was when I finally headed downstairs and went straight into my room. I figured that if he wanted to talk, he could come to my room and say whatever he wanted to say. Except he didn't.

Was he disappointed in me for not being a virgin or for just being a dumb kid and adult? Was he mad at me for keeping it a secret? Or was there something else going on?

I had no clue.

What I did know was that I felt exhausted even though I didn't want to go back to sleep. I didn't feel like I had the strength right then to sit with him in silence in case he wasn't ready to talk. Some part of me expected that was how it would go. Hadn't we gone two weeks without talking in the past? I only had a couple more days left here, and I didn't want to spoil them, but I wasn't about to apologize either.

Frustrated, I unplugged my laptop from where I'd left it charging on the floor, opened it up, plugged in my headphones and began streaming a movie through Netflix. The sun filled the room with color, but I ignored it until the credits scrolled down the screen an hour and a half later. I wasn't hesitant opening the door to go to the bathroom with my clothes rolled up under my arm. I couldn't hear a sound in the house, but I didn't put any thought into it. It didn't take me long to shower and get dressed, and I took my time putting aloe vera on my neck in my room, noticing that it was already feeling a lot better than when the hot water had initially touched it.

Feeling brave, I finally left my room with the intent of going to the living area, wanting to just get this awkwardness over with. But I hadn't even taken a step when I heard the familiar voice talking in almost a hiss upstairs.

"I don't understand what you're expecting from me," Aaron said in an angry whisper.

When there wasn't a response, it confirmed that whoever he was talking to wasn't someone in the house. I should have gone back into my room instead of eavesdropping, but instead, I just stood there as he kept speaking, his voice a steady, angry thrum throughout the house.

"Do you need more money, is that it? . . . Not more money, you just want me to let him know you're running low, right? . . . Again? Running low *again* . . . How many times is this now? Five? You've asked five, maybe six times, to put in a good word for you and I haven't. I don't understand why you'd think this time I'd change my mind . . . I've told you, if you want something, call Colin. He might have some sympathy, but Paige and I won't . . . *What?*"

There went the mention of Colin and Paige again. Was it his mom? I couldn't think of who else it would be, especially not when there was a mention of a "him" and "more money" like there could be someone else other than his dad this could be about.

"That's not my problem. I told you already I didn't want to talk to you, but every single time you think I'm joking, you think I've changed my mind . . ." Aaron practically growled. "That's never going to happen. You think I've forgotten how you used to cry on demand around Dad? It stopped meaning anything a long time ago. You've overused that card, don't blame me."

I didn't need him to use the "M" word to know it was definitely his mom—his *birth* mom—he was speaking to. Jesus. Was she asking him for money? Who did that? And what the heck had happened to make him so mad at her?

Suddenly feeling like a little bit of a jerk for listening in on something I knew down to my bones was extremely personal for Aaron, I turned around and headed back to my room, trying to be as quiet as possible as I closed the door and leaned against it.

What was I supposed to do now?

I must have stood there for at least half an hour, playing a game on my phone before I straightened and decided to try this again. Based on the tone of voice Aaron had been using, there was no way that that conversation had lasted too much longer. I was only slightly worried as I headed up the stairs, keeping my ears peeled for any noise, but there was none. I made it halfway into the living room when I found it empty, and looking out onto the deck, I found it was empty too.

It was the bowl sitting randomly on the kitchen island that had my eyes zooming in on it. There was something that looked like a piece of paper sitting beside it. As I approached it, I could see scrambled eggs, a biscuit, and a tablespoon of jelly inside of it and everything in me stopped. My heart gave a squeeze.

And the only thing I could think of was that as pissed as he'd been, he'd still made me breakfast.

Picking up the note, I read the words scribbled on it quickly and sighed.

Have a headache. Going to take a nap. Stay out of the sun.
                                                                  –Aaron

At some point, Aaron must have decided he was going to start staring at me again.

Because that was exactly what he was doing.

He'd been boring a hole in my direction from the moment he'd climbed up the stairs late that afternoon, looking beyond exhausted in a way I could tell wasn't just physical. Max had braved the trip to wake him up after we'd all agreed to go out to dinner that night instead of having anyone cook. I hadn't been sure what exactly Aaron planned on doing with the scallops, so I hadn't signed up to make something out of them when I'd never messed with them before.

When he hadn't come up at noon for lunch, when we usually ate, I made him a sandwich with a side of those gross salt and vinegar chips he liked and a pickle, and went downstairs to offer it up to him. He hadn't answered when I knocked on his door lightly, and in a move there was no way I would have made months ago, I'd opened his door and peeked inside.

Sure enough, he'd been curled up on his side, facing away, sleeping soundly, not a snore, not a whistle, nothing coming out of him except the soft inhale and exhale of his breathing. So I'd left the plate of food on the dresser in front of his bed and tiptoed out, closing the door as quietly as possible. I'd spent the day watching TV, with only a thirty-minute break to walk the beach with Mindy, wearing the giant, ridiculous hat that Aaron had given me to wear the day before.

So when he'd finally come up the stairs in his slightly rumpled clothing and gone straight for the newest package of bottled water, I'd kept my eyes on him. He'd barely finished guzzling an entire bottle when those deep brown eyes moved around the room and landed on me.

And they hadn't left me since then.

Even on the car ride to the restaurant—a new one we hadn't gone to yet—I'd been able to see him glancing at me through the rearview mirror every few seconds. With Max and Mindy in the truck, I hadn't been ballsy enough to ask him if he was fine. And when we were led to a table, I wasn't sure what to do with myself, but he'd taken the decision right out of my hands when he'd pulled a chair out, gestured me toward it, and taken the seat directly beside it. The place was loud and crowded, and it shouldn't have been surprising considering that the Fourth of July was the next day. Over to the far side of the restaurant was a small dance floor with three couples, two-stepping on it.

I could sense Aaron's gaze on me as I scooted my chair forward and he did the same. Chancing a peek at him, I gave him a smile that was a lot weaker than any I'd given him yet, and he returned it to me, those eyes drilling into mine in this way that was completely new to me. Almost like . . . I wasn't sure. I wasn't sure at all, because I'd seen every man my mom had ever married look at her the same way. I'd seen my brother's boyfriend look at my brother that way.

And Aaron wasn't supposed to be looking at me the same. Not even close.

We all ordered and ate, with Max and Des taking ahold of the conversation about a sports team I'd never heard of. Meanwhile, I tried to collect my thoughts. Tried to plan what I could tell Aaron when he decided to talk to me again. Would we brush everything off and act like nothing had happened the night before? I wondered, bringing my fork to my mouth. I'd just closed my lips around it when I felt a hand cover my right one. The palm of Aaron's hand covered the back of my hand, his fingers going over mine.

This was a good sign, wasn't it?

With his free hand, he gestured to the waiter who was busy collecting Max's empty plate. "A double please."

"Of?" the man asked.

"Anything."

I shot Aaron a frown as he let out a choppy exhale, his eyes now on his own mostly empty plate. If it wouldn't have been for the weight of his hand on mine and the thumb moving along the bone that stretched from my pinky to my wrist, I would have asked him if he was fine, but I didn't want to ruin it, as selfish as that made me.

But Aaron's hand didn't go anywhere even though he didn't say anything until after the waiter had brought a glass filled with amber liquid and he'd sucked it down in record time, tossing it back like whatever was in it was water. He didn't cough, he didn't squirm, nothing.

I glanced over at the other end of the table to see Brittany and Des both watching him with a funny expression on their faces, and when they caught me looking at them, all I could do was lift a shoulder in a shrug, not wanting to take credit for leading Aaron to drink a double.

When the hand over mine squeezed it one more time, he leaned to the side and whispered, "Come dance with me."

Uh. "Okay? I don't really dance though . . ."

"We'll make it work," he said, already pulling me up to my feet, his gaze so intense, I almost started to worry.

I nodded and followed behind him as he maneuvered between tables and toward the tiny area in the back with a dance floor empty now except for a single older couple, swaying together. This wasn't exactly the type of atmosphere I danced in when

I usually did. On the rare occasion it happened, it was usually on a crowded floor at someone's wedding or party when everyone was too hammered to pay attention to what was going on.

And this wasn't a crowded floor.

But surprisingly, the instant that Aaron stopped at nearly the middle of the very small floor and reached out to me with both of his hands going to my waist, I stopped thinking. Stopped caring. Anyone could have been sitting there watching me and judging me and it wouldn't have mattered in the least. With my stomach still feeling off about his reaction to everything that had been said and done over the last twenty-four hours, I was equal parts nervous and apprehensive to be so close to him.

Mostly nervous though, even as my arms went up and my hands went to his shoulders. For some reason, linking them around his neck just seemed too personal.

And Aaron must have noticed because he shuffled closer to me, so close that our fronts grazed one another's. I'd danced with enough men in the past, friends of my brothers and distant relatives to know that this wasn't how it was done.

I stopped breathing and asked, "What are you doing?"

For one brief moment, Aaron looked me right in the eye and then brought us even closer together, so close I could feel the side of his jaw at my temple.

I wasn't going to overanalyze him not wanting to make eye contact and bringing us so close together, there was no way this was friendly.

I wasn't.

But I did.

Because *what the hell was happening?*

"What are you thinking?" I tried not to hiss but failed.

Something raspy touched my temple, and I didn't imagine the sigh that made his chest meet mine. His voice was lower, hoarser, the words dragged and slow. "You really want to know?"

Did I? "Not if it's something bad," I told him, just barely loud enough for him to hear me over the music, people's voices, and the tinkling of plates and silverware.

He made this chuffing sound that could have been a single laugh on the verge of tears. "Ruby girl . . ."

It was pathetic, but I pressed my forehead tighter in to him, knowing I had no right to, knowing I shouldn't because there were a hundred reasons why this was a terrible idea, yet somehow making my grip more possessive, stronger. "Why are we so close together?"

"Because." One of the hands at my waist tightened. "I want to."

I stuttered. "Why?"

"Ruby," was all he said.

Did he feel bad for me? Did he think I was an idiot? Was he doing this because he thought—

There were tears lurking in my eyeballs, all pathetic and too easy to trigger. But I still told him, "I don't want you to think I was stupid." I sniffled and felt tears clinging to my eyelashes. "I already beat myself up enough about it over the years. I know how dumb I was. I never planned on telling anyone because . . . I'd never met anyone I would want to tell. Until you."

I *felt* his whole body go hard. I *felt* tension fill one muscle after another in his incredible body. I *felt* him tip his face down and felt the breath out of his mouth hit the shell of my ear. The hands on my hips contracted even more and Aaron pulled me in closer, so close even I knew without a doubt that was something friends didn't do. Ever. They didn't have one zipper meeting another zipper. Friends with beautiful faces that you were in love with didn't croak into your ear, "You're not stupid. I don't think that you're stupid or dumb or pathetic, you understand me? Not even a little." The fingers around my waist gave me an even tighter squeeze, and I was sure his lips brushed my forehead as we stood there, an unmoving island in this world. "I hate you thinking that of yourself, because you're not."

And then he repeated for good measure, "You are not, Ruby." His chest pressed closer to mine on another inhale and he said, "You're the opposite of all those things. Every single one. You're smart, you're funny, you're talented . . ." That mouth went to my temple again and just stayed there, whispering words directly into me. "You think I've forgotten about you and your '*just Ruby*' shit?"

I just about choked.

And he kept going, oblivious. "You're beautiful, Ru. And you're sweet and kind. You're all those things you don't think you are . . . all those things you think everyone else in your family is, and more. I didn't understand why you couldn't see that in yourself, but I get it now."

With all the questions bouncing around in my head, I could only focus on one. He got it now?

"I wasn't thinking anything bad about you, RC." He continued speaking in that low voice. "I'm not mad at you. Most of what I've been thinking about is how I'm going to beat that piece of shit's ass the first chance I get for what he did to you, and nothing you do or say will talk me out of it."

I stopped breathing again.

"And I was thinking you messed up, like most of us do, being with somebody who you ended up regretting," he explained.

I guess I'd never thought about it like that. Then again, it was rare I ever let myself think about that. It was one of the lowest points of my life.

"Mostly though, Rubes, I want to go back in time and beat every single person's ass who's ever made you doubt yourself, because the girl who makes me smile till my face hurts even on a shit day needs to see that in herself. I feel like I owe it to you."

Aaron kissed my temple, and I couldn't breathe, couldn't think, couldn't get my cells to move.

My legs were weak.

And if that wasn't enough, he kept going. He kept going. "I was a goner from the first time you gave me hell." Aaron smiled. "Maybe even before then."

I was going to pass out. Right here on this crappy dance floor, I was just going to faint. And I highly doubted anyone had smelling salts.

I honestly couldn't do a single thing but just . . . stand there, and that was just barely. Because my knees . . . they had turned into jello.

That hand that had held mine countless times over the last few days came up and Aaron brushed at my cheek with his thumb. I heard him gulp. Heard him breathe. I felt him over the entire length of my body. "You are so goddamn special, Ruby. I'll tell you every day if I have to."

I couldn't look at him. I couldn't. It was taking an act of nature to even keep myself standing. "Okay." I gulped as my mind reeled, reality and just everything settling down enough for me to put the pieces back together. Then I stopped moving and raised my head so I could meet his eyes as I opened and closed my mouth. "Wait a second."

He raised a blond eyebrow, his facial features a mix of hope and nerves. *Nerves.* Coming from Aaron. *What was going on?*

"I don't understand," I told him slowly, still processing everything, forcing myself to back up a second.

"What don't you understand?" he asked easily, a partial smile on his features.

I squinted. "What do you *mean*?"

"What do you mean what do I mean?"

I blinked. "Do you . . .?" I couldn't say it. I couldn't say it, but I needed to. Had to. The words came out of me in syllables, a blush rising to my face at the fact that I was even about to *ask* this because it seemed so unreal. "Do you like me? Is that what you're trying to say?"

He squeezed my hip, his gaze intent. "Yes."

My entire world went hazy as I got out, with more hope than I ever could have dreamed, "As more than a friend?"

All of Aaron's facial features gentled and dropped, even his shoulders seemed to slump a little, those mahogany eyes boring right into mine, capturing them and not letting them go as he said one word and only one word, "Yes."

It was a miracle my mouth didn't just drop open so I'd gape at him.

"As a lot more than just a friend," he clarified like his "yes" hadn't been enough. His voice sounded watery and a little unsure, and it . . . it wrecked me.

I felt like . . . everything was a lie. Like I knew nothing. Like everything I thought I knew was BS. Skepticism I didn't even know I was capable of seemed to drip from my words as I looked up at him in 1000 percent confusion. "But you . . . you said . . ." *Aaron liked me?* I couldn't even wrap my head around the "Aaron" part of the sentence, let alone the rest of it. "You said I was like your sister," I pretty much accused him.

He made a groaning noise deep in his throat, his gaze never straying. "Not even a little, Rube," he replied. "I was drunk, and I'd been . . ." He swallowed and shook his head. "I'd been having a real hard time trying to talk myself out of thinking about you like that, but it didn't work."

That time, I'm pretty sure I did fail at keeping my mouth closed.

I must have because Aaron's smile grew a fraction and he dipped his head closer until his nose touched my forehead. "At first, you really were just a nice stranger. Then you were my friend, and I really did want you to be happy and do your thing," he explained softly. "And then it changed. The next thing I knew, you were telling me about some dick kissing you and it pissed me off more than anything ever had before."

"But . . . but . . . but . . ." I sputtered, my pulse going crazy, my breath getting thick, my mind swimming against the current. "But you . . . but I . . . but—"

His laugh was low. "Ru."

Jerking my head back, I glared up at him, unsure about how the hell I was feeling. He liked me. He liked me? I wasn't ready for this. It was what I wanted, what I should have wanted, but . . . "Aaron, why are you telling me this?"

That had him blinking. "Because I need to. I want you to know."

"But why?"

"Because you make me happy, Ruby. Because there's no one else I want to be around more."

In any other circumstance, I might have fainted, but I didn't. Every piece of my sanity was going nuts, and I couldn't line everything up and put it back in order yet. Not while I had a thousand questions and insecurities bouncing around in my head. "But you don't . . . ," I stammered, trying to think of why I would be ruining this moment and then remembering. "This was a real crappy idea."

His eyelids hung so low over his irises I almost couldn't see them. "Why's that?" he asked slowly.

"Because I'm crazy about you too, but this wouldn't work out. I think I might have rather not known," I told him honestly.

"Why is this a bad idea? Why wouldn't it work?" he whispered almost cautiously.

"Because!" I hissed at him.

"Because what?"

"Because you know I want to get married someday," I told him quickly. "And you don't."

He raised an eyebrow.

"But mostly because you don't want to tell me things for whatever reason," I responded, almost quietly. "I care about you so much . . . I love you, Aaron, but I don't want to get shut out. I told you yesterday. Every time I ask you something you don't want to answer, you don't. You tell me almost everything, I think, but the things you don't . . ." I shrugged. "I don't want you to be alone. I want you to know I'm here, even if it's just as a friend. But I can't love you when you just brood about things and bury them inside you. I get how it is, I get there's a lot you don't want to tell me because I wouldn't understand, but I'm sure there's a lot of stuff where that isn't the case."

Aaron stared down at me for so long, I thought I'd made him change his mind, and I wanted to believe I would have been all right with that because I didn't want to be with someone who held so much back from me. That wouldn't be fair. But finally, *finally*, one palm left my waist and cupped the back of my head, gently coaxing it forward until my cheek rested against his pectoral. Aaron hugged me to him, his chest expanding greatly beneath me. His words were soft. "I'm sorry, Ru. You're right. I shouldn't. I've told you almost everything. What do you want to know?"

There were multiple things, I knew there were. And I was glad he wasn't pretending like there was just one. So I picked the big one, the one that had been turning my stomach for days, and I asked.

"Who's been calling the house making you mad?"

I felt his sigh beneath my cheek. "My birth mom."

"What happened?"

He sighed again, the hand on the back of my head slid down my spine to land on my waist. "She's been calling since she knows I'm back in the States," he explained. "We don't . . . All right, I don't like to talk to her or about her, I'm sorry. I'm sure you can tell from our messages. She left when I was little. She cheated on my dad. I remember her saying how unhappy she was. How it had been him that wanted kids and she was the one stuck at home raising us while he worked all the time. How we weren't what she'd wanted out of her life.

"One day, she just upped and left. We didn't hear from her or see her for the next six years, until I was thirteen. The only reason she tried to come back was to ask for more money than she'd gotten in the divorce. I hadn't even known they'd gotten divorced, you know?"

I squeezed my eyes closed and nodded into him, focusing on the arms at my sides.

"About ten years ago, she came back again, claiming she'd found religion again and said she wanted to have a relationship with us. She talked my brother Colin into it, but Paige and I didn't fall for her shit. We know how things are with her. She only comes around when she wants something from my dad, mostly money, once a car. She's been calling the house, and I know that's what she's working up to, and it just . . . it pisses me off, Ruby. It messes with my head. She broke my dad when she left. She . . ." He let out another breath. "But he got over it and moved on and . . . some days, I still can't."

I knew what it was like to not have two parents around at the same time, but my dad had always been a call away. Always. "I'm sorry, Aaron."

He shrugged in front of me. "I'm sorry for not telling you. I don't talk about it. Her. You know what I mean."

"I might have not wanted to tell you either," I admitted to him. "I'm sorry she's like that though."

"I told you, the crazy ones like me. It runs in the family," he said, almost like he was trying to make a joke.

"I'm not crazy and I like you," I told him, trying to sound like I was joking when I really wasn't.

Aaron pulled me in close to him again, his mouth lowering so that he could speak directly into my ear. "You're not crazy. You're the best, and you deserve better than me, but I hope you don't care."

I was not going to have a panic attack or much less faint. Not me. Not me. Maybe I'd just slide to the floor, worst case. *This is not a dream*, I told myself. *I repeat, this is not a dream. You are awake.*

I didn't want to believe him. I really didn't. But . . .

"You think I'd do for anybody else what I do for you?" he asked, reminding me that he'd always been able to read my mind.

I was no match. Maybe it made me naïve that I wanted to believe he cared about me so much, but I didn't care. I didn't. I didn't need to think about the way he was with me to know it was real.

Because I knew what it was like when it wasn't real, and this wasn't it. Not even close. It was as far from being fake as you could get.

Because this was Aaron.

"You're sure?" I whispered.

His "hmm" was rumbled into my hair.

"For-sure for sure?"

He chuckled into my hair, roughly. "For sure."

"I need to make sure I'm not misunderstanding this, okay?" I asked, almost croaking, and he laughed again, all low and sexy and almost confident, nodding. "Don't laugh. I'm being serious."

"Okay." He still chuckled, his hands flexing at my waist. "I'm sorry for not telling you things, RC. I really am. You're the only person I've ever wanted to tell things to." Aaron pulled away from me just enough so he could look down and I could look up at him. "I know I told you I don't know about marriage and all that, but . . . ." His Adam's apple bobbed. "The idea of you being with somebody else . . . even just texting them . . . him . . . even before I saw your face or heard your voice, Rube . . . I don't want you with anybody else. You're my Ruby, and you have been for a long time."

There was no doubt in my mind I swooned. Hard. My sister Tali would have smacked me in the face, and Jasmine would have told me to grow up. Maybe I should have questioned this more. Maybe I should have thought about this more, but I wasn't going to. I knew what I felt. I could sense what Aaron felt. What more did I need?

Nothing. Absolutely nothing.

"Does that mean you want to kiss me?" I just went and blurted out.

He didn't vocally laugh, but I could sense the vibrations coming from his chest before he said, grinning down at me, "Uh-huh."

He wanted to kiss me. Aaron wanted to kiss me.

"Not as a friend?" I clarified.

"Not as a friend," he confirmed, amusement tingeing his words.

"Are you telling me this because you know I'm not a virgin now?"

There was a pause. He froze again. And then the next thing I knew, Aaron had dipped his face into my neck, over my hair. And he was laughing, *laughing*, as he kissed where my throat would be, and everything in me just went *nuts*. "No," I thought he said. "I was going to tell you at some point. Tomorrow I think. You're just always rushing me."

I snorted even as I felt like I was falling into quicksand, into this place I didn't know what to do in.

Aaron liked me? Aaron. Liked. Me?

I guess the signs had been there.

And still . . . "What are we supposed to do now?"

His chuckle was soothing, his palm going to the small of my back as those brown eyes stared into mine with more love and affection than I knew what to do with. "Whatever you want, RC. Keep doing what we've been doing. We'll figure it out."

Chapter Twenty-Three

Aaron liked me was the first thought I woke up to.

The possibility that Aaron might love me was the very second one.

I'd stayed up for over an hour after I'd made it to my room the night before, going over everything that had gone down on the restaurant dance floor, and it still hadn't been enough time. But I understood what my heart thought, what it sensed. And that was that Aaron Tanner Hall loved me. Maybe he hadn't used the words, but he hadn't needed to. All I needed to do was think about what he thought about me, how he treated me, and compare it to how every guy my friends had dated had treated them, and I felt pretty confident about it.

After all, hadn't I kind of sneaked in me loving him in there and he hadn't commented?

Maybe someone would tell me I was jumping the gun and coming to a conclusion that wasn't at all reality, but my gut thought differently. I didn't think I was imagining anything. Then again, if he was this wonderful and he didn't love me, I could live with it forever. What was love if it wasn't just a single word people used to try and describe something that wasn't easily explained or grown in one action or declaration?

I'd grown up knowing love was complicated. But I knew what it looked like. What it felt like. And I'd learned the hard way, through my own life and the lives of the people I loved, that there was a really thin line between love and hate. Telling someone you loved them didn't mean you'd end up together. It was just a freaking word.

So I wasn't going to worry about it.

With a lot more pep in my step than usual, I got off the bed and showered, feeling revived, feeling even stronger and better than I had before because I'd done what I'd never thought I would be capable of. I'd told someone I was crazy about, madly in love with, that I wasn't sure we could be together because they weren't holding up to the expectations I had for them.

Who the heck was I? A badass? Had I reached that level yet?

I never, ever would have thought I would have been able to do that. Ever. Not even in my wildest dream, but if there was something I'd learned about myself quickly, it was that I deserved better. I needed it. I wasn't about to settle for less.

And I'd done it.

Even Jasmine would have called me a bad bitch.

With the sun seeming to shine straight out of me, feeling rejuvenated and awesome, I finished showering, got dressed and headed up the stairs feeling like I could take on anything. I really did. After grabbing my bottle of water, I went to the deck and took a big whiff of the salty air, simply thinking to myself *this is amazing.*

So, it was the sun and me feeling pretty indestructible in general that I could blame for how the next few minutes went.

Because it was at that second that the phone inside the house rang.

And when I turned to look inside, Aaron wasn't already in the kitchen like he'd been the other two mornings when he'd answered it.

It was during the second ring, while I'd been too busy focusing on the fact that the phone was actually ringing, that this image of Aaron being angry and upset at these calls he'd been subjecting himself to, filled my brain. Then, it made me mad. That was when I practically stomped into the house, feeling like a different kind of Ruby than I thought I was capable of.

And I answered the stupid phone sitting in the cupboard beside the fridge with a grumpy "Hello?" that I also didn't know I had in me.

There was silence on the other end of the receiver.

"Hello?" I repeated myself, sounding just as aggressive as I had at first.

"Hello?" the female voice on the other end responded, sounding hesitant.

"Can I help you?"

There was a pause before the woman cleared her throat and said in a very stern, clear voice, "May I speak to Aaron?"

"Can I ask who's calling?" I already knew who it was, but I'd seen my family play enough games to know how to play this one.

"This is his mother," the woman replied with a certain amount of steel in her voice.

"I see," I said to her, thinking about the words he'd used last night. "He's not available right now."

"Can I leave a message?"

"I would rather you didn't," I told her, honestly and evenly.

She didn't say anything again for a moment. "Excuse me?"

"I would rather you didn't," I repeated myself.

"Who am I speaking to?" the woman asked, her voice getting a hint of attitude in it.

"His girlfriend," I said before I could stop myself. "And if you're going to keep calling him and upsetting him, I would rather you didn't."

"Excuse you," his mom snapped. "Who are you to—"

"Look, I don't know what your intentions are for calling him, but all I'm going to tell you is that you should really think twice about forcing him to talk to you when all you do is make him mad. If you're really trying to get back into his life, maybe you should ease up and go about this another way. If you're not . . . I don't know. All I know is that I'm not letting you ruin his morning. Have a nice rest of your day," I told her. Then I hung up.

Not even two seconds later, the rush hit me.

What in the *hell* had I just done? Had I actually just said that to Aaron's mom?

I couldn't believe it.

I couldn't freaking believe it.

Who was I?

"Everything okay?" came a voice that had me jumping in place and slamming the cabinet door closed.

It was Aaron.

"Oh, yeah," I stuttered. "Um." I knew I needed to tell him. I couldn't *not*. My face still went red anyway. "Your, ah, mom called."

He was halfway to the kitchen when he stalled in motion. Already in his swim trunks and a white T-shirt, he blinked at me sleepily. "Did it go all right?" he asked slowly.

"Yes," I told him, faking the brightness in my voice and failing miserably. "Don't say I never did anything for you, okay?"

He stared at me for so long, I fidgeted, thinking I'd done something wrong.

"I didn't want her to make you mad and ruin your day," I tried to explain.

Aaron took a step forward and then another and another until he stopped in front of me, and lightning quick, his hands came up to my face, cupping my cheeks in those rough, broad palms. A small smile had started covering his mouth at some point. Right before he kissed each of my cheeks with that perfect mouth, he said, "Have I told you today how happy I am you're here?"

"Jasmine, *Jasmine,* listen to me—"

"Nope."

"I'm not joking. If your thunder thighs"—she didn't have anything close to huge legs. Jasmine's were the stuff people's dreams were made of. Strong, athletic legs that looked great in everything and nothing. But I wasn't about to compliment her—"rip my tights, I'll give you bangs like I did when we were kids, remember that?"

There was a pause, and I'm sure even though she couldn't genuinely remember asking me to cut her hair when she was five, and the awful haircut that had followed, it had been well-documented by our mom in picture form. She knew it had happened. Then my little sister made her decision. "I'll risk the bangs. I'm wearing your tights. Bye, Squirt."

And then she hung up on me.

All I could do was basically cough out a laugh in surprise, when I shouldn't have been surprised at all.

"What are you cracking up about?"

I was still smiling as I turned in the seat to find Aaron standing at the doorway with a beer and a bottle of water in each palm. Reaching toward the chair he usually sat in, I patted the armrest as I answered his question. "Jasmine had texted me asking where I had some of my tights, so I called her to ask why she was asking. One thing led to another and I threatened to cut her hair if she wore them and ripped them. Then she just said 'Bye, Squirt' and hung up on me."

"Are they special . . . tights? What are tights again?"

"Basically pantyhose." I smiled at him. "The ones she was looking for have cats on them. I think she's going on a date if she's asking."

Aaron nodded as he sat down, the hand with the water bottle extending in my direction. I took it. "Cat pantyhose, huh?"

"Cat pantyhose."

"That's cute."

What was I supposed to say after that? "I have some with elephants on them too."

He raised an eyebrow as he lifted the bottle of his beer to that mouth that had touched various places on my face the night before. "I'd like to see those."

It was times like that I wished I actually had some experience flirting, instead of losing my words and not knowing what to say. "Hopefully one day you can," I said, unsure if that was too presumptuous or not.

But the smile he gave me said it wasn't. "One day," he confirmed.

I opened my mouth and closed it. Questions had been plaguing me while we'd been out doing a little more scalloping for a couple of hours and then when we'd spent the afternoon cleaning our catch under the carport using tablespoons. I'd even thought about my questions while I'd showered and eaten lunch. And then while helping Aaron make dinner, my head filled to the point where it felt like I'd burst. I knew I wasn't being very graceful or classy or mysterious. The truth was, I wasn't any of those things. I liked people being upfront with me with their expectations and thoughts. I wasn't so good at picking up hints or trying to play games with people. So I just did it. I just asked Aaron. "What exactly does this mean? You and me?"

His eyebrows went up as his lips left the rim of the bottle and he swallowed thoughtfully, one of his bare feet coming up to rest on the opposite knee. "Whatever you want it to, Ru."

That wasn't helping any. "What does that mean?"

Aaron smiled.

"I don't want to . . . take things out of proportion. Does that make sense?" I asked him hesitantly, his smile crumbling into a smaller one as his eyes narrowed.

"How would you take it out of proportion?"

Why was this conversation making me itchy and restless? "Like maybe we both really like each other, but you still want to be single—"

"No."

I shot him a look and continued with my examples even though I didn't want to. "Like maybe you like me, but when we're not together, we go our own ways and date other—"

"Hell no."

I blinked. "No?"

His entire expression changed, and Aaron set the beer down on one of the side tables. "I haven't liked you dating other people in months." He spat the words out with so much disgust I couldn't help but fall even more in love. "It's making me mad right now just thinking about it, Ruby," he said in that low voice. "I was jealous when I hadn't seen you, when I didn't know how much I like having you close by . . . when I hadn't heard your voice . . ." He swallowed. "Even if you didn't . . . look the way you do, I would've been here, feeling this way about you. Does that help you understand?"

He was feeling what kind of way?

My confusion must have still been apparent because those brown eyes bore into mine. "You're my Ruby girl. And if we would've met and hadn't kept hitting it off, then I'd feel differently, but I don't. That's not how it worked out between us."

I shook my head slowly, watching his face, lost, still confused and a little overwhelmed.

"I'm not going anywhere. Today or tomorrow. We can do this at whatever pace you want. That's what I'm trying to tell you. We're going to move forward, but we can do it when you want to," he explained.

"Just to make sure I'm not misunderstanding you . . ."

He grinned and I smiled.

"Just to make sure," I reiterated. "We're talking about sex?"

Aaron tipped his head back and laughed before looking at me once more and cocking it to the side, grinning wide. "I was talking about holding hands, kissing you, sex, too, I guess." He laughed again. "What am I going to do? Tell you no?"

I snorted. I couldn't help but watch him, suddenly feeling in control for the first time in forever and not really sure what to do with it. "Do you *want* to have sex with me though?"

The tips of his fingers went up to press into the space between his eyebrows as he laughed and peeked at me from the side of his hand as he kept on cracking up.

"Why are you laughing at me? I want to make sure I understand," I cried.

"I know you are, but it's making me laugh when you call it sex."

"Why? That's what it is."

"Damn it, Ruby," he said, laughing again. "I thought we'd be having this conversation months from now."

"Why?"

"Because!"

"Because what?" I asked him, too amused to be embarrassed. "Why are you being shy?"

Aaron blushed even as he grinned and shook his head. "Come here."

I felt myself perk up. "Where?"

With both hands at about chest level, he motioned me toward him. "Here."

I eyed him and blinked, and that only made him grin more.

"Come here and we can talk about sex."

My entire body went hot and red. Definitely red. I honestly wouldn't have been surprised if my eyeballs had bulged out of their sockets, and all I could do was laugh. "This sounds like the kind of moments my mom used to warn Jasmine about when she started having boyfriends, and she worried she'd end up pregnant."

"She didn't have those talks with you?"

I scowled at him and shook my head. "No. Not once. That actually makes me feel kind of crappy now that I think about it.

She never had the sex talk with me. I'm twenty-four years old and I'm still waiting."

Aaron laughed. "I'll tell you all about it."

I groaned, and that only made him laugh harder. "You're awful. You're doing this to me on purpose."

He shook his head, grinning so wide that dimple of his could have been a star. "You know I am. I know, Ruby girl. I know you. This is on you, as long as you know I'm not going anywhere. I'm not giving you up. I was ready to go fight those guys you were dating if it would've gotten serious."

Maybe it was wrong of me to flash him the biggest smile I was capable of, but I didn't care.

He tipped his face down, his expression suddenly going serious. "This isn't for this weekend. This isn't for the rest of the month." My expression must have been skeptical because he motioned me toward him again, his face solemn. "You don't make a dress in a day, right?"

With a lump in my throat, I nodded. "Usually."

"Your best ones take you hundreds of hours to make, don't they?"

"Yes." Where was he going with this?

"A business isn't successful overnight. You don't get promoted in a week. Everything takes time. Everything that is important and good and worthwhile, takes time. I'm not the kind of man who doesn't know that. Just looking at you makes me happy. Listening to you makes me happy. So come over here if you want, but only if you want."

He was killing me. Maybe he already had and this was some alternate dimension. Or heaven. I could see this being heaven if Aaron was saying what he was saying and all the arrows pointed at me. Maybe I was naïve. Maybe I'd been incredibly stupid in my life in the past.

But I wasn't going to be now.

So I got up and went to stand in front of him while my heart beat, beat, beat, frantic, frantic, frantic.

And Aaron smiled at me as he scooted to sit straight in his chair, his hands going to my waist, and he pulled me into him. My butt going to one of his thighs, my hip going next to his, my shoulder making friends with the one he called his own.

For the first time in my freaking life, I was sitting on a man's lap. I'd thought about this moment a dozen times in my past, but each time had been with someone who didn't look anything like the one next to me. I'd thought, back then, that nothing would have made me happier than sitting on this other man's lap and being the object of his affection.

That's what I'd thought.

And I would've been a moron. An idiot.

It was like . . . *this moment* was what I'd been waiting for my entire life. Like anything else, if there would have been anything else, would have been a pale, pathetic imitation. It would've been a drop in a bucket that I would never remember.

But this, this was not that.

Sitting on Aaron's lap on the deck of his beach house, with a handful of stars out, and the sounds of people on the beach . . . it was just one of a dozen other memories I'd already made with Aaron that I would never forget.

I'd hung out hundreds of times with other people doing things that had been fun in the moment, but I couldn't recall anything but a vague, hazy summary of the event. And maybe that's how I knew this was something else. How everything with Aaron was different. It was special. In my gut, as we lived in the moment, I knew I could never or would never forget the way he smiled at me as I sat on his lap. How his hand felt on the side of my thigh. How his eyes looked at me the way I'd always wanted to be looked at, like my heart was surrounded by bees and my skin covered in butterflies.

I could never, ever forget it.

"What are you thinking?"

Pressing my lips together, I chewed on the inside of my cheek for a second as I swept my eyes all over his face and said, "About you."

"Yeah?" he asked, amused.

"Yeah, Mr. Modest. Don't sound so excited." I snickered. "This is the first time I've sat on someone's lap."

Those brown eyes roamed over my face and the hand on my thigh gave it a squeeze.

With shaky fingers, I touched one of those beautiful, sharp bones just below his eye, unsure if this was something I could do. But he didn't say anything. Instead, he leaned into my fingers a little more. "Do you ever look at yourself in the mirror and think, *man, I got lucky*?"

There was a sharp noise that had me glancing at the face Aaron was making before he laughed and shook his head. "What the hell are you talking about?"

"You. Do you ever thank your birth mom or your dad for giving you the best bone structure in the world?" I asked, tracing my finger over the bridge of his nose.

"No," he chuckled. "I've never heard that before."

I stopped my fingers and glanced at his eyes. "You haven't?"

Aaron scrunched up his nose and shook his head. "No."

I made a thoughtful noise. "I bet you've heard all about how handsome you are plenty of times."

The hand on my hip gave it a squeeze. "Sometimes people only see what's on the outside and don't always care about everything else, Ruby. Looks can be deceiving."

With my fingers over the opposing cheekbone, I glanced at his face again, wondering what the hell had happened to him in the past to say that. Then I remembered, and I kept on moving my fingers along his cheekbone as I said in a low, steady voice, "Well, luckily for me, the best part of you is on the inside, huh?"

Then I stopped my fingers and cupped his face with both hands all of a sudden, cupping his cheeks together, not looking him in the eye on purpose. "I don't know if I'll ever be able to get used to looking at this face. It's like . . . you shouldn't be real. Like I shouldn't be real. Like I shouldn't be sitting on your lap right here because—"

Aaron reached around me and wrapped his long fingers around both wrists, his chin dipping down. "Get used to seeing it," he said.

And then he came for me.

Aaron leaned forward, his fingers still around my wrists, and slowly, so slowly I could have moved at any point or stopped him, the tip of that perfect nose touched mine. I could almost see every fleck of color in his eye from how close we were, and if he had any pores on that immaculate skin, I would have been able to see them as he rubbed the tip of his nose against mine, making me grin and feel like the world could have been on fire in that second and I would have died with a smile on my face.

"I could get used to Eskimo kisses," I said in a whisper.

And in a move I never would have ever given myself credit for, I tilted my face just enough to press my mouth to his. It was a peck. Dry lips on dry lips. It lasted all of a second of contact before I pulled back just an inch or two.

Then it was Aaron who pressed his mouth to mine. Two seconds before he pulled back.

And then we took turns. Me for three seconds. Him for four. Me for five. Him for six. Seven. Eight. Nine.

By the tenth peck, I moved my mouth up to kiss that full upper lip. And then I pulled it into my mouth with a playful nip, like I really knew what the heck I was doing. My subconscious must have been totally aware that Aaron wouldn't be the one to take it too far this time, so I did. It was my mouth that tilted to the side, that brushed my tongue across the seam of his lips. It was my hand that went to the nape of his neck to hold him in place. My fingers that brushed against the soft, short hairs right there.

But it was Aaron who opened his mouth and brushed the tip of his tongue against mine.

I hadn't kissed a whole bunch of men, but I'd kissed enough, especially over the last few months. And even though I'd enjoyed most of those kisses, it was nothing compared to this one. No one had made the hairs on my arms stand up. No one had stolen the breath from my lungs or made me squirm closer for more. No one else had made me feel like this was exactly where I was supposed to be.

Aaron kissed me and kissed me and kissed me with his hand around my hip, the tips of his fingers just under the hem of where my shirt had ridden up. He held me to him, and I'd swear I could feel something hard and thick right along my hip. And we kept on kissing. My face tilted one way, his tilted the other as his tongue stroked mine slowly and tenderly. I'd suck one of his lips between mine gently and he'd do the same to me. Our breathing grew harder. My hands moved deeper into his hair. My nipples went hard, and I wasn't sure if I shivered because of the breeze or because of Aaron.

What I did know was that it was him who pulled away, his nose touching mine as he let out a ragged breath against my cheek with a dry laugh that didn't sound all that entertained. "Jesus, Ruby."

I couldn't help but smile, feeling pretty damn pleased with myself. "Is that a flashlight in your pocket or did you think that kiss was as good as I did?"

He laughed straight out, his chest bubbling. "Pretty sure we're on the same page about that kiss," he muttered, sounding slightly out of breath.

It was my turn to laugh. "Can we do it again?"

Chapter Twenty-Four

I woke up with a stomachache the next morning.

It was our last full day in San Blas and . . . the idea of it sucked.
It really did. I'd always been relieved to go back home after a vacation, missing my bed, missing my stuff, missing my life, but
while I missed some parts of it, I didn't exactly miss the rest of it.
Not really. Not enough to calm the ache of knowing this was my
last day with Aaron.

I'd turned into one of those girls apparently.

And honestly, I didn't care. Not even a little bit.

I didn't need to look at the clock on my phone to know it was
right around six in the morning based on the shade of purple
coming through my curtain. Aaron and I had stayed up until
almost two, going back into the house to watch a movie when
people started shooting fireworks off on the beach. Aaron had
tensed every time the *pew, pew* sound from outside became par-
ticularly loud, but I didn't make it known that I noticed. I wasn't
even sure he did, like it was more instinctual than anything. The
rest of the group had shown up only about an hour into the
movie after watching the fireworks, crashing on the couch to
watch *Stargate*.

When we'd finally gone down the stairs and headed toward
our bedrooms, I'd thought about asking Aaron if he wanted to
sleep in the room with me, but I'd chickened out and just kissed

that mouth like it was the greatest chore I would gladly do every morning for the rest of my life and the next if anyone gave me the choice.

But it was the hand of his that cupped the back of my head as he tipped his mouth deeper into mine that had got me going to my tiptoes. Just as quickly as he'd leaned in, he pulled back, kissing one of my cheeks quickly.

I was a sucker. A real, real sucker.

With my head full of crap, I did my usual shower and shaving and headed upstairs, knowing that was about as far as my morning routine would go. Instead of going out on the deck like I had almost every other morning, I opened the fridge and started pulling out ingredients. I'd just finished sliding the first omelet onto a plate when the stairs squeaked with weight. Sure enough, it was Aaron, freshly showered and looking not as tired as he usually did.

But there was something there in his eyes I hadn't seen before.

"Morning."

"Morning, RC," he replied in that quiet, rough voice, slowly walking toward me. "What are you making?"

"Omelets," I said. "I already made you one. I figured you'd want two at least, right?"

His gaze flicked to the pan I had in my hand before he nodded. "Need any help?"

"No." I looked toward the stove again. "It's my turn this morning."

I wasn't going to be sad. Today was going to be a good day. A great one. One that didn't end with me blubbering into my pillow because tomorrow I'd be flying back home.

No. Today was going to be a good day if I had anything to say about it.

"You mad at the eggs or what?" came Aaron's amused voice.

I stopped with the whisk in my hand and looked down at the overly whipped concoction in the bowl.

He must have already been standing right by me because his hip checked mine, almost scaring the crap out of me. "Scoot over. I'll help so you can get done faster and you can sit with me."

So I could sit with him.

Tears prickled in the backs of my eyes and I stopped freaking blinking so they wouldn't get any ideas about what they were going to do next. The next few minutes went by quickly, but the most memorable thing about it was avidly avoiding Aaron's eyes as we moved around each other, making two more omelets in half the time it had taken me to make the first one.

"Who taught you how to cook?" I pretty much croaked out, knowing full well he had to have heard the hitch in my voice.

"My stepmom, ex-stepmom," he answered. "She'd only make breakfast and dinner. If we were hungry the rest of the time, we were on our own for food. She wasn't going to be anyone's maid, she used to say."

That made me smile. "My mom would say the same thing."

I could see him try to make eye contact with me, but I couldn't get myself to meet him halfway. I couldn't. I knew I'd cry. I just needed . . . another second. Or five.

"I've found a few recipes on my own too, if you can believe that," he said sarcastically.

I wasn't in the mood for sarcasm yet, not when it felt like there was this giant chasm in my chest getting bigger by the second. "It's hard to believe," I replied weakly.

There was a pause. A silence. And then a sigh seconds before two arms came around me from behind, a mouth speaking against my ear, "There's nothing to be sad about, okay? This isn't our last day."

I sucked in a breath and didn't make a single sound before I whispered, "It bothers me how well you know me."

"Tough shit."

That had me laughing, even if it did sound watery and almost heartbroken.

"See? Everything is going to be all right. Let's go eat our breakfast on the deck, yeah?"

And that's exactly what we did.

"Do you think you bought enough firewood?"

Aaron snickered as he dropped the last two bundles of wood on the blanket I'd laid out when he first asked me to help him set everything up. "This is all they had," he explained. "I'm surprised they even had this much left after the Fourth of July yesterday. Pass me four pieces, would you, stalker?"

It was my turn to snicker as I handed him what he asked for. We'd come out to the beach right after dinner, finding the spot we'd found earlier that others before us had used as a fire pit. Large heavy rocks had already been lined up in a large circle. I'd noticed that morning when we'd come out to the beach, with me in the ridiculous, large hat, that there were only about half the amount of people who had been sunbathing and swimming the day before. It'd been another painful reminder that this whole trip was coming to a close.

But I tried not to let it show on my face. I smiled at Aaron every time he'd been watching, and every time he hadn't. I was going to eat up every moment we had left together and store it all up for when we weren't. And then, *then*, I'd think about all the things he had said and all the things he had hinted at and all the things he had promised me. I just wanted to swallow up everything else in the meantime.

"Do you need help?" I asked him as he walked in a circle around the pit, looking at the center of it with a furrow between his brows.

Aaron snickered. "I know what I'm doing."

"I didn't say you didn't."

He walked directly in front of me, grazing his fingers across my cheek before stooping. "I was an Eagle Scout."

"Really?"

"Yeah," he answered.

"It's hard to get your badge for that, isn't it?"

One of those brown eyes peeked at me over his shoulder. "Yeah."

"I always wanted to be a Brownie."

I could see him pause where he was, his hands loose in front of him as he arranged the wood into a teepee-shape. "You couldn't?"

"No. No money. My mom didn't have time to take me to meetings." I wrung my hands. "She had work and night school. It was tough. Maybe one day when I'm older I can lead my own troop or something. That would be fun."

"Your mom went to night school?" he asked, his back to me.

"Oh yeah. That's why we were so tight. She went back to get her degree right after my dad left. She'd dropped out of college when they got married. That's actually how they met. She was an intern at a firm he worked at. She was young and wanted to have kids. Then after that, she got her master's; she wanted to be an auditor. She's kind of amazing. I didn't think of it too much when I was a kid, all I knew was that she was gone a lot and my aunt and grandpa would watch us all the time during the week. Then Saturdays were for homework and Sundays were our family day. She apologized to us a few times once we were older, but we all told her she didn't have anything to apologize for. She busted her butt for us."

"My dad worked all the time too, so I know what you mean, but he just likes working."

The reminder of his dad's work made this uneasy feeling fill my stomach. Did I play stupid or did I say something? Watching the lines of his back, I knew my answer the second I questioned it. "Aaron."

"Yeah?"

"You know I don't care that your dad is loaded, right?"

Slowly, slowly, he pivoted around in his crouch and stared at me.

I smiled. "I know I look pretty oblivious, but I'm not."

"Ruby—"

"I just wish you would have told me yourself."

His mouth opened and it gaped, the skin on his neck turning pink and getting darker as the color rode up his jawline and filled his cheeks. "I was going to. It's just—"

I held up my hand to stop him. "It's none of my business. I just wanted you to know that I knew is all, okay?"

I could tell Aaron was uncomfortable. Embarrassed maybe. And honestly, I could have repeated to him a dozen times that it was fine he hadn't been upfront about his family or who owned the beach house but . . . why? It had hurt my feelings a little when I'd found out and put the rest of the pieces together. I understood why he'd done it. I did.

But . . .

He still hadn't told me, and it made me ache a hair. Just a hair. I couldn't cure trust issues overnight.

"Ru—"

Getting up to my feet, I grabbed a log off the stack and walked around to the other side of the pit. "You need another one. I wasn't an Eagle Scout, but I can tell that's going to fall over in no time."

Aaron's mouth seemed to open before he closed it and pasted a tight smile on his mouth with a nod and a gulp he probably assumed I hadn't noticed, but I had.

"You still haven't gotten the fire started?" came Max's voice a moment before he started kicking up sand just a few feet away, stopping at the edge of the pit with his hands on his hips. "Do you need me to do it?"

Aaron huffed a tight laugh at the same time Max shot him a dirty look. "You do it? Right."

Max rolled his eyes. "Some of us go into manhood knowing how to do things and don't need to be in the Scouts."

"Is that why you made me change your tire twice?"

Max blinked. "Fuck you."

They bickered back and forth for the next hour while Aaron started the fire, after grumbling about kindling. Then Brittany, Des, and Mindy made their way to the beach with plastic grocery bags in their hands just as the sun completely fell behind the horizon and everything darkened. Down the beach, I could see another small bonfire going. I'd snagged a spot on one of the chairs they had brought from the house, rubbing my hands over my calves to warm them up while the fire grew larger. Mindy came over and took the seat beside me, spending almost all her time typing on her phone. As every minute passed, it got harder to accept that this was my last night here without making a big deal about it.

Aaron was in his element with his friends, arguing with Des and Max about everything and anything. I just watched him. At one point, just as they started busting out the bags of marshmallows, graham crackers, and chocolate bars, we made eye contact. I winked at him.

"I think I'm gonna go sit . . . over there," Mindy said abruptly, getting up without hesitation and going over to the other side.

I watched Aaron smile as he got to his feet too and patted her on the shoulder while they passed each other. Then it was my turn to smile as he came to a stop in front of me, both his hands going to cup the top of my head before sliding down until they rested on my shoulders. "What are you doing sitting all the way over here by yourself?"

I shrugged. "Nothing. The chair was lonely over here."

He frowned as he lowered himself to his knees on the sand,

pushing my legs apart on the way. Aaron scooted into the space, his back against the seat, my knees on either side of his shoulders. His hands went to my ankles, circling them. The side of his cheek rested against the inside of my knee. I could feel his breath on it, and that's what told me he was talking.

Leaning forward, I moved just close enough to hear him. "What did you say?"

He peeked at me out of the corner of his eye as he took my hand away from where I had it resting on my thigh, bringing the palm to sit right over those perfectly built pecs, the muscle taut, his body warm. But it was the feel of his heart beating steadily that relaxed me. "I said, I could sit right here for the rest of my life."

"Oh? That's all you said?"

I could see the corner of his mouth perk up into a slow smile. "Yeah."

I rubbed my hand in a circle over his chest, feeling more of his body on me.

"I'm sorry I didn't tell you about it," he said into my knee.

"It's okay."

He shook his head. "It's not okay. I'm sorry, Ru. It's just . . ."

I moved my hand to smooth over the short hair on his head, and he leaned into me.

"Where I'm from, everybody knows about my family. It's no secret."

"I'm sure."

"No, I want to tell you I just . . . you live in your family's shadow for so long, and when you don't want to be in it anymore, everyone thinks you're a dumbass."

"You're not dumb. Who made you feel like that?" I asked a little defensively.

"Everyone." His mouth touched the inside of my knee. "That's why I went into the military. I didn't know what I wanted to do, but I knew I didn't want to go to college and join the family business like my brother had done, and my dad had before him. It's what everyone expected. It's what everyone's always done. Joined one of the family businesses."

Were there more? But instead I asked, "But you don't want to?"

One of Aaron's hands wrapped around my bare calf. "No. Not really." There was a pause. "I don't know anymore, Ru."

"Then don't," I told him as easily as he always told me I could do everything and anything. "Or do. This is going to sound really cliché, but it's the truth: you can do whatever you want. Anything. You'll figure it out. Just because you didn't want to go to college years ago doesn't mean you can't in the future. You can stay in the military if you want. You can do anything. As long as you're happy, you can never be a failure. You don't have to make a ton of money to be successful, you know. Look at me, I'd rather be poor and stressed out than have a steady job that I hate." I hesitated. "Maybe I'm not the best example. All I'm saying is, do whatever you want to do. That's what you're always preaching to me, isn't it?"

He made a chuffing sound against my leg as he stroked it from the calf down to the ankle and back up. Aaron didn't say anything for a while, his gaze stayed forward on the fire.

With the hand not on his chest, I touched his soft blond hair and leaned in closer to his ear. "I don't know what to do with my life either, you know. But someone I know told me not to give up on my dreams. You know I'll help you figure it out in any way I can, just like I know you'll help me any way you can. Ruron, remember?"

That had him tilting his face to the side, peering at me over his shoulder thoughtfully. Before I could react, before I could even think, he pressed his mouth against mine. Lip to lip, just a press, then a peck on the corner before he smiled softly and nodded almost hesitantly like he believed what I said but was still a little unsure.

And that was okay. Because I wasn't going to quit telling him what he needed to hear. Not ever.

Neither one of us talked much as we ate smores roasted over the fire, and hours later, once the fire had finally died down enough for us to smother it completely, we trudged back to the house. My head had been full of all kinds of things I wanted to think about and all kinds of things I didn't want to think about.

But there was one thing I couldn't stop thinking about.

And that one particular thought stuck with me as we went back to the house and I detoured to shower because I smelled like smoke. With that same thought still in my head as I got dressed, I told myself that I only got to live this life once. Just once.

And somewhere deep down inside of me, I was the brave twenty-one-year-old who had done something I couldn't ever imagine redoing. Except this time, it was with someone that every part of me was convinced loved me back. Loved me back and wouldn't be afraid to hide it, if there was anything to hide.

But there wasn't.

There wasn't, but if there had been, Aaron would never make me his dirty secret.

Never.

So when I saw the sliver of light coming in from beneath the doorway of his room, the door slightly cracked, I shook off the tingling coming from my fingertips and told myself that I was a different person than I'd been even just a few days ago.

I pushed the door open a little more, nerves buzzing along my skin trying to convince me that I was scared. I ignored them as much as I could.

If I was going to be brave for anyone, it should be Aaron.

"Yoohoo?" I tried to ask, but it came out like a whisper.

He was kneeling in front of the bed, his suitcase wide open as he rummaged through it, but the moment I spoke, he stopped what he was doing and glanced over, smiling easily. "You okay?"

"Yes," I said, pushing the door open wider. "Can I come in?"

"You don't have to ask, Rubes," he said in a chiding tone. "Like I'd ever tell you I don't want to see you."

How did he do this to me? How? Swallowing the knot in my throat, I finally opened the door wide and stepped inside, closing and locking the door behind me. Aaron's eyes stayed on my face the entire time, obviously aware that I'd just gotten out of the shower from how wet my hair was, up in a knot at the top of my head. I smiled at him as I walked over to his bed, sitting on the edge of the corner closest to him.

"Good shower?" he asked, getting to his feet with a clean shirt and boxers in hand.

I nodded, trying my best to ignore the butterflies in my stomach going crazy at what the hell I was going to say.

Something must have been apparent on my face because Aaron made a goofy expression. "What's wrong?"

"Nothing's wrong," I croaked out.

He raised an eyebrow.

"Nothing is wrong."

His eyebrow still didn't go anywhere.

"Aaron."

"Ruby."

"Aaron, for real."

"Ruby, for real."

I groaned and fell back on his bed with a sigh, staring up at the ceiling like it would give me magical steel balls I'd been missing my entire life. The mattress dipped and I didn't need to see Aaron's face to know he was right beside me . . . moving closer to my hip from the way the bed moved and from the heat hitting my skin.

His hand landed on the hand I had resting on my stomach, and he made a little sound. "Tell me what's up."

Did I want to look him in the eye as I said what I wanted to say? No. Not really.

Should I?

That answer to that was an unfortunate yes.

Sliding my elbows up over the comforter I'd just realized had been neatly made at some point, I propped myself up and let out the deep breath I hadn't noticed I'd been holding. I'd brushed my teeth and rinsed out my mouth while I'd been in the bathroom, so there was that at least. Those brown eyes were on me and intent, and his mouth twisted just enough for that dimple of his to pop.

Now or never, Ruby. It was game time.

Swallowing the grapefruit in my throat, I pretty much whispered, "Can I sleep with you tonight?"

Brown eyes blinked.

Now or never, I repeated to myself. The world was for the strong.

So I kept going. "And by sleep, I mean later-later, if you know what I mean."

He knew what I meant. He always knew what I meant.

"You don't have to if you don't want to," I rushed out, feeling my imaginary, tiny balls rolling away and hiding.

Pink and red crept up from the collar of Aaron's T-shirt, going up, up, *up* as he sat there on his heels, looking at me like he couldn't believe what I'd just said. I couldn't either. Slipping my hand out of his grasp, I raised both my fists to my eyes and let out a moan. "We can just pretend I didn't say that too. That's an option. That's probably our best option. You know what? Let's do that. Deal?"

His chuckle wasn't immediate. It took a few seconds for it to rumble out of him, all content like a big cat. At the same time, the mattress sank and shook even more. His body heat reached me from my toes to my hair. My hands were moved away from my face gently, and when I felt the bed dip right beside my head, I opened one eye to find Aaron leaning over me, his dimple all out, basically ready to demolish my life.

And he was smiling even though his neck was pink and he looked like he was torn between several different emotions I couldn't exactly pinpoint.

It was my turn to blink. "What are you smiling at?"

He laughed. Loud. "Someone's in a mood."

I closed my eyes and groaned. "So, how about that bonfire?"

Aaron laughed again, the entire length of his body stretched beside mine, and I found myself peeking at him again. The hand he was holding to prop himself up moved, shifting over to cup my cheek as he kept on grinning, those brown eyes bouncing from one of mine to the next. "Ruby girl, we're not pretending that didn't happen."

"What?"

"That. What you said."

Keeping my face neutral, I let my eyes completely open and shrugged under his stare. "I don't know what you're talking about."

His chuckling made me smile even though I didn't want to. "You fried my brain there for a sec," he explained calmly, smiling down at me like I was the most entertaining thing in the world. Or the dumbest. "You can't say that to me and expect me to be able to think afterward."

"I shouldn't have put you on the spot like that," I tried back-pedaling with an apology. "We don't have to—"

Aaron kissed me. Not a peck. He went in there. His mouth molding to mine, his tongue lapping at my upper lip for all of a second before I let him in. And just like that, we were making out with him hovering over me. He kissed me and kissed me, going deeper with each movement of his tongue. From one side to the next, kissing and kissing me.

The truth of the matter was: I had no idea what I was doing. What I was supposed to do. I'd kissed other guys before, but it had never been with us lying down. Most notably though, it had never been with Aaron. With someone I was crazy about. Someone I couldn't stop thinking about. Someone who made me feel alive and special and like I could take on anything.

He knew I was pretty inexperienced. I knew he wasn't. But I wanted him to remember this. Whatever happened.

Hopefully exactly what I'd wanted to happen.

Because that's what I hadn't been able to stop thinking about. I'd waited my entire life to have sex once. And now . . . well, now I didn't want to wait around. That one time hadn't been awesome or legendary. It had hurt and been awkward, and it had been rushed.

And it hadn't meant a single freaking thing.

And Hunter hadn't kissed me anywhere near the way Aaron was. Like he was taking my life force every time his mouth scraped mine, like he couldn't stop kissing me. Like he couldn't get enough.

It was with that thought that I wrapped my arms around him. One hand went to the back of his head and the other went to the small of his back, slipping beneath the hem of his shirt to touch all that smooth, warm skin. He was everything. *Everything.*

"Jesus, I love your lips," he whispered, suddenly pulling his mouth away with a gasp. His face was only an inch or two above my own, his chest brushing mine with every breath. Those brown eyes bounced all over my face for a moment before he lowered his mouth again, peppering closed-mouth kisses along my jaw, one, two, three, then down the column of my neck, stopping on the second kiss, giving it a hard suck that had me tipping my head back for more, more, more. Aaron groaned into my skin, his body shifting around until the elbow beside my head moved and a hand slipped under the hem of my shirt, that big palm covering most of the skin on my stomach.

Aaron moved that beautiful mouth across my throat, his lips lingering over the middle of it, alternating between kisses and that suction that had me holding back a whimper each time. The fingers on my stomach moved slowly in a circle, teasing and touching, never going too high up.

All I could do was tilt my head up to catch Aaron's mouth in another kiss.

I'm not sure exactly who started taking whose clothes off first, whether it was me who pulled his T-shirt over his head or if he did it to my tank top beforehand. All I knew was that in a matter of seconds, we were both in some stage of sitting shirtless. Aaron's eyes grazed over my chest, his breathing so much harsher than I would have expected.

"I came ready," I croaked out, gesturing toward my bra-less chest, trying to lighten the mood.

It was like he didn't hear me, he was staring at me so intently.

I swallowed as his hand reached toward me, cupping my breast in his palm, basically swallowing it entirely in the dark gold of his skin color, making me look almost pale despite the hours I'd spent under the sun this past week. His hand was warm and his movement gentle, but his fingers were the total opposite when his thumb and index finger went to pinch a nipple that had gotten hard the moment he'd started kissing me.

"You're so damn beautiful, Ru," Aaron whispered, palming the slight weight of my entire breast again, his eyes going back and forth between my chest and face. "I can't think when I'm looking at you like this." He smiled, our eyes meeting again, and he leaned forward to kiss me. "Lie back for me," he said, pulling away just an inch.

I was a little scared. Just a little. More nervous than anything, honestly, mostly because I was sitting there, practically naked, just saying *Hello, look at me*. This beautiful, perfect man, who had more than likely dated handfuls of beautiful women before me, looking at me and only me. No pressure.

But I did what he said. I rolled down flat on my back, watching him as he turned onto his stomach, his palm sliding from where it had been cupping my breast, fingers splayed, going toward the middle of my stomach and stopping directly over the center of my belly. Aaron was watching me, and he hadn't stopped watching me, his eyelids going heavy, his breathing getting louder. And he moved, his head hovering directly over my chest, and in one heartbeat to the next, his mouth descended.

He kissed the side of my nipple. Then he kissed the other side. Above it. Below it. His tongue drew a circle around the hard nub, and then, finally, he sucked it into his mouth.

I was arching my back like crazy. Sucking in a breath, a hiss, something, making a noise I didn't think was possible for a human being to create. I felt him exhale in small puffs against the dampness of what he'd left on my breast. And he did the exact same thing with its sister, that hand of his moving up and down on my stomach, from the space between my breasts, down, down to the hem of the sleep shorts I had on.

"Ruby, Ruby, Ruby," he whispered, sucking at the nub again, soft and hard, using the tip of his tongue to flick it while it was inside his mouth, and then stopping.

I was squirming like crazy, wanting more, wanting everything I'd seen in movies and in porn before. I shivered, I shook. "Please," I whispered. "Please."

But instead, Aaron drew back. He watched me. And he slowly rolled onto his back beside me, his hands going to his hips, and as I sat up, I watched him shove his swim trunks down. I watched a line of light brown hairs emerge and watched as more trimmed hairs appeared, then a fat, cylinder-shaped base, and slowly, inch by pale pink inch, the length of his dick surfaced until it bounced upward, pointing straight into the air. He was long, thickest at the base, and with a deep red head that seemed to have a little white tear at the tip. Those slabs of his abs seemed to heave with a rapid breath I would never have expected from him as he kicked his trunks across the room to lay there naked.

I didn't know what I'd done in another lifetime to deserve the body lying beside mine, but all I knew was that whatever it was, I would have done it a thousand times over for just one single chance to see Aaron like this again. Those slim hips, the ridges of muscles along his obliques that seemed to point straight at the big penis that was tipping toward his belly button, and that face . . .

"I feel like it's my birthday," I whispered to him, unable to quit smiling. Aaron flushed deeper but smiled back. "Can I . . .?"

"Whatever you want," he said, swallowing hard, watching me straighten and sit up, slowly scooting over.

I reached for his stomach first, moving my hand across from one rib to the other. I moved my hand down the center of it, passing over the hollow of his belly button, going over the trail of blond-brown hairs leading down, side by side with thin veins, toward the thicker patch at the root of his penis. I had just grazed his pubic hair, and Aaron had just arched his hips upward with a rough breath, when I started moving my hand back up, toward his pecs, watching his face to make sure I wasn't doing anything wrong.

With my hand flat on him, I rubbed up over one pec, feeling the flat hair on his chest tickle my palm. I even rubbed my thumb around the pink of his nipple before moving over and circling his other pectoral, the muscle firm and warm. And then I swept my palm down one more time, trailing my fingertips over the slabs of his abs, watching in a trance as he held his breath while I did it.

"Why are you so handsome?" I asked him, joining my other

hand so I could feel all over his stomach with both like I'd never get this chance again.

Aaron let out a breath that could have passed for a laugh if it didn't sound so pained. "You can thank my parents another time," he basically groaned, arching his back and into my touch.

I smiled. How could I not? Lowering myself to my side, it was my turn to stretch against him, stretching against this beautiful naked man who felt like he was mine. That seemed like he was mine. Like he belonged to me. Raising my eyes to his face, I lowered my mouth to brush my lips against the slab of ribs closest to me, listening to him hiss. He was smooth there, and so warm, all I wanted to do was wrap myself around him and soak him in.

But I didn't do that. I moved my lips to his belly button and gave the skin right above it a kiss.

"Ruby," he hissed. "Come here."

"I am here," I said, kissing a spot below his belly button.

He groaned. "No, here," he said, his hands coming up to pat directly over the center of his abs.

Nervous, so freaking nervous, I swung a leg over his waist so I straddled his stomach, straightening my back so I kneeled over him, unsure of what he was asking for but knowing it wouldn't be nothing. He was smiling softly at me from where he lay, a flush covering his chest and neck. The feel of his hands landing on the outside of my thighs made me jump a little. But he watched me as he dragged his hands upward under the legs of my shorts until his fingertips seemed to graze the lower half of my bottom cheeks.

And then, one hand disappeared for all of a moment and the next thing I knew, there was pressure over my slit, right at the top, dragging down the length of it. Aaron watched me with those brown, brown eyes as he moved what had to be the pad of his thumb up and down the seam of my lips over my underwear, pausing right at the top with a gentle circle that had me sucking in a breath.

He smiled.

And he did it again.

And again, and again . . .

"More," I pleaded, more than likely sounding crazy.

And he gave me more, his touch gentle, light, circling and drawing a line straight down the center of me before going back up again for seconds, thirds, fourths, fifths, tenths and twentieths, until I could feel how wet my underwear was, I could feel how achy the middle part of my body had gotten. There was no way Aaron could have missed it, especially when his other hand slipped inside the leg of my shorts and tugged my underwear to the side a moment before the hand that had been driving me crazy, did the same thing again except this time over bare skin.

Then he slipped a finger inside of me and I lost it. In and out, one finger and then eventually two fingers, crooking and then sliding, forcing me to drop down to hold myself up on my hands and knees over him. His mouth found one of my nipples and gave it a nip that had me shuddering. It was the first time anyone other than me or my vibrator had been anywhere near the center of my body. Not even the other idiot, the original idiot, had gone there.

I only knew I was panting because I could hear myself as I moved my hips around his fingers for more. And just as I started to tighten, to feel an orgasm starting right at the juncture of my thighs, he stopped.

He freaking *stopped*.

"Aaron, please," I started to cry out, getting caught off guard when he sat up, his hands frantic on my hips as he shoved my shorts and underwear down my thighs, helping me maneuver them off in this tangle that only wasn't awkward because we were both so desperate. So damn desperate.

In the blink of an eye, he was on his back again and I was straddling his hips that time. Aaron watched me as he licked his palm and wrapped it around the broad, hard flesh that was lined up right along my lips. His fingers brushed the sensitive skin on the crease as he rubbed his palm up and down his length twice before pressing himself to where I was warm and wet and so needy it might have been pathetic if I'd cared. The smooth cap of his head brushed against my clit as he slicked his palm up and down, licking it once more before doing the motion all over again.

Then he lined himself up with where I'd played enough in the past to know was my entrance, and with flexing hips and his hands on my waist, he pushed upward at the same time I sat on the shaft standing there upright waiting for me. One inch at a time, I held my breath as he stretched me and kept on stretching me, going where only one other person had gone before, but somehow, I couldn't remember anything about that one and only time.

And then, with a slight sting that was nothing to write home about, and just enough discomfort to make me not want to move for a little while, my bottom hit his thighs and we both gasped. Neither one of us moved, breathed, did anything but just . . . exist.

"You okay?" he asked roughly after a moment, sounding almost entirely like a different person.

I nodded, flexing my inner muscles like that would help them get used to the new friend they'd made who wasn't anywhere near being small or skinny. And Aaron groaned, ragged, long, his abs heaving as he blinked like he was in pain. "Are you okay?" I asked him with a hiss of something that wasn't pain when he seemed to flex the big muscle buried inside of me in response.

Aaron smiled, swallowing, gulping, his breathing off.

I prodded at his shoulder, earning a moan from deep in his

throat as he moved inside me. "Hey, if you croak on me right now, I'll never recover."

A pained smile grew across his mouth, and he pretty much groaned, "I'm not okay. I'm never going to be okay."

I laughed and that only made him moan more.

Aaron tipped his head back, arching his upper body. "Ruby," he whispered, "move, just move a little, and I'll tell you anything you ever wanted to know. I'll do whatever you want me to do, I swear to God . . . I might die if you don't," he wheezed out.

Well.

When he put it like that . . .

I swallowed the knot in my throat as I lifted my hips just an inch and dropped back down. Okay, all right. Then I did it again, up and down, taking a little more each time, it feeling so much better, *so much better* after every movement. I had no idea if I was doing it right, but I tried to do what I'd seen in movies before. It wasn't like it was rocket science. Moving my hands to his chest, I started taking it all, every inch of his length until it felt like he'd almost come out, that big cap the only thing still inside of me, and I dropped back down with a hiss.

It was Aaron's hands on my waist, kneading, that made me start grinding against the base of him when I'd sit back deeply enough that I was on his lap. And then, *then*, it was amazing. Beyond amazing. With each grind of my clit against his pubic bone, the need to orgasm became more pronounced. Achier. And from the way Aaron was breathing, he was close too.

I froze, hovering over him, but he pushed me back down and made me circle my hips as I was impaled on him, over and over again, and I came. I came with a cry, with a swallow, with a groan that had me falling forward, my chest against his, the side of my face doing the same.

And then Aaron groaned, grunted, his body stiffened, every

muscle tensing as he jerked out of me suddenly, hot, sticky warmth covering my upper thighs as he clutched me to him.

I pulled back after a moment and looked down at him, breathing so heavily I wasn't sure I'd ever stop, and I said the words he had to know were in my heart. The only time I'd ever said them out loud and to one person . . . and maybe that was the proof I didn't need right there. Loving Aaron wasn't something I could just keep to myself, it burst out, stretching every seam in my soul and body. When you loved someone, you told them. There was no other option.

And I told him my greatest truth, like it was something I was proud of and would tell anyone . . . because I could and would. "Maybe this is the wrong time, but I don't care. I love you, stalker."

With the side of my face to the warm, damp skin of his chest, he whispered the words right back to me as another hand landed on the small of my back. "I love you too, Ruby Cube. You know that."

Chapter Twenty-Five

I was sad.

Sadder than sad.

I was so damn sad it made my mouth taste like ash. It made my heart ache.

I'd never really experienced grief before, but this sure as heck felt pretty close to it. So far, I'd been lucky enough to never have anyone close to me die, but this ... I could understand how some people never recovered from it if this was a fraction of what it felt like to lose someone.

Neither one of us had said much the last hour and a half since we'd left the beach house en route to the airport. He'd brought me breakfast at the crack of dawn again, but instead, this time, we'd woken up in his bed together. We'd showered together, with him washing my back and kissing my shoulders and hugging me while we were wet and slippery. I'd sat at the kitchen island while he'd cooked, and then we'd headed to the deck together to eat the waffles and side of berries he'd made.

We both knew what today was. What going to the airport meant. It meant this vacation was over. Our time together had come to an end.

It meant that Aaron would have to drive back to Shreveport, say goodbye to his loved ones, and then drive all the way to Kentucky to get back to his base.

It meant I'd go from spending all day with him to . . . not.

Every single thought that ricocheted around in my head since reality had really settled in had been focused on the fact that I had no idea when the next time I would see him or be near him would be.

And honestly, I'd been fighting back tears the entire time. This didn't seem fair. It didn't seem fair at all that now that I had him, I had to let him go. I had to go back home. For the first time in forever, there wasn't so much comfort in it.

"Did you check in to your flight already?" came Aaron's low, distant voice from behind the steering wheel. We'd left later than we should have, but I hadn't really cared or worried too much about how close we were cutting it.

I swallowed hard, fighting back the sadness that seemed capable of crushing my lungs. "No," I muttered as we passed a sign pointing us toward the airport.

It wasn't my imagination that Aaron slowed his truck down. "Ruby . . ."

I didn't want to look at him. I couldn't. "I wish I could stay here with you longer," I said, keeping my gaze focused on the blurry scenery outside the window. "And I feel really bad I'm not as excited as I should be to go see my dad because I'm sad to leave you."

"Ru," he whispered, gulping so loud I could hear him.

I wasn't going to look over. Nope.

"Hey," he said, steering the truck to a cluster of lined up cars that told me our time was about to run out. "I don't want to drop you off either, you know that, don't you?"

I shook my head, still looking outside. Where was a rainstorm when I needed one? I couldn't even hiccup without him hearing it.

"Ruby," he repeated, and I pinched my lips together as he pulled into the drop-off lane, trying so hard not to cry. I knew I failed when at least five tears just jumped right out of my eyes.

"Ruby Cube," he said. "Would you look at me?"

I shook my head again, two more tears jumping to their deaths of shame.

"Hey."

I swallowed and slowly turned my head to look at him, totally conscious that there were tears in my eyes, and I had no hopes of hiding them, and knowing full well that the second I looked at him, I was going to cry.

And that's exactly what happened.

One second I was looking out the window, and the next, I was shifting in his passenger seat, meeting those warm brown eyes, and then four tears turned into a hundred and I whispered, "Why does it feel like I'm never going to see you again?" I blubbered.

Before I could register what he was doing, Aaron undid his seat belt and reached for me, his hands going to my face across the center console, palming me, cupping me, bringing us forehead to forehead. His lips hovered millimeters from mine, full and a shade of pink I'd only ever seen on him before, and he said the words that ate me up completely. "This isn't goodbye. You know that, don't you?" his voice croaked, pretty much ending my life.

I didn't get a chance to answer before he answered his own question, his voice breaking and creaking and raspier than ever. "You know that. You know you'll see me again," he claimed, to me, to himself, to everyone in the world.

Pinching my lips together, I wanted to tell him that it didn't feel that way. That this felt like goodbye forever, but maybe it was just the part of me that didn't completely understand or accept separation. I could admit it. When my dad had first moved back to California, I'd cried every day for months. I'd gotten used to the idea, but it had taken time. There was no hiding it. And yet this . . . this felt just like that but worse somehow because I didn't know what would happen to Aaron in his career.

I wanted it all, as selfish as it made me.

All of it.

With his forehead still pressed to mine, his mouth kissed one of my cheeks and then the other. He brushed my lips with his, tenderly, tenderly, tenderly. One corner and then the other. His hands the gentlest thing I'd ever felt in my life. And he spoke into my skin, into my heart, my soul, everything in me. "I don't want to leave you. I want to turn this truck around and take you back to the house with me, and then I want to take you to Kentucky and have you there while I figure my life out this next year. With you." He gulped, trailing off.

The sound that came out of me was somewhere between a laugh and a sob, and I didn't miss the smile he made into my cheek.

"This is just for a little bit. You know that, don't you?" he pleaded into me. "Tell me you know that."

Did I know that? It didn't take much soul searching to know that I did. I did know he didn't want to drop me off at the airport, to let me go back to the place I'd almost always called home.

The thumb he had on my right cheek made a swipe across it. His nose touched mine, and his voice was weak as he whispered, "You can come visit me whenever you want, and don't say anything about the money. Visit me every month. Every other week. Fucking every week if you want," he offered. "This is only temporary. Understand me?"

I closed my eyes and nodded, not having the strength in me to say words that wouldn't come out like cries and pleas of *take me with you, please, please, please.*

"I love you, Rubes, and I know you love me too," he whispered. "You're the one who told me a few thousand miles wouldn't really matter in the grand scheme of life, remember?"

That had me almost cracking up. Almost, but it sounded

broken, and I didn't sound like myself. "Yes," I croaked, admitting it but not wanting to.

"You and me, we'll figure this out. We'll make this work."

I was back to pinching my lips and nodding, a few more tears streaming out of my eyes at the infinite sadness that weighed down on me even though I knew he was speaking the truth.

"I love you, stalker. Time. Distance. Nothing is going to change that. We'll figure this out, I promise." He kissed my lips again, and that time I kissed him right back. Warm lips on warm lips, and I wished we had a motel to stop at to get under the covers together, skin to skin, his chest to my face, his legs wrapped in mine, one last time, just one last time. I should have been embarrassed by how clingy I was being, but I couldn't find it in me. Not even a little.

"Do you believe me?" he asked, brushing the tip of his nose against mine like I would have loved on any other occasion.

I nodded.

"Tell me." He kept on Eskimo kissing me. Holding my face. Keeping me together. "Tell me," he repeated, sounding almost anguished.

"I believe you," I said. "My head knows I'll see you again, but my heart thinks you're leaving me here and I'm never going to see you again."

"Never see you again? I couldn't forget you in a hundred years if I tried, Ru. And nothing would get me to try. Not a single thing. Everything happens for a reason, remember?"

"What happened for a reason?"

"You got me in the program. They could've given my name and address to anybody else, but you got me."

I just barely held back a choke. "I thought you got me."

His voice was low. "No, Ruron. You got me."

I screwed my eyes closed and nodded, leaning into him so that I buried my face into his neck. "I'm probably going to be a really shitty, clingy girlfriend."

"You couldn't be shitty at anything."

I laughed.

"You're mine, RC. That's not changing."

I gulped, feeling like I was drowning. With a sob stuck in my throat, I nodded, quick, quick, quick. I was going to cry. I was going to freaking cry for real, and I didn't want to.

"I wanted to park—"

"It's okay. I need to run in anyway," I gritted out, staring at the dashboard. I swallowed. "Will you give me a hug outside at least?"

He grunted, opening his door and getting out before I'd even undone my seat belt. By the time I closed my door, he'd already pulled my suitcase and bag out, stacking one on top of the other. I took him in, every single inch I'd seen the night before. With his hands fisted at his sides, I could tell Aaron was breathing hard from the way his shirt hugged his chest. I took my time trailing my gaze higher up until it landed on those features I'd think of all the time. He was watching me, the saddest smile I'd ever seen on his face, because it was filled with so much affection and love. It cracked my heart in half.

"Come here," he said, holding one hand toward me.

I went. I wrapped my arms around his waist, and I hugged him like I'd never see him again. His mouth was at my ear as he squeezed me to him, like he was trying to conjoin us.

"I'd take you with me if I could, Ru, but have fun with your dad," he said, nuzzling me as his hand made a trail up and down my spine. "We'll make this work. I promise."

I didn't cry on the plane ride, and I didn't cry when my mom drove up to the arrivals section of the airport and then talked my ear off the entire ride back home, telling me all about Jasmine going to train with her coach again finally.

I didn't cry when I got into my room that night either.

But when I lay down in bed, this feeling of missing Aaron like crazy hit me right in the solar plexus.

And then, I did cry. Just a little. Two little tears. But they were enough.

Ruby: I feel like I have the flu. Tell me something funny.

I texted Aaron, using some of the same words he'd used on me before.

Thirty seconds later, a response from him came in.

Aaron: Why didn't the toilet paper cross the road?

I didn't get a chance to reply before another message from him came in.

Aaron: Bc it got stuck in a crack

Ten seconds after, my phone chimed again.

Aaron: Have I told you today how happy I am you got stuck with me?

And how could I be sad after that?

Epilogue

May 17, 2012

10:03 a.m.
Aaron: Morning
Ruby: Morning
Aaron: Feeling any better?
Ruby: No. I just took my temperature and it's back up to 101 again.
Aaron: Take some aspirin
Ruby: Already did. I found the bottle on the nightstand next to the thermometer.
Ruby: Thank you for that.
Aaron: :]
Aaron: I touched your face before I left and thought you were feeling warm. Go to the doctor.
Ruby: I know. I should. I don't want you getting sick too.
Ruby: I told Jasmine I was sick and she immediately asked if I was pregnant. Why is that her first assumption every time?
Aaron: Because she's Jasmine.
Ruby: Lol. You're so right.
Ruby: Speaking of her, we got into a fight at the end about her wanting to switch to pairs skating.

Aaron: How'd that go?

Ruby: Fine. I think I still catch her off guard when I talk back to her, so it makes me feel like I win when she doesn't have a comeback immediately. We'll see what she decides. You know how she is.

Ruby: Going to shower and see if that makes me feel any better. I'll call the doctor after and see if I can go.

Aaron: OK.

Aaron: Call if you need anything.

1:15 p.m.

Ruby: Guess what?

Aaron: What?

Ruby: It's not the flu, just an upper respiratory infection.

Aaron: They gave you meds?

Ruby: Yes.

Aaron: Sorry, honey

Aaron: Want me to pick up your script on the way home?

Ruby: It's okay. I'm already at the pharmacy waiting.

Ruby: The doctor made sure to tell me three times that my birth control won't be as effective while I'm on antibiotics.

Aaron: Did you tell him we'd planned on you not taking them anymore after your next period?

Ruby: Yes. It was so awkward. It was like he was pretending he didn't hear me.

Aaron: Lol. It's that cute, innocent face.

Ruby: :)

Ruby: How's your day going anyway?

Aaron: Fine.

Aaron: My CO is in a shit mood

Ruby: Sorry. One more year and then you can rethink what you want to do again.

Aaron: :] only a year

Ruby: It'll go by fast.

Aaron: :]

2:55 p.m.

Ruby: [picture attachment]

Aaron: [picture attachment]

Ruby: What is that???

Aaron: Tacos from a new food truck in town

Ruby: Bring me some, those make my sandwich look like crap.

Aaron: Snooze you lose

Aaron: Come have lunch with me tomorrow

Aaron: If you're feeling better

Ruby: "if you're feeling better"

Ruby: . . . . .

Aaron: :] love you

Ruby: Yeah, sure.

Ruby: Love you too, but I'd love you more if you brought me tacos

4:50 p.m.

Aaron: What are we having for dinner?

Ruby: Whatever you decide to bring home. ☺

Aaron: That's what I thought

Aaron: Vietnamese?

Ruby: Yes please.

Aaron: OK

Aaron: Are you lying down?

Ruby: Yes. I tried cutting some bandanas for that big order to Canada I got but I cut myself because I wasn't paying attention, then I started worrying about contaminating the cloth and getting other people sick so I stopped.

Aaron: Jesus, RC

Aaron: Chill

Aaron: You'll catch up on everything. Worry about feeling better. That's all that matters

Ruby: You're the best, have I told you that today?

Aaron: I know

Aaron: Not today.

Ruby: Cocky

Aaron: You've never complained.

Ruby: I knew you were going to go there.

Aaron: :]

Ruby: Why don't skeletons watch scary movies?

Aaron: Because they don't have the guts

Ruby: You knew that one???

Aaron: I GUESSED

Ruby: Bye

Aaron: I got a tear in my eye

Ruby: . . .

Aaron: . . .

Aaron: Leaving here in a sec, Ruron.

Ruby: Okay, Ruron.

Aaron: Think of a better joke before I get home.

Aaron: Meant to tell you that you might as well throw away your pills now that I think about it.

Ruby: You're a real bossy pain in the you know what.

Aaron: I know.

Ruby: And I'm sick.

Aaron: So? I'm not scared of a little infection.

Ruby: Oh brother.

Ruby: I'm feeling bad but not that bad.
Ruby: But if you get sick don't blame me.
Aaron: Never
Ruby: :)
Aaron: :]

Acknowledgments

I think it's a well-known fact I have the best readers on the face of the planet. Thank you all for knocking my socks off with all your love and support with every release. Whether you've been with me from the beginning, or are taking a chance with me for the first time, my gratitude knows no bounds. From the bottom of my heart, thank you.

A big shout out to my Slow Burners! You're all my spirit animals. Thank you for being so understanding when I disappear on you guys for long periods of time, haha. You're the most awesome reading group on the Internet.

A big thank you to Nissa for all of her advice and knowledge on Filipino foods, and for being so cool in general.

A big thank you to my friend Eva. You know how much you do for me. I know how much you do for me. The group does too. Thank you for everything.

Thank you to Letitia Hasser at RBA Design for the amazing cover and putting up with my dumb ideas and anal crap. Jeff at Indie Formatting Services, thank you for always being so professional and great. Virginia and Becky at Hot Tree Editing for never reducing me to tears with edits. Lauren Abramo and Kemi Faderin at Dystel & Goderich for being the best team.

To my pre-readers/friends who can't get rid of me, I can never thank you enough for what you do and never wanting any credit for it. My books wouldn't be the same without your gentle "Mariana, why?" comments.

A great big thank you to the greatest family on the planet. Mom and Dad, Ale, Eddie, Raul, Isaac, Kaitlyn, my Letchford family, and the rest of my Zapata/Navarro family.

To Chris and my boys, Dor and Kai. Every book is for you guys.

Discover more thrilling love stories from the queen of the slow burn!

Order now from

HEADLINE
ETERNAL

FIND YOUR HEART'S DESIRE...

VISIT OUR WEBSITE: www.headlineeternal.com

FIND US ON FACEBOOK: facebook.com/eternalromance

CONNECT WITH US ON TWITTER: @eternal_books

FOLLOW US ON INSTAGRAM: @headlineeternal

EMAIL US: eternalromance@headline.co.uk